D1111461

EARTHQUAKE WEATHER

EARTHQUAKE WEATHER

Terrill Lee Lankford

BALLANTINE BOOKS • NEW YORK

A Ballantine Book
Published by The Random House Publishing Group

www.ballantinebooks.com

Library of Congress Cataloging-in-Publication Data

Lankford, Terrill.
Earthquake weather / Terrill Lee Lankford.—1st ed.
p. cm.
ISBN 0-345-46777-9
I. Title.

PS3562.A542E37 2004
813'.54—dc22
2004041068

Book design by Julie Schroeder

Manufactured in the United States of America

First Edition: May 2004

1 3 5 7 9 10 8 6 4 2

For Heidi and Mike, who gave
this book—and this writer—more
second chances than either of us deserved.

~

And for John A. Alonzo, A.S.C., who shot the hell
out of this town. Your friends miss you, John.

EARTHQUAKE WEATHER

PART I

There was a desert wind that night. It was one of those hot dry Santa Anas that come down through the mountain passes and curl your hair and make your nerves jump and your skin itch. On nights like that every booze party ends in a fight. Meek little wives feel the edge of the carving knife and study their husbands' necks. Anything can happen.

—RAYMOND CHANDLER
"RED WIND"

Earthquake weather makes the Santa Ana winds look like pussies.

—CLYDE MCCOY

ONE

I don't believe in Heaven or Hell, but on any given night Los Angeles can do a pretty good imitation of either locale.

In the early morning of January 17, 1994, L.A. slipped into Hell mode in a big way. At the time I was living in an apartment in Sherman Oaks, a suburb of Los Angeles in the San Fernando Valley. Despite the early hour, I was still awake when the event occurred, having been unable to nod off due to a strange mixture of listlessness and unfocused anxiety: It's said that dogs experience similar precognitive distress prior to seismic events. I had just closed the book I was reading, Rudy Wurlitzer's *Hard Travel to Sacred Places,* and reached for the light when I heard a terrifying rumble in the distance. Something big was about to happen.

It was an incredibly loud noise, yet it seemed to be emanating from a distant place and moving closer with great speed and violence. I realized it could only be a few things: an earthquake, a comet striking Earth, a nuclear blast, or some other big-ass explosion, maybe from a stunt gone awry on a movie set filming in the West Valley. It was four thirty in the morning on Martin Luther King's birthday and the idea that anybody, even Joel Silver, might be blowing up buildings at this hour was somewhat unlikely.

I had only a split second to consider these possibilities and I quickly circled number one—earthquake—just as the first shock wave hit. The entire apartment complex was lifted into the air and brought back down hard. The halogen lamp fell from the top of my bookshelf and exploded. Glass hit me in the face. A rip of plaster tore straight up the wall directly behind my head. When the crack reached the ceiling, it zigzagged across the surface out of the bedroom. The streetlights in the alley outside the room flickered and went out, followed immediately by the flashing lights and neon trim on the marquee of the La Reina Plaza on Ventura Boulevard a half block away. My bedroom was plunged into darkness.

The initial shock wave seemed to last an eternity. It was probably only twenty or thirty seconds in reality, but that can be an eternity if you live on the second floor of an apartment building that feels like it has turned into wood-and-plaster-flavored Jell-O. When the huge bookshelf itself fell over and crashed six inches from my head, I decided that this was an earthquake worth getting out of bed for. I scrambled over the fallen bookshelf to the doorway, got the door open, and stood in the arch. Five feet across the hall I saw my roommate, Jeff, standing naked in the arch of *his* doorway. A vaguely familiar TV actress, also naked, dangled from around his neck, looking up into his stoic face as if she were seeing the face of Jesus in the gloom. It was easy to see how she could have been confused. Jeff had his arms outstretched and pressed against either side of the doorjamb for support. A flashlight at his feet bounced illumination up against the rubber walls, hauntingly lighting his face from below. He looked like he was suffering on an invisible cross.

"It's the fucking Big One!" Jeff screamed in an un-Jesus-like fashion. He seemed to take little notice of the girl carving her initials into the back of his neck with her fingernails.

I nodded approval of his assessment. It did indeed appear that this could be the notorious "Big One" that we had all been waiting for. I had experienced hundreds of earthquakes over the years, most of them small, a few of them sizable, but I had rarely moved to a doorway for any of them. This sucker was intense. It felt like the entire building was going to tear itself apart. We could hear glass breaking everywhere, in our apartment and outside, in the dozens of apartment houses and office buildings that surrounded us. The shaking did not seem like it was going to stop. I had a brief aerial vision of the entire area, along with half of California, heading out to sea.

The quake abruptly came to a halt. Nine million car alarms filled in while the rumbling earth took a quick cigarette break.

"That wasn't so bad," I said.

The woman around Jeff's neck let go and bolted for the front door. "I'm outta here!" she screamed, seemingly unaware of just how naked she really was.

Jeff stayed in his doorway and yelled, "Don't!" as loudly as he could, but she ignored him.

I smiled at Jeff and said, "She'll never make the door."

We braced ourselves for what we knew was about to happen. The first aftershock hit with almost as much force as the earthquake itself. It was enough to turn the apartment into a Salvador Dali landscape. Everything became liquid. The girl was tossed into the air and catapulted into the front door with a resounding *splat.* Luckily her shoulder was leading or her head probably would have gone right through the wood panel. The vibrations were on the gentle side by the time Jeff and I decided to apartment surf out of the place before the next shock wave could hit. Jeff reached into his room and grabbed a bathrobe and a towel. I made my way gingerly through the darkened minefield of fallen items and broken glass, snagged my leather jacket off the kitchen chair, and slipped it on. I was wearing boxer shorts, so a jacket was all I'd need. I grabbed Jeff's lady friend by one arm and started to pick her up off the floor. Jeff, dressed in his Hugh Hefner robe, grabbed her other arm, and we hoisted her to her feet. She looked like a dazed raccoon that had bounced off a car fender. Jeff had the flashlight in his free hand. He swept it across the apartment and we saw that everything was on the floor. Everything. He bounced the light into the kitchen where pots and pans were still gently rattling against the thousands of pieces of broken glass that had been our dishes. The place was thrashed.

The apartment stopped shaking for a few seconds, but it continued to rock and sway gently, its beams and girders singing out that this was not the way things were meant to be. The place was old, and part of it appeared to be older than the rest. We had two front doors, almost side by side, one in the kitchen, the other in the living room. An open arch separated the two rooms. The arch looked like it had been designed in the forties and I had a feeling that the kitchen area had been an add-on. I hoped the place wasn't going to split at its seams.

We got the living room door open and piled out onto the balcony. The hammock, strung diagonally between two opposing pillars of the balcony, was still swaying from the aftershock and the wood floor was creaking as if it wanted to collapse under us. We negotiated the darkened stairwell with the girl. There was another door at the bottom of the stairs. I turned the knob but the door would not open. Jeff shined the flashlight around the edge of the door frame. The building had settled on the door slightly. Jeff and I looked at each other for a moment of Butch and Sundance bonding, and then we both kicked the door hard, knocking it open and sending splinters everywhere. Luckily the building had been standing for more than fifty years. The wood was soft, practically rotten.

We dragged the naked actress into the large parking lot next to the building and received a standing ovation from our neighbors, who were gathering in clusters in the safety zone, shining flashlights wildly about in the dark. Beams of light danced all over the stunned girl's naked body until Jeff wrapped her in the towel and growled at the crowd. He held her close as another large aftershock rocked the ground.

Even over the earth's rumble I could hear someone in the crowd say, "Hey, isn't that? . . ." referring to Jeff's dazed actress girlfriend. The great thing about natural disasters in L.A. is that they are star-studded events. An Irwin Allen Production made flesh.

In the hours, days, months, and years of earthquakes and aftershocks that would follow, we would never again trust the ground on which we walked in quite the same way as we did before this quake (which, at a magnitude of 6.8, was impressive, yet far short of the Big One), but at least we were finally going to get to meet the neighbors.

TWO

Over the last few years Los Angeles had been plagued by a series of disasters verging on the biblical. We had suffered through riots, drought, fires, floods, mud slides, and now a sizable earthquake. Send in the locusts and I think we might finally get the message. Los Angeles. Possibly the worst place in the world, and I wouldn't consider living anywhere else. Most of my friends felt the same way. The assortment of L.A. denizens I now found myself sharing a parking lot with were no different. They all muttered and mumbled about "getting the fuck out of L.A.," but they knew that they'd be going back into their apartments the moment the aftershocks settled into the mid-4's.

The parking lot in which we now gathered sat beside our building and behind Viande, a restaurant and bar that served California cuisine cooked by Mexican chefs under a French logo. They ran a jazz club out of a surprisingly small room upstairs, and some of the world's finest jazz musicians played there on a regular basis—if you liked that kind of thing. Viande also served as a local watering hole for the occupants of the many apartment buildings in the area. One of the owners, Dale Jaffe, was kind enough to allow the tenants of my particular building to park their cars in his spacious parking lot. It helped that our building had only four units; the two-bedroom deal on the second floor that Jeff and I occupied was the penthouse of the complex. The other three apartments were one-bedroom affairs that stretched from the foot of our place toward Morrison Street. The alley on the other side of our apartment separated us from the local Tower Video outlet, where Tower sold their leftover books, videotapes, and CDs at a discount. Viande was two doors west of Tower, separated by a grumpy chiropractor's office and his small parking lot, which he kept locked up with a chain at night so no one could park there for free. The front door of Viande opened up on Ventura Boulevard, the Valley's answer to Sunset Boulevard: thirty-four miles of commerce and speculation that stretched from Universal City to Woodland Hills.

On nights when we had power, the chiropractor's parking lot was illuminated by the monolithic La Reina marquee shining from the other side of Ventura Boulevard, a remnant of the La Reina theater, one of the most famous movie palaces in the Valley, which had been transformed in the eighties into the jewel in the crown of a high-tech strip mall. Instead of proudly displaying the latest hit movies, the marquee now featured a computerized animation display in white Vegas bulbs that flashed ads for The Gap.

The Viande parking lot was the largest bit of open space in the neighborhood. People from all the nearby apartment buildings had gathered there hoping to avoid toppling buildings. Considering that there was nothing higher than a three-story building in the immediate area, it was a safe bet. It was still dark and very cold, so no one was exactly in the mood for a block party. A few women were crying, Jeff's actress girlfriend among them. She had never been in a really good earthquake before. The last one of any consequence had been back in 1992, and she had been in Vancouver at the time doing a TV pilot for a series that failed to make the grade. The violence of this quake was something she was totally unprepared for and it had frightened her to her very core. Jeff stowed her away in my car, the keys of which had been in the pocket of my jacket when I scooped it out of the kitchen. He had the heater on full blast and he was rubbing her legs for warmth and comfort, but it wasn't doing her any good. She was bawling her eyes out and swearing to move back to Wisconsin.

I stayed in the car long enough to get warm and remove small bits of plaster from one of my eyes, which was scratched and watery but appeared to be functioning properly, then I decided to give Jeff and the girl some quiet time alone. The car was an '88 Camaro, silver with the T-top accessory. The heater worked great, but the space was tight and the proximity to Jeff's girlfriend got annoying very quickly. I preferred knocking knees in the cold to listening to some crybaby actress whine.

I walked through clusters of people speculating on the magnitude of the quake and estimating the death toll. The attitudes ranged from intense fear to a general exhaustion with the city and its violent quirks. The term "U-Haul" was being bandied about freely.

I saw my three immediate neighbors huddled together near a brick wall in front of our building. Most of the wall on the other side of the lot had crumbled into a zillion pieces, but this section had miraculously survived the quake. I hadn't formally met any of the other residents of my building, although I had been living there for almost a year. They had each seemed preoccupied with solitude, and I had respected their wishes at the risk of appearing standoffish. I knew a little about them just by catching glimpses of their lives through their windows as I would come and go. I had also read their names off the mailboxes next to their front doors, but that's as intimate as the relationships had gotten.

There was T. Zimmerman in apartment One, the apartment closest to Morrison Street. I had heard people walking with him on the sidewalk call him *Zim.* Zim was rumored to be a war veteran of some sort. Which war I wasn't exactly sure. He looked like he could be anywhere from his mid-forties to early sixties. He was very thin and had long straggly hair and a beard to match. He wore glasses and listened to classical music at all hours of the day or night. On more than one occasion I passed his place and smelled ganja thick in the air. *High-quality ganja.*

A blonde lived in apartment Two. The name on her mailbox read REBECCA OSTERHAGE. She was gorgeous, yet appeared to be somewhat of a recluse. There was an air of mystery about her. She waitressed at the jazz club upstairs at Viande, but always seemed to go straight there, then straight home again. I had never seen a man go in or come out of her place. The last guy to knock on her door was a pizza delivery man. She had called for a pizza and, when it arrived, she refused to answer the door. I knew she was in there, because I had been reading a script on the inside ledge of my living room window, overlooking her apartment, when she had gotten off work. I saw her go in and a half hour later the delivery man showed up. When she wouldn't open the door, the guy looked up and asked me if a Becky Osterhage lived in that apartment. I told him I thought so, but I hadn't seen her in awhile. I wondered if she had fallen asleep or if she had just had second thoughts about making further contact with the outside world that night and decided to stay huddled in her room until the guy went away. She looked like Catherine Deneuve in her glory days. With her looks she could have been living in Beverly Hills on the dole of some old fat cat who would visit her twice a month—once to get what was left of his rocks off and once to pay the bills. I didn't know what her story was but I wanted to find out.

Then there was apartment Three, the one directly next to the foot of my apartment. That was the real mystery. The guy who lived there never seemed to leave his place either. But never in his case meant *never.* He had everything delivered: food, water, supplies. He would get deliveries at all hours of the night, but never in the day. It appeared he slept most of the day and worked through the night. There was no name on his mailbox, but I knew he was a writer of some sort, because I could often hear him banging away on an old Selectric when I sat out on the balcony at night or early in the morning. Sometimes he would work as late as 6 A.M. before giving up. Whatever he was working on, it must have been *long.*

Now I had them all together, clustered in a group, out of the protective confines of their little cubicles. Maybe they would open up and let the secrets out. I went over to introduce myself. The guy from apartment Three shined a flashlight in my face as I approached.

"Friend or foe?" the voice behind the light asked.

"Friend," I said, trying to sound cheery. "I'm your neighbor from apartment Four."

He took the beam off my face. "You may enter the inner sanctum."

I joined their circle and said, "Everybody enjoy the rockin' and rollin'?"

"It was terrifying," Becky said. Her hair was in curlers and she was dressed in a white bathrobe, but she appeared to be in full makeup. She was still beautiful, curlers and all. I wondered if she slept in that makeup, just in case Prince Charming showed up in the middle of the night to whisk her away to the palace.

"It was a big one," I said, trying to keep the conversation alive.

"Mid-6's," the stranger from apartment Three said. He had dark, wavy hair, strong cheekbones, hollow eyes, and a nose that had been broken more than once. He appeared to be on the intense side and his voice had a slight Yankee accent. He was from back East somewhere, but he had been here long enough to adjust to the dialect.

"Seventy-one was bigger," Zim said. He was wearing a long, tattered army jacket over what appeared to be nothing. His stubby, gnarled legs extended from the bottom of the coat to unlaced work boots that had been new a decade ago. "I was here for seventy-one. That one made me shit my pants."

"That was before you burned all your gray matter into charcoal, dude," the man from apartment Three said. "And of course, back then, you actually *had* pants."

Zim chuckled. "That's true, hon. That's true." I soon realized that Zim called everyone *hon*—man, woman, and child.

"My name's Mark," I said, extending my hand to the man from apartment Three. "Mark Hayes."

Somewhat to my surprise the man immediately took my hand and shook it firmly. He was not as standoffish as I expected.

"Clyde McCoy," he said with a smile. "Pleased to meet you." Clyde McCoy was the only person in the parking lot who was fully dressed in street clothes. It was as if he were leaving for work at any moment. He was wearing a pair of freshly pressed blue jeans, a country-and-western-style button-down blue shirt, loafers, and a sports jacket. He was bright-eyed and ready to get on with his life.

The blonde shook my hand and smiled warmly at me in the dim light. "Becky," she offered, nothing more. I enjoyed the contact a little too long and she withdrew her hand nervously.

"You can call me Zim, hon," the aging hippie said as he shook my hand. He smiled, and even in the darkness I could see that a number of his teeth were missing. The rest were stained with a combination of tobacco and ganja resin.

Clyde McCoy looked around the parking lot at the various pockets of survivors milling about. He drew us in close and whispered in a conspiratorial tone, "Anyone want hot coffee?"

Our eyes grew wide. We knew what he meant and how important the offer was. The whole city was likely to be without electricity for hours, if not days. A man with a pot of freshly brewed hot coffee would be a king under these circumstances. We were standing with that king.

"You're kidding," I said.

"It's no joke," he replied. "I had just made a pot to get me through dawn right before the quake hit. It's espresso grind."

An aftershock in the 4.5 range rumbled through the parking lot and got the buildings vibrating again as if the earth itself was in awe of Clyde McCoy's words. Becky leaned in and grabbed me for support until she realized what she was doing. She pulled away again and rode out the last few seconds of the aftershock on her own. Zim and Clyde looked from Becky and me to each other and grinned slowly, as if sharing some private joke.

"So how about it?" Clyde asked. "Is it worth it to anyone?"

"We'd have to go into your apartment to get it?" I asked like a dummy.

"Well, it ain't going to walk itself out here and jump down our throats."

"I'm not going in that building again," Becky said.

"C'mon, it's no big deal," Clyde said. "We'd be safer in there drinking coffee than trying to bring it out into this parking lot. We'd be torn apart once the neighbors saw what we had."

"But the earthquakes . . . ," Becky wailed.

"They're not earthquakes; they're aftershocks," Clyde said stoically. "Besides, we're on the first floor."

"The way things are going," I said, "my living room might topple over and land in your kitchen."

Clyde laughed at the thought of inheriting my living room the hard way. "Possession being nine-tenths of the law, I hope you've got some nice shit. I could use a new CD player."

"How can you joke about this?" Becky asked. "People are probably dying all over the city."

"People are dying for a cup of coffee all over the city, and I've got one of the few pots loaded and ready to go. I'm going in. Whoever wants to join me, come along. I'm just trying to be neighborly."

"I'm not going," Becky said. "I'd rather freeze to death."

"You can sit in my car if you want," I offered. "My roommate and his friend are in there. I'm sure it's warm."

"Thank you. Are you going to come?"

I looked at Becky, then at Clyde and Zim. It was obvious that they considered this to be some sort of test. Hot coffee or the Frost Queen.

"No. I'm gonna go in and get a cup of coffee. I'll see you when we get done."

Clyde and Zim smiled. I guess I had passed the test. Whatever it was.

Becky frowned. "You're crazy."

"Yeah," I said. "But I need caffeine. It's going to be a long day."

I led her to my car. Clyde and Zim headed for apartment Three. "We'll see you in there," Clyde said.

"Be right in," I said, then I knocked on the window of my car. The glass was fogged up all around the vehicle. I had no idea if Jeff and the girl were just breathing the steam onto the windows or if they were going at it in some kind of apocalyptic sexual frenzy. I opened the door and found that they were halfway to the apocalypse. They were making out with the heater running full blast. The girl had lost her towel and she was giving Jeff a hand job while he suckled furiously at her augmented breasts. Jeff dislodged himself and looked up at me, trying not to scream. He was covered in sweat and his long red hair was hanging in his face in wet strands.

"Could you give us a few minutes?" he asked in the most pleasant of voices.

"'Fraid not," I said. "I've got one of our neighbors out here who's freezing and wants to get in out of the cold."

Jeff looked past me at Becky, who waved timidly. From her angle she couldn't see the naked woman sitting next to Jeff, or the woman's hand still furiously tugging away at his earthquake-rattled member.

"Why don't *you* warm her up?" Jeff asked in a strained rasp.

"Because *I'm* going in to our other neighbor's apartment for a cup of hot coffee. Possibly the only cup of hot coffee I'll see all day."

Jeff sat straight up and pulled the girl's hand away from his crotch.

"You're shitting me!"

"I shit you not," I said with an arrogant smile.

"I'm going with you," Jeff said. He sprung up out of the car and attempted to wrap his robe around his body, his erection pointing at eleven o'clock, making the task all the more difficult. Becky averted her eyes to spare herself further trauma.

The girl in the car looked up at us and yelled at Jeff, "You're nuts if you think I'm going back into that death trap!"

Jeff and I leaned forward and simultaneously said, "Who asked you?!"

THREE

The door to apartment Three was slightly ajar. I knocked and pushed it open. We could see Clyde and Zim standing in the kitchen beyond the living room, a flashlight crazily illuminating the area, refracting off shiny tiles covering the countertop it rested on. They were sipping cups of coffee and staring at the doorway as we entered.

"You made it," Clyde said. He sounded slightly disappointed.

"I brought my roommate, Jeff," I said. "I hope that's okay."

"No problem. We'll just have to ration the pot. Come on in."

Jeff and I entered the living room and had to maneuver through a field of books and magazines that had exploded off a bookcase. There appeared to be no broken glass in the place. Knickknacks were not part of the decor.

Clyde was pouring coffee into two tin cups by the time we made it to the kitchen.

"How do you take it?" he asked.

"Black," we both replied.

He had one of the old-fashioned metal coffeepots with the lid that had a small bubble of glass sticking up in the center where the coffee would dance while it percolated. That was how the coffee had survived the quake. The pot wasn't open-topped like most modern coffeepots.

And it wasn't all glass. He must have grabbed it when the shaking started to keep it from spilling. Clyde put the pot down and we picked up our cups and savored the brew.

Another aftershock hit. We steadied ourselves and balanced the cups so that none of the precious liquid would spill. This aftershock was much weaker than the previous ones. We lost nary a drop.

"The worst is over," Zim said.

"Not hardly," Clyde said. "The worst is going to be hearing everyone's earthquake stories for the next three months."

"True," Zim nodded.

The earth rumbled gently in agreement.

Clyde picked up the flashlight and shined it on us. "So," he said, "tell us about yourselves."

Jeff looked up from his cup of coffee and extended his hand. "Jeff Lasarow, glad to meet you."

Clyde and Zim took turns shaking Jeff's hand and then Clyde said, "So what do you boys do?" He sounded like he was implying we were a couple of some sort.

"I work for Black, Hershfield, Dykstra and Grossan," Jeff offered.

"Are you a lawyer?" Clyde asked. A hint of hostility tinged his voice.

"No. I'm a computer programmer. I just keep them online and up-to-date."

"That's good," Clyde said. "I'd hate to think I was giving coffee to an *attorney.*"

"You don't like attorneys?" Jeff asked, somewhat offended. He wasn't an attorney, but he made his living off of them and he liked most of the people he worked with.

"Got no use for them," Clyde offered. "They're suckfish."

Jeff let the comment pass and sipped his coffee. The air in the room was suddenly heavy with tension.

"Lighten up, hon," Zim said. "The man's got to earn a living."

Clyde ignored Zim and looked at me. "So, what's your story?"

"I work in development. At Warner's."

"Oh, a D-boy, eh? A suit? A future wizard?" Clyde laughed. "Christ, Zim, we got some heavy hitters living next to us."

Zim smiled apologetically. "You got to excuse Clyde when it comes to certain things," Zim said. "He's touchy about the industry."

"He's rude," Jeff said.

Clyde looked at Jeff like he was going to punch him. Then his expression morphed into a smile.

"You nailed me on that one, partner," Clyde said. "I'm a rude motherfucker. Goddamn, I'm sorry. I invite you into my place for coffee and start insulting your professions. What the hell's the matter with me?"

"You've got D.G.S.," Zim offered.

"No shit," Clyde replied.

"What's D.G.S.?" I asked.

"Damaged Goods Syndrome," Zim said. "He's got it bad."

"I'm sensitive around 'show' people," Clyde added.

"You're in the business?" I asked. The *business* in L.A. being show business.

"Not anymore," Clyde said. "I'm retired."

"He made a lot of movies," Zim said.

"Leave it alone, Zim," Clyde said. He appeared to be growing uncomfortable with the direction of the conversation. It suddenly dawned on me. I *knew* this guy.

"You're Clyde McCoy, the writer, aren't you?"

"As opposed to Clyde McCoy, the brain surgeon, or Clyde McCoy, the physicist?" he asked sarcastically.

"I remember seeing your name on a bunch of movies in the eighties."

"Ah, the eighties," Clyde said. "The golden years. I remember the eighties."

"So do I," Zim said. "Yuck."

"Why'd you quit?" I asked.

"I got sick of all the bullshit," Clyde said.

"You're still writing *something,* aren't you?" I asked. "I hear you typing every night."

"I'm working on a book."

"What's it about?"

"Raymond Chandler. It's a biography of his life and work."

"I love Chandler," I said. "He's one of the main reasons I wanted to make movies. I'm a big film noir fan."

"Chandler was a liar and a fraud," Clyde said. "He was a dishonest writer."

"Dishonest?"

"He didn't have the goods. Not like Hammett, for instance. Chandler's work should have been shelved under fantasy, not crime fiction. He was a mama's boy."

"Chandler was a great stylist. He's had a huge impact on the twentieth century."

"He's the most overrated writer of the twentieth century."

"Why do you want to do a biography on him then?"

"I want to expose him. I want to blow his bullshit out of the water."

"You're a crank," Zim said.

"And *you're* a dope fiend," Clyde retorted.

"At least I'll admit it."

"Touché."

"You think there's a market for Chandler biographies?" I asked. "I've read a bunch of them. He seems to have been covered pretty thoroughly."

"Not like this," Clyde assured me. "This is *non*fiction. I peel the bastard back and reveal him for the drippy charlatan that he was."

"You're just bitter because he made money off his drippiness," Zim said. "You had to go to AA."

"Shut the fuck up, Zim, or I'll piss in your coffee."

Zim pulled his cup away and embraced it protectively.

I finished my coffee and Clyde hit it again. He divvied up the rest of the brew between the four of us and put the pot back on the dead stove. We savored our coffee and stared at the empty pot like it was a dead relative as another aftershock rolled under our feet.

FOUR

Once the coffee was gone and the sun was up, Jeff and I returned to our place to get organized. His girlfriend would not come upstairs, so he had to bring her clothes down to her. The harsh light of day revealed the extent of the damage done to our apartment. Broken glass was all over the kitchen; the television was on the floor in the living room, and we had no way to know if it was broken; there was no electricity and there wouldn't be for days. Books, videotapes, and magazines were everywhere. The water was off and someone had had the good sense to shut down the gas lines at the main to keep the whole building from blowing up, but that meant the stove and the heater didn't work. I tried the telephone. It was dead. We had been plunged into the Dark Ages. I put on a pair of blue jeans and a sweatshirt, ran a brush through my hair, and stared at myself in the mirror. I don't fare well without sleep. I begin to look like an old man very quickly. My eyes were turning a patriotic red, white, and blue. The deep lines in my forehead—earned by years of dismayed frowning—looked smoother than usual in the dim light of the bathroom, but I knew the harsh sun outside would not be so kind later in the day. I don't have a beard, but if I go without a shave, after about sixteen hours I start to look like Lon Chaney Jr., during a full moon.

I went downstairs to see how everyone in the parking lot was faring.

The crowd had thinned considerably. Only the truly terrified were still gathered in the wide-open spaces.

Jeff and his girlfriend were getting into his car as I came out of the apartment.

"Where you going?" I asked.

"Palm Springs for a day or two," Jeff replied. "Give this place a chance to settle down."

"Good idea. Where's Becky?"

"She left a long time ago," Jeff's girlfriend said. "Some guy came by in a nice Jag and picked her up."

That came as a bit of a surprise. I had to wonder who that had been. Maybe Becky *did* have a candyman somewhere in town. I approached Jeff and asked him if I could use his cell phone. He handed it to me and said, "Good luck. I've been trying to get out on it for half an hour. Everybody is tying up the lines. These are probably the only phones working in all of L.A."

Due to the deskbound nature of my job I had not yet decided to go to the expense of a cell phone. That was a decision I figured I'd be regretting for the next few days. I tried my boss's own cell phone number and got a quick busy signal, indicating that I wasn't even getting a clean line out to the server. I tried it repeatedly as Jeff stood waiting by the side of his car.

"I'm telling you that thing won't be any use for hours," Jeff said.

"*Someone* must be getting through or the lines wouldn't be busy, right?"

"Yeah. Someone wins the Lotto every week, too, but it ain't gonna be one of us."

The line suddenly clicked through and began to ring. "Jackpot," I said.

"No shit?"

The line rang five or six times before a pissed off voice answered with, "This better be fucking good!" It was my boss, Dexter Morton.

"Dexter, it's me. Mark Hayes."

"Hayes? What the hell do you want? Don't you know we're in the middle of a fucking disaster movie?"

"I just wanted to make sure you were okay."

There was a long silence on the other end of the line.

"Dexter?"

"I'm fine, Hayes. Except for the fact that I'm standing in my bedroom and I can walk right through the crack in the wall out into my fucking garden. My goddamn house split in half when the ground settled."

"Jesus. You need some help up there?"

"Yeah. Are you a building contractor? If you are, get your ass up here. If not, I'll see you in the office on Wednesday."

"Wednesday? You don't want us in tomorrow?"

"Hayes, there's a big difference between being driven and being obsessed. Let's give everyone a day to clean the wood out of their skulls and buy new china."

"Wednesday, then."

His response was a dial tone. I handed the phone back to Jeff.

"Happy you got through?" he asked.

"Thrilled. And I've got another day off. This is turning into a very long weekend."

"You could come with us to the Springs."

"Thanks, but I think I'll drive around and see how my friends have fared."

"What friends?"

"Acquaintances, then."

"Okay. See you tomorrow. Or whenever."

He got into his car and they drove away.

Chaos reigned for the next few days. Los Angeles proper ground to a halt as damage was tallied and public utilities were slowly repaired. We had no water or electricity until January 19. The food spoiled in our refrigerator, and I took to eating at a local barbecue joint that cooked outdoors, right out on Ventura Boulevard, while the glass guys replaced all the windows that had blown out of the place. Glaziers, amateur and pro, were the most common sight on the road, zipping around, placing temporary plywood over future window sites. Glass and plywood installation became the boom industry of the new year. Guys who knew absolutely nothing about it were signing on to twenty-four-hour-a-day work crews.

People were paying top dollar for the service, and the contractors couldn't move fast enough.

A twenty-five-story office building in Westwood collapsed two days into the aftershocks. It was the biggest single structure to come all the way down, but thousands of smaller buildings were flattened. Hundreds of thousands were severely damaged.

A three-story apartment house near the epicenter of the quake in Northridge became a two-story apartment house in the first minute of the shaking. Seventeen faithful renters died in the tragedy.

Overpass collapses occurred on every major freeway. The Santa Monica Freeway was completely shut down. A motorcycle cop on the 14 didn't notice that entire sections of that structure had disappeared and he drove off the edge and fell hundreds of feet to the ground.

The death toll was relatively low for an event of this magnitude. The pundits noted the early hour of the quake and cheerily stated that if it had occurred three or four hours later, while people were traveling to work or after they had arrived there, many thousands would have perished. Instead, what we got was an old-fashioned Hollywood-style spectacle. Lots of special effects with very little actual loss of human life. More people were killed in the riots of '92. Of course mankind *strives* for chaos. Nature just doles it out at random.

My apartment seemed to come out of it okay. It had some big cracks running along the walls and a couple of chunks of ceiling fell in, but the damage appeared to be cosmetic only. The FEMA inspector promised to come look at the structure when he finished with the more seriously damaged buildings. His advice until then: "Want to play it really safe? Go back East for a few weeks, like everybody else."

Thanks, pal.

Using another friend's cell phone I got through to my parents on the day after the quake. They had retired to a condo in Boca Raton, having left their hectic life in Baltimore four years earlier. My mother had been worried sick since news of the quake broke. She had been scouring the casualty reports for my name. I assured them that I was fine and that the news stories were being blown all out of proportion. My father just said, "Anytime you want to get out of that madhouse and get a real job, just let me know." He had always said he could set me up as a real estate broker. He had been fairly successful in his day and still had quite a few connections in Baltimore. I replied with my standard line: "And waste a perfectly good M.F.A. degree from the American Film Institute?" That always brought a chuckle from the old man.

Putting the apartment back together was an ordeal. It took me an hour just to pick the bookcase up off the bedroom floor and rearrange all the books. I got some large wood screws and fastened the thing to the wall so it could ride out all the aftershocks without toppling over and killing me. The living room was a big mess. I put the television back on its stand, then picked up all the Academy screener videotapes that had been stacked on the various shelves and tables around the room that had ended up on the floor. It was the beginning of awards season and the studios had been canvassing the Academy members with videotapes of their product in the hopes of picking up nominations. I wasn't a member of the Academy, but my boss was. He had no interest in the tapes, since he would be voting not with his conscience but with his bankbook in mind. His votes would go to those who were positioned to make his life better in the coming years. He allowed the staff to borrow the tapes as they wished. I had taken more of them home than anyone else and now they were all over the place.

A pile of screenplays on the coffee table had become a sea of screenplays on the floor. These weren't screenplays that I was covering for my job, but two dozen or so of my favorite works of the past, scripts I could pick up and read whenever I needed to cleanse my palate after covering something particularly noxious. *Chinatown, Lawrence of Arabia, The Long Goodbye, Sunset Boulevard, Body Heat, Cutter and Bone, Some Like It Hot, The Maltese Falcon, Paper Moon, My Bodyguard, The Last Detail, North by Northwest:* there wasn't a loser among them. That stack of scripts was my compass. I referred to it whenever I felt myself getting lost in the morass of works by lesser word slingers. Reading screenplays of that quality made me feel like Salieri in a roomful of Mozarts. It clarified my position in the world of film; I could hear and appreciate the music, but I could never create it on that level. If more of my contemporaries could come to the same conclusion, my job as a "creative executive" would be a lot easier.

The kitchen was littered with broken glass. I swept it all up as best I could and tossed it into the trash. I was a lot less interested in making things right in this room than I had been in my bedroom and the living room. I took care of the big stuff, but Jeff could worry about the cabinets and shelves filled with broken dishes when he got home. I was bored with the job. Luckily for us our cabinet filled with liquor was packed so tightly with bottles that nothing had fallen out and nothing was broken. It was like a miracle.

After straightening up the apartment, I spent my time cruising around looking at damage in the city, visiting with friends to make sure they were okay and to hear of their near-death encounters with Mother Nature. Despite Jeff's callous inference that I didn't really have friends, only acquaintances and associates, there were many people around town that I cared enough about to find out if they had been buried under rubble. Okay, most of them were good contacts, but still, I *cared.* All of them made it out alive, but most of the ones who lived in houses in the Valley had lost their chimneys. Many of them looked at the quake as a positive thing. A wake-up call. A chance to reevaluate their lives and buy new wineglasses.

I had dinner Tuesday night in the swimming pool of a friend of mine who worked for the Fox Network. The quake had split her large pool wide open, and it had drained down the hill into her neighbor's backyard, drowning one of the pit bulls who lived there in the process. The pool was now functioning as an oversize barbecue pit. Beers and sodas were being cooled in the two feet of water still remaining in the deep end while her boyfriend cooked burgers and steaks in the shallow end on a homemade grill. All her friends within cell phone range had come over to party, and we ate, drank, and gabbed by the light of tiki torches. It was quite festive.

The water came back on just in time for my Wednesday morning shower. I smelled pretty gamy by then. I can't remember a shower and a shave ever feeling so good. It was time to suit up and head back into the lion's den. I put on my Hugo Boss, loaded up my satchel and briefcase, and headed for my car.

Jeff was pulling into the parking lot as I was pulling out. We rolled down our windows and spoke.

"How was it in the Springs?" I asked.

"Not much better than this war zone. The place was packed with chickenshits and whiners."

"Which table did you sit at?"

"Very funny, joker. How's the apartment? Is it safe?"

"I think so. The landlady said they're sending an inspector around later today."

"Good. I'm late for work. See ya."

I nodded and pulled away. As I drove through the city to the studio I noticed something very peculiar. People were behaving quite normally. All was in order again. In less than three days we had gone from chaos to calm. Restoration was at full throttle, and many people were returning to work. If not for the dusty remains of the occasional condemned building or burned-out house, the San Fernando Valley would have looked like any other city during a growth period. Other than the unusual number of repairmen of every ilk skittering about the streets like hungry rats, the place appeared psychologically unblemished.

But I knew that wasn't true. This thing had shaken something deep in the nervous system of the collective. The U-Haul trucks that dotted the landscape weren't moving people in to new abodes; they were shipping them out to more stable ground. A chunk of the population was going to cut and run. They'd had it. They'd talked it out and determined that enough was enough. Maybe traffic would be lighter in the coming year. Once they rebuilt all the freeways, of course.

FIVE

The general wisdom in Hollywood is that the locals never refer to it as *this town,* much like the old axiom that no one who is truly from San Francisco would ever refer to it as *Frisco,* but the simple fact is that if I had a nickel for every time someone who lived here used the term *this town,* I could finance an Arnold Schwarzenegger movie. It's usually uttered in disgust when the chips are down, but sometimes it is used cheerfully as in, "Holy cow, this town can really tear you a new asshole, can't it?" And of course *Hollywood* is only a metaphoric term for the film industry. Paramount and the Warner's Hollywood lot are the only major studios that reside within the actual city limits of Hollywood. The other studios are spread out all over L.A. County. Universal is in North Hollywood, the Disney/Touchstone/Hollywood Pictures lot is in Burbank down the street from the Burbank Studios, the compound that used to house Columbia and Warner Brothers until Sony took over Columbia and moved it down to the old MGM lot in Culver City. MGM/U.A. was kicked out of its digs and moved into a big bland office building next door. Twentieth Century Fox is in Century City, which itself sprang up from their back lot, which they had to sell after *Cleopatra* took a huge dump at the box office in '63.

Mini-majors like New Line and Miramax are also spread out all over

Los Angeles. Very little power rests within Hollywood proper, which has become a flea circus for tourists and a magnet for the dregs of society. Hollywood itself is more a state of mind than an actual physical location.

I worked for a producer who had a first-look deal at Warner's and luckily our offices were on Warner's Burbank lot, probably my favorite standing lot in town. It retained the greatest feel of the old studio era. There were a lot of ghosts floating around on that lot, and I liked hanging out with them.

I pulled through the employee gate at the Burbank Studios and stopped to talk to Jack, one of the guards I had befriended in my brief time on the lot. If you really want to know what's going on behind the walls of a movie studio, get to know the security guards.

"How'd the place hold up, Jack?"

"Broke a couple of lights, couple of windows. A crack down the side of Eastwood's building, but other than that you wouldn't notice anything."

"They don't build 'em like this anymore."

"You can say that again, Mr. Hayes."

"Power back up yet?"

"Been back on in Burbank since yesterday afternoon."

"How'd your house handle the quake?"

"Not a scratch. Shook Kelly and the girls up a bit, but they'll get over it."

"Glad to hear it. What's the current skinny behind the palace walls?"

"Layoffs. This thing is giving the boys upstairs plenty of excuses. Be prepared to say good-bye to some of the support staff around here."

"Let me know if my name comes up."

"Will do." He smiled and waved me through. "Have a good day, Mr. Hayes."

"You, too, Jack."

I parked in my reserved space and got out and looked around the lot. The place was half empty. A lot of people were using the earthquake as a chance to catch up on their reading. The movers and shakers were here, though. In my office our boss, Dexter Morton, was the mover. The rest of us were shakers.

Dexter's suite of offices was on the second floor of one of Warner's more modern buildings. All glass, steel, and concrete. He had been given the option of setting up in the classy old bungalows near Clint Eastwood's building, but he had told the execs in charge that he was in the business of tomorrow, not yesterday. There was no room for nostalgia in Dexter Morton's world. He had even named his company Prescient Pictures with that kind of forward thinking in mind.

Dexter had an infrastructure staff of six working for him full-time at the studio. A receptionist, two secretaries, both male, a researcher, and two development people—creative executives, if you will—Alex Richards and myself. A bevy of assistants also rotated in and out of the offices on a picture-by-picture basis. I was the new man on the team. Alex had been there the longest—almost two years. Dexter had a big turnover problem. If you couldn't take the heat, you had to get out of his kitchen.

Dexter also had a personal assistant named Mrs. Bolender, but she spent most of her time working out of his house, organizing his private affairs, so we saw little of her, which was fine by me. She was a lean, hard slice of gray cloud, and she could bring the temperature in a room down just by walking past the door. She spoke with a slight British accent, but I had the feeling it was affected. I also saw and heard no evidence that there was a *Mr.* Bolender.

Dexter had worked his way up from corporate attorney to agent to the owner of a modestly successful production company all in the span of ten years, the Hollywood boom years of the eighties. Sensing that the end of economic prosperity for the independents was approaching, he siphoned off all the assets of the production company so the investors and filmmakers expecting profits would be left with nothing, then he dumped the company on the public market right before the bottom fell out. He made a fortune, and the stockholders and filmmakers who had supported him got burned badly. His reputation as a sharp businessman soared and he began producing bigger pictures for the studios. He bounced from studio to studio until he ended up on the Burbank lot. He had made five movies during the last three years. Two bombed, one was a modest hit, one was unreleasable, straight-to-video fodder, but the last one was *the* number-one hit of the summer. Dexter's fortune was on the rise. On top of his first-look deal with Warner's, he had every other studio in town waiting in line to pick at the leftovers.

I had lucked into my job. I had been filling in as a reader for a friend of mine who worked for Dexter and had to go on a stress-related leave of absence. She decided to make it permanent. Dexter offered to let me stay on. It looked like a good opportunity, so I gave it a shot. It had been the toughest five months of my life. Most producers and executives have quirks. They are egocentric. They are often hot tempered. None that I have met rivaled Dexter Morton. He was the King Kong of assholes. But he got movies made, and that's where I wanted to be, in close proximity to the people who can get things done. I didn't necessarily want to make the kind of movies Dexter specialized in—big action flicks and high-concept no-brainers—but you have to have success first if you are going to earn the right to make what you want to make. If I could ride Dexter's coattails on to a couple of big hits, I might eventually be able to strike out on my own as a producer.

My last regular full-time job had been as an assistant to Hal Grover, one of the old-time pros who had been producing movies all the way back in the fifties. Hal had the best story sense of any producer I've ever worked for. He could smell bullshit a mile away. He didn't buy into the clichés of the day: the hero's journey or the character's arc or even location as character. That kind of sound bite development had no place in Hal's office. He just wanted it truthful. He abhorred the phony nonsense that passed for writing at most of the studios. Unfortunately the only thing keeping him on the Fox lot was a thirty-year relationship with the head of the studio, and even that yielded only a housekeeping deal and endless development without tangible results. He couldn't even get his pals to green light one of his pictures. Hal's projects "skewed too old," as one of the execs on the lot used to say. During a palace coup Hal's studio boss friend was "retired" and Hal's dismissal soon followed. At seventy-eight, his was not the face young Hollywood wanted to stare up at during pitch meetings. He cut all his employees very generous severance checks, then retired to his house in Bel Air. It had been a warm and instructional experience for me. I missed working for Hal. He was a hell of a nice guy. But he couldn't get a movie made anymore.

Dexter Morton had none of Hal Grover's attributes. He also had none of his problems. Dexter could get movies made. He just made everyone suffer in the process.

Before Grover I worked for a man named Pete Turner, an executive at a boutique production house called the Film Factory that had coproduction deals with three of the major studios. One day the accountants at Paramount pulled a surprise audit on Pete, and discovered he had been embezzling millions from the productions they were cofinancing. He was also working kickback deals with all his major vendors. Pete was fired but not jailed. He even got to keep his Malibu beach house and his seven cars. Everyone working under him was fired as well. We were all marked as coconspirators, even though none of us had known what Pete was up to and none of us had shared in his profits. Work was hard to find after that scandal. I was lucky to land a position in Hal Grover's office. Grover believed I was innocent, but the job with Grover had not advanced my career in the least and had done little to cleanse my reputation. Dexter Morton had hired me despite the dark cloud hovering over my head, but he used my tainted past against me whenever he needed to put me in my place. He was keeping those coattails I wanted to ride just out of my reach. My career clock was ticking, and if something didn't break for me soon, I was going to be a low-level flunky the rest of my life.

Alex Richards rushed up to me as I entered the office. Alex usually looked *GQ* suave: perfect hair, perfect teeth, perfect build, but when the heat was on and the tension was high, he had a tendency to fall apart and resemble a stock broker circa 1929. He produced copious amounts of flop sweat in pressure situations. During these stressful events he always seemed to have one eye on the window, as if it would make a perfectly fine exit.

"He's on the rampage," Alex said, sweat blistering on his forehead.

"So what else is new?" I asked.

"No, I mean it's bad. Like in *firing time* bad."

"What's the problem?"

"He read the new draft of *Terminal Youth* during the earthquake."

"Really? During all that shaking? I could barely get out of my apartment."

"You know what I mean."

"Yeah. I know."

"Did you read it?"

"Uh-huh. Read it over the weekend. It was spotty, but I thought Jason fixed a lot of the problems we had addressed."

"Jason's had it. He's toast. Dex has already hired Klane and Epperson to do a fix."

"Does Jason know?"

"No. He's coming in at ten. He'll find out then."

"Holy shit."

I looked at the clock. It was a little after nine.

"It gets worse," Alex added. "He went through our notes on the project. *All* of them."

"So?"

"So? Don't you get it? He's not through. He wants a fall guy on this. Maybe *two.* He's going to can us both."

Alex wiped the sweat from his brow and fumbled for a cigarette. We walked past Janet, the receptionist, who was busy on the phones, and went out onto the terrace overlooking the back lot. Alex lit his cigarette and took a long drag. In an attempt to cut down on my nicotine intake, I became a social smoker in '92. I try not to smoke unless someone else around me is smoking. It limits me to five or ten cigarettes a day and an occasional cigar. I also try not to buy cigarettes, which has turned me into a tobacco bum, so I had to "borrow" a smoke from Alex. His hands were shaking as he flicked his lighter under the cigarette. I'd never seen him so frantic.

"You've got to calm down," I said. "He sees you like this and you're as good as dead."

"We're dead anyway."

"Bullshit. Has he said anything to that effect?"

"No. But I know him. He wants blood. We've been wrestling with this script for a year now and he thinks we've all been jerking off. The studio has put the hammer down on spending. They want him to start cutting corners. He's going to can us."

"So what?"

"That's easy for you to say. I just bought a condo. I can't make those payments on unemployment."

"You'll bounce back."

He looked at me sharply. "You've heard something, haven't you? It's true, isn't it? I'm out. Oh, shit, I knew this was going to happen. I never should have bought that fucking thing! I'm going to lose my down payment!"

"Calm down. I haven't heard anything."

"This is so fucked. This is the wrong time to be looking for a job."

Alex stubbed out his cigarette. He seemed to have tears brimming in his eyes.

"Relax, man," I said. "It won't be as bad as you think. I'm sure."

"You are?"

I nodded, patted him on the back, and led him inside. As we walked down the hall, Dexter's door flew open and Tom, one of his secretaries, stepped out to greet us.

"He wants to see you," Tom said.

"I just got here," I said. "I haven't even dropped my stuff in my office."

"Bring it with you."

I made eye contact with Janet, the receptionist, and she winked at me with a combination of *hello* and *good luck* as she continued to field phone calls. Most of the callers were being told that "Mr. Morton is in a meeting and cannot be disturbed."

Alex and I followed Tom into Dexter's office. Alex looked like a condemned man being led to the gallows. I had a feeling that *we* were the ones who were about to be disturbed.

SIX

Dexter Morton wasn't an ugly man, but there was something distinctly repulsive about him. He disguised it as best he could but it was there. You just had to get past the façade.

He always dressed to impress, the standard black-on-black three thousand-dollar designer suits, and his regular workouts at the gym left him well built for a studio exec. But there was something about his face that was disconcerting. No, not his face, his *skull.* That was the problem. He had a somewhat misshapen skull. It was an odd shape, round where it shouldn't be, angular in just the wrong way. Combine that with a toupee that was expensive yet obvious, and he gave the impression that he could have just as easily been a mortician as a film producer. There was something ghoulish about the man. He looked like the kind of guy who would fuck a dead snake if there were a twenty-dollar bill up its ass.

Dexter was on the phone when we entered his office. He motioned for us to sit as he finished his conversation. He was obviously on with a woman. His tone was more pleading than demanding. Dexter was hell on wheels with anyone he did business with, but when it came to women he wanted to bed, they had his number. They made him pay in ways unimaginable to most of us.

Dexter wrapped up his call quickly and got right down to business. He tossed the latest draft of the *Terminal Youth* script on the floor in front of us.

"Have you read that piece of shit?" Dexter asked me directly, as if Alex wasn't even in the room.

"Yes, sir."

"And?"

"I thought it still needed work."

"Really? You should work for the fuckin' U.N. with diplomacy shooting out of your ass like that."

Dexter got up and paced behind his desk.

"Who told this writer to go limp on us? What's with this 'gritty realism' that keeps popping up in your notes to that pimply faced little fuck? And what happened to the action? He's cut it all out and replaced it with talking heads. This isn't TV we're doing here. This brat's been sucking cash out of my office for the better part of a year and tossing garbage back in our faces. This office can't afford to play games like this anymore. Especially after the earthquake. The fiscal ramifications of that motherfucker are going to be felt around here for years. Why have you guys let this situation get out of hand?"

I pulled the notebook out of my satchel and quickly flipped through my notes, looking for a way to extricate myself from this mess. Alex had relaxed a bit, like maybe he thought he was out of the woods and that I, being the newest man on the team, was going to crash and burn alone.

"Um, uh," I stammered, "during my last conversation with you about the script, you said you wanted a more realistic take on the material, like *Goodfellas.*"

Dexter stopped in his tracks and stared at me like I was a bug.

"*I* said that?" he asked. He seemed genuinely shocked.

"Yes, sir."

"*Goodfellas* only grossed fifty domestic. I can't afford to top out at fifty domestic! We make hits here! I must be out of my goddamn mind if I said something like that!"

"Maybe you were thinking of the Academy, sir," Alex interjected, his newfound bravery betraying him. "The prestige of the awards."

"Screw the awards," Dexter said. "Net profits *are* awards. That's how we keep our asses at the top. *Profits.* I must've been having an acid flashback if I said something like that. Why didn't you guys straighten me out? What the hell do I have you around for? If you can't keep the ship on an even keel I'll goddamn get someone who can. I can't micromanage every dink project that comes down the pike. I expect you fuckers to pull your weight!"

"Yes, sir," I said.

"Sorry, sir," Alex added.

We were saved by the buzzer as Janet contacted Dexter over the intercom. "Jason Ward is here," she said.

"Send him in," Dexter said into the intercom. Dexter sat down behind his desk, which was elevated a good three feet higher than any other seat in the room. Like all good despots he liked to control the high ground.

Alex and I sat silently as Jason Ward entered the room. He was just a kid, barely twenty-six, but old by Hollywood screenwriter standards of the day. He wore the traditional outfit of the hip young writer: jeans, sweatshirt, and untied tennis shoes. He had bad skin and an attitude to match. Two years earlier, fresh out of UCLA, he had sold his first spec script to Fox for 2.5 million at auction and he became one of the hot shit new kids on the block. The Next Big Thing. He thought he could do no wrong. His self-perceptions were about to be rattled.

The moment he walked in, Jason spotted his screenplay on the floor. He went over and picked it up.

"You dropped your script, Mort," Jason said. Dexter liked his writers to call him "Mort" or "Morty." He said it gave them a false sense of familiarity that he could use to his advantage.

Jason started to lay the script on Dexter's desk.

"Forget it, Mr. Ward," Dexter said. "That's *your* copy. Matter of fact, they're *all* your copies."

"What do you mean?" Jason looked genuinely confused.

"I mean we've decided to go another way."

"Why don't you drop the studio jargon and just tell me what's happening? Are you canceling the project?"

"No. I'm canceling *you.* As I said, we're going another way."

Jason was starting to get steamed. I could tell he wasn't accustomed to being spoken to like this. He had spent the last two years having his ass kissed by everyone in town. Well, that 2.5-million-dollar script was still gathering dust over at Fox and word on the street was that it wasn't ever going to get made. I had a feeling that this wouldn't be the last time Jason Ward got an earful from a studio suit.

"You're firing me? From my own project?"

"Yes and no. Yes, you're being fired, but from your own project? Not hardly. *I* own all the rights to *Terminal Youth* and I plan on protecting those rights. You should thank me. With you out of the way, maybe the picture will get made. At the end of the day, isn't that all that matters? You'll still get a credit—of some sort—depending on how the Guild arbitration goes."

"I don't get it, Mort," Jason said, waving the script in the air. "What's the fucking problem?"

"It reads like bad Tolstoy, Mr. Ward. And even good Tolstoy is *out* this year. Or didn't you get the memo?"

"Hey, that script is about the *truth.*"

Dexter looked at Alex and me for the first time since Jason had entered the room. "He doesn't understand, does he?"

Jason glared at us like we were Dexter's coconspirators. His face was flushed with embarrassment and rage.

"I guess I have to explain it in simple English, eh?" Dexter said.

Jason turned back to him and tried to calm down. "Yeah, Mort, why don't you explain it to me? I'm new around here." The sarcasm dripped off the punk like he had eaten Bill Murray for breakfast and was sweating him out of his pores.

"We deal in lies," Dexter said. "That's our business. Lying to the audience. I thought you understood that. We have to take their myths and streamline them, clean them up, remove the troublesome realities and details, add a little perfume, and then put a nice glossy veneer over it all so it's palatable for mass consumption. They don't want to smell death or sex, but they want to *see* it, and they want the pictures pretty and entertaining and unthreatening. They want to be in a nice cool theater with a hot box of popcorn and they don't want to get hurt or dirty. They just want to relax, throw back their heads, and be lied to as nicely as possible."

"That's bullshit, Mort!" Jason stammered, enraged by Dexter's callous slandering of the audience and the profession. "That's not why I got into this business and I won't be any part of it."

"Really? What is it you want, then?" Dexter asked. "Why *are* you in this business?"

"Because I love movies and I thought I could make some good ones. I wanted to give something back to the industry. I wanted to be like the great filmmakers of the past and do some good work and leave my mark on the world. And somewhere along the way I wanted to try to get a little truth into the pictures so that those who came later would know where we had been and what we had done. I wanted to progress the evolution of the medium."

Dexter had begun laughing halfway through Jason's speech. It started quietly enough, but he soon lost control, and by the time Jason was finished, Dexter was holding his sides to keep from splitting a gut. Jason had chosen to ignore him and throw himself into his spiel with religious fervor. He must have figured that if he was going to humiliate himself, he might as well do it with style and make his feelings known with total, unabashed honesty, no matter how corny or ridiculous he might sound.

When Dexter finally quit laughing, he said, "Kid, you can really lay out the shit!"

Dexter slowly got to his feet and tried to catch his breath. His face was crimson and he was trying not to laugh anymore, probably for fear that he might give himself another heart attack. He had experienced an "episode" during the stock market crash in '88 and had been advised to avoid stress. Jason just stood and watched him. He had nothing more to say and decided to cling to whatever fragile dignity he had left by going mute. But Dexter wasn't done.

"To tell you the truth, Mr. Ward," he continued, "I think you've got a lot of talent. I don't think you're going to be able to do jack shit with it in this town, but I think you're one hell of a talented kid. Maybe you ought to make documentaries. They *pretend* to tell everyone the truth. Of course they're bullshit too, but the guys who make 'em are usually confused like you and they walk around real happy, like they've shined a light on something for the world. Now that I think of it, they're just *exactly* like you. They don't realize that the world doesn't give a shit about reality, even the phony reality of documentaries. The only people who care about that crap are wet-nosed UCLA students and pussies who watch PBS for their weekly dose of reality. These people wouldn't know reality if it bit them on the ass. And when they *do* get a taste of *real* reality, they're going to hate it, 'cause at the end of the day they're going to be staring up into the face of some ugly paramedic and they're going to realize that life is tough, that it hurts, and that sooner or later it's *over,* just like the movies, but for real. Black screen. Blanko. Forget it! That's when they'll know they've wasted their time and been just as deceived by truthmongers like you as they would have been if they spent their time with *my* product. But at least with me they would have been *entertained* while they were killing the time."

"You're a fucking asshole," Jason said. He rolled his screenplay into a tube, tossed it in the wastebasket, and stormed out of the room.

Dexter looked at the script in the trash, then turned to us and smiled.

"See," he said. "The meeting wasn't a complete waste. The kid learned exactly what his work was worth."

SEVEN

I felt bad for Jason Ward, but he had brought it on himself. He had been given plenty of time to shape that script into something Dexter would like, but he had ignored many of the notes we had given him and proven himself to be someone that Dexter could not mold to suit his purposes. Dexter was not usually that directly confrontational with anyone unless he was sure he was never going to need them in the future. A dressing-down like Jason had received was a good indication that his career was in serious trouble.

After the Jason Ward bloodbath, I spent the rest of the day alone in my office, writing reports on the scripts I had taken home for the long weekend that had grown longer than anyone expected. I had read six new screenplays and a novel in my downtime at home. They were all bad. The novel had a few good ideas, but it would take too much work to develop it into a profitable feature film. I handed out six PASS reviews on the scripts and a CONSIDER WRITER notice on the novel, turned the reports in to Tom, plucked a couple of scripts from the slush pile to read, packed them in my briefcase, and called it a night.

Alex was still in his office when I passed his door. He was hard at work, reading something dreadful judging by the pained expression on his face. Alex had been a screenwriter in the fat eighties. A couple of his scripts were turned into low-budget films before the bottom dropped out of the indie video boom and he had to seek refuge in the executive branch. Occasionally he made noises about going back to writing, but we all knew he had seen his best days as a screenwriter and they weren't good enough to base a career on. If he wanted to keep up those condo payments, he was going to have to stay in the catbird seat—passing judgment on other writers' work for a steady paycheck.

That's one of the more tragic ironies about the film industry. There are hundreds of men and women—kids, really, most of them—who are hired to read material and pass judgment on it so that the executives can keep their hands and heads away from the written word. Most readers are wannabe writers or producers themselves, so the conflict of interest is quite obvious. The majority of them are not qualified to do anything other than render an undereducated opinion, but that is all they need do, because the job isn't really about finding good material. It's about weeding out all the rotten stuff that weasels its way into the studio. Many readers work for no pay whatsoever, just trying to get their feet in the door. *Interns.* Their opinions are usually worth exactly what they are being paid—zilch. But the executives and producers depend on these cherubs to defend them from the tidal wave of material that flows over their transoms every day. People at the very bottom of the food chain are passing judgment on what should be the most important decision in the entire process—what stories are going to be developed and made into feature films. The creative executive, C.E. for short, which was the job title on my paycheck, is not much more than a glorified reader: a D-boy, or *development boy,* as we were called by the disrespectful, a reader with an income to justify his work. A writer might spend a year, two, three, on his screenplay or novel, only to have it dismissed in an afternoon by some angry schmuck who just wants to get to the bottom of his slush pile. I myself had just rendered such life-altering judgment on seven writers.

It was exhilarating.

EIGHT

Famished from my afternoon of playing God, I dropped in to Viande for a bite to eat before going home. The power was back on in the neighborhood and the place was lit up like a Christmas tree. I took a seat at the bar and ordered my usual—a blackened New York steak and a Tanqueray and tonic. Jennifer was working the bar and had my order in before I even sat down.

It was the first time I had seen her since the earthquake, so I asked her how she fared through the disaster.

"Okay," she said. "Lost all my dishes."

"Me, too."

"Suzie was in earlier. She asked about you."

"That's nice. Tell her I said 'Hi' when you see her again."

"Why don't you tell her yourself?" she said curtly, then turned away to make my drink.

Suzie was one of Jennifer's best friends. We had gotten drunk a few weeks earlier and ended up in bed. I had been uncomfortable around her ever since. Suzie had wanted to know what the experience had meant to me, and after hearing the question phrased that way, I had to admit that I wasn't exactly sure. That was not the answer she was looking for. I explained to her that I couldn't handle any complications in my life at the moment, and things deteriorated from there. The fact was that I had no interest in having a lasting relationship with anyone until I had my career on track. If art is a jealous mistress, then the film business is an outright selfish bitch. Women always say they understand the sacrifices one has to make while working in the film industry—they always give lip service to giving you room, space, and time to get the job done—but when you actually put in the fourteen-hour days then come home with more work that you have to do before you go to sleep, when you cancel dinner plans over and over again, when you have to dedicate your weekends to work that didn't get done during the week instead of walking with them on the beach, then the luster soon fades from the romance of the job. My last relationship of any standing endured for eight months. Collette was a fantastic woman, far better than I deserved, beautiful, sweet, kind, sexy, smart, and generous to a fault. She just wanted to have a man in her life who actually paid attention to her. No harm in that. I just couldn't work it into my schedule. I didn't have the kind of clout that would enable me to get away with industry success *and* a healthy personal life.

None of this information was comforting to Suzie. As a matter of fact, it just made her very angry. I was hoping it wasn't going to affect the quality of my bar service from her good friend Jennifer.

Jennifer placed a tall Tanqueray and tonic in front of me. She did not disappoint. It was a gooood drink. Heavy on the gin. Just what I needed to knock the dust from my lungs.

The bar at Viande occupied fully one-third of the dining room. It was a big square thing, almost like a cage for the bartender. The bar itself was sheeted in bronze, which was nice and reflective so you could stare into your own eyes if you felt the need to rest your head around closing time.

I turned my attention to the various flirtations oozing around the bar. Single women liked to come into Viande, usually in pairs or groups, but they didn't usually remain single for long. There were always plenty of guys who came to the place hoping to keep them company.

Two women occupied one of the external corners of the bar. They looked married and bored. They were being hit on by two jazz fans who had not found what they were looking for in The Club Upstairs, as the jazz room at the top of the stairs was called. The jazz boys were so damn cool that the women couldn't get worked up enough to cheat on their husbands. It looked like it would take a couple of nasty packages to get them to stray, and these guys didn't fit the bill. They were coming on all slick and suave. These ladies weren't looking to be gently seduced. They wanted to be blown away or left alone.

Jennifer was playing a handful of male customers like so many cards in a marked deck. She knew how to walk that fine line between friendly flirtation and outright seduction. She could bring her customers to the brink of intimacy, peel away a fat tip, and not leave them sore thinking she had made any promises she didn't keep. She was a pro.

I wanted to check on the nest egg I jokingly referred to as the Development Fund. I opened my briefcase and brought out my checking and savings account books. I had a combined total of $22,436.18 in the two accounts. Not much of a nest egg. Far short of what I would need to make a career move. My entire life outside of the office was controlled by the idea of making a move. It's why I lived in a crappy apartment in the Valley and had a roommate to split expenses with to boot, why I drove a car that would impress no one, why I had no cell phone and no steady girl. I was saving every cent I possibly could for the moment when I could make a move: buy a project, develop it, put up a piece of the production capital if necessary, be the producer. Control. That's what it was all about. But you can't control much with twenty grand.

The only point in being a creative executive for a Dexter Morton is the hope that you might be able to step up a bit and eventually get a producing credit on a feature. And not just a credit. They hand those things out like jelly beans now. I wanted to actually *do the work.* Most of the people taking producer credits on movies nowadays haven't the faintest idea what it is to physically produce a movie. They are producers by proxy. They are owed politically in some way. They rep one of the actors, they found the screenplay, they bought the book the script was based on, they're related to the director or the star; they are generally anything but actual film producers. The credits of the average mainstream studio picture usually have at least two producers listed, two or three executive producers, a coproducer or two, a line producer, and any number of associate producers. The two producers are usually the people who initiated the project. They bought the book or the script, used to be the director's agent, or found a way to coerce some major stars to sign on to the film, thus ensuring a green light from the executive producers, the suits working for the studio. The coproducer is often the guy who actually does most of the physical work that the producer used to do in the old days, but the coproducer isn't fixed up enough politically to warrant the desired producer's credit, so he does all the work for half the dough and a watered-down credit. The line producer, if there is one—and if he hasn't been given the coproducer credit—is often the unit production manager, and they are throwing him a bone with the title. He will bust his ass to make his superiors' dreams come true and his superiors will do their best to minimize his contribution at every opportunity. The associate producers are usually pure suckfish: the relatives of the movers and shakers, the attorney who controlled the will, or sometimes the lowly writer of the piece. Of course there are other titles you may see occasionally: coexecutive producer, production associate, executive in charge of production. The specific function of these credits changes from picture to picture, situation to situation, deal to deal, depending on the nature of the players and the quality of their legal representation. The jockeying for credits on a feature film is a horse race like no other, and it's madness trying to make sense of it. All these characters will have a bevy of assistants running around, often doing most of their real work for them. If you want to know the assistants' names, you'll have to wait for the end credits to roll. They can only put twelve or thirteen producers at the top of the picture.

As sick as it sounds, I wanted to be one of those twelve guys. That's the only way you can work your way up to where you can develop and make your own films if you don't have the bread to buy your way in. You gotta get that producer credit. And if you can't find a major mover to grandfather you into the business, you've got to find your own projects, your own production money, and make your own films. I was living like a monk—well, maybe a perverted monk—so I could build up a stash large enough to buy into a project and make it happen on my own if my time with Dexter Morton proved fruitless. I had optioned a few screenplays from young writers with the standard one-dollar contract that passes for a deal on those kinds of things, but I had not been able to set any of them up. Most scripts that can be optioned for a dollar are worth no more than the buck you paid for them, especially if you have no clout. The Development Fund was growing, but it would have to get a lot fatter before I was going to be able to afford a substantial position on a project of any worth.

I put away my things as a couple of the locals came in and filled the bar on my side of the room. We all said our hellos and got down to some serious drinking. My steak arrived and I scarfed it down like it was Claudia Schiffer on a French roll. Jennifer refilled my glass and I gave her the cutoff sign. I never had more than two drinks on a work night at Viande. It was like having four anywhere else.

I looked at the corner of the bar. The ladies were saying good night and heading for the door. The jazz boys went back upstairs to try to get their rhythm back.

NINE

I stumbled out the back door of Viande and crossed the alley to my apartment building. It was a warm, clear night for January and the air smelled clean for a change.

Clyde McCoy was sitting on the brick wall in front of his apartment, staring up at the stars and nursing a cup of his famous coffee. I almost didn't stop, afraid I'd disturb him or startle him into falling off his perch, and then I reconsidered. I wanted to be a friendly neighbor. After all, the man had saved me from a morning without caffeine. I owed him.

"Nice night, huh?" I said.

"Fuck, yeah," he replied. "You can even see the stars. You know when the last time it was you could see this many stars in a Valley sky?"

"Tell you the truth, I don't look up there that often."

"How come?"

"I'm afraid of heights."

He looked at me for a moment, probably wondering if I was drunk or just a smart-ass. A thin smile creased his lips and he sipped his coffee.

"That's a good one. I might have to use that someday."

"Feel free," I said. The Tanqueray was making me a little dizzy. I leaned on the wall for support.

"You look like you could use a cup of coffee."

"I've got to be up early tomorrow. I drink coffee now and I'll never get to sleep."

"You've been drinking gin, haven't you?"

"You've got a good nose."

"I used to like my liquor."

"How long ago you quit?"

"About two years now. I don't count it out like some of them."

"Does it bother you when people around you are drinking?"

"Nope. I find it comforting. *Someone* might as well be having fun. I'm not one of those born agains. I've just been taking a little break, trying to get some work done and let the old liver heal."

A woman came out of Clyde's apartment. She was short, blonde and cute, about thirty, and very well built for her size. She was wearing shorts and a sweater. I was surprised by her arrival. Besides the night of the quake, I had never seen anyone other than Clyde or delivery people go in or out of his apartment. She was new to the scene.

"What's going on out here?" the woman asked with a smile.

"We're just talking about stars and bars," Clyde said.

I offered my hand to her as a greeting.

"I'm Mark Hayes. I live upstairs."

She shook my hand with a grip of steel. "I'm Emily," she said. "Glad you introduced yourself. Clyde would never get around to it."

"Oh, shit," he said. "You know how I am. I always think everybody knows everybody."

"I know what you mean," I said. "It's okay. Nice to meet you, Emily."

"Nice to meet you, too."

There was a moment of silence as we tried to figure out where to take it from there. Clyde came to the rescue.

"Emily just got back from the Philippines."

"Really? What were you doing down there?" I asked.

"Working on a film."

"Emily's a movie star," Clyde offered.

Emily blushed and punched him on the shoulder. It almost knocked him off the wall. He spilled half his coffee trying to catch himself.

"Damn, girl," he said. "I told you not to beat on me. I'm getting too old for that shit."

"That *line* is what's old," she said with a laugh.

"That's why I don't write screenplays anymore," he said. "All the good lines have been taken."

I finally recognized the woman. She was Emily Woolrich, a martial arts movie star who had found fame in wild Hong Kong flicks and lesser quality straight-to-video junk made in the States.

"I've seen some of your films, Emily," I said. "On Showtime and HBO."

"Hope you saw the Asian ones," she said, almost timidly.

"One or two. They were good."

"The movies I've done here aren't so hot."

"They can't choreograph here like they do in Hong Kong," Clyde added.

"No one here would do what they do over there," she said. "People get hurt bad on those films. I almost lost my kneecap."

She extended her leg and showed me a crescent-shaped scar around the kneecap. Her leg was tanned and shapely, but when she extended and flexed it the muscles popped out like she was a female Incredible Hulk. She looked like she could kick a hole through the brick wall if it pissed her off.

"What happened?" I asked.

"Guy threw me down a flight of stairs at a Buddhist temple we were shooting at in Thailand. That was the last time I worked for Hong Kong producers. I want to last in this business."

"Hey, you would have never made it to where you are today if you hadn't done that crazy shit for all those Hong Kong guys," Clyde said.

"I was younger then. And more flexible. Let the new girls bounce off the stairs. I've had enough of that. The Philippine movies are a lot easier on the bones."

Clyde smiled like that was the answer he wanted to hear all along.

"You shit," she said, and she punched him again. "You tricked me!"

"Owwww, I'm gonna have a big fucking bruise!" He dumped the rest of his coffee in the bushes and climbed off the wall.

Emily looked at me like she felt she owed me an explanation.

"Clyde's been trying to get me to quit acting for years," she said. "He thinks it's dangerous."

"You can't be jumping over cars when you're forty," Clyde said.

"That's still a ways off, dear," she said. "*You're* the forty-year-old, remember?"

"Oh yeah."

"He's just jealous," Emily said. "He's afraid I'm going to fall in love with some leading man from Singapore."

"Try a stunt man from Indonesia."

"That was *one time.* Get over it."

"You hurt me deeply." He didn't sound very hurt.

"You managed to console yourself with a wide variety of playthings during my next trip away." She *did* sound hurt.

"Let's not fight in front of Mark," Clyde said sweetly. "He's been drinking."

"I'm sorry," she said to me.

"Don't be," I said. "I barely heard a word."

"That's what I like," Clyde said. "A friend with selective hearing."

I don't know exactly why, but hearing him refer to me as his friend made me smile. I drunkenly said good night and retired to my palace at the top of the stairs.

I hit the light switch in the kitchen and found that the electricity was back on in my place, too. The first thing I did was check to see if the television had broken when it crashed during the earthquake. It worked! I quickly flipped through the seventy channels and found there was still nothing on worth watching, then turned it off.

I went around the apartment and gathered up the candles that had been functioning as my lights while the power was out. I put them all on the kitchen table so that they would be handy if they were suddenly needed again.

Power is one thing that you can never be sure of in this town.

TEN

At lunch the next day, Alex and I commiserated in the commissary about the various pieces of dreck we were reading. I didn't eat in the commissary often, preferring the privacy of my office when I didn't have a lunch meeting scheduled with a writer or producer who wanted to pitch ideas or needed help writing themselves out of a corner on a project we had commissioned. I could read half a script during lunch, sometimes the whole damn thing if it was good. The good ones are usually the quickest reads. It doesn't take a lot of words to get a point across. The better writers don't waste time showing off.

"Ever hear of a guy named Clyde McCoy?" I asked Alex during a lull in the conversation.

"Sure," Alex said. "He wrote a ton of shit back in the eighties. Low-budget garbage mostly. He did a thing called *North of Ensenada* that wasn't too bad. Kind of an *arty* piece of garbage. He was doing three or four pictures a year, but I haven't seen his name on anything in a long time. Did he die?"

"He's my next-door neighbor."

"No shit?"

"Yeah. I didn't know it until the earthquake. That was the first time we spoke."

"Was he drunk?"

"Sober as the pope."

"He was a notorious drunk. He used to proudly say he *never* wrote a script sober, and looking at the films they made out of them, I believe it."

"He must've been doing something right to get so many movies made."

"Don't get me wrong. He was an adequate writer for what he was doing. A good, by-the-numbers type, sometimes a little quirky, but I heard he was a real pain in the ass to work with. Dexter knows. They did a couple of pictures together."

I was shocked by this revelation. "No . . ."

"Sure. Dexter hated him."

"Why?"

"I've just heard stories on the grapevine, but I think the guy wasn't very good at taking orders."

"Dexter doesn't exactly dole them out with finesse, either."

"True, but you know writers. They get a couple of credits under their belt and you can't tell 'em anything. They think it's going to go on forever."

We ate in silence for a few minutes, watching the politics flow through the commissary like blood through a racehorse, then Alex asked, "So what's he doing now?"

"Who?" I asked, having already forgotten the conversation.

"McCoy, your neighbor."

"Oh. I think he's working on a book."

"Ah," Alex said. "The last refuge of the scoundrel."

ELEVEN

When I got back to my office I looked up Clyde McCoy's résumé in our database. He was a hyphenate. A writer and occasionally a producer or director. But his main area of success, if you could call it that, was clearly screenwriting. I found seventeen writing or cowriting credits under his name and the database was notoriously incomplete. He probably had four or five more that weren't listed. He had also produced a couple of low-budget grinders and he had a directing credit on a movie under the pseudonym Colon Noble. Alex was right. A number of Clyde's writing credits were for movies produced by Dexter's old company, Cinetown, back in the heyday of the video boom. So Clyde and Dexter had worked together. It probably explained why Clyde was afraid to come out of his house.

I cross-checked some of Clyde's titles with the Maltin and the Martin/Porter movie guides. Most of his films got at least two stars, an average rating but not bad for low-budget fodder. Some got two and a half or three, but none registered higher than that except for a raw-sounding piece of work called *Student Chainsaw Nurses* that Leonard Maltin deemed worthy of three and a half stars due to its "drive-in purity on a global scale." Clyde's credits ended in 1990. Which meant his last film was probably shot in 1989 and written God knows how long before that. He hadn't had a picture produced in years.

Dexter came into my office without knocking, as was his habit, and immediately started in on me about a script I had covered before lunch, a new untitled piece by a pet writer of his named Gregory Cloud who had penned two of Dexter's worst movies, one of which went straight to video, the other of which became his biggest hit, the one he was riding to the bank everyday since it opened last June.

Dexter waved the coverage in the air. "What the hell is this all about, Hayes?"

"The script stank," I said, prepared for the worst.

"So?" He said it as if my reaction made no sense whatsoever.

"I thought he could do better," I said, holding my ground.

"I'm still not getting your point. See, due to the nature of our relationship with Gregory Cloud, we've got first look at a spec script by one of the hottest writers in town. We can buy this before it goes to auction and steal it out from under everyone's nose, or we can sit around and get into a bidding war with Silver and New Line and Geffen and pay three times what we can purchase it for right now."

"What if we just passed?" I asked cautiously.

"Oh, sure, we could do that. Why don't we just close up the office and stay home for the rest of the year? We don't need to make any more movies. We can leave that to the other guys."

"Dexter, it's a bad piece. It's filled with clichés and flat characters. It's nothing but gunfights and explosions and corny dialogue."

Dexter sniffed the air as if getting a whiff of a delicious pie baking in the kitchen.

"Smells like another big hit to me. I'm buying it."

"Please don't do that, Dexter."

"Too late, I already did. Cut him a check for one point five and called it a day."

I was flabbergasted. "When?"

"This morning. It was a preemptive strike. I just wanted to know what you really thought of the material before I told you it was ours."

The bastard was playing with me. It was a test and it seemed that I had failed miserably. I just stared at him, not saying anything, waiting to be fired. Dexter folded the coverage neatly and laid it in front of me on my desk.

"Well, what do you think of your coverage now, Hayes?"

"I stand by it," I said, knowing I had nothing left to lose.

"You're all right, Hayes," Dexter said, surprising me once again. "And you're right about the script. It's shit. But I couldn't let it get past us. It gets made next year at Fox and turns into a big hit, I'd look like Frank Price letting *E.T.* go at Columbia."

"I understand."

"I've got a small problem though. The good news is, Cloud doesn't care what we do to the script and he doesn't want to be bothered with the rewrites. The bad news is I had to guarantee him under the table that he'd get solo credit. You know the Guild won't allow such guarantees, so we're going to need a stealth rewrite. Get Wilkie on the phone and see if he wants to do an under-the-table dialogue polish on the turd. Tell him we'll give him fifty grand cash, but it's got to be off the record and out of Guild jurisdiction. He'll go for it. He needs every dime he can get his hands on."

"Okay."

"You're always begging for more responsibility, so today's your lucky day. You're going to be the go-to man on this. I don't want to know anything about it and no one else can know anything about it, either. Just get it done."

"I understand."

I *did* understand. Dexter didn't want to get into hot water with the Writers Guild or with Gregory Cloud and his representatives. If a scandal broke out, Dexter wanted me to be the fall guy, a role tailor-made for Mark Hayes considering my checkered past. I'd go along with his plan. Up to a point. But I was also going to make sure my ass was covered this time.

Dexter leaned forward and looked at my computer screen. Clyde McCoy's credits were still up. I had been so busy with the Maltin guide that I had forgotten to hit my screen saver when Dexter entered the room.

"What the hell are you looking at?" Dexter asked.

I tapped the screen saver and psychedelic fish floated across the screen.

"Nothing."

"Bullshit. Put it back up."

I reluctantly clicked the screen saver off and Clyde's credits filled the screen again.

"Why the fuck are you looking at Clyde McCoy's credits? He's a has-been. A never-was."

"He's my next-door neighbor," I said.

"Really?"

An evil grin crossed Dexter's face as if he were happy that Clyde McCoy had ended up living in the same apartment building that a lowly D-boy occupied. He was slapping us both in the face at the same time.

"Yes," I said. "I was just curious. I heard he made a lot of movies."

"He *wrote* a lot of movies," Dexter corrected. "Other people *made* them."

"He worked for you, didn't he?" I asked.

Dexter suddenly looked concerned. "What did he say?"

"Nothing. I noticed your old company's name attached to some of his credits. I didn't even know he knew you until today. It's just a bizarre coincidence, I guess."

"It's a small town. You're bound to run into a lot of people I've done business with. If I were you I wouldn't listen to a thing McCoy has to say about *anything.* He's a notorious liar."

"I've heard that." I hadn't, but I wanted Dexter to relax.

Dexter smiled at the confirmation. "He wasn't a bad writer, though," he added, as if now that Clyde McCoy's mysterious threat had been removed, he was safe to be complimented.

"How many films did he do for you?"

"Four or five. I don't know. Rewrites mostly. He wasn't much for originals. He just did fixes so he could keep in the booze. I don't think he was ever sober enough to have an original idea of his own."

"He stopped drinking."

"That would explain it," Dexter said.

"What?"

"Why I haven't seen his name on a movie in years."

TWELVE

"Wilkie" was Gordon Wilkenson, one of the best dialogue men in the business. Unfortunately he had lived beyond the dreaded gray line of fifty and jobs were becoming harder and harder to come by. Thirty is considered just about over the hill for the average screenwriter, forty is retirement time, fifty is death. Even for the good ones, like Wilkie. Sure, Bob Towne and Bill Goldman will keep working until they drop dead, but they're legends. Wilkie was just a good, solid craftsman. He never had a P.R. agent touting his wares. He preferred to work quietly, under the radar of the Hollywood hype machine. An honorable goal, but one that proved costly as he got older. It pays to be a household name if you're going for the long haul in this business.

Wilkie had suffered through a devastating divorce a few years back and was desperate for any kind of work that would give him cash in hand, capital he could hide from the IRS and his wife's divorce attorney. Dexter had used him for quick polishes three times in the last seven months and each time his payday had gotten lower. Dexter knew how to squeeze. Now he wanted me to offer one of the best in the business fifty grand under the table to secretly fix a piece of shit action script that Dexter had paid a mil and a half for. It was sinful. But I was beginning to dream up a scheme that would make it an outright crime.

I reread the script, then called Wilkie. He was home. Judging by the sounds I heard in the background I thought he was watching *Oprah.* A good sign for Prescient Pictures.

"Hey, Wilkie," I said into the phone.

"Who's this? Mark?"

"Yeah. What're you up to?"

"Just hanging out. Taking a break."

"How's the spec coming?"

"It's rough. I've rewritten it eight times. Whole new plot every draft. Still haven't found one that works."

"You'll get it. Hey, how would you like to take a breather on that thing and pick up some loose change?"

"I don't know. You guys are getting pretty cheap on me. What's the pay?"

"Let's discuss it over some pool. I want to run the script by you before we talk dollars."

"Oh, man, this sounds like it's going to hurt."

"Tell you what," I said. "I'll play you for the gig. Nine ball. Best out of five. I win, you do the job. You win, and I'll convince Dexter to buy your spec when it's finished."

"Sounds like you win no matter what happens."

"Hey, it's show biz."

"How come I always feel like I'm the one getting the 'biz' part of that?"

"Because you're a writer. You think too much."

"You're starting to sound like Dexter."

"Wilkie, I thought we were friends?"

"Sure we are. How's House of Billiards at eight o'clock?"

"I'll be there."

We hung up. The phone hadn't even come to rest in its cradle when I realized that I had manipulated the conversation *exactly* the way Dexter would have.

THIRTEEN

House of Billiards is just a block down from Viande on the opposite side of Ventura Boulevard, so I stopped by my apartment after work and changed into comfortable clothes and splashed on some aftershave to cut the sweat of the day down to a manageable scent. I walked over to the pool hall, having to maneuver around the various construction crews tearing down and loading up the massive Bank of America building across the street from House of Billiards. It had been deemed structurally unsound by the quake masters and now they were bringing it down before it came down on its own and killed a bunch of people.

House of Billiards is a fairly classy joint as far as pool halls go. Sixteen pool tables and four billiards tables arranged in two rows with just enough elbow room in between to keep the natives from banging into each other. The bar served beer and wine and a rather amazing array of hot food, considering all they had to cook with was a microwave and a small pizza oven.

I was deep into a pitcher of piss-thin beer by the time Wilkie stumbled through the front door, but he was already half in the bag. The prospect of work must have sent him on a bender right after we spoke.

Wilkie appeared emaciated. He had always been thin, but now he was gray as well. He was getting a head start on his cadaver look. A liquid diet will do that to you. He nodded solemnly as he sidled up to the bar.

"You started without me," Wilkie said, pointing at the pitcher of beer.

"You seem to be keeping pace on your own time."

"Had a sip at the house." He motioned for the bartender to bring him a glass.

"Where's Marge?"

"Parking the car. I decided not to drive."

"Good thinking."

Marge is Wilkie's long-suffering personal assistant. She's been with him through thick and thin. Everyone in town knew she was helplessly in love with Wilkie. Except Wilkie, of course.

The bartender set a frosted mug in front of Wilkie and filled it with beer from my pitcher. Wilkie took a long, deep swig. When he came up for air he had to actually catch his breath. The effort seemed to exhaust him.

"It's so hard to get a bite out of domestic brew," he said.

"That's all they serve here."

"That's why I brought this."

He produced a silver flask, checked to make sure no one was looking, then took a hit. You could smell the bourbon from five feet away. Wilkie offered me the flask and I shook my head and sipped my beer. I needed my wits about me.

Marge came through the front door and made a beeline for us. She looked good. A handsome woman in her early forties, she had dark red hair and sculptured features that would have afforded her quick entry into the modeling or acting worlds if she hadn't wasted herself on a master's in English lit. Her education had kept her from pursuing the shallower side of the industry. She made a good living taking care of this broken-down wordsmith, but it was nothing compared to what she could have raked in had she decided to step before the cameras when the time was right. The grapevine hummed with rumors that Marge was the secret key to Wilkie's talent, that she had pulled his fat out of the fire more than once when he was consumed by alcohol and self-loathing, that she had written whole sections of much of his later work and had provided critical editorial advice when his material had turned arch or sloppy. Many of these rumors were started by Wilkie himself, stating in interviews with various film-lit mags that Marge was a better writer than he was and that she should leave him to pursue her own career. Marge would have none of it. She was loyal to a fault and denied contributing anything to his cause other than a touch of organization and a dollop of sanity.

"Good evening, Mr. Hayes," Marge said with a faint smile. She immediately gave off a vibe that let me know she felt I was there to take advantage of Wilkie. She was right, of course. More right than she could know.

"Hello, Marge. Please call me Mark."

"Whatever you wish."

"Would you like something to drink?"

"I'm fine."

"Aren't you going to ask me how it went in court yesterday?" Wilkie interrupted.

"You went to court yesterday?" I asked, taking his bait.

"Fuck, yes. She took me back in. Wanted more money. Someone told her about the rewrite I did for Touchstone and she rained lawyers on me."

"But I thought that was settled?"

"Her alimony is settled. She can come after me for more child support until Dean's eighteen. Anytime she thinks I've got additional disposable income she can try to raise her payments. They only let me see him two weekends a month, and she bleeds me dry every time I get a residual check. I pay my ex-wife for the privilege of keeping my son from me. It's such horseshit."

"Don't you want them to have enough money to live well?"

"Look, I want my son to live with *me.* Not Angie and whoever she's shacked up with at the time. If she wants primary physical custody she should be willing and able to support herself and the boy. If I had him all the time you think they'd ask *her* to pay *me*? Wouldn't happen. And you know what? I wouldn't ask for it either. It's a money grab on her part. The law in this state is totally skewed to treating men as worthless scumbags and women as the earth mothers who are saving the planet. I'm not the greatest guy in the world, but when it comes to my kid I'm a prince.

I could raise him every bit as well as she can. I think I could even do a *better* job."

"But you're a drinker."

"Not when my son is around. I never drink around him."

"It's true," Marge said.

"Plus I work at home. She spends most of her day shopping and working out. I've got more time to give him than she does. They've made a big mistake here. And they want *me* to pay for it. You think she spends the money I give her on *him*? Not hardly. She's on an extended vacation and I'm paying for it. It's insulting. I feel like I'm rubbing salt in my wounds every time I cut her a check."

"Well, then, I've got just what the doctor ordered. Cash in hand."

"How much and who do I have to kill?"

"Forty grand. And it's just a quick polish." The nerves in my back tingled as I realized I had just initiated the scam. It had begun. Now could I pull it off and not get caught?

Marge and Wilkie looked at each other and a ton of information flashed between them. It was easy to read, even for me. "A new low," she said with her eyes. "I could use the dough," he said with his. "It's your life, throw it away," was her reply. "Fuck it all," he shot back with a shrug.

"Who's the original writer?" he asked me.

"Gregory Cloud."

"His new spec?" Marge interjected.

"Yes."

"You had to have paid over a million for it," she said, with a side order of vitriol. She couldn't sit quietly by and watch me railroad her man. Wilkie gave her a pleading look, begging her to stay out of it.

"I'm not at liberty to discuss what Dexter pays for anything. I just came here to offer Wilkie some bread because I know he can use it. If he doesn't want the job, we can go elsewhere and pay someone the same amount over the table and get the tax break." I poured the rest of the beer into my glass and ordered another pitcher, trying not to let my nervousness show. If I screwed this up, Dexter would have my head.

"Let me see the script," Wilkie said.

I reached into my satchel and pulled out the copy I brought for him.

He glanced at the cover then weighed the thing in the air using his hand as the scale.

"Feels like a million dollars," he said with a smile.

"Fuck it, Wilkie, it's a million and a half," I said, tired of dragging it out. "You'll read about it in the trades in the next few days, so I don't want you riding another wave of anger. Look, I'll square with you. It's shit. Dexter bought it for political reasons. He paid for the name, not the material."

"And now you want Wilkie to fix it for pocket change," Marge said.

Wilkie looked at her again, this time with a touch of hostility. She was mucking up the works. I knew then that I had him.

"We're not expecting miracles on this pass. We just want it presentable enough to submit to actors. I'm sure there will be additional work needed on it in the months ahead. Additional work, additional money."

The fresh pitcher of beer arrived and I filled Wilkie's glass, then topped off mine.

"Wilkie is a far better a writer than Gregory Cloud," Marge said. I thought she might cry.

"You'll get no argument about that from me," I said. "But you know how the business works. Wilkie hasn't had a credited hit in years and Cloud is the hot boy."

"Wilkie hasn't had a credited hit because he keeps saving people like you by doing these little rewrites. He's fixed more scripts in this town than your boss has ever read. How is he supposed to get anywhere if he keeps sacrificing himself for the likes of you?"

Wilkie made a stop sign with his hand.

"That's enough, Marge," he said. "You're making me lose my thirst. Why don't you go down to Tower and rent some videos. Get some Simpson/Bruckheimer stuff so I can get in the mood for Mr. Cloud's deathless prose. Get *Lethal Weapon,* too. That's one of the good ones."

He was looking to get the mind-set back.

She stared daggers at him, then huffed and stormed for the door. When she was gone Wilkie looked at me sheepishly.

"Sorry about that," he said.

"Hey, she's right, Wilkie, it's a weak deal. If you don't want to do it I wouldn't blame you."

"I can use the money."

"You know I don't usually do this. I'm a development guy, not a deal maker. Dexter just asked me to talk to you because we got along so well on the last one."

"That was a piece of cake."

"Wilkie, as always, this deal is being done under strict confidentiality—in this case, even stricter. Do you understand?"

"Of course."

"Does Marge?"

"Don't worry about Marge. She would never betray me."

"It's not you getting betrayed that I'm concerned about. Dexter doesn't want any involvement in this part of the process whatsoever—if you know what I mean, and I think you do. He's putting me completely in charge of the deal. If something goes wrong, I'm the one who will get burned, not Dexter."

"It's getting more like the CIA over there every day, isn't it?"

"It seems that way. How come you never come over anymore to pitch ideas?"

"I don't want to get into any development deals with Dexter. By the time we're done bouncing the ball around it's just not worth it. Besides, if I wrote something for him, he'd just have you in here meeting with someone else, trying to get them to fix it. You know the first guy on is never the last anymore."

"You got me there," I said.

"I *like* being the doctor. There's less pressure. The material is always so bad when they give it to me that I can't help but improve the situation. And I never have to face the blank page. It's a relief."

"Is that why you don't do specs anymore?"

"Who says I don't do specs? I told you I'm working on one now. Have been for five years."

"How's it going?"

"I'm on page eight. Again."

We shared a laugh.

"When you get it done, would you give me first look? Not for Dexter. For me."

"Really? Thinking about striking out on your own, eh?"

"If I can find the right property. You blame me?"

"Not in the least. And I'll give it some thought. You have financing?"

"Some." Yeah. And some more that will be coming out of your own pocket, my man.

"Well, let me see if I can finish the damn thing first, then we'll talk about it."

"Okay. Want to shoot some pool?"

"Not really. I'm not feeling so great."

"I noticed you looked a little pale."

"My liver's been acting up. I've got to cut back on the booze."

"Yeah. Stick around and see how it all turns out."

"Wouldn't that be something?"

I excused myself to go to the men's room. By the time I did my business and got back to the bar, Wilkie was halfway through Gregory Cloud's screenplay and another pitcher of beer.

"You should give me forty Gs just to read this thing," he said.

"I know. It's a rough one. But just think how easy it will be to make it better."

"Thanks for the Vaseline."

Marge entered carrying a bag from Tower Video. She dumped the contents on the bar in front of us. She had the *Lethal Weapon*s, the *Beverly Hills Cop*s, the *Predator*s, the *Die Hards,* the Clancys, and *Top Gun,* all the usual suspects.

"Instant lobotomy," Marge said with a frown.

Wilkie closed the script and got to his feet. He looked very unsteady. "I'll finish this thing tonight and call you tomorrow if I have any idea how to fix it."

I stood up and shook his hand. "Good deal."

Marge piled the action flicks back into her Tower bag and they headed for the exit. She didn't say good-bye. I paid the tab and finished off the pitcher, thinking about Wilkie and his women.

FOURTEEN

Our morning meeting was not going well. Dexter was frantic. He had a picture shooting entitled *Maelstrom* that had been behind schedule and over budget even before the earthquake hit. Postdisaster L.A. had exacerbated the situation. But more serious problems lay elsewhere. The earthquake was putting the kibosh on L.A. location shooting for his next big picture, *Downtown Blues,* starring Nick Nolte. Two of the most important exteriors in Reseda were blocked off due to earthquake damage, and one of the buildings we were using as a production office in Santa Monica was red tagged, meaning no one could enter the place, period, not even to move equipment and material out of the offices. The production crew had set up a temporary office in a warehouse in North Hollywood, but a lot of vital information was stuck in that Santa Monica death trap and now the work would have to be redone.

The problems were not going to clear up in time for the shoot, which was to begin in two weeks. We had to either find new locations, do a major reschedule, or a big rewrite, since most of the action took place on the streets of Reseda and downtown L.A. It was not customary for the creative staff to sit in on the physical production meetings, but the situation was so dire that we were invited to participate on the off chance that one of us would actually say something intelligent. The director of the film wasn't physically in attendance—he was dealing with water damage at his house in Brentwood—but his voice floated out of a speakerphone on the long conference table every now and then whenever too much logic filled the room.

"We don't solve this problem today, we're going to lose Nolte," Dexter said. "Universal has him booked for April through July. We can't push back."

"What if we change the location to San Francisco?" Alex offered.

"There's no way we can scout, permit, and schedule a move like that in two weeks," Hugh, the unit production manager, said.

"And you want me to stage my chase scene on the streets of San Francisco?" the director's voice grumbled from the speakerphone. "Ever see a picture called *Bullitt*? I've got no interest in working in its shadow."

"*Bullitt* is ancient history," Dexter said. "It's from the sixties, for Christ's sake."

"Dexter, if I was in the room with you I'd throw you out a window."

Before Dexter could reply, the intercom buzzed. Tom, Dexter's secretary, announced over the airwaves, "Dexter, your whore is here."

"I'm going to fire that faggot," Dexter told the room good-naturedly. "Tell her to wait in my office," he said into the intercom.

Most of us could not contain our laughter. It manifested as tittering and choked snickers. I looked at Alex and he wasn't laughing. He was sitting there stone-faced, as was his reaction whenever Dexter's "whore" was mentioned.

Charity James was Dexter's "whore." It was a running gag around the office, although not everyone thought it was funny. Charity was an actress. She had dated Alex briefly, but the moment Dexter got a look at her he had to have her. He put her in one of his movies, playing a prostitute who bangs Ray Liotta in a men's room at Dodger Stadium. Charity thought she had a good thing going and dumped Alex for Dexter. Dexter had gotten her work in three more films, one of his own and two others produced by friends of his. Each part required that she play a tramp or a prostitute. And each role was less vital to the movie in question than the last had been. Charity moved into Dexter's house and, with easy access to what he wanted, Dexter's incentive to make her a star diminished with every stroke. Alex had taken it all in stride. "The cost of doing business" is the way he put it, but he did not seem amused when we called her Dexter's whore, even though the nickname was actually her idea due to the fact that she was not just living the part but playing it out in the few films in which she appeared. Alex never used the phrase himself, at least not around any of us, but I had the feeling he might have used it directly to her a few times when the affair with Dexter first began, and he probably mouthed it silently to himself every time he saw her.

Dexter looked around the room at all of our happy faces and said, "I'm going to step out for a few minutes."

"Dex, I gotta run anyway," the director's voice said through the speaker. "The carpet guys are here."

"Good luck, Martin," Dexter said.

"Same to you." The dial tone droned over the speaker and Dexter clicked it off. He got up and headed for the door. "We need some answers on this one, people. Start earning your paychecks."

Dexter left us staring at each other, wondering how the hell we were going to do that.

We kicked around every lame idea we had, the production manager and his staff sitting stoically while we made fools of ourselves, then decided it was time for coffee and cigarettes. We hit the snack room, and then I joined Alex out on the terrace overlooking the back lot.

"We're fucked, aren't we?" I said.

"This is a production problem. I don't even know why he's bringing us into it."

"It won't be a production problem if we can't start the production. I'm glad he's letting us get closer to the process."

"He's just desperate."

Charity James suddenly stepped out onto the terrace.

"Oh, I'm sorry, didn't know anyone was out here," she said, trying not to show her embarrassment at running into Alex.

"It's okay," I said. "We're just taking a break."

"Yeah, don't leave on our account," Alex said.

Charity seemed confused, unsure whether she should stay or leave. "It's so crowded in there," she said. "It's kind of crazy."

"We're having scheduling problems," I said.

"I know. Dex told me."

She went into a corner of the terrace that could not be seen from anywhere on the lot down below. She was holding something in her palm. As she turned I could see it was a large vial of coke. She opened the vial and laid out two lines on the terrace railing. Luckily for her there was no wind. She bent forward and inhaled the coke like a Dustbuster, first one nostril, then the other.

Charity James was one fine-looking woman. She was tall and leggy; her hair was cut short, just above the shoulders, and it was almost a platinum blonde, but the color hadn't come out of a bottle. It was natural, and you could tell. Nothing looked phony on her, even the stuff that was: her perfect, saline-enhanced breasts, her collagen lips, her liposuctioned thighs. Everything had been done with subtlety. Her face was round and beautiful, and she usually looked like she had just smelled something delicious. She was a Hollywood cream pie, and everyone in town who counted had had a taste. She was the kind of woman that men all over the world dreamed of having . . . at least once. Unfortunately, this was not an uncommon look in Los Angeles. She did it better than most, but there were others who did it even better than she.

Charity knew the unspoken rule in town: Unless you're the one percent of the one percent who can go to the top on sheer ability alone, you've got to have a sponsor. She had chosen Dexter Morton as that sponsor, and Dexter was glad to oblige. Despite Dexter's power, even desperate women sometimes passed on what he could offer in trade for what he wanted from them. Charity had come to terms with the deal. Somehow. I have to admit I had always had a bone on for Charity James, from the first time Alex introduced us. I had considered attempting to poach her from Alex myself, since he never seemed very proprietary about her, but Dexter got there first. Once Dexter Morton claimed her, she was completely verboten. It would have been career suicide to go for it now. No matter how hot she was, it just wasn't worth the various risks involved.

"So," Alex said to Charity, "how's it going?"

"Good." Charity rubbed her nose a bit. "Real good. How are you guys doing? Dexter making life miserable?"

"Oh yeah. But that's the job."

Charity waved the vial in our direction. "Want some? It'll help get you through the day."

"No, thanks," I said.

"I'll take a hit," Alex said.

Charity laid out another line and Alex snorted most of it with his right nostril, then cleaned up with his left. He didn't have the same precision working that Charity James had demonstrated. He wasted almost a third of the line. Charity giggled at his clumsiness.

"Oh, Alex, you always were such a slob."

"Hey, I'm out of practice," he said, laughing.

Charity leaned into him and gave him a big hug. "I gotta go. Nice seeing you." She kissed him on the cheek.

"Yeah," Alex said. "Thanks for the buzz."

"Bye-bye now," Charity said. "Don't let Dex ride you too hard."

"You either," Alex said.

"You are such a nasty boy," Charity said, then she was gone.

"You *are* a nasty boy, buddy," I chided. "I think she still wants you."

"That would be *her* problem. I've moved on to other things."

"Nothing that hot, I'm sure."

"You'd be surprised what I've caught in the net at the new condo. It's very tasty fishing on the West Side."

"Uh-huh. Let me ask you something. Doesn't it ever bother you the way that whole thing went down? The way Dexter stole Charity away from you?"

"That's not how it happened. Charity and I were done with each other. It was all over but the shouting. Dexter actually did me a favor. This way I had no guilt attached to the breakup. It made her feel like it was all *her* fault. Dexter provided a service. And Charity got some work out of it."

"That's a very practical way of looking at things."

"You've got to be practical around here. You can't go falling for every nice tight skirt that smells like White Diamonds. You'll go crazy."

FIFTEEN

The production meeting eventually broke up with no problems having been solved other than where everyone was going to have lunch. Le Dôme won that one.

Wilkie called late in the afternoon to tell me how bad Gregory Cloud's script was and that he would take the job. He said he could get it castable, but not filmable, in the time allotted, which meant it would be good enough to convince actors to commit to the project, but more work would be required before the screenplay would yield a good film, if that was possible at all.

I told Dexter the news and he handed me a large manila envelope containing twenty-five thousand dollars, half of Wilkie's pay, as if silently stating that there had never been any doubt about Wilkie taking the job. After briefly contemplating how long twenty-five grand would last me in Spain, I decided to stick with my slightly less greedy plan. After I left the office I took five thousand dollars out of the manila envelope and placed it in my briefcase. I dropped the remaining twenty K off at Wilkie's house. He seemed too preoccupied to be grateful. He was already in work mode and was in no mood for casual conversation. See? It didn't matter to him what the amount was. Twenty or twenty-five. Or fifty. I'd repeat the siphoning process when he delivered the script and we paid him again. I convinced myself that what I was doing was fundamentally okay because Wilkie would eventually see all that was coming to him anyway, if that spec of his was any good. I planned on using the pilfered cash to help option Wilkie's screenplay for my own production. With my twenty and Dexter's ten, I'd be in the ballpark. With a new Gordon Wilkerson screenplay in my briefcase, I could get my foot in a few doors around town. If the thing was any good. And if he ever finished it. *If.* There's big trouble in that little word.

I went home, put the five grand in another large manila envelope, and stashed it in my bookshelf behind the collected works of Alexandre Dumas. Then I settled in for a good read. I had brought the galleys of Stephen Hunter's latest book home with me. I doubted I could sell Dexter on Hunter because Hunter was just so damned good and Dexter didn't really understand that, but one of the perks of being a creative executive is that you occasionally get to read something you *want* to read and you can call it work.

The Hunter book was terrific, of course. A sure nonsale at the House of Dexter, unless we could terribly miscast it with the denizens of Young Hollywood, casting that would be completely wrong for the strong, mature characters in the book. I finished reading in time to watch the eleven o'clock news. They were doing an earthquake-related body count and damage estimate. FEMA had moved in and was handing out free money, sometimes by ZIP code. I considered filling out the form and picking up the twenty-five hundred dollars they were automatically giving to renters who requested assistance in my area. What the hell, that would get me that much closer to being able to afford Wilkie's script or some other decent property. I took down the number and put it next to the phone.

The contractor who had made a deal with the city to fix the Santa Monica Freeway was way ahead of his own self-imposed schedule. His company was going to pocket a million dollars a day in bonuses for each day he beat the deadline he built into his contract. He anticipated a twenty-million-dollar bonus—he somehow was managing to shave twenty days off his thirty-day schedule—and everyone was congratulating him on his great work. He was a concrete Moses leading his people back to the Holy Gridlock. Let's see: Cut a deal with the city to do some very expensive—and profitable—work, tell them it will take a certain amount of time to complete this work, build in a big bonus for every day you can beat your own schedule, then bill the taxpayers for the whole ball of wax and become a hero. And I thought the studios had funky business practices.

I suddenly heard stomping on the stairwell. Jeff came in late from a long day of catching up at work. I turned down the TV so we could talk.

"How's Rome holding up?" Jeff asked.

"Pretty good. Looks like the FEMA inspector came by and green-tagged the building."

"I saw that. What's it mean?"

"We can still live here, but the landlord has to do some minor repairs, so we'll have repairmen in and out of here for a few weeks."

"That sucks."

"At least we don't have to move."

"I've been meaning to talk to you about that. I'm thinking of moving anyway. The Valley was already weird. This quake thing is too much. It's a big fucking hassle."

"Where you going to go?"

"The other side of the hill. Maybe West L.A. or Hollywood."

"That'll be real normal."

"At least I won't be so close to ground zero."

"There's a million ground zeros in the naked city. You have only experienced one of them."

"Yeah, but I think that Northridge Fault is going to go again and go big!"

"If it does it will probably trigger the San Andreas Fault and then Hollywood will be flattened."

"Maybe, but I'm gonna take my chances."

"Okay. When do you plan to be out?"

"I'm going to start looking tomorrow, but I'll give you a full month's notice so you can find somebody to take the room."

"Don't worry about it. I don't even know if I'll rent it out. I can probably handle the rent alone now if it comes to that."

"You sure it's not a problem?"

"I'm sure."

"I'm going to hit it. Got to be up early tomorrow. 'Night."

"Good night."

I turned the TV back up and watched David Letterman's opening monologue. He was beating the last bit of life out of the earthquake and it was making me bored and anxious and thirsty. I turned off the tube and went next door to wash the dusty old jokes from my lungs.

SIXTEEN

I was surprised to find Clyde McCoy and Emily Woolrich sitting at the bar when I walked into Viande. They both had glasses of Bass on tap in front of them and they seemed to be celebrating something, which was even more surprising because it was my understanding that Clyde had given up alcohol. That wasn't usually a pledge to be taken lightly.

"What's up, guys?" I asked.

"I finished the fucker," Clyde said.

"The book?"

"Oh yeah. It is done. And tonight we are partying! Shelly, a drink for my friend!"

A new bartender—obviously named Shelly—was behind the bar, but she was on the phone. She raised an index finger to let us know my drink would have to wait.

"So, I see you guys are breaking training tonight."

"Just sipping, my son, just sipping," Clyde said.

"One's my limit," Emily added.

"One here, one at Boardner's," Clyde pleaded.

"Oh, come on, Clyde. You know I hate that place."

"Just tonight, baby. Just one drink. I told the gang we'd be there. C'mon, it's a party! I'm free of the beast! I want to stretch a little."

"You stretch too much and you'll snap something . . ."

"I can handle it. Trust me."

She eyed him skeptically and sipped her beer. Shelly approached and asked me what I wanted. To keep in the spirit of things, I ordered what they were having: Bass on tap.

After a little small talk, Emily asked me how things were going at Warner's. I decided it was time I revealed all.

"Uh, you know, I've got a little confession to make. I don't just work at Warner's. I work for Dexter Morton."

Clyde stared at me like I had thrown up on the table in front of him. Emily looked at Clyde with concern. I could tell she thought he might lose his temper and make a scene.

Finally Clyde sipped his beer and said, "How in the hell did that happen?"

"I just kind of fell into it."

"You know I did a lot of movies for that asshole, don't you?"

"I didn't until recently. I looked up your credits in our database."

"What made you do that?"

"Just curious."

"Man, I just can't seem to shake that guy. This town's too damn small."

"I take it you weren't happy working for him."

"That's the understatement of the century. Are you going to tell me *you* like it?"

"It's a tough gig, but he's getting movies made and that's where I want to be. Near the action."

"Aren't you the go-getter?"

Emily touched his arm to ease the bile starting to flow up out of him.

"Don't be like that, Clyde. You did your fair share of work for Dexter Morton. Why disparage Mark for doing the same? He's just trying to have a career in the movie business. You're out of it. Don't let it drag you down."

Clyde seemed to calm a bit. "You're right. I'm being selfish. Sorry about that, guy. I just kind of hate your boss. I shouldn't hold it against you."

"It's okay. I don't blame you for hating Dexter. Seems a lot of people do."

"It doesn't bother him, though, does it?"

"No. I think he likes it."

"I always got that feeling. It's perverse."

"Maybe that's just how he copes."

We moved off the subject. We toasted the completion of Clyde's book, then toasted Emily's upcoming film, then we hit a bump in the road when we tried to find something to toast in my life. We finally toasted my apartment not being condemned.

"So come with us to Boardner's," Clyde said. "We're going to meet a bunch of my old crowd there. It should be fun."

"I've got to go to work in the morning," I said.

"Christ, everything in town closes by two. Everything legal at least. You're telling me you can't stay out until two?"

"I'll follow you down in my car so I can leave early if I have to."

"Fine."

We finished out drinks, then went out to the parking lot and Clyde pulled the tarp off his car, a battered black Maserati Bi Turbo that had been collecting dust in the lot for at least as long as I had been living at the apartment complex. I had never seen it out from under the tarp until this very moment.

"The Black Beauty," Clyde said.

"This thing runs?" I asked.

Clyde snorted. "Just try to keep up."

"Let's not get carried away," Emily said as she got into the passenger seat. "You don't want another DUI."

Clyde ignored her and looked at me. "You know where Boardner's is?"

"Down in Hollywood?"

"Yep. Down in Whorewood."

"See you there."

He slid behind the wheel of the Maserati and fired it up. It choked and sputtered but finally roared to life.

I got into my car and followed them onto the 101 Freeway, heading south, toward Hollywood and the unknown. Clyde was flying, weaving in and out of traffic, doing eighty-plus. He wasn't kidding. I had a hard time keeping up with him.

We took the Highland exit and cruised past the Hollywood Bowl.

The huge marquee that dominated the island across the street from the Bowl was dark, a token attempt at conserving energy for the city's overtaxed, earthquake-ravaged power grid. Even at this late hour—and in the off-season—the sign usually had something cheery to advertise. Until the Department of Water and Power got its act together, however, that was a luxury L.A. would have to do without. Now the marquee just loomed ominously out of the darkness like that fat bastard monolith guarding the entrance to the moon in *2001*.

We turned left on Hollywood Boulevard and I surveyed the ruins. Actually, it was hard to tell the difference from the way the Boulevard had looked *before* the quake. There was a little more yellow crime scene tape apparent, a few more broken windows dotting the landscape, and a couple of buildings had been red tagged, but Hollywood Boulevard had been a disaster area for years. The riots of '92 had left a few scars, but the hardest hit building during that event had been Frederick's of Hollywood, where looters had completely cleaned out all the fancy lingerie, including one of Madonna's prized bustiers.

Hollywood Boulevard had far deeper problems than the natural and man-made disasters of late. Cheapjack speculators had run rampant in the sixties and seventies and turned Hollywood Boulevard into a long, low-rent strip mall for tourists. Then the green card crowd had brought their special sense of style to the area: one tacky knickknack shop after another. You want a statue of Charlie Chaplin with a cheap clock in its navel? Come to Hollywood Boulevard. Want a life-size cardboard cutout of your favorite dead movie star? Come on down! Want some cool postcards that feature the Hollywood sign emblazoned across the tits of some hot chick who never made it big? Five for $1.99 on the Boulevard!

The denizens of Hollywood, the locals who lived in the low-rent apartment buildings to the north and the south of Hollywood Boulevard, were a healthy mix of young newcomers, burned-out losers, working folk, and junkies. Pimps and crack dealers flourished on the streets, but could usually afford to live in better neighborhoods.

The Hollywood Walk of Fame, stars dotting the sidewalk with the names of your favorite film and recording artists emblazoned in gold in the center, was in terrible disarray. A large number of the stars were being pulled up to make way for the construction of the subway, a multibillion-dollar MTA project that had been plagued by miscalculations and costly delays. Time was doing in many of the remaining stars, just as it had their real-life namesakes. Avid fans might adopt the star of a Fred Astaire or a Grace Kelly, regularly scrape the cigarette butts and bubble gum off of it, clean it with toothbrushes, polish it with mink and caviar, but who was going to take care of Neville Brand? Or Jeanne Crain? And what of Harry Guardino? Their stars, and countless others, were wearing out under the steady tread of tourists, bikers, and crackheads.

A few of the classic establishments of yesteryear had held on for dear life in the thick of this stew. You could still go to Musso and Frank for a great martini or the Hamburger Hamlet for a seven-dollar cheeseburger. You could sleep with Marilyn Monroe's ghost at the Hollywood Roosevelt or take in a live show at the Pantages Theatre. And the Hollywood Wax Museum wasn't going anywhere, which just proved that our generation had not invented kitsch, merely redefined it. Like the portrait of Dorian Gray, Hollywood Boulevard blistered with the dark, corrupted soul of a world gone mad on the cult of celebrity.

Most of the great movie palaces of Hollywood had fallen on hard times and either been shuttered or reduced to playing second-run movies on the cheap. But there was hope for the Boulevard looming in the future. Big business had sniffed its rotting carcass and decided there was still meat on those old bones. Disney had recently renovated El Capitan Theater and turned it into a grand showplace where they could not only run their premier films but also put on stage shows to enhance them—and add a twenty to the admission fee. Ripley's people had built a "Believe It or Not" museum on the corner of Hollywood and Highland, complete with a T-rex bursting through the roof and eating a neon clock, and there were plans for a giant multiplex to be built a few doors down from Mann's Chinese Theater—where you could still go to see how small Myrna Loy's feet had really been. There was hope for Hollywood yet. The suits had plans for her. A face-lift and a boob job, and the old whore would be back to work before you could say corporate gentrification.

We turned right on Cherokee and I saw that there was a small crowd hanging around the entrance to the bar. They were clustered under the ancient metal and neon sign that read BOARDNER'S, a rather precarious spot to be standing considering the earthquake weather we had been experiencing of late. But the place had held up under the strain of the quake and even the large, heavy sign had stayed fast, despite the fact that it was being supported by only two frayed steel wires that probably dated back to the fifties. Hollywood had not been hit with the same ferocity that had ravaged the Valley. On top of the fact that Hollywood was much farther from the epicenter in Northridge, it also had the mountains separating the city from the Valley acting as a buffer, absorbing and diminishing the intensity of the shock waves and sparing Hollywood from Armageddon once again. It would take the San Andreas Fault to bring Hollywood to its knees, and the "Big One" seemed to be waiting for the new millennium.

There was no free parking to be had on the street, so we pulled into one of the five-dollar lots, which still offered no guarantee that your radio would be in your vehicle when you returned. We paid the parking fees, then walked across the street to the bar.

SEVENTEEN

Boardner's is a dive. Or at least that's what the hipsters who frequent it would like you to believe. It's one of those run-down Hollywood joints that turned highly fashionable in the late eighties. I became acquainted with it when I first moved to L.A. in 1981 and began working at a place called Larry Edmund's Bookstore, which was right around the corner on Hollywood Boulevard. I worked in the mail-order department for about six months before I got a job as an assistant to a record producer. Boardner's was always the first stop for the gang at the bookstore after work. Back then it was just a ratty little dive with faded pictures of old movie stars on the walls and a few drunken bums slumped at the bar. Sometime between then and now the place had caught on with the hipper-than-thou crowd and business was booming. It was still a ratty little dive with faded pictures of old movie stars on the walls, but now it was packed with leather-clad rockers, wannabe actresses, and young moguls-in-training. Currently, there was also a very heavy contingent of writers in the room. I could smell them as we came through the door. The air was ripe with frustration and angst.

The place was incredibly dark, but Clyde found his group at the big round table in the back of the room. Unlike King Arthur's knights of the Round Table, this assortment of drunken swine screamed *screenwriters.*

Some were wearing black T-shirts or black leather jackets; others had sweaters tied around their necks—always a good idea to keep a noose handy. I recognized a number of them from pitch meetings over the years. I hadn't actually done deals with any of them, but most of them were working writers, people who actually made their living by writing, which is not an easy feat. Most writers have to work a day job to afford to indulge in their craft. This looked like a fairly successful group. If a bomb had gone off in this room the town would have ground to a halt—for about five minutes. That's how long it would take the studio hotshots to replace these scribes and they knew it. They were all stinking drunk.

Everyone at the table shouted greetings at us and a few of them stood up to shake my hand and mumble introductions, but I couldn't understand anything they said. They made room for us at the table and we sat. A waitress was on us immediately.

"Nothing for me," Emily said.

"Bullshit," Clyde said. "Bring her a beer. Amstel Light. She's not drinking tonight. And I'll have a Black and Tan."

I thought Emily would argue with him but she just sat there quietly and the cocktail waitress turned to me.

"Heineken," I said.

The gang acclimated to our presence immediately, congratulated Clyde on the completion of his book, and then resumed their previous conversations as if there had been no change in the room whatsoever. It was like a frigging knitting circle. They sounded like a bunch of old ladies gossiping and gabbing it up: "How'd that guy get *that* deal?" "The legal department screwed me on the option date." "So-and-so was caught in a three-way with a couple of circus midgets." "The *assholes* don't understand story."

It was standard fare.

"So, buddy, this is Boardner's," Clyde said to me. "What do you think?"

"I used to come here all the time, back when I worked at Larry Edmund's."

"No shit. When was that?"

"Eighty-one."

"Hell, I was working part-time at Hollywood Book and Poster down the street in eighty-one. We were competitors. I'm surprised we never ran into each other."

"We probably did, but don't remember."

"Could be. But back then I mainly hung out at the Dark Room."

"I didn't go there much." The Dark Room made Boardner's look like the Taj Mahal.

"You must've been a kid back then," Clyde said.

"I was twenty-two when I started there. It was my first job in L.A."

"So tell me, what is it you really want to do with your life? What's left of it, that is, after you're done serving your evil master?"

"I don't know anymore. When I was younger I wanted to direct. I made some short films like everyone else and kicked around trying to get gigs, but I just never got the break."

"So you ended up in development."

"Uh-huh."

"Why didn't you go independent?"

"Never had the money."

"Oh, that's horseshit. The eighties were like a license to print money. Everybody and their brother were making movies and they were all making a profit. With video and cable booming, you couldn't lose."

"You mean low-budget stuff, right?"

"Yeah."

"The problem was the screenplays I wrote back then, they were more expensive kinds of movies. They needed studio backing. That's why I got into the system."

"A lot of good that's done you."

"Well, I had another problem, too."

"What's that?"

"The scripts were no good."

"That never stopped anyone in this town."

"It stopped me. I'll make a much better producer than writer."

"That's what we need. Another producer."

"What about you? Why don't you direct your own material?"

"Tried it. It's not for me."

I wanted to ask him about the movie he had directed under the name Colon Noble, but the waitress returned with our drinks and broke my concentration. Clyde paid for the round. As the waitress sat his drink down in front of him, Clyde looked across the table and yelled at one of the younger guys in the group.

"Hey, I hear Paramount's buying your book!"

"Yeah," the kid said, "for one of the Scott brothers."

"Which one?"

"Does it matter?"

"I don't care if you don't."

Two drinks later, I was trapped in a conversation with a short, balding character who had started out with lofty aspirations and was now relegated to making a fortune writing sitcoms that no one at the table could stomach watching. He was rich, but even more spiritually bankrupt than the rest of this pack of hyenas.

"I sit there sometimes," the guy was saying, "staring at the computer, realizing that precious seconds are ticking away in my life. Time that I can never have back. And it seems like the biggest waste in the world, staring down at a green screen, trying to come up with stuff to sell to people I hate who will then try to sell it to the masses, another group I am not overly fond of. Who am I trying to impress? My folks are dead. I need the approval of the general population? It's ridiculous."

"Maybe you're trying to leave a mark," I said, playing along but completely bored.

"For what? For who? A bunch of people I'll never know? Don't you see how amazingly stupid the whole thing is?"

"Then what do you think you should be doing?"

"That's the problem. I don't know. I'm not qualified to do anything else. I'm not really qualified to do this. I'm just lucky that the people I sell to are dumber than I am."

"At least you're working."

"That's not enough. I have such anxiety about not contributing anything of value to society. I don't know why. There are so many people who contribute nothing. But I've always felt that it was my duty, my responsibility, to do something worthwhile. To make a difference, no matter how small. It pains me to realize I have spent all this time on this planet and contributed nothing meaningful. My life has just been a huge waste of time."

Clyde, eavesdropping, leaned into the conversation and said, "Then why don't you kill yourself, Tim? Nobody will miss another whining TV writer. But don't forget to put me in your will. I could use the dough."

"Fat chance," Tim said.

A man on the other side of the table leaned forward to speak. He was tall and graying, with wild, wiry hair and a full beard and mustache. They referred to him as the Professor because he taught screenwriting at USC even though he had never had a screenplay of his own see its way to actual production. He had written a best-selling book about the craft of screenwriting and had sold a lot of scripts, but no movies had been made from his material, so it was impossible to prove his many theories in any tangible fashion. Nevertheless, when he spoke, everyone at the table listened.

"If you think television is so easy, Clyde, why don't you write for TV?"

"I never said it was easy. I can't even watch the stuff. How am I going to write it? I've got no interest in TV."

"See that?" the Professor said. "You defeat yourself before you even try. This industry won't tolerate self-doubt. Self-doubt will kill you every time. Everyone in Hollywood is waiting to criticize you, to put you down, to pass judgment on you, to reject you. If you beat them to the punch, they have no use for you. If you are even remotely self-critical, they will take you at your word that you are no good and dismiss you. If you don't believe in yourself, no one else will. That's why it's such a tragic atmosphere. The only people who survive are egotists and specialists in self-denial. You've got to believe your work is golden. If you show any cracks in the veneer, they'll ostracize you. This town has destroyed stronger, more talented people than you, Clyde. Torn them apart, limb from limb, wadded them up, and tossed them in the trash."

"Gee, thanks, Professor. That explains it."

"What?"

"Why I keep finding body parts in my Dumpster."

There was laughter at the table, but not so raucous this time. More like nervous tittering, as if the Professor's words had struck some nerves.

The conversations slowly grew loud and boisterous again, as if the evil sermon was drifting away on the wind. There was much whining and carrying on about the state of things in the industry, even though most of the people at the table were making a very good living off of it.

Clyde went well beyond the one drink maximum that he had promised earlier, but did not seem to be getting hammered. Emily didn't even bother him about it until it got past one A.M., then she leaned into him and said, "Listen, I've got to get going. I'm tired."

Clyde handed her the car keys and said, "Why don't you take the car and I'll ride back with young Master Hayes?"

"Why don't you just come home with me now?"

"We're in the middle of a celebration. The guest of honor cannot leave his own party."

"They'd never know you were missing."

"You're probably right, but *I* would."

"Please, Clyde . . ."

I watched his face and could see he was getting perturbed, but then he thought about it and relented.

"Okay," he said. "I guess I've had enough fun for one night. Time to head on back to the Ponderosa."

I got up to join them.

"No need to leave on our account, Hayes."

"I've got to be up early for work," I said.

"Oh yeah, I forgot. Gotta keep those suits happy."

Emily pinched his ear and led him out of the room.

"So long, suckers!" he yelled.

A cacophony of good-byes and fuck-yous pushed us out the front door into the cold night.

EIGHTEEN

The studio solved the location problem on *Downtown Blues* by canceling the project. They had four million dollars tied up in preproduction, but the head of the studio said he never liked the project anyway and the marketing research numbers they had been receiving weren't looking good. They were exploiting the force majeure or "act of God" clause in their insurance package to cover the loss. I thought Dexter would be upset, but he was actually quite happy. He had a pay-or-play deal on the picture, so he was paid in full for *not* working. The cancellation also reduced his future risk, for there was no way that *Downtown Blues* could possibly bomb if it was never made and even Dexter had been having second thoughts about the commercial viability of the project.

He didn't have the same luck with *Maelstrom,* his picture that was already deep into filming. That show would have to be completed, despite the fact that Dexter was less than thrilled with the dailies he was seeing from the production and the massive cost overruns created by that film's overbearing director.

My schedule began to return to normal. Writers and producers were rescheduling their pitch meetings and beginning to trickle through my door. A lot of them had earthquake-related stories to pitch. Dexter's mandate on that: "Leave it to the television producers. That thing will be ancient history by the time we could make and release a movie."

The big guns of Hollywood pitched directly to Dexter, sometimes with Alex and/or myself in attendance. The lower minions pitched to Alex and/or me. If we thought they had something interesting, we would discuss it with Dexter. If he liked the idea, the writer or producer would get a shot at pitching to the big man himself. It was rare when someone could run that gauntlet and actually get into a development deal with Dexter. Most of his projects were generated through his connections with the Hollywood upper crust.

We were all in the habit of recording our pitch meetings with mini-cassette recorders. It was more accurate than just keeping notes and it also provided a good record of any meeting that could later blossom into a plagiarism-related lawsuit. There are a million ideas out there. Unfortunately there are eight million writers in Los Angeles. There's bound to be some overlap. Dexter had no interest in being involved in nuisance suits. So we each kept audio records of every meeting to back up our written notes.

My fifth pitch meeting after the quake proved that our sense of paranoia was more than warranted. I had an 11:30 with a producer named Jim Becker, an annoying character who pitched often and with little success. He never had anything we were interested in, but he just wouldn't give up. He was one of those guys who used the shotgun approach to producing. He attached himself to anything he could—without respect to quality—and hoped something would hit somewhere. He'd made a decent living this way and had gotten his name on a number of movies, most of which were lousy. He had been attached to a few films that Dexter produced in his low-budget days, but Dexter was swinging for the fences now. Jim Becker's product was of no interest to him anymore. Nevertheless, the meeting had to be taken and it was up to Dexter's grunts to handle the likes of Jim Becker. Alex and I took turns meeting with Becker, and now I was up to bat. I always scheduled Becker for late morning/early afternoon so I would have a good excuse to cut things short by saying I had to go to lunch if he couldn't take the hint when I had had enough.

Janet buzzed me at 11:20 to say Becker had arrived and was waiting in the lobby. He was early. I told her to let him sit until I was ready. I went down the hall to the bathroom and splashed water on my face. This was one of the more painful and meaningless exercises connected to my job: the courtesy meeting. It was doomed from the start, but it had to happen. You never know when one of these little pigs will come up with a golden truffle.

I grabbed a Coke from our kitchen, went back to my office, and told Janet to send in Becker. I clicked on my minicassette recorder before he entered my office. The recorder was always in plain sight on the desk among other things piled there—scripts, books, reports, videotapes—but I never made a point of turning it on in front of someone pitching to me. The first time I did that the writer I was meeting with just froze up. Then he spent half of his pitch staring at the recorder. I decided to be subtler about it from that point on and start taping before the meetings began. No one had mentioned it since. I think the recorder just blended in with the rest of the clutter. At lunch meetings I couldn't be so obvious. I wore the recorder inside my jacket pocket and let the microphone pick up whatever it could. It wasn't quite as ethical as the office recordings, but the tapes would only come into play if we were hit with a lawsuit full of lies anyway. Considering the noise level of some of the restaurants I frequented, I was lucky to get anything at all on those tapes other than a cacophony of chatter and rattling china.

Jim Becker entered my office looking like a cat that had just eaten a cageful of canaries. He was a tall man and he looked strong. He always wore shirts that were just a little tight on his biceps so that you could see he liked to lift weights. The first thing he always did when he entered an office was take off his jacket, drape it over his arm, and let you take a look at his big guns. I think he thought he could intimidate you into a deal that way. Not in this office you couldn't. But today was no different from all the rest. He stripped off his sport coat and hung it over his arm, trying not to be too obvious when he flexed up and his muscles stretched at the cuffs of his short-sleeved shirt. That must've been one heavy jacket.

Becker tossed a script on my desk, then took a seat in one of the chairs off to my left. "I think you're going to be very happy when you read that," he said.

I opened the script to the title page. *Burnin' Down Vegas* by Victor Hart and Sal Munroe. I had turned this one down four months earlier, although I didn't remember seeing two writers' names on it at the time.

"Haven't I read this one already?"

"Yeah. But it's been revised. I fixed it. I hired a new writer and he had a fantastic take on the material. I'm giving you guys a one-week exclusive on this because I don't think anybody can handle it the way Dexter can. It's right up his alley."

"Listen, you may not want to give us an exclusive. I've got a lot of work piled up because of the quake and I can't promise I'm going to get around to a reread in a week. I've got to consider fresh material first."

"This *is* fresh. It's a brand-new take on the story. This kid is good, I tell you."

"I'll see what I can do. Got anything else for me?" If not, that would be his cue to put his jacket back on and head for the door.

Becker's demeanor changed. His brow furrowed and he looked almost mentally disturbed.

"You're brushing me off, aren't you?"

"No. It's just that I have a lunch meeting over the hill at the Farmer's Market and I have to get going soon."

"That's bullshit. You always have a lunch meeting. And why can't I ever meet with Dexter anymore? It's always you or pretty boy. Never the man in charge."

"You know Dexter. He's busy. He doesn't take many pitch meetings anymore."

"Too busy whoring out his girlfriend, I guess."

I stared at him mutely, too shocked to respond.

"What's wrong? No smart comeback for that one?"

"What should I say? You just made an outrageous accusation about my boss. I'm tempted to call security and have you thrown out and banned from the lot."

"You don't have the power to do that, big shot. And besides, your boss wouldn't like it much, because the first thing I'd do is call Army Archerd over at *Variety* and tell him how Dexter puts his sweet Charity to work getting all those favors for him from the big brass."

"You don't know what you're talking about."

"Oh yeah? I know some things about Dexter Morton. Bad things. Specific things. People, places, and dates. And I think Dexter should read this script and meet with me in person a week from today or maybe my next project will be about a Hollywood producer who pimps his girlfriend out on the side."

Becker leaned forward and picked up my tape recorder from the desk and spoke directly into it. "Got that, Dexter? A week from today. As they say, have your people call my people."

Becker put the recorder back on my desk, got up, and slid his jacket on. "I don't want to meet with errand boys anymore. Let the boss know all about it."

I sat there red-faced. I wasn't going to dignify his slights with a response. Becker walked out of my office. I heard him laugh as he went down the hall. He was having a good time. Whatever he had on Dexter must have been so ugly and powerful that he didn't fear reprisal, because he had just threatened blackmail on tape and in front of a witness.

I turned off the recorder, placed it in my jacket pocket, and went down to Dexter's office. His door was partially open and I could see Dexter sitting at his desk, talking on the phone. I sat on the couch outside his office and rewound the tape to the beginning as I waited for him to finish his call. His secretary, Tom, was not at his desk beside the office door. He appeared a few minutes later with a cup of hot tea in hand and a telephone earplug dangling around his neck.

"What's up, Mark? He's on with a Sony exec. It's going to be awhile."

"I've got to see him. It's important."

"You'll have to wait."

"That's fine. But I have to see him as soon as he's off the phone."

Tom looked at me suspiciously now. "What is it?"

"I can't tell you. Maybe Dexter will, but I can't."

"Jesus Christ, now you've got me curious."

"I can't talk about it."

"Okay. Hope you don't have cancer or something."

"It's nothing like that."

"Good."

I waited ten minutes for Dexter to finish his phone conversation. Tom had received a barrage of incoming calls during that time and he had taken down a long string of messages. Dexter came out of his office and asked Tom for an update. Tom read off the list of messages and I could see Dexter mentally organizing the order in which he would return the calls. He stared at me the entire time but did not address me. When Tom was finished with the list, he said, "And Mark wants to talk to you but he won't tell me what it's about. Must be bad news."

"It better be important," Dexter said. "In my office, Hayes."

I got up and followed Dexter into his office. I shut the door behind me. Dexter sat at his desk and looked at me oddly, wondering why I felt it necessary to close the door. I produced the tape recorder from my jacket pocket and said, "I just had a meeting with Jim Becker. You're going to want to hear this."

"That guy's a loser. He never has anything good."

"No. But this time he's got something bad. Just bear with it and listen to the end."

I put the recorder on his desk and played the tape. Dexter looked bored at first, but when Becker started talking about Charity James, Dexter lost the bored expression and just looked blank. He was doing his best not to show me any reaction whatsoever.

When the tape was over, Dexter leaned forward and turned off the recorder. "So it's come to this, has it?" he said. "The guy can't come up with the goods and he has to resort to blackmail."

"It's ugly."

Dexter popped the tape out of the recorder and said, "I'm going to give this to my attorneys. They'll know how to handle Becker. He's a shakedown artist. Maybe it's time he went to jail."

I went over to Dexter's desk and picked up the empty tape recorder. "Good. He's got it coming."

"Hayes, not a word of this to anyone, understand? I wouldn't want Charity hurt by gossip like that."

"I understand." I headed for the door.

"Better bring me that script, too."

I stopped and looked at Dexter, wondering why he needed the script.

"For the lawyers," he added, reading my confusion.

"Oh," I said as I went out the door.

NINETEEN

I didn't hear anything more about the Jim Becker incident and I soon forgot all about it and focused on the grind. Meetings, coverage, and more meetings. Dexter also had me scouring used bookstores for old novels that might have flown under the Hollywood radar when they were first released and could be bought now on the cheap. He was hoping, in particular, to find a series character that he could turn into his own franchise, à la James Bond or Batman. And while I was looking for Dexter, I kept one eye open for something I might be able to option myself, not a big budget franchise picture, but something more along the lines of a good character piece that I could produce for HBO or Showtime if the actors and budget were right for the suits over there.

Dexter's fiftieth birthday was approaching and his personal assistant, Mrs. Bolender, was planning a major fiesta at his house up on top of Mount Olympus, now freshly repaired from being ripped in half by the earthquake. I was surprised, because Dexter didn't usually have large parties there, preferring to rent space elsewhere and charge the studio, but he was in an unusually good mood of late. To "compensate" for the loss of *Downtown Blues,* the studio had extended his first-look deal for another three years and green lighted two of his projects, one for release at

Christmas, the other for the following summer. Despite what some might consider a setback, the cancellation of a major motion picture, Dexter Morton was hot around the lot and people were referring to him as the next Joel Silver. He wanted to celebrate in style, at his own home, and show off his pre-Columbian art.

Mrs. Bolender came into my office late one afternoon with a very unusual request related to the upcoming party.

"Do you have a current address for a Mr. Clyde McCoy?" she asked.

"Sure," I said. "He's my neighbor. What do you need it for?"

"Mr. Morton wants to invite him to his celebration."

"You've got to be kidding."

"No, he was very adamant."

"But they hate each other."

"Dexter Morton hates no one."

"He sure doesn't *like* Mr. McCoy very much."

"Mr. Morton said he's thinking about doing business with him again and thought the party could serve as an icebreaker. He also said that you might be of some help in convincing him to attend."

"I could talk to him, but I don't think he'll go for it."

She handed me an envelope with Clyde McCoy's name inscribed on it in red ink. "Could you see to it that Mr. McCoy gets this invitation? It would mean more coming from you than arriving cold in the post."

"Okay," I said, befuddled.

She left the room without saying another word. I turned the envelope over gingerly, looking for booby traps or some sign of poison.

I got home just in time to watch *Jeopardy* and have a drink. I wasn't ready to talk to Clyde about the invitation to Dexter's party. I wanted to prepare myself to get kicked in the ass before I broached the subject. I wondered what Dexter was up to. He seemed to be inviting everyone in town to this shindig, but I found it hard to believe that his invitation to Clyde McCoy was sincere. I figured he probably wanted to rub his success in Clyde's face. I was certain Clyde would decide to pass on an opportunity like that.

I finished watching *Jeopardy,* then bit the bullet and went downstairs. Becky was entering her apartment as I stepped out of mine. It was the first time I had seen her since the night of the quake. I waved at her but she ignored me and closed her door quickly. Ah, the neighborhood was back to normal. I could even smell ganja drifting down from Zim's place.

I knocked on Clyde's door. Clyde jerked it open and said, "Come in, come in," without looking at me. His attention was elsewhere.

I entered the living room and Clyde backed into viewing angle of the basketball game playing on his television. Orlando was losing to Phoenix. Clyde yelled, "Fuck!" as Barkley hammered past huge new phenom Shaquille O'Neal and went in for a layup.

"That's not supposed to happen," Clyde said.

"You a big Orlando fan?"

"No, but I've got money on this game and Phoenix is beating the spread."

I handed him the envelope. "Sorry to have to give you more bad news."

"What's this?"

"It's an invite to Dexter Morton's fiftieth birthday bash."

"Ah, the return of the prodigal scum," Clyde said, opening the envelope. He read the thing and laughed. "This is rich. Dexter must be getting senile in his old age. Doesn't he know I hate his guts?"

"He knows. I just don't think he cares. I told his assistant you wouldn't want to go."

"Are you crazy? I can't wait. Maybe I can catch Dexter next to his swimming pool. I've always wanted to see if that toupee of his floats."

"I'm surprised that you'd want to see him again at all."

"Hell, this'll be a great opportunity. I can piss in his bedroom and fuck his girlfriend in the bathroom."

"What about Emily?"

Clyde looked at the date on the invitation.

"Shit, you're right. She's working in Indonesia, but she might be back by then. Maybe I can keep it a secret from her. I won't tell her if you don't."

"Would you really do that?"

"What?"

"Fuck Dexter's girlfriend if you could." He didn't realize it, but he was talking about a friend of mine: Charity James.

"Sure. Hey, it's not about love. It's about *revenge.*" He laughed and went into the kitchen. "Want a beer?"

"No, thanks."

He opened the refrigerator and pulled out two Guinness Stouts. He popped the tab on one and handed me the other. "For the road then."

I took the beer and thanked him. He was drinking again, and Emily was out of the country. I had a feeling that could be a powder keg in the making. As much as I disliked Dexter, I didn't really want to get in the middle of his old feud with Clyde. I wanted Dexter's party to proceed as peacefully as possible. Working for Dexter was barely tolerable when he was in a good mood. When he was unhappy he made the rest of us completely miserable.

I said good-bye to Clyde and went upstairs. I stretched out in the hammock on the balcony, opened the beer, and sat there staring into the night, regretting that I had given him the envelope, thinking how much better it would have been if I had just torn the thing up and told Dexter that Clyde had turned down the invitation.

TWENTY

As the date of Dexter's party drew close the guest list swelled to 160 of his closest friends and their insignificant others. It would have grown larger, but Mrs. Bolender finally put her foot down. She knew that list potentially represented 400 to 500 celebrants throughout the night. There was no way even Dexter's large house would accommodate any more people.

Wilkie turned in his rewrite and I repeated my shortchanging procedure, delivering twenty thousand in cash to him out of the twenty-five that Dexter gave me. If I was going to be the bagman for this deal, shouldn't I have my cut? I just had to pray that the two of them never got together to compare notes. Since mutual anonymity was key to the deal, I thought I'd be safe.

The screenplay read just as Wilkie had predicted. Much improved, but still not ready to shoot. I had a feeling he had held back. He gave us forty thousand dollars worth of work and no more. The script was adequate to send out, but only because hot new genius Gregory Cloud's name would be on the title page. If Gregory Cloud wrote it, it *must* be good. Now that the story made a little sense and the dialogue was not so incredibly stilted, the project would cruise straight to the top of the food chain. Our P.R. firm would leak a piece to *Variety,* reporting that anonymous sources had read the new Gregory Cloud script and that it was his best yet. Nothing's good in this town until someone else says it is, but once that happens it's *great*! Actors would be clamoring for a read by Wednesday, and this would be a "go" project before the end of the week. This is movie making by hype. People like Dexter Morton build fortunes this way.

I went to Dexter to update him on the progress of the Gregory Cloud script and remind him of a promise he made to me when he asked me to stay on permanently. It was time to make my move.

"Dexter, I'm putting a lot of time and energy into this project, aside from the fact that I'm sticking my neck out for you. I want to work as a producer on the movie."

"You do, huh?"

"You said my job would eventually lead to that."

"I said it *could.* Not *would.*"

"C'mon, Dexter. What could it hurt? One more name on the credits. It wouldn't mean anything to you. But it would mean *everything* to me."

"I'll consider it, Hayes, but you're going to have to earn it. They don't give that shit away around here. Christmas has come and gone."

"Granted. But you know I can do the job."

"We'll see. You've got balls, that's for sure. Not so hot in the brain department sometimes, but you've got balls. Be careful you don't get them caught in a wringer. At the end of the day, survival is sometimes preferable to advancement."

That's right, Dexter. Keep watching your back. Keep me in my place. Keep me down. This is how embezzlers are born. Nevertheless, I left his office with newfound hope. Despite his warning, I thought he might actually let me take a shot at this one. It was a piece of shit action flick, but it would have a budget of fifty mil-plus and could easily gross three times that amount worldwide come next summer if we landed the right above-the-line talent.

A credit like that could lead to big things.

TWENTY-ONE

Charles Callaway was missing. That was the word we received from Mel, the panic-stricken Unit Production Manager who called the office not long after lunch on a hot Thursday—Day Ninety-Eight in the trouble-plagued production schedule of Dexter's latest magnum opus, *Maelstrom.*

It was a red alert. The director had gone off before lunch and failed to return. The crew had a huge stunt rigged and ready to go, but there was no sign of the commander in chief. They thought maybe he had come to Dexter's office to confer with him, but no such luck. The last thing Dexter wanted to do was screw around with Charles Callaway. He was steamed at the guy for being so far behind schedule and over budget, but he couldn't get rid of him. Not at this late stage of the game. No, he'd have to ride it out, take his lumps, get more money from the studio, and hope to God the foreign box office would make everything all right. Now the auteur had flown the coop and the situation on the set was reaching critical mass.

When Dexter heard the news he practically had a coronary. He called for his limo to be brought around, then ordered me to accompany him to the set. Why, I didn't know. I guess he wanted a witness. Or perhaps he was testing me to see how I would handle set pressure. I took it, optimistically, as a sign that he was considering my request to be involved as a producer on the *Untitled Gregory Cloud Project.*

The production company was shooting at the Burbank airport, less than ten minutes from the studio. They had shut down an entire runway and were slowing the progress of two other landing strips as they announced, intermittently, that explosions would be going off within twenty minutes. That plan was hinging on the presence of one man, Charles Callaway, director supreme, now MIA.

Dexter's driver went through the gates, right onto the runway. The first assistant director came scrambling over before we could get out of the limo. "Any sign of him, Mr. Morton?" he asked frantically.

"What you think? We got him in the trunk?"

Dexter got out and the A.D. gave him space. First A.D.'s are generally a macho lot due to the intense nature of their jobs. They control the set, making sure everything is in place and everybody is where they are supposed to be when they are supposed to be there. Before any crew member—other than the director of photography—could talk to the director on this particular set, they had to go through the A.D. It's not a job for wimps, and this guy was one of the toughest around, but he immediately grew timid around Dexter. He knew who the true alpha gorilla was in this jungle.

I got out of the limo and surveyed the set. There were more than two hundred people standing around waiting. The main crew itself was approximately one hundred thirty strong, but because the scene they were shooting was a stunt with explosives, there were seventy to eighty extra hands in for the day. Effects people, stunt people, safety people, firemen—with two trucks—paramedics, cops, extra riggers, additional camera crews to capture the scene from twelve different angles, and a large contingent of art department folks to put it all together again if the first take didn't work out, or to clean up the place if it did.

The scene itself was relatively simple. Although *scene* is somewhat misrepresentative. This army had been gathered for what was basically a single shot, although it would be photographed from the aforementioned twelve angles. The subject of the shot would be a beautiful 1969 Corvette, supposedly driven by the star, but actually piloted by his stuntman, hitting a camouflaged pipe ramp at high speed and crashing through the side of the bad guy's Lear jet as it is attempting to take off from the airfield. Somehow both the hero and the villain would survive the crash for a climactic fistfight in the demolished but still rolling Lear jet, a scene that would be shot in the days and weeks to come. I checked the shooting schedule and noted that they had planned the big effects shot for immediately after lunch to give the tech crews extra time with all their riggings. The morning had consisted of getting shots of the plane taxiing down the runway and the Corvette hauling ass after it. I checked with the script supervisor and was told that Charles Callaway had gotten "most" of the morning's shots, but would have to get some pickups at a later date.

I found Dexter conversing with Mel, the Unit Production Manager, who was still frantically trying to raise Charles Callaway on his cell phone and pager. Dexter was saying that they should just get the shot, with or without Callaway's guidance.

"You know we can't do that," Mel said. "The D.G.A. would have our heads."

"Fuck the Director's Guild," Dexter said. "They want to get tough with someone, they should start with this director. He's three months behind schedule on a movie that was originally scheduled for three months of shooting. That's a pretty impressive trick."

"Hey, take it up with the Guild, Dex, but I can't go forward without his presence on the set. Fire him. Call the Guild and get a replacement. I don't care. I'm sick of this fucking show. But I'm not flushing my career down the tubes for you or anyone else. You pull the trigger on this stunt and something goes wrong, you want to explain that you couldn't wait for the director? You want another *Twilight Zone* on your hands?"

I thought Dexter would fly off the handle and kick the guy off the set, but I guess what he said made so much sense that it overrode Dexter's anger.

"You're right," Dexter said. "But if this asshole doesn't appear in the next ten minutes, I want you to cancel the rest of the day's shoot and send everyone home."

"Are you nuts? We haven't even gone eight hours yet. You won't save any money that way."

"It'll make a point. Maybe if he shows up and no one is here waiting for him, it will sink into his fat head that he can't carry on like this. A dose of reality is good for a runaway ego."

"I see your point, but at least let everyone put in the eight-hour minimum. Maybe we can get *something* done today. This fucking show is never going to end."

"Oh, it will end. I promise you that. If things don't start running smoothly on this picture, the studio will step in and shut us down. Then we can all go work for Roger Corman, because no one else in town will take us in after we sink a studio."

"This is so fucked. I wish I never signed on to this goddamn show."

"I feel your pain."

A roar suddenly filled the air. I thought for a moment it might be a runaway plane about to crash-land into the crowd. We all turned to see Charles Callaway speeding through the gate in a bright red Lamborghini. He pulled right up to where Dexter was standing and said, "Hey, Dex, came by to watch the big bang, eh?"

"I came by to find out where the fuck you were. Get out of the car."

Callaway shut down the Lamborghini and got out. He didn't look concerned in the least. He was the *director,* after all. Add to that his height of six feet five inches in his jackboots, and you've got a guy who is hard to intimidate. He towered over Dexter, but Dexter was not one to be intimidated either.

"Where have you been?" Dexter continued. A few hundred people stared silently, waiting for the answer.

"I went to test drive this boat. I knew the shot wouldn't be ready until after lunch, so I decided to make use of the time. I think I'm going to buy it."

"You son of a bitch! You had two hundred people standing around with their thumbs up their asses for almost three hours. What about your cell phone and pager? You gone deaf or did you just choose to ignore them?"

"I must've left them in my Porsche," Callaway said with a grin.

"You selfish bastard! You just tacked another half million to the budget while you were out car shopping!"

Charles Callaway rubbed his bearded chin and considered Dexter's words. It was as if he were trying to decide what was more important, the studio's half million dollars or his test drive. Finally he said, "Why don't you let the actors handle the melodrama, Dexter? You want me to make the magic happen or not?"

Dexter bent at the waist and waved his arm in an arc starting at Charles Callaway and ending up pointed at the "A" camera.

Callaway strode to the camera area, asked if everyone was ready, got affirmatives all around, then said, "Call it," to the First A.D. who promptly went through the dozen or so commands over his walkie-talkie to prep the rest of the shot, warn the control tower that there was soon to be "fire in the air," get everyone not involved to the safety areas, and begin the action.

The plane began rolling on its prearranged course, the stunt driver took off in the Corvette, hit the ramp perfectly and crashed through the middle of the Lear jet just as they had practiced and rehearsed for the last four months. It all went perfectly. Charles Callaway called, "Cut," and said, "Check the gates," meaning for the various camera crews to check to see if hair or dirt had been on the gates inside their cameras during the shot, which could ruin the footage. Reports quickly came back that everything was clean. The fire crews moved in and foamed down the Lear jet wreckage to make sure the small amount of fuel it was carrying did not ignite. The stunt driver was helped out of the car to thunderous applause. The whole thing went down in less than five minutes from the time Charles Callaway said, "Call it," to the First A.D. The director's involvement in the process was so subtle as to be almost unnoticeable. This is what they had waited three hours for him to do, say, "Call it," and "Cut"?

It was insanity.

Callaway walked over to Dexter with a big grin on his face. "Beautiful, wasn't it?"

"You're a genius, Charles. A fucking genius. It reminded me a little of the climax of that picture *Shakedown* from a few years ago, but otherwise it was fabulous."

"I consider these things evolutionary."

Dexter looked like he was going to be sick. Charles Callaway always pulled that evolutionary line out of his hat whenever someone noticed a lift from other movies tainting his work. It was the way he justified himself whenever he took someone's old idea and just made it *bigger.* The concept kept him from having to be original. Less risk that way.

Charles Callaway looked at the First A.D. and asked when the next shot would be ready—the exit of the big star from the Corvette. "One hour," was the response. Callaway climbed back into the Lamborghini. "I'll be back," he droned, imitating Arnold Schwarzenegger. A couple of the director's sycophants standing nearby giggled like they'd never heard *that* one before and Callaway sped away.

Mel, the beleaguered unit production manager, approached Dexter solemnly. "Well, we got it."

Dexter said, "At the end of the day, that's all that matters."

"At the end of the day" was Dexter's favorite catchphrase. It was how Dexter—and many of his colleagues—wrote off uncomfortable moments, by referring to the mythical "end of the day" that justified every event or motivation they could not explain away politely. The end justified the means. It was an attempt to make wonderland seem less abstract, a stab at convincing themselves that it was all part of a bigger plan.

Dexter turned and walked silently toward his limo. I followed along. For just a brief moment I felt a pang of sympathy for Dexter Morton. His job did have its dark side.

TWENTY-TWO

On the night of Dexter's birthday party, Clyde McCoy decided to follow me to Dexter's house in his own car so he could leave at will. He didn't expect to stay longer than it took to insult the host and drink his bar dry.

Dexter lived in Mount Olympus, a rich man's housing community two miles up in the mountains off Laurel Canyon Boulevard just above Sunset. His house was at the end of a half-mile-long private drive on Icarus Way. By the time we got to the party the driveway was lined with vehicles from the house all the way down to the street. Clyde parked his car at the end of the line and rode up the hill to the house with me. He didn't want the valets parking what was left of his Maserati. It was the last remnant of his earlier success and it was barely holding together. Once it was gone he would have nothing left with which to remember his heyday in Hollywood other than the tragic images gracing *The Late, Late Show.* I, on the other hand, had no problem handing my keys over to the valets. They could drive my Camaro off the side of the mountain for all I cared.

Dexter's house was a sprawling ranch-style affair at the very top of Mount Olympus. It was sectioned off from the housing project itself—

Mount Olympus being the design equivalent of HUD houses for the wealthy—but his address was still a Mount Olympus address. Dexter liked to consider himself the Zeus of Mount Olympus. He knew his neighbors were somewhere below, but, like a God among gods, he never had to encounter them physically unless he so desired.

We entered through the front door and saw that the party was already functioning at full throttle. Clyde took one look around and said, "And me without a gun."

"Behave," I said.

"Absolutely."

We split up, moved through the crowd and mingled. Anyone who wanted to be anybody was there. Most of them were failing. Dexter had gathered together just about everyone he had ever crushed under his heel. This was a gloating party. He was rubbing their noses in it. There's a lot of hate in Hollywood, but hatred can easily be put on the back burner if there is even a faint promise of work in the air. And Dexter was a very big employer. Everyone was on their best behavior. *Almost* everyone.

Charity James was the exception. She was blitzed out of her mind. She must have started early in the morning to have a buzz that deep crackling through her system. Dexter was completely ignoring her, choosing instead to work the crowd and bask in his glory.

Gregory Cloud was there, holding court for a group of young screenwriters-in-waiting. And Charles Callaway was in attendance, trying to decide which of the fresh young crop of bimbos would win the ride home with him in his new Lamborghini. There were quite a few likely candidates. He was probably wishing Lamborghini made a station wagon so he could take them all.

I looked around to see if Jim Becker had weaseled his way into the place to make more trouble, but I didn't see him anywhere.

A jolt went down my spine as I saw Wilkie and Marge over by one of Dexter's huge fireplaces. What the hell were they doing here? I could see Wilkie coming to this thing for the booze, but Marge set foot in Dexter's house? I never would have believed it. And why had Dexter invited them? Wilkie's work for us was supposed to be a secret. Wasn't he worried that Wilkie might get sloshed and start blabbing about how he fixed Gregory Cloud's million-and-a-half-dollar script? Maybe even to Cloud himself? Had Wilkie and Dexter spoken and compared financial notes? Was the jig up and my ass in the wringer? It seemed crazy that Dexter would invite Gregory Cloud *and* Wilkie. Crazy or just plain arrogant.

I went over to say hello to Wilkie and Marge and to take the temperature of my scam.

"I'm glad you guys could make it," I said, shaking Wilkie's hand. I hugged Marge but she did not hug me back. She didn't flinch or pull away either, so I considered that progress.

"It was Marge's idea," said Wilkie. "She says I don't get out and mix it up enough. She thinks I should learn to be a better 'networker.' "

"Well, she's right. Maybe you can dig up some work around here."

"That's a rather nauseating reason to go to a party."

"Don't try to talk sense into him, Mark," Marge said. "He'll never be one of those guys. Believe me, I've tried to get him to sell out in the proper fashion, but he's too much of a masochist."

Something must have happened between the two of them, because Marge had lost the halo of despair and the veil of hostility that she usually wore out in public. She didn't seem to be bothered by the fact that she was at a party that was populated by the kind of people she despised, people who had taken advantage of her man Wilkie, present company included.

"I just got here," I said. "Anything exciting happen so far?"

"Do you mean did the hookers come flying out of the cake yet?" Wilkie said.

"Something like that."

"No. It's been pretty sedate. We've just been hanging back watching the execs work the ingenues. That's always fun."

"You've been salivating over a few of them yourself," Marge said with a smile.

"Now why would I do that when I have you?" he asked, squeezing her hand. She leaned into him and giggled like a schoolgirl. So *that* was it. They had finally done the deed. It was about damn time.

"You seen Dexter around?" I asked, hoping they hadn't.

"Not yet. But he's got to be here somewhere," Wilkie said.

"Maybe he's under his rock, keeping warm," Marge said. If my plans were going to explode in my face, I had a feeling she'd be the one that said what it took to light the fuse.

"I've been meaning to tell you how much everyone likes the new script, Wilkie. You really did a good job."

Marge straightened up and got serious. "Maybe you should pay him a bonus."

"You know if it was up to me, that's what I'd do, Marge, but Dexter keeps a tight hold on the purse strings. And, of course, this is all just between the three of us."

"Oh, of course. Isn't it always?"

"A deal is a deal," said Wilkie. "I'm happy with the way things are."

Marge looked at him sternly, wanting him to be fiercer, to fight for his rights, but then she softened and resigned herself to the way things were. If it was good enough for Wilkie, it would just have to be good enough for her.

Marge excused herself to go to the powder room and Wilkie and I hit the bar for fresh drinks.

"So, Wilkie, looks like things have changed a bit around the office."

"It's that obvious?"

"Wilkie, it's been obvious to everyone in town for years. It's about time you did something about it."

"She's a damn fine woman," Wilkie said.

"You're a pretty good guy yourself," I said, clicking glasses with him. "You deserve each other."

"Why, thank you, Mark. That's very nice of you to say."

"Nah. It's the truth. The good guys don't always find happiness around here. If you can make it work, even for a little while, you'll be ahead of the game."

"I guess the earthquake rattled some sense into us. Made us realize we didn't have forever anymore."

"I heard that."

"Was that Clyde McCoy I saw you come in with?"

"Yes. Do you know him?"

"Sure. We were drinking buddies in the old days."

"He's my neighbor. I still haven't figured out what he's about. What's his story? How'd he end up at the bottom of the ladder?"

"It's hard to live by the rules of this business and retain a sense of manhood. Clyde was never very good at the politics of the thing and it's cost him. But he's okay. The people with the good front, they're the ones to watch out for. They're the snakes who will strike you when you're not looking."

"I follow your thinking there." I was *practicing* it.

A junior agent from C.A.A. slithered into the conversation, as if he were an expert in ethics. He was actually just trying to weasel his way into Wilkie's pocket. I took that as my cue to drift off.

I went on the schmooze and hugged some of the women gracing the living room. The hot ones were all actresses or make-up artists. Most of them left silicone dents in my chest. The plainer ladies present were D-girls or trophy wives who had begun to tarnish under the harsh light of their duties. I found no fulfillment in the idle gossip that passed for conversation in this group. I did the kiss-kiss, hug-hug and abandoned the living room for higher ground.

I cruised through the house and headed for one of the six bathrooms. I went down a hallway, stopped by the closed bathroom door, tried the knob, and found it locked. I turned at the sound of sobbing. Charles Callaway was arguing with a beautiful woman in one of the guest bedrooms across the hall. The door was open partially and I could see the two of them in the dimly lit room. She was sitting on the bed, crying, and he was standing over her, obviously accusing her of something horrible. He appeared to have no sympathy for her position in the matter. He was intensely deriding her for some infidelity, real or imagined. She looked like she was on the verge of a complete breakdown. The tears were streaming fast and she was gasping for breath. At one point Callaway looked out into the hallway and saw me staring into the room. He frowned and kicked the door shut. I guess that meant it was a closed set.

I went to another bathroom, took a leak while two sitcom actresses snorted lines off the sink nearby, washed my hands, and rejoined the fray. I found Clyde standing alone by the bar, nursing a beer.

"Hitting the hard stuff, eh?" I joked.

"Just pacing myself. This isn't the kind of crowd you want to turn your back on."

As if on cue, Dexter came over to say hello to Clyde. The air was thick with tension before a word could be spoken, and I wondered which one of them would snap first.

"Clyde McCoy," said Dexter, extending his hand. "How have you been?"

"Terrific," said Clyde, ignoring the outstretched hand. Dexter let it hang there like a side of beef. "What have you been up to?"

"Very funny," Dexter said. "I've been making movies. That's what we're supposed to be doing isn't it?"

"Depends on who you are, I guess."

Dexter finally let his hand drop to his side. He took the insult with no sign of embarrassment whatsoever.

"There's an old script of yours floating around that we're thinking of buying—*The Long Haul.*"

"I wouldn't work for you again in a million years, Dexter," Clyde said. He was smiling when he said it, but the words vibrated with hostility.

"You won't have to work for me. We'll just buy the script and I'll put someone else on the rewrites."

"I paid twenty grand to buy my way out of our last contract. You really think I'll let you get your hands on anything else of mine?"

"You don't have much to say about it. It's in turnaround at Tri-Star. I've already made an offer to buy."

"They just have an option on that thing and the option is up in June."

"I pay the turnaround fees and I can exercise the option myself."

I could see Clyde filling with frustration and rage. "Buy it if you want. It's a shit script anyway. Perfectly up your alley."

"We'll *fix* it."

"Sure you will. Hey, what do I care? It's your funeral."

Clyde turned and walked away.

"Thanks a lot, Dexter," I said.

"What?" he responded, all innocent-like.

"I have to live next door to that guy. Did you have to be such a sadist?"

"It's just business."

"Right."

"Hayes, you're going to have to figure out which side you're on. You can't be soft on the writers. If you find a piece of material that's suitable for production, our job is to buy it, make it better, and shoot it. We're not here to nursemaid these characters. Without us their scripts are worth two bucks in paper and ink and that's it."

"Yes, but without their words how could we make movies?"

"Don't be a simpleton. Taxi drivers and waitresses write screenplays every day. How many people can harness the power of a studio and actually put eighty million dollars up on the screen? Who do you think is more valuable to the process?"

Not wanting to debate, I said, "*You* are, Dexter."

"That's right. So decide. Do you want to ride in the back of the limo or the taxi?"

"The limo, Dexter."

"That's what I thought. I've had my eye on you, Hayes. You like to fancy yourself a nice guy, but deep down you're a son of a bitch just like the rest of us. You'll do what it takes to get what you want. And your instinct for survival is not half bad. You know when it's time to dance and you know when it's time to fuck and you know when it's time to hide. That's important. You may just make it in this business after all."

"At the rate I'm going I'll be using a walker by the time I'm producing."

"Don't be so sure about that."

"What do you mean?" I was suddenly seized by a childish rush of hope.

An attractive young lady caught Dexter's eye and gave him the excuse to ignore me. "Let's talk about this later," he said, then he oozed toward the starlet-in-waiting.

He hadn't committed to anything, but he had certainly dangled the carrot closer. Was I in? Was he going to give me my shot on the Gregory Cloud film? It sounded like it. Or was he just toying with me?

I went looking for Clyde. I wanted to make sure he didn't throw someone through a plate glass window. I found him out by the pool talking to Wilkie, catching up on old times.

"Sorry about that in there," I said.

"No problem. It's par for the course."

"I promise you I had no idea that he was trying to buy your screenplay."

"I know. I'm sure you would have told me."

"We're going to the Formosa for a civilized nightcap," Wilkie said. "Want to come?"

"No, I better not." But I was glad they were going. All three of them. Now I might be able to relax a little and enjoy the party.

"Where's Marge?" I asked.

"She's getting her things from the room."

"You guys safe to drive?"

"Absolutely. We're tip-top!" Wilkie spouted.

We could see Marge waving from inside the house, carrying her coat and purse.

"Certain you don't want to come along?" Wilkie asked.

"I'd like to, but I better stick around here a bit."

"Don't get anything on you," Clyde said. Then they were lost in the crowd.

I sat down on one of the deck chairs by the pool and watched the party swirl around me. The backyard was peopled not only by the cream of New Hollywood, but also by a dozen or so Greek and Roman statues. Some of them were full-length bronze likenesses of the gods; others were merely plaster cast busts on pedestals. One of the busts, a likeness of Achilles, lay at the base of its pedestal a few feet away from my chair. It had either fallen during the earthquake or it had been placed there deliberately to complete the design statement that was running amok in the backyard.

I began to grow hypnotized by the trance music blaring from inside the house. I studied the light reflecting off the water of the pool for a good five minutes before I was suddenly disturbed by an angry voice.

"D-boy!"

It was young Jason Ward, ex-hot screenwriter, and he was stinking drunk.

"Writer boy!" I replied, not feeling up to suffering his hostility without retort. A party is the perfect place for the gloves to come off. You can always blame it on the booze later if you have to. "What the hell are you doing here?"

"I was invited."

"I'm shocked that you would accept such an invitation."

"I just wanted one last look at all the morons before I split."

"Leaving town, are you?"

"Yep. I've had it. I don't want to play their games anymore. I bust my ass trying to write something good and some asshole throws it on the floor and dances on it? Fuck that. Then you guys turn around and make the shit you make? I don't need you geniuses in my life."

"I certainly understand. What are you going to do?"

"I'm going to Montana to write a novel."

I suppressed a laugh, stood up, and started to walk away. "Well, good luck."

Jason grabbed me by the shoulder.

"Don't fucking walk away when I'm talking to you! You just sat there grinning while Dexter ripped me apart, but you're just as big an asshole as he is!"

I pulled away from his drunken grasp and the sudden freedom was too much for him. He fell backwards into the pool with a big splash. Applause wafted up from the crowd. I walked away without checking to see if he could swim. I alerted security and let them know that the guy in the pool should be escorted off the premises before he caused more trouble. Jason went without a fight. I guess it was too cold out to be lounging around in wet clothes.

The party ebbed, then a second wave of revelers arrived, working the circuit. As always, there were competing parties going on all over the city. A guest's time of arrival would give a pretty good indication of how many they had hit already and where this party fit into their schedule in either importance or geography.

I was at the food table making a roast beef sandwich when Charity James came up to me. Her eyes were red and moist. She had obviously been crying.

"You've got to do me a favor, Mark."

"Sure. What?"

"If Dexter comes over here you've got to act like you're talking to me. Don't let him take me away from you."

"Why?"

"I'm scared."

"What happened?"

"I stabbed him in the ass with my nail file."

"What? What the hell are you talking about?"

"I found him fucking Amy Barth in *my* bed upstairs. *My bed!* My bedroom was off limits for the party, but he went in there with that whore. I went in to take a rest and found him with his ass in the air, fucking her like crazy. So I grabbed my nail file off the vanity and I stabbed him in the ass."

"Is he hurt bad?"

"I don't think so, but he's probably going to kill me. I should just get out of here, but I don't know where to go."

"How about a hotel?"

"I don't have money for a hotel. I don't have *any* money of my own."

"Haven't you been saving up while you lived here?"

"I don't make any money and Dexter hardly gives me any. He's a cheap fucker."

"Don't you have friends you can stay with?"

"Most of my friends cut me off after I moved in with Dexter. They all hate him."

"I could give you money for a hotel for the night."

"Will you take me?"

"Don't you have a car?"

"No. I don't even drive. They suspended my license. Too many DUIs."

Realizing how messed up her life was, she went for another round of tears.

"Let's go in here," I said, leading her into the bedroom where everyone had piled their coats.

"I don't want to go to a hotel. You think I could stay at your place for a night or two?" She was sobbing between words.

"I don't really have a lot of room. I live in a two-bedroom apartment and I've got a roommate."

"A girlfriend?"

"No. Just a guy who rents the spare bedroom from me."

"I could sleep on your couch . . . or in with you."

The offer was electric and dangerous.

"Dexter would fire me if I took you to my place."

"He doesn't give a damn about me. It's humiliating enough that everyone knows I'm sleeping with him, but then he has the nerve to *fuck around behind my back!* Why doesn't he just rub shit all over my face and throw me out onto Hollywood Boulevard? You have no idea the things I've done for that pig."

I thought of Jim Becker and his accusations that Dexter had been pimping Charity out to the suits. Was it true? If it was, then the nickname she had chosen for herself, "Dexter's Whore," must have multiple meanings for Charity.

"Just stay here for a minute," I said. "I'll be right back. Don't move. Promise?"

"I'm not promising anything."

"Please, Charity. I've got to talk to someone. I'll be right back."

"Bring me a drink."

"Okay."

I left her in the bedroom and went into the party proper to see if Alex had arrived yet. I found him in the kitchen talking to a hot redhead with the biggest boobs I'd seen all night. And that was saying a lot. Before I could reach him, Dexter grabbed me and pulled me into the walk-in refrigerator. He was wearing a robe and I could tell he was hurting.

"Where the fuck is that cunt?" he snarled.

"Who?" I asked, feigning ignorance.

"Charity!"

"I don't know. I haven't seen her."

"The bitch stabbed me!"

He pulled the robe to the side and showed me his buttocks. Two butterfly bandages were taped over the stab wound. It looked pretty minor.

"Shit," I said.

"She used a nail file. I'll probably get varnish poisoning!"

"Varnish would probably sterilize the wound."

"Who are you, Marcus Fuckbe, M.D.? I want you to find that psycho and get her out of here before she causes any more trouble."

"What do you want *me* to do with her?"

"I don't care. Drop her in the L.A. River, for all I care. Just get her out of here."

"I'll see what I can do."

"I'm going to go get dressed."

He snuck out of the refrigerator and crept down the hall to his bedroom, somehow managing to avoid detection by his oblivious guests. I rejoined the party and found Alex. He was still talking to his chesty friend.

"Alex, can I have a word with you?"

"I'm a little busy here, Mark."

"Just a sec. It's important."

We stepped into the hallway for some privacy. He did not look happy.

"You're messing up my deal here, Hayes. What's so fucking important?"

"Charity's gone nuts. Dexter wants her out of here."

"So?"

"Can you take her home?"

"Isn't *this* her home?"

"I mean *your* home."

"No way."

"She used to be your girlfriend."

"Uh-uh. She's not my problem. I've got better things to do. Take her to your place."

"I've got no room for her."

"Put her in your bed. Dexter won't care."

"This is crazy."

"Hey, don't look a gift whore in the mouth. I gotta get back."

He left me in the hall. When I went back to the bedroom, Charity James was gone. I searched through the house but I couldn't find her. I heard a commotion out by the pool and followed my ears to find Charity throwing glasses at Dexter, now dressed, and his new lady friend, who were both cowering behind the wet bar. A sizable crowd had gathered to watch the festivities.

I came up behind Charity and grabbed her by the arm. The glass in her hand shattered at her feet. She turned and tried to slap me, but I caught her other hand before she could make contact.

"Hey, hey, hey, hold on a minute. I'm a friend, remember?"

"Goddamn it, let me go! I want to kill that fucking cocksucker!"

"Let's get out of here, go for a drink. Okay?"

"Fuck that. Let's drink here. There's plenty of booze!" Charity picked up a bottle of vodka and threw it at Dexter to prove her point. It missed his head by inches and exploded against the wall of the house. Amy Barth yelped with fear as vodka and glass splattered her.

Two security guards approached us at a trot.

"It's about time," Dexter yelled, standing up from behind the wet bar. "Where the fuck have you guys been?"

"Patrolling the perimeter," one of the guards said.

"Bullshit, you've been trying to score with the bimbos!" Dexter yelled. "And what about you, Hayes? I told you to get her out of here."

"Fuck you, Dex!" Charity screamed. "I'm going, but I'm going to burn this fucking house down first!"

She shook free of me, grabbed a book of matches off the wet bar, and started striking them and throwing them at the bushes. It was a very weak attempt at arson.

"Will you lazy bastards get her the hell out of here?!" Dexter bellowed. *"Right fucking now!"*

The two security guards grabbed Charity and restrained her arms. She screamed in pain.

"Let her go!" I yelled.

"Step back, sir, or we will have to pepper spray you," one of the guards said politely.

"Just let me talk to her. I can get her to calm down."

They didn't care. They dragged her through the house, past the crème de la crème of Hollywood, who all had a good laugh at her expense, and dropped her unceremoniously on the driveway in front of the valet's station, tearing her stockings in the process.

"Now, decide," the polite guard said. "You go home quietly or we call the police."

"This *is* my home!" Charity screamed.

"Not anymore," the guard said.

Mrs. Bolender came out of the house carrying a suitcase filled with Charity's clothes. She said, "Mr. Morton requests that you leave the premises immediately."

Charity stared at the suitcase in horror. "That's not all my things! I want *all* my things!"

"Your belongings will be packed and sent wherever you wish tomorrow." Mrs. Bolender handed Charity a thick envelope. "Here is three thousand dollars to get you started. Behave, and Mr. Morton will give you three thousand more each month until you get on your feet. Say six months?"

"I don't want his fucking money!" Charity threw the envelope on the ground.

Mrs. Bolender looked at me pleadingly. I scooped up the envelope and took Charity's hand.

"Let's get out of here," I said to her gently.

Charity looked up at me and I could see some of the fog lift. She realized the situation was hopeless. She took in Mrs. Bolender and the two security guards and contemplated jail for a moment, then she said, "Okay. Maybe we can make last call somewhere."

"Sure," I said. I helped her to her feet and gave the guards a step-back look. They were rent-a-cops, not real police. Not too hard to intimidate if you knew the right fuck-with-me-and-I'll-sue-you glare. I got my keys from the valet. Mrs. Bolender thanked me and I walked Charity down the long driveway to my car. She leaned on me to keep from tumbling down the steep incline. Her breasts felt warm against my arm and the contact made me a bit light-headed. It was all I could do to keep us from falling down the mountain together.

TWENTY-THREE

Charity passed out on the ride to my apartment, which was for the best. I didn't feel like playing Q&A with a zoned out bimbo at this hour and I didn't want to engage in any conversations that might get either one of us angry or aroused. I had heard enough stories from both Alex and Dexter to know that Charity James was exactly the kind of woman I had sworn off long ago: a great time in the bedroom and nothing but nightmares everywhere else, a woman who would do her best to drag you down to her level, then trade up the moment something better than what you had become came along. No matter how much I had craved her in the past, I could not get involved with her. A relationship with Charity James would be counterproductive to everything I was trying to achieve.

I had a hard time waking Charity when we got to the apartment. Finally I got her moving enough so she could zombie her way up the stairs. She crashed on the couch as soon as we were through the front door. I got some blankets and covered her up. She was shivering, but it wasn't cold in the room.

I poured a glass of water and put a couple of aspirin next to it on the coffee table in front of her. If she woke up in the middle of the night with a hangover, help would be close at hand. Her body vibrated and a small sob emanated from deep within her, followed by another. She was not finding solace in her dark dreams.

Jeff's door was closed and I could hear female whispering from within. Probably one of his actress girlfriends practicing a monologue on him while he slept. Jeff loved actresses. He said he liked the fact that they didn't know the difference between reality and fantasy. His goal was to sleep with as many beautiful actresses as possible by the time he was fifty, then settle down and marry a rich, sexy stock analyst. He had come to the right town.

I took one last look at Charity stretched out on the couch. She was very beautiful, but lines were beginning to form early on her sweet features. This life was aging her prematurely. What she had to offer would be gone far sooner than she thought. She could not afford to go through too many more Dexters without a sizable payoff. There's not a lot of work for aging starlets in this town, especially ones with Charity's microscopic résumé. Most of the hot young things who fail to hit big come to grips with their situation in their thirties and try to marry someone with dough before their looks fade permanently. If Charity didn't find her man soon, it would be too late. And then where would she be? She could work as a casting agent, maybe, or she could turn pro and hook for a living. If Becker was telling the truth, she already had practice in that department. There was always room for another hooker in town. But honest work was out of the question. She couldn't make enough money as a secretary or a waitress to keep herself in the lifestyle to which she had grown accustomed. Her drug intake alone would far outweigh her salary. And at this late date she'd never hack law school.

Charity sobbed gently again and I could see a tear running down her cheek, but she was totally unconscious. I fought the urge to go over and wipe her tears away. I knew from experience that a move like that could turn into an all-night sympathy fest. I clicked off all the lights except for a small lamp in the corner so she could find her way around the alien surroundings if she awoke, then I went into my room and went to bed. It had been a long, ugly day. The sooner it was behind me the better.

PART II

A screenwriter and a producer were lost in the desert. They had not had food or water for three days. On the verge of dying of thirst, they suddenly saw what appeared to be a beautiful oasis shimmering on the horizon. Thinking it a mirage, they scrambled for it nevertheless. When they arrived they discovered it was no illusion. It was a beautiful orchard of fruit trees surrounding a crystal blue pond bubbling up out of the desert. The screenwriter crawled desperately down to the water's edge and was about to drink. Suddenly a noxious stream of urine passed by his face into the cool, clean water. He looked up and found the producer standing over him, pissing furiously.

The screenwriter jumped to his feet and screamed in the producer's face, "What are you doing! It was perfect! It was beautiful!"

The producer leaned back and continued to drain his poisonous loins into the crystal blue waters with a deliriously happy grin on his face.

"I'm fixing it!" he yelled.

—Classic Hollywood joke

TWENTY-FOUR

I came to a little before 10 A.M. and entered the living room to see if Charity James was okay. She was gone. Jeff's door was still closed, and I could hear synchronized snoring in the bedroom. His latest conquest had spent the night. Sounded like Jeff had finally found a woman who had as deviated a septum as he did. Maybe it was Kismet.

I called Dexter's house to see if Charity had gone home, but the answering machine picked up. Her suitcase was still in my car, so I thought I should take it back to Dexter's. There was a high probability that Amy Barth, the new girl from last night, was long gone and Dexter and Charity had already made up. She had probably called him in the morning and told him to come get her. Let bygones be bygones. Whatever. She wasn't my problem, and I wanted to keep it that way.

I showered and shaved and dressed in my weekend casuals: jeans and a Museum of Neon Art T-shirt. I caught a glimpse of Jeff's girl skittering out the front door as I came out of my bedroom. She was a short little Sophia Loren-looking thing. That Jeff. He got a lot of action for a computer geek.

I reached into my jacket and pulled out the envelope containing Dexter's cash. If Charity was there, Dexter would want his money back.

The sun was high in the sky by the time I got into my car. As I pulled out of the lot, I noticed Clyde McCoy's car was not in its designated parking spot. It was very unusual for him to be out and about during the day, especially after tying one on like he probably had with Wilkie and Marge after they left the party. I would have thought he'd sleep until late afternoon. Then again, maybe he never got home last night. For all I knew he could be sleeping it off at Wilkie's house or, God forbid, still out partying.

It was Sunday so traffic was light but frantic as everyone rushed around trying to cram as much relaxation into the weekend as possible. A naked guy was walking around on Laurel Canyon Boulevard when I approached the entrance to Mount Olympus. He was causing a bit of a traffic jam and slowed my progress in reaching the long, winding road up to Dexter's compound.

As I came up the driveway I could see that Dexter's Mercedes was under the carport and the front door of the house was wide open. I got out and called Dexter's name a few times, getting no response. I walked through the house and out to the pool area. Then I saw him.

Dexter was doing a William Holden in the middle of the pool. He was floating face down; his body looked bloated and his hairpiece was missing. The top of his head was wrinkled and pink.

My first instinct was to jump into the pool and drag him out, but I hesitated long enough to realize that not only would that be a pointless effort, it might also be downright disgusting. I began to feel queasy and decided to call nine-one-one, even though this had probably passed the emergency phase many hours earlier.

I calmly told the operator that I had found my boss drowned in his pool. She asked if he could be revived and I told her I was neither David Hasselhoff nor Charlton Heston. She didn't think that was funny, but she said she'd send the police and an ambulance right away.

I went back out and studied the scene. The longer I stared at Dexter's imitation of a flotation device, the sicker I felt. I finally had to throw up in the bushes nearby.

When I came back, I felt much better. I had never seen a real dead body before—outside of a funeral home—and never wanted to, but I have to admit there was something fascinating about seeing Dexter floating aimlessly in his pool. It surprised me that he could screw up like this and drown in his own backyard. Not very *prescient* of him, was it?

I walked the perimeter of the pool trying to figure out what had happened. He was still in the clothes he had changed into last night after he was stabbed in the ass by Charity James; tan chinos and a white polo shirt, but they seemed to be fitting quite a bit tighter now. I don't know if the clothes had shrunk or Dexter had puffed up. Did he decide to go for a 3 A.M. swim with his clothes on after the party? Or did he get too wasted last night and fall into the pool? I looked at his feet. He was barefoot, which might support the midnight swim theory, but why would he leave his clothes on? There seemed to be a cut of some sort on the top of his head, but his skin was so wrinkled I couldn't be sure of exactly what I was seeing.

I looked at the large stone tiles surrounding the pool and there appeared to be chalk marks in a starburst pattern on two of the tiles, like a big rock had fallen and exploded next to the pool. Before I thought about what I was doing, I rubbed at the powder with my shoe, seeing if it would come loose. It scuffed and smeared. The marks were made recently.

I walked over to the statue of Achilles that had fallen during the earthquake. It was still on the ground but there was now a bust missing from the pedestal next to it.

What the hell happened here?

Sirens snapped me out of my Columbo-like trance. Two police cars and an ambulance were winding their way up the steep canyon road, trying to find Dexter's house. I walked out to the driveway so I could wave them in. They found the entrance to the compound and did sixty up the asphalt drive, screeching to a halt in front of me.

Two cops got out of the first car and approached me.

"What's the problem here?" the first cop said. He was a big black guy with Elvis muttonchops and straight, waxy black hair. He looked like a very tan version of the King in his later days, but he had no accent to match the build and the facial hair.

"It's my boss," I said. "I think he's dead."

"You *think* he's dead?" Black Elvis said.

"No. I mean, yeah, he's dead. I found him floating in the pool, and he's got a cut in his head and he's not breathing."

"Sounds like he's dead," Black Elvis said.

"Show us," Black Elvis's partner said. He was Latino, not as big as his partner, but muscled where Elvis had girth, like he spent all his free time in the gym.

I led the two cops through the house to the pool. A third cop was trailing behind us by a matter of feet. He was a skinny white guy with nervous eyes. He and his partner had gotten out of the second police car, but his partner had gone back to talk to the paramedics in the ambulance. The three cops were keeping a close eye on me. Their hands hovered nonchalantly in proximity to their guns. They were taking no chances.

A blast of warm wind greeted us as we stepped out into the backyard. The four of us stood beside the pool and watched Dexter Morton drift in the breeze.

"He's dead all right," Black Elvis said. "Looks like he got banged in the head. Better call it in."

Black Elvis's partner gave a speech into a microphone attached to his collar. It was in copspeak, so I couldn't understand half of what he was saying but I got the impression that he was calling in the A-Team. A crackly voice that sounded like it was coming from a busted speaker at a Jack-in-the-Box drive-through replied. It was completely unintelligible to my untrained ear.

"Homicide is on the way," Muscle-boy said. "They said not to touch anything."

"You got to tell me that?" Black Elvis asked. "When the fuck I ever touch anything at a crime scene?"

Muscle-boy didn't say anything. The cop behind me looked away, making it clear he didn't want any part of this conversation.

"I asked you a question, Ramirez. When the fuck you ever see me touch anything at a crime scene?"

"How about the time you ate the caviar at that Beachwood Canyon house?" Ramirez said.

"Hey, I was hungry. We had worked a double and Homicide left us hanging for three hours."

"It could have been poisoned."

"Bullshit. She *knifed* that guy."

"She could have had a backup plan."

Black Elvis couldn't come up with an answer to that one. He looked retrospectively concerned.

The paramedics rolled a gurney out to the pool and looked at Dexter.

"We got a D.O.A. here, guys," Ramirez said. "No need to resuscitate. He's dead."

"That your medical opinion, Chief?" one of the paramedics asked sarcastically.

"Yeah. And Homicide said not to touch anything. Got it?"

"No problem."

The paramedics set the gurney aside, fired up cigarettes, and walked to the edge of the bluff to enjoy the view. All of Mount Olympus stretched out beneath them. But Zeus was dead and Homicide was coming. They thought this was a murder scene. My mind reeled at the possibilities. Somebody *killed* Dexter Morton. But then I realized I had instinctively known that from the start. They had just solidified what had been in the back of my mind since the moment I saw Dexter floating in the pool. The story editor in me subconsciously assumed it was a murder. It was just such a fantastic notion that I hadn't been able to grasp it fully until the word *homicide* was articulated.

While we waited Black Elvis took down my name, address, phone number, Social Security number, driver's license number, and a whole bunch of other personal information that I didn't feel comfortable sharing with the police. Then they went about the business of waiting for the real deal, the homicide detectives.

I stared at Dexter in the water and flashed on William Holden again, floating dead in Gloria Swanson's swimming pool at the beginning—and end—of *Sunset Boulevard.* Certainly the papers would latch on to that bit of Hollywood folklore and wring it dry in Dexter's case. Which is the only time Dexter Morton would ever be compared to William Holden in any way. That train of thought led me to one of my favorite Hollywood stories. After the premiere of *Sunset Boulevard,* the director of the film, Billy Wilder, was confronted by an enraged Louis B. Mayer, who spat at him something like, "You bastard! You have disgraced the industry that made you and fed you! You should be tarred and feathered and run out of the country!" To which Wilder, not usually one to be short on words, took a moment, then simply replied, "Fuck you." I'm not sure why I find that story funny. The simplicity of the response, I suppose. All the best stories have simplicity at their core.

The paramedics had gone through half a pack of cigarettes by the time movement on the road below triggered one of them to say, "Aw, geez, look who it isn't—"

A gray sedan was making its way up the hill. This would be the homicide detectives. I moved to greet them but Black Elvis said, "Please stay where you are, sir."

"I just wanted to let them know where we were."

"They can find us. Take a seat."

I went to a deck chair and sat down nervously. These guys have a way of making you feel guilty even when you haven't done anything wrong. The pool filter started making an ugly sucking sound, as if something was stuck in it. It would snore loudly, then take a break. Then start all over again. Black Elvis started to go over to the filter to investigate, then thought better of it. Homicide would be joining us momentarily.

Two men came out to the pool area. It was a complete *Lethal Weapon* act. One of the men was black, athletic looking, clear eyed, and happy. His suit was immaculately pressed and he was carrying a large briefcase. The other man was white, with curly brown hair going gray and a mustache to match, pallid skin, and dark brown eyes that almost looked black, as if he had absorbed the bad things he had seen in his life and held the evil deeds prisoner behind those eyes. He was dressed in jeans and a rumpled white T-shirt that featured a replica of a detective's badge over the left breast with the words LAPD HOMICIDE printed underneath. He looked sleepy and hostile, as if he had been rousted out of bed to make this call and wasn't happy about it. As he turned I saw the homicide squad's motto plastered across the back of the T-shirt.

OUR DAY BEGINS WHEN YOUR DAY ENDS

Black Elvis approached the detectives and discussed the crime scene while they stared at Dexter's body floating in the pool. After a few moments the white detective turned and yelled at the paramedics, who were still standing at the edge of the drop.

"Hey, guys, anybody think about pulling this poor son of a bitch out of the pool?"

"We were told not to touch anything," one of the paramedics replied.

"Real lifesavers, you are," the detective said, then he turned back to look at the body.

"Fuck you, Campbell," the paramedic said. "We're leaving. This is a bag job."

The paramedics gathered their gear and headed for the door. The detective spoke without looking at them. "Thanks for everything. We couldn't do it without you."

"I hope your house falls the rest of the way down that hill," the paramedic said.

The detective looked up at him with anger, and the paramedic thought twice about his words and hightailed it out of there.

The sucking sound came out of the filter again, even louder than it had been before.

"What's that fucking noise?" Detective Campbell asked.

His partner opened the briefcase, pulled out a pair of plastic gloves, and snapped them on. Then he went to the pool filter and opened the cover. He produced a pair of tongs from inside his coat and prodded around. After a few moments he managed to dislodge what looked like a giant, hairy tarantula.

"We've got a toupee," the detective with the tongs said. "Could be the perp's."

"Dexter wears a toupee," I said from my seat.

The two detectives fixed me with *who asked you?* glares.

The detective with the tongs produced a plastic evidence bag from his magic jacket, bagged the hairpiece, and handed it to his partner. Then he put the tongs down, got the skim net out, and pushed Dexter's body so it would float to the side of the pool. They looked at the top of his head and inspected the cut, which, with a little prodding, revealed itself to be a large gash. Campbell stood up and stared at me for almost a full minute. I felt sweat form on the back of my neck but I refused to look away. He then scanned the area around the pool. He seemed to be paying particular attention to the statues in the backyard. He walked over and looked down at the vomit I had left behind the bushes. Then he looked at the tile surrounding the pool. He walked over to where I had rubbed at the scuff marks and he stared at the area for far too long, as if it were a crystal ball or a time machine. Finally he turned and spoke to his partner.

"Better bring them in," he said.

His partner put the net away and disappeared into the house. Campbell put on a pair of plastic gloves from the briefcase and then approached me. I stood up to greet him.

"You found the body?" he asked without introducing himself or shaking my hand.

"Yes."

"How long ago?"

"About an hour or so."

"And you worked for the deceased?"

"Yes. I'm a creative executive at his production company. We've got offices at Warner Brothers."

He cocked an eyebrow at me as if I had just admitted to being a communist from Mars.

"Creative executive? Is that like military intelligence?"

I didn't respond to his insult, but I wanted to say it was a more accurate phrase, like police brutality. Of course, that would be like putting in a request for samples.

"Did you puke in the bushes?"

"Yeah. I tried not to, but the sight of Dexter floating like that . . ."

"Sit down."

I sat back down. The detective lifted my shoes and quickly pulled them off my feet.

"Why did you try to rub off the marks beside the pool?"

"Uh, I wasn't trying to rub anything off. I didn't even know what it was. I was just testing it."

"Testing it?"

"You know. Just to see what it was. It was an automatic response. I didn't realize I was doing anything wrong."

"Those marks were probably left by the murder weapon."

"Murder?"

"Don't tell me you think this man died of natural causes."

"I don't know what happened."

"Please, Mr. Hayes. Don't play stupid."

He knew my name. Black Elvis had obviously filled him in on everything. Black Elvis and the other cops were hovering at the far end of the pool, giving the detective room to work and enjoying the show. Dexter had floated to the middle of the pool again. He was really getting in some laps today.

"Listen, I came here looking for someone and I found Dexter just like he is. I don't know anything else about it."

"Who were you looking for?"

"A girl who lives here. Or used to live here."

"What's her name?"

"Charity James. But she's not here. She stayed at my place last night and I thought maybe she came back here, but I was wrong."

"Did you and your boss have an argument over the girl?"

"No. Not really. I mean, last night *he* had a problem with her and he told me to take her out of here. I didn't want to get stuck with her, but I wouldn't call it an argument."

"I think you better tell it from the beginning, son. Your tongue is tangling you up."

"Wait a minute. You're treating me like I'm a suspect. I didn't kill Dexter."

"I didn't say you did."

"Oh, come on. I've got eyes. I see the way you guys are carrying on. You think someone killed him and you're treating me like I did it."

The detective placed my shoes into a large plastic evidence bag.

"You're talking like a guilty man. Should I read you your rights? You want a lawyer? Or do you just want to make things easy and tell me about it?"

"I didn't kill Dexter. I just found his body. And why are you taking my shoes?"

"You tried to destroy evidence with these shoes. Now *they* are evidence."

The man's partner came over and said, "Harvey, the lab guys are on their way. Want to show them what you want?"

"I'm working here, Jer. Give me some space."

"C'mon, man, let me play good cop for a while."

Detective Campbell grunted and got out of my face. The other one took his place.

"Sorry about that," he said. "Harvey's under a lot of stress. His house got really messed up during the quake. City's been threatening to tear it down for months."

"That's too bad," I said, trying to be sympathetic.

He showed me his badge. "I'm Detective Lyndon."

"Pleased to meet you. I guess."

"So, can you tell us if the deceased had any enemies?"

I burst out laughing and Detective Lyndon shot me a look that said I hadn't chosen the smartest way to respond.

"Dexter was a Hollywood producer," I said. "He had nothing *but* enemies. Even his friends hated him. Some secretly, some right to his face. He didn't seem to mind. He had a party last night and you could take the guest list and narrow your suspects down to all one hundred and sixty people he invited—and their dates. If he was murdered, you're gonna have to talk to whoever was here last. The party was still going strong when I left."

"I'm going to need to see that guest list."

I had just implicated half of New Hollywood and a third of Old Hollywood in a murder. I realized I was going to have to watch what I said around these guys. They were so literal minded.

TWENTY-FIVE

The place was soon crawling with detectives. I answered a million or so questions while a complete forensics team worked the house and the backyard. Whoever killed Dexter hadn't seemed too concerned about hiding the details of the crime. The cops quickly deduced that the murder weapon was one of the Greek busts in the backyard. The bust, a sixty-pound cast of Adonis, was found in some bushes near its pedestal not far from the pool. It was poetic justice that Dexter had been killed by a bust, even if it wasn't exactly the kind of bust he would have hoped to see listed in his obituary as the cause of his death.

It appeared that the killer had struck Dexter while his back was turned and the bust bounced off his head and landed on the tiles. He—or she—had then picked the bust up and put it in the bushes but neglected to clean up the marks where it had fallen. It seemed very sloppy. Why go to the trouble of moving the bust if you're not going to clean up the scuff marks? Maybe the killer anticipated that some idiot would come along and wipe them off with his shoe. Unfortunately for them, I didn't do a very thorough job.

A half-dozen news helicopters and a police chopper were in the air nearby. The police chopper was keeping the news helicopters at bay. The cops said they didn't want the downdrafts from all those competing rotors contaminating the crime scene in Dexter's backyard, so they instituted an official no-fly zone directly overhead. I think they just wanted to stick it to the media. After the way the local television news hounds handled the Rodney King verdict and the subsequent riots, I didn't blame the police for demanding some privacy while they worked. Trial by media was getting old around here. I'm sure the zoom lenses were working overtime up there anyway.

I decided to stir the pot a little and told the cops about Jason Ward. I told them about the drubbing he took in the office a few months ago and that he had been replaced on his own project and that he had started trouble last night and ended up in the pool. They took notes but didn't seem overly interested.

Detective Campbell asked if I would allow my car to be searched and let me know that if I didn't feel the need to volunteer for a search, he would be glad to make a few calls and provide me with a proper search warrant. Under those circumstances I said I'd love to cooperate, and they went over my vehicle with fine-tooth combs. They found Dexter's three thousand dollars in its envelope in the glove compartment and I went through another round of uncomfortable questions as I tried to explain the property chain to the money.

Luckily for me, Mrs. Bolender arrived with the official guest list from the party and she backed up my story about how she had given the money to Charity James the night before so Charity could find accommodations elsewhere. She was so convincing the cops didn't even seize the money as some form of potential evidence.

Upon seeing Dexter's dead body lying next to the pool, Mrs. Bolender passed out and a fresh set of paramedics had to be called in to medicate her. Dexter's death hit her harder than I thought it could possibly hit anyone. Or so it seemed! Maybe it was all an act. My thinking cap was on and everyone was now a suspect as far as I was concerned.

The cops took all my pertinent info, again, kept my shoes, and let me loose on my own recognizance. They also said they wanted to talk to Charity James as soon as possible.

I took off my socks and went to my car. As I drove down the long driveway I saw a mob scene at the bottom of the hill. The police had cordoned off the driveway and a pack of bloodthirsty reporters was pressing against the boundaries. Television broadcasting vans lined the street and a number of newscasters were doing stand-ups for live feeds. This was already hitting the airwaves. My car was mobbed as I exited the driveway. Everyone wanted a shot of whoever the guy in the Camaro was. Suspect? Houseboy? Gay lover? Killer? I burned some rubber and let them choke on the smoke.

I drove home, pissed off and shoeless. When I got there I found Charity and Jeff drinking beer at the kitchen table. They were laughing it up and having a good old time.

"Where the fuck have you been?" I asked Charity.

"Right here."

"Since when? You weren't here when I got up."

"I went to Starbucks for coffee and banana bread. I brought you back a latte, but you were gone when I got here. Jeff had to let me in."

"I just got back from Dexter's house. He's dead."

Charity sat there staring at me, not sure if I was joking or not.

"Did you hear me?" I asked, trying to read her face.

"I heard you, but I don't know what to say. What do you mean?"

"I mean Dexter's dead. I found him floating in his pool. Someone hit him on the head and killed him." I must have sounded more accusative than I meant to sound, because Charity immediately became defensive.

"Well, don't look at me. I was here all night."

"How do you know it happened last night?"

"What's that, some kind of movie trick? You said he was dead. I just figured it happened after we left and before you saw him this morning, which would, for the most part, leave last night. Wouldn't it?"

"I'm just wondering why you seem more concerned about me thinking you killed him than you are with the fact that he's dead."

"You think I *liked* that guy? Puh-leeze. But still, I didn't kill him."

"I tell you the guy you've been living with is dead and all you can say is 'I didn't kill him'?"

"Well, I *didn't.*"

"You've got nothing else to say about it?"

"What do you want me to say? You want me to cry or something? People die. Shit happens. Talk to Amy Barth. She's the last person he fucked! Maybe she didn't like it."

"I just got done with four hours of questions from the cops and they don't buy all of my story. You're my alibi for last night and I'm yours, but the fact is that I didn't see you after about two in the morning. Not until just now. We don't make very good alibis for each other, do we?"

Jeff jumped into the fray. "Hey, man, she told you where she went this morning. What do you want?"

He was *defending her.* My roommate, my buddy, was taking this girl's side over mine! I had known him for ten years. He had known Charity for no more than a few hours. Either I had overestimated Jeff's intelligence or underestimated Charity's power over men.

"Stay out of this, Jeff. It's got nothing to do with you."

"Hey, you brought her here last night. I've been with her all day. When would she have time to kill someone? Why don't you give it a rest?"

"Don't you get it? She's using us! She set me up to be her alibi and you're playing right into it."

"You're paranoid, man."

Charity was now producing tears, but I'm sure they weren't for Dexter. They were for herself. Either I was right and she thought she was busted, or she just couldn't stand being accused of anything.

"I've been in this apartment since last night, except for a half hour at Starbucks this morning. I can prove it."

"You'll have to. The police want to talk to you."

She looked horrified. "I can't talk to the police."

"Why not?"

"I just can't, okay? They scare me."

"That's tough. You're gonna have to get over that quick."

The tears were streaming now. She got up and ran down the hall to Jeff's bedroom and slammed the door behind her.

I looked at Jeff. He looked both angry and sheepish. A tough stunt, but he managed it.

"You fucked her, didn't you?" I asked.

The anger disappeared from his face and only sheepishness was left.

"Jesus Christ, man, I leave a girl here for a few hours and you're already banging her?"

"She said you guys weren't involved. What's the big deal?"

"Don't you get it? That chick's trouble. She's a coke whore."

"So?"

"So, she might have killed my boss. She might be using us. She's crazy."

"You're nuts. That girl didn't kill anyone."

"Someone did. And, by the way, didn't you already have a woman in your room this morning?"

"She left."

"Your dick is going to get you in trouble one day. It's a good thing you work for lawyers. You may end up needing one."

Jeff noticed my bare feet. "What's with the Huck Finn look?"

"The cops took my shoes."

"Why?"

"Because I stepped on some evidence."

"Sounds like *you're* the one who needs a lawyer, stepping on evidence and shit."

I stood there looking at him, trying to think of something witty to say. "Fuck you" was all I could come up with, but if it was good enough for Billy Wilder, it was good enough for me.

TWENTY-SIX

Detectives Campbell and Lyndon decided to swing by my apartment after they left the crime scene to see if Charity James was there. She freaked a little at first, but once she calmed down she handled the interview with the same calm demeanor she would have exhibited on an audition for a bit part in a TV movie. She was a better actress than I thought. Jeff was out running errands and didn't get to meet the detectives. I was allowed to sit in my bedroom, which was just down the hall, so I heard most of their conversation. Charity admitted to stabbing Dexter in the ass with her nail file, but denied going back to the house after I brought her to my apartment. Since she had no car, she would have had to take a cab or get someone to give her a ride to have made it to Dexter's and back between the time I left her on the couch and my arrival at the crime scene the next morning. They didn't say it, but I knew they would be checking taxicab records for just such a trip. Still, I got the feeling that she was not a serious suspect in their investigation. They seemed to be giving her the kid glove treatment.

As they spoke I suddenly remembered that I had ten grand stashed in my bookshelf that could be traced back to Dexter Morton. If the cops wanted to search the place and they found that money, it would look like I had ten thousand little motives to knock off the boss.

I went to the bookshelf and considered pulling out the envelope. But then what would I do with it? If I tried to walk it out of the apartment, they might catch me in the act. And where would I take it anyway? I couldn't put it in the bank. They would eventually be looking into my accounts if they actually considered me a suspect.

The phone rang in the kitchen and I nearly jumped out of my skin. Charity answered it and called down the hall for me. I went into the kitchen and took the phone. It was Neil Silverman, a business affairs exec at Warner's. He had heard the news of Dexter's death and was calling an emergency meeting of the staff for 10 P.M. at our office. I said I'd be there, then hung up. I told the cops who had called and asked if it was okay for me to leave the apartment. Detective Campbell smiled strangely and said, "Sure. Why wouldn't it be? We're not here to talk to you."

The way he spoke gave me chills. I went back to my room and considered the money again. I decided it was better to leave it where it was for now. I locked my bedroom door and returned to the kitchen-cum-interrogation room. I snatched my jacket off the chair and left them to it. It was already eight-thirty and I hadn't eaten anything all day. I grabbed a Fatburger from the joint on Ventura Boulevard and headed into Burbank.

Neil Silverman had us gather in Dexter's glass-walled conference room. The group was unusually subdued. No one actually shed tears for Dexter, but no one made any nasty jokes either. It was the best that he could have hoped for.

The staff asked me about finding Dexter's body. I gave them just enough information to satisfy their curiosity, but left some of the more grotesque or humorous details out of the telling. I'd save the bit about the toupee in the pool filter for the next wrap party.

Dexter owned his company, but the studio was fully funding the enterprise. All the projects developed since Dexter moved onto the lot were rotating back to the studio. If any of the films ever saw production, Dexter's heirs would receive his share of the profits. The studio accountants would do their best to make sure that Dexter's relatives were never bothered by that tax burden. The rest of his projects would be controlled by his estate. His parents were deceased and he didn't have children or siblings, but if his uncles, aunts, and cousins were anything like him, there would probably be one hell of a wrestling match over the details of the estate.

Silverman quickly laid out a plan that called for all of us being out of work within the next few weeks. *Maelstrom* was the only film Dexter currently had in production and it was almost wrapped. The studio was taking over all the duties Dexter or his people would have needed to perform for postproduction and the distribution of the movie. They were already considering changing the title and moving the release date up by three weeks to try to cut down on the interest payments accruing on the over-budget nightmare. Dexter Morton's office staff was now obsolete. Dexter's executors would be working with the studio to coordinate our duties as we wrapped up the office. There would be a small severance payout, and Silverman gave lip service to trying to find each of us new positions within the studio walls, but we knew that was bullshit. They had been laying people off left and right since the earthquake. This was the perfect excuse to cut some more deadwood.

The staff met the news with a variety of emotions, from shock to relief to horror. Some of them had complete confidence in their ability to land on their feet, others feared reentering the depressed job market.

Alex looked devastated. His worst fears had come to pass. He was about to be unemployed. The condo payments would be tough to come by if he didn't find another gig fast.

As the initial shock of Dexter's death began to fade, it suddenly hit me with full force that my big opportunity had just died in front of me as well. I would not be hitching a ride on Dexter's coattails onto a producing position on *The Untitled Gregory Cloud Project.* Whoever killed Dexter also killed off the shot I had been working toward since arriving on this lot. My time with Dexter Morton had been a complete waste. I was getting steamed, and I guess it showed on my face.

"Do you have a problem, Mr. Hayes?" Silverman asked.

"I guess you could say so. I've been shepherding a project here and I was up for a producer's position on the picture if it got made. I have a feeling that deal is now history."

"Trust your instincts," Silverman said.

Detectives Campbell and Lyndon entered the room, introduced themselves, and asked to speak with each member of the staff individually. The emergency meeting had been structured for two purposes: to clarify the studio's intentions and to gather Dexter's closest associates in one place so the cops could take their crack at them and check their demeanors and alibis. They probably also wanted to see if anyone *didn't* show up. I wondered whose idea the meeting had actually been, Silverman's or the cops'? The speed with which the studio had acted suddenly became very suspect. This could have waited until morning if it was just about business.

Other investigators began arriving at the office and started going through things, looking for clues. I felt queasy as I saw two men enter my personal office. I didn't think I had anything in there that would incriminate me in any crime, including my misappropriation of funds, but I felt a sense of outrage at the violation of privacy. Still, I knew better than to complain. I didn't want their spotlights trained on me again.

Since I had already spoken at length with Campbell and Lyndon earlier in the day, I was excused early. My coworkers looked at me very suspiciously as I left them to their fates.

"Watch out for the tall one," I said. "He wields a mean rubber hose."

TWENTY-SEVEN

Clyde McCoy was sitting on the brick wall in front of our apartment building, sipping coffee and smoking a cigarette, when I pulled into the parking lot. It was well after midnight.

"Heard about Dexter," Clyde said as I got out of my car. "You must be rattled."

"Yeah. It's pretty fucked up. How'd you find out about it?"

"It was the lead story on every channel at eleven. They're going nuts with it. They *love* this kind of shit."

"Vultures."

"Dexter was an asshole. I can't say I'm sorry to see him go."

"He wasn't that bad," I said.

"You have no idea the kind of evil that guy did to people."

"Still, it's no reason to be glad he's dead."

"Are you kidding? You know how many dead people I know? Dozens. Good people. I'm sick of burying my friends. It's always the people I like who die, never the people I wish were dead. You ever get that feeling? Like maybe this is Hell and our punishment is to watch those we love die and those we hate survive and thrive?"

"I think I know what you mean."

"Dexter was a bad guy and he was bad for this town. I'm glad he's gone. There's about forty other motherfuckers I'd like to see buried right along with him. But they'll live forever. It's just nice to see one of the bad guys buy the farm for a change."

"You've got a cold heart."

"Just for scumbags."

"I'm sure Dexter had his good side."

"If he did he kept it well hidden."

"He was keeping a lot of people employed."

"Yeah. Doing *his* bidding. Speaking of which, what's going to happen to your job? They going to move you to another producer?"

"I don't think so. The executors of his estate are coming in to clear up all kinds of rights issues with the studio, and the studio is handing their end of it over to the business affairs people."

"*Cocksuckers!* All those business affairs people are cocksuckers! Goddamn, I hate them!"

"Well, they're in charge now. I've got three weeks to straighten out my notes and help them find everything, then I'm out on the street."

Clyde pulled a package of tobacco out of his pocket and began to roll a cigarette.

"I didn't know you smoked," I said.

"On again, off again. I hate it, but when I'm not writing something, I have to keep my hands busy. I roll my own to slow down the process."

"Good idea. I ought to try it. I've been trying to quit for a couple of years now."

"You're welcome to roll one if you like."

"No, thanks. I don't want to add another weapon to my arsenal of addiction."

"If you didn't have an addictive personality you wouldn't fit in around here."

"It's funny, I've been in L.A. for fifteen years, but I still feel like a stranger. I don't feel like I fit in very well at all."

"Oh, you fit. Don't kid yourself."

I had the feeling I had just been insulted.

Clyde finished rolling the cigarette and fired it up. I went up to my apartment to talk to Charity, but she was in Jeff's room with him, playing around. They did not sound concerned about Dexter's death or the police investigation in the least. I had a beer out on the darkened balcony and watched Clyde McCoy roll and smoke three more cigarettes down below. He was just staring out at the Viande parking lot, thinking. But about what?

Finally he stubbed out his last cigarette and went into his apartment.

The phone rang. It was my father. Friends of his had called him many hours ago, awakening him from a deep slumber to tell him his son was on the news and had been involved in a murder. He had already left six messages and wanted to know why I hadn't called him back. I told him I just got home and hadn't checked the answering machine yet. It took a while for me to explain the circumstances behind Dexter's death and I don't think he believed me. My mother was so traumatized, she wouldn't even get on the phone.

After we hung up I checked the answering machine. There were seventeen calls waiting for me. Other than the six from my father, the messages were all from members of the press who had tracked me down and wanted an interview. I wasn't going to talk to any of those vultures. Not yet at least.

I pulled the plug on the phone, finished my beer, went to bed, and crashed hard.

TWENTY-EIGHT

The office was a war zone the next day. The cops had searched the place thoroughly and not bothered to put anything back in place before they left. Everything was a mess. Dexter's attorneys were functioning as his executors, and they placed a hard-nosed prick named Miles Gallo in our office to supervise the last rites. He provided us each with a list of duties he expected us to perform and strict instructions not to do anything else. He had a small army of associates going over the place with fine-tooth combs.

I spent most of the day organizing my office for the eventual shutdown and listening to Alex whine. He was in the midst of a terrible economic nightmare.

"Why did fucking Dexter have to go and get himself killed?" he asked. "If I don't find a gig fast I'm going to lose my condo."

"That's all you ever think about, Alex. Why don't you sell that damn condo?"

"I just bought it! I'm going to have to file for bankruptcy."

"At least you're alive to go bankrupt. Dexter's dead."

"So?"

"I just think you should have a little respect for the dead."

"Why? You think he's a better person now?"

"He's quieter."

"Dexter hated us. Worse than that. He didn't even consider us *people.* Why should I feel anything for him now that he's dead? Fuck him."

They say laughter is the way some people deal with tragedy, but I don't think many people viewed Dexter's passing as a tragedy. The consensus appeared to echo Alex's and Clyde's *fuck-him* sentiment.

Even Dexter's family appeared far from devastated. They were shipping his body back to Connecticut, where there would be a small, private ceremony. They weren't even going to throw a West Coast memorial for the wealthy black sheep of the family. Like Dexter, the bottom line carried weight with these people.

Miles Gallo entered my office soon after I returned from lunch, set a document on my desk in front of me, and said, "I'd like you to read that very carefully."

"What is it?"

"It's your confidentiality agreement. You signed it before your first official day of work in this office."

"Okay. So why do I need to read it?"

"Because you're going to be getting calls from the media. In fact, you already have. We've been screening them for you."

I leaned forward, starting to get angry at the fact that I had been restricted from receiving incoming calls. "And why is that?"

"Because you have no business with the media. Your agreement states very clearly that you are never to discuss anything related to Dexter Morton with any member of the press. Ever."

"But Dexter is dead."

"That does not vitiate your agreement with this office. You found his body. They're all going to want to talk to you."

"And why do you care if they do?"

"Dexter Morton is a commodity, dead or alive. There is a value to his name. We want to protect that name wherever possible. You should be able to understand that. Besides, considering your situation, I wouldn't think you would want to talk to the press."

"Why is that?"

"Well, I think they view you as a suspect. If you let them have their way with you, others may come to believe this too. You know how the media functions."

"I see what you mean."

"Good. We don't want to get strident about this, but we will if necessary. Read the agreement. The penalties are quite clear."

"Don't worry about me. I just want to finish my work and get out of here."

"Fine. Carry on then."

He left my office and I began to read the confidentiality agreement I signed those long months ago. It was severe. You'd think I was working for the CIA or a cigarette manufacturer. I was to speak to no one outside of the office about anything either personal or professional that I learned or discovered while working for Dexter Morton. There were pages and pages of legalese covering every possible scenario, including the death of a fellow office worker or even Dexter himself. It was amazingly complete. If I were to break any portion of the contract, huge financial penalties would automatically be assessed. I would be rendered penniless, and it wouldn't end there. They could still come after me once I was solvent again. Even bankruptcy offered no lasting protection. It was vicious. I had signed it without paying it much heed. Most producers have agreements like this for their employees. But I never foresaw myself standing over the boss's dead body. This was a good story for the tabloids and I could sell my version of it for a lot of dough if not for this agreement. I decided to take the document home with me. Maybe I would contact a lawyer and see if there was a way to break it without it breaking me.

TWENTY-NINE

The officials finally released the official cause of Dexter Morton's death: drowning. The blow to his head hadn't killed him, just stunned him. Water in his lungs finished him off. It was still a murder investigation, though. No one thought for a moment that Adonis himself had jumped off his pedestal and attacked Dexter.

I went about the hundreds of minor administrative tasks required to put Dexter Morton's office in a state of readiness for the transition. Final filings, lists of properties owned or coowned by Dexter, a calendar of option expirations, final returns of unread manuscripts to the various talent agencies around town. Much of what I was doing was redundant. The studio's legal department tracked most of the same work, but I wanted to keep busy in my final three weeks and I wanted to do nothing to draw suspicion to myself. I also wanted to stay close to things so I could have fair warning if Dexter's clandestine payment to Wilkie surfaced.

The rest of the office was on a constant job search. Janet, the receptionist, found a position right away working for Bette Midler's All Girl Productions over on the Disney lot. Natalie, the researcher, picked up an archivist gig at Universal. The job hunt was not going as well for the rest of the staff. It was not a good time to be looking for a job in the industry. Layoffs were occurring all over town. The biz was going through one of its "adjustments," which translated to "we didn't have such a great year last year" and "that earthquake really fucked us up." There had been a lot of overspending and underachieving at the box office, and now the fat was being trimmed. Not from the top, mind you. The execs still had their massive salaries and outrageous stock-option packages, and perks that would make the average grunt worker puke and slash tires if they knew the truth of it all. No, the cuts were in the form of manpower below the line. If certain studio heads hadn't turned their profit packages into multimillion-dollar bonuses at the end of the year, heads had to roll. And roll they did. They were rolling all over town. We were reentering the job market at a bad time.

Tom and Roger, Dexter's secretaries, were having no luck, but at least they weren't griping about it. They knew that if they faxed enough résumés around town, something would eventually surface.

Alex was his usual panicky self. He was certain that he would never work again. He thought for sure that he was going to lose his condo and eventually have to resort to selling big-screen TVs at Circuit City.

I sent out a couple of résumés and took a few meetings with prospective employers. I soon discovered I could get any meeting in town I wanted—as long as I was willing to talk about how I had found Dexter Morton floating in his pool. No one actually wanted to hire me, but they all wanted to hear the story.

I was tired of the studio scene anyway, tired of seeing talentless hustlers like Charles Callaway waste millions of dollars getting a single shot that we'd still have to fix digitally before it could be used in a film, tired of slogging through reams of bad screenplays looking for something good to bring to the boss only to have it thrown back in my face because it wasn't "commercial" enough or didn't have the right elements attached, tired of seeing the worst dreck imaginable getting the green light because of relationships or politics instead of quality. But what else was I going to do? The nest egg was not yet ready to hatch, and now it was in danger of exploding, loaded as it was with the phantom 10K.

Natalie was the only other person on the staff showing up regularly in those last three weeks. Her new job didn't start until a week after our end date, so she put the same effort into wrapping things up that I did. It was the first time I managed to learn anything personal about her. She had kept very much to herself before Dexter died. She was always buried in research and remained very quiet during meetings, letting her paperwork speak for itself. She was a mousy little thing, timid looking behind her horn-rimmed glasses, a classic librarian cliché straight out of central casting. She couldn't have been older than thirty but she had premature gray in her hair that made her look more like forty. I'd like to say that she transformed magically into a hotty the moment she took off the glasses, but sadly that was not the case. Underneath her frumpy exterior was just more frump.

Occasionally, while performing our mundane tasks, we would discuss Dexter's murder and trade theories. She was a mystery fiction fan, and Dexter's demise was the one department in which she showed some glimmer of interest. I would have thought that she would have been all teary eyed when talking about her late boss or frightened by the prospect that we might know the murderer personally, might even be *working* with them, but she was amazingly calm and cool when discussing "the case," as we referred to it around the office.

Natalie's favorite theory was one that I had originally proposed in jest: Charles Callaway murdered Dexter out of spite because of the way Dexter snapped at him the day he went car shopping while a few hundred people waited for him to say, "Action." She didn't necessarily think it was the most logical choice, but it gave her the greatest satisfaction as a mystery aficionado and she disliked Charles Callaway immensely because he had dismissed her research work on *Maelstrom* as trivial and "unimportant to audience satisfaction." I had a feeling she thought I was actually the most logical suspect, but she was too polite to mention it. If she really thought I killed Dexter, it didn't seem to bother her much.

I was leaning toward Mrs. Bolender as my personal favorite suspect. I found it hard to believe anyone could work for Dexter for so long without growing to hate him deeply. I had many theories about what might have touched her off: from spurned affection to one too many trips to the dry cleaner. Anything could have been the straw that broke the personal assistant's back and then the producer's skull. Also, she was in the catbird seat now, working closely with the executors of Dexter's estate to clean up his affairs outside of the office. I'm sure she knew of many secret stashes of gold and booty that Dexter had squirreled away that no one else would ever find out about. Plus, Mrs. Bolender was the only person who seemed genuinely upset that Dexter was dead. I speculated that she was performing in an attempt to throw the law off her trail. She was the perfect suspect.

Natalie and I laughed away the hours playing our own private version of Clue. "Was Mr. Bastard killed by the pool by Mr. Son of a Bitch Director or Mrs. Disgruntled Personal Assistant?" It made the days pass very quickly. And in the process I grew quite fond of my mousy little friend. I almost scratched her from my list of suspects, until I realized that's just what the murderer would want me to do, so I moved her up two notches to number six, right between Jason the Wronged Boy Genius at number five and Marge the Vengeful Lover of the Abused Writer at number seven.

THIRTY

On Thursday, Miles Gallo came into my office and stood before my desk.

"Mr. Hayes, I'm wondering if you might be able to help me with something."

"Sure, Mr. Gallo. What can I do for you?"

"Our accountants have uncovered a rather large cash withdrawal that Mr. Morton made a few weeks before his passing. We've tried to trace what it was used for but we've had no luck. We're asking the staff if they were aware of any large cash transactions as of late."

I sat there staring at him, unsure of what to say. They were on to the money and they were following it right to my door.

"How much was it?" I asked, stalling for time so I could think.

"Fifty thousand dollars."

"I thought you said it was a large withdrawal?"

"You don't consider fifty thousand dollars a large amount of money? I've seen your pay stubs."

"No need to be rude, Mr. Gallo. It's just that I assumed Dexter handled that kind of money all the time. He *was* rich, you know."

"I don't need attitude from you either, Mr. Hayes, only answers. Mr.

Morton rarely ever took more than five thousand dollars in cash out of his accounts at one time. Plastic was his preferred method of payment. A cash withdrawal in this amount is a red flag. He needed that money for something, and I'm thinking he might have been being blackmailed. I wanted to check with the staff before I alerted the authorities, just in case there was a logical, legal explanation. If there isn't, I'll move forward. Thank you for your valuable time."

He started for the door. I realized I had just raised the old red flag myself, and wanted to lower it before it was too late.

"Mr. Gallo, wait a moment."

He stopped at the door and looked at me.

"Sorry if I came off as flip. I'm just a little cranky lately since I'm about to face unemployment."

He nodded as if he understood, which of course he did not and probably never would.

"I don't know anything about the money specifically, but when you said *blackmail* it triggered something. I had an unusual meeting with a man named Jim Becker not long before Dexter died. He implied he knew some things about Dexter that Dexter would not want to be made public."

"What kind of things?"

"Personal things. See, he was meeting with me, but he was really trying to reach Dexter. Dexter wouldn't give him the time of day. But he picked up my tape recorder and spoke into it as if he were speaking directly to Dexter, knowing I would play it for him."

Gallo approached my desk again. He was hooked. And now that I thought of it, I was a little bit too. This wasn't that crazy a theory. Except I knew it had nothing to do with the fifty K. Still, Becker made a very good suspect, even if he hadn't been invited to the party. I hadn't seen him there, but he could have showed up late or he could have waited until everyone had left to make his move.

Gallo leaned forward and smiled thinly. "You say you recorded this meeting?"

"Yes."

"Where is the tape?"

"I gave it to Dexter."

"Come with me."

He turned and walked out of my office.

I got up and gave chase. He led me down the hall to Dexter's private office. People I did not recognize were in the room going through massive amounts of paperwork. Gallo went to a corner of the office and pointed to a stack of boxes marked AUDIO.

"I would like you to go through these boxes and find that tape. It could prove very important."

"Okay. Should I take the boxes to my office?"

"No. Clear a spot in the room and work here."

"All right. Can I finish what I was doing in my office first?"

"This takes top priority. Let me know when you find it."

He turned and walked away.

I started going through the boxes. They were filled with hundreds of minicassettes. Luckily for me, Dexter labeled most of his cassettes with the names of those he was meeting with and the dates the meetings occurred. The first box contained cassettes that dated back four years. The second box was slightly newer. Most of the tapes in that box were dated 1992 and early 1993. The last box had tapes from 1993 and 1994. They were not stacked in any order, so I had to go through the entire box. The cassette I had given to Dexter was unmarked. I hadn't had time to label it when he took it from my recorder. I only found three tapes in this box that did not carry a label.

I asked one of Gallo's assistants if she knew where Dexter's minicassette recorder was.

"Mr. Morton's extraneous office machinery has been boxed and moved to storage" was the reply.

I took the three cassettes to my office, got out my tape recorder, and played the tapes. Two of them were blank. The third one seemed to have some sort of sexual encounter recorded on it. There was a woman's voice, but her words were muffled. I could hear Dexter moaning and instructing the woman to do very specific things with her tongue and her lips. I realized this was a tape that he recorded—possibly by accident—during an in-office fellatio session. As the woman's voice became clearer it was obvious that she was not Charity James. Dexter had been auditioning recently, and either accidentally clicked his recorder on or wanted to capture the session for posterity. If it were the latter, then it would lead me to believe that the woman in question might have been someone of note, not just a run-of-the-mill ingenue.

I had to think of a way to stall for more time and throw Gallo off my trail. Not only did I not want to be caught with Dexter's ten grand in my possession, but the revelation that Wilkie had taken the other forty for an under-the-table rewrite would get him kicked out of the Writers Guild. My participation as the bagman would only serve to add more dirt to my tarnished reputation. Adding embezzlement to the charge would qualify me as a felon. I had to find a way to protect Wilkie from exposure, because protecting him was the same as protecting myself. Wilkie might get blackballed, but I would end up in jail for my crimes—to say nothing of the fact that the police would consider embezzlement and the possibility of getting caught or the fact that Dexter might have *already* caught me as perfectly good motives for murder. There was a lot of pressure on the police and the D.A.'s office to find Dexter Morton's killer. I didn't want any callbacks for the role. I had to get rid of that money.

I took the three tapes back to Dexter's office. Gallo was there again, conferring with one of his flock. I approached him and waited for him to finish. He turned to me immediately and said, "Find it?"

"No. But I found something else you might be interested in." I handed him the tape containing the recording of one of Dexter's sexual adventures.

"These other two are blank. I don't know what he did with the one I gave him. It must be somewhere else."

"Was it labeled?"

"Not when I gave it to him. Actually, I didn't give it to him. He took it out of my recorder. He said he was going to give it to you guys along with the script that Becker wanted him to buy."

"What script?"

"It was called *Burnin' Down Vegas.* It was a project Becker had brought to us once already that we had rejected. He said he had paid a writer to fix it and Dexter would be overjoyed with the results. It seemed to me that he wanted to use whatever he knew about Dexter as leverage to force him to buy the project no matter how good or bad it was."

"And what makes you say that?"

"Just the things he said and the way he said them."

"This is looking more and more like a matter for the police."

"We probably ought to find that tape before we bother them with this."

"Now you are practicing law?"

"No. It's just . . . I just . . . I just think they'll think it's nothing unless they can hear that tape."

"If it exists, we will find it."

"You say that like you don't believe me."

"I don't even know you, Mr. Hayes. Why should I believe a perfect stranger?"

"Well, nobody's perfect . . ."

"Go back to work, Mr. Hayes. We'll look for the mysterious tape."

I nodded and headed back to my office. I was hating that little prick more and more by the moment.

THIRTY-ONE

When I got home Jeff's door was shut and Charity was nowhere to be seen. I finally realized that she was in Jeff's room with him, and by the sound of things, they seemed to be getting along just fine.

I went into the living room and tried to watch some TV, but the sounds from Jeff's bedroom proved distracting. Even though I was the first to rent the apartment, I felt like moving out of the place instead of waiting for Jeff to leave. He was turning the joint into a bordello. Even when *I* brought a girl home she ended up in *his* bedroom. Besides, it was getting crowded. Charity's one-night sleepover was dragging on indefinitely. Her three-thousand-a-month stipend from Dexter was a deal that died with him, and his executors had made his house off-limits to her so she had no place to go and very little money with which to get there. Mrs. Bolender made good on her promise and had Charity's personal belongings delivered to her at my place. She had loaded most of her things into my garage, which Jeff and I used as storage space, and seemed to feel no need to be on her way. For all I knew she had killed Dexter, and here I was letting her bunk out on my couch—when she would use it. She was usually in there with Jeff, fucking, then fighting about something trivial, then fucking again.

I went out on the balcony and discovered that it was raining outside.

I sat in the hammock, the sound of the rain a great improvement over the noises inside the apartment, and fell asleep.

By the time I awoke it was after ten and the rain had stopped. Deciding I needed a nightcap, I went next door to Viande and found Clyde McCoy sitting alone at the bar.

"Hey, neighbor," he said. "How goes the job search?"

"Not so good," I said, taking a seat next to him. "It's hard to get work when the town thinks you killed your last employer."

"Hell, in this business that should be a glowing recommendation."

"What are you drinking?"

"Shot of Jack with a Bass chaser."

"The hard stuff, eh?"

"The good stuff."

I ordered the same and we sat quietly, nursing our drinks. When Clyde finished his he got up off his stool and said, "Think I'm going to head on down to Boardner's. See what's going on down there." He seemed very unsteady on his feet.

"You going to drive?"

"Well, I sure as hell can't take the corporate jet."

"Maybe you ought to stay here—you know, in walking distance of your apartment."

"It's boring here. I want to go down to Whorewood. Why don't you tag along?"

I had nothing better to do, so I said, "I'll drive."

"Good man."

I finished my beer, paid my tab, and got to my feet. I felt a little wobbly myself, but I was certainly more qualified to be the designated driver than Clyde.

As we exited the back door of Viande, we could hear loud, angry voices coming from my apartment on the second floor. The door to the kitchen was open and Charity and Jeff were screaming at each other at top decibel.

"What the fuck is going on up there, Hayes?"

"I don't know. I better go up and find out. I'll just be a second."

I ran across the alley and up my stairwell. The argument seemed to be escalating. I entered the kitchen and caught Jeff and Charity in mid-scream. They both froze in place when they saw me in the doorway.

"Guys, I can hear you all the way across the alley. What the hell's going on?"

Charity said, "Your asshole buddy just got done with me and he's leaving to go out partying and he won't take me along—like I'm some kind of fuck doll to be used then put away in the closet. I'm not a Stepford wife!"

"I want to go out for a drink," Jeff said, "to clear my head and shit."

"Sorry the experience was so traumatic for you," Charity spat.

I stepped all the way into the kitchen and closed the door. "This whole situation is getting ridiculous."

"Well, don't worry about it," Jeff said. "I found a place. I'm moving out next week."

Both Charity and I were shocked by the abruptness of the statement.

"That's great," Charity said. "I guess you want to get as far away from me as possible?"

"I just need my own space. It's time."

"So what about me?"

"You can stay here. Take over my room if you want. We can still see each other when our schedules permit."

"Aren't you the Gandhi of cock?"

"Wait a minute," I protested. "This is *my* place. I'm going to be stuck here with all the rent, and frankly I don't know if I want another roommate. Especially one who doesn't *pay* rent."

Charity looked hurt and infuriated at the same time. "I'll give you money, if that's what you want. I've been buying groceries. If you wanted money, you should have asked me."

"You're not working."

"I know. But I still have some of what Dexter gave me and I can always get money if I need it that bad."

I didn't want to ask her how.

"You guys work it out," Jeff said. "I'm leaving."

He went out the door before we could say another word. Charity looked like she had been punched in the gut.

"He's just like all the rest," she said.

"Maybe you should think about that before you jump into bed so quick."

Her expression suddenly hardened. "Maybe you should mind your own fucking business!"

THIRTY-TWO

Clyde chain-smoked all the way to Hollywood. I smoked one of his hand-rolled cigarettes out of self-defense. It was *harsh.*

Boardner's was even deader than Viande had been. There were eight people at the bar and a handful of tired folks in a booth at the back of the room. Even hipsters don't like to come out in the rain.

Clyde went to the bar and said hello to a friend of his whom he introduced to me as Earl. Earl was an ex-carney who had worked with Clyde at Hollywood Book and Poster back in the early eighties. Earl was driving a cab now, but yearning for those halcyon days working the Ferris wheel and ruing the day he left the memorabilia store. Earl was dressed like a modern-day cowboy, including a white Stetson, which he was wearing tilted back on his head like he was James Dean, despite the fact that he was indoors.

I nursed a beer as Clyde and Earl caught up on old times while downing shots of Jack Daniel's. Clyde was feeling no pain. It was just like the old days, or so they both said.

A lanky brunette in her early thirties wearing a low-cut blouse and hot pants was arguing with a man a few stools over from us. It had obviously been going on long before we arrived. She was very drunk. He looked fairly sober, a studly looking barfly who had the air of the local cock of the walk about him. I got the impression that they were an item, or at least that she *thought* they were, but it sounded like she had caught him in some sort of dalliance with a "big-titted whore."

"You think all women are good for is to give head," she said to the man drunkenly. "I'll give you head till you die!"

Studly didn't respond. He just sat there sipping a Dewar's and water.

An older man joined them. I recognized him as one of the owners of the place. I had seen him around over the years, usually hunkered down at the end of the bar, watching the register through the bottom of a rocks glass. The old guy tried to interject some calm into the proceedings, but just managed to agitate the woman. She was getting louder and more physical. She reached over and pulled at the stud's silk shirtsleeve. He pulled away from her and downed his drink, then got up from the bar and moved for the door. The woman gave chase, grabbed him, and pulled him around, trying repeatedly to slap him but not managing to coordinate her timing properly. The old guy wedged between them and tried to pry them apart like a referee at a boxing match turned sloppy. The stud shoved him back to remove him from harm's way and the girl took a wild swing. The stud ducked under the slap but the woman's hand struck the old guy flat on the side of his face—hard! The guy went down and hit his head on the floor. He was out for the count.

"You stupid cooze," Studly said. Then he turned and went out the front door.

We sat there, flabbergasted.

The woman straddled the old man's chest and started slapping his face, trying to wake him up. He wasn't moving. He looked like he wasn't even breathing.

"Shit, I think he's dead," I said.

Clyde and Earl went over and looked down at the woman and the old man.

"You're right," Clyde said. "He's not breathing. Better call nine-one-one."

"Call nine-one-one!" I yelled at the bartender, a slimmer, younger version of the old man on the floor. He stared at the old man's body for a few moments before moving slowly toward the phone. I guess he didn't want to bother the paramedics unless the guy was really dead or at least near dead. Or maybe he was hoping to inherit the joint.

"He's alive," the girl said. "He's just faking it." She shook the man by the collar, lifted his head up and let it drop with a thud. It did not bring him around. If he was faking it, he deserved an Oscar.

"Get the fuck off him," Clyde said.

"No, I'm going to wake him up," she said, slapping the old man in the face again.

Clyde lifted her up and handed her to Earl. She pulled away and tried to get back on the old man's chest. Clyde shoved her away again.

"Keep her off me, Earl."

Earl slapped the woman hard, and she promptly spun around and sat on the floor Indian-style, in a daze, contemplating the mysteries of life.

Clyde began pumping the old guy's chest, trying what little CPR he knew. It wasn't working.

"Give him mouth-to-mouth," Earl said with a smile.

Clyde looked down at the old man's scraggly, spit-encrusted beard and his yellowed teeth and said, "Fuck that. *You* give him mouth-to-mouth."

Clyde got up and let Earl straddle the old man.

"I'll pump his chest, but I'm not giving him no lip-lock," Earl said. He pumped on the guy's chest furiously. The old man was not responding.

"Anyone in here want to give Bob mouth-to-mouth?" Clyde called out.

The looky-loos all looked away.

"How 'bout you, Hayes?" Clyde asked. "Want to give old Bob the kiss of life?"

I stood there frozen, staring down at Bob. Earl was slowing down, all tuckered out. He got up and Clyde shoved me toward the dead guy. I straddled the man, started to bend forward to give him mouth-to-mouth and found I just couldn't do it. I put both hands together and pushed down on his solar plexus. Everyone in the bar laughed at my cowardice. I even thought Bob might sit up and laugh in my face, but he seemed pretty dead. Pressing on his chest was like pushing into a bony trampoline. I was getting nowhere and it was scaring me. I was sitting on a dead guy! His life was in our hands and none of us could make the commitment to blow air into his body to save him. Even worse, it had become a bar joke.

Clyde tapped me on the shoulder. I got up and he replaced me. Clyde struck Bob over the heart with his fist.

"Stop it!" the drunken woman said from her cross-legged position. "You're hurting him!"

Earl touched her with the tip of his cowboy boot, causing her to roll over on her side. "Just lay there and shut the fuck up," he said. She managed to maintain her cross-legged position as she capsized.

Clyde struck Bob in the chest again, then a third time. Then he started pumping again.

Bob suddenly gasped for air and everyone in the bar jumped. We had all given him up for dead. Clyde leaned down, put an ear to Bob's chest, and said, "I've got a heartbeat!"

Bob mumbled, "So do I, motherfucker."

Two paramedics came through the front door, carrying a ton of gear.

"That was quick," I said.

"We were just over on Highland working backup on a hit-and-run," one of the paramedics said.

After a quick question-and-answer session with Clyde about what had happened, they put an oxygen mask over Bob's face and let him breathe from a canister for a few minutes.

Clyde and Earl sidled up to the bar and went back to their drinks. I continued watching the paramedics, but for the rest of the crowd the show was over. They returned to their inane conversations and their cheap flirtations. The woman who had started it all was sleeping peacefully under one of the tables. Within an hour Bob was up, his head was bandaged, and he was nursing a drink at his spot at the end of the bar, having refused to accompany the paramedics to the hospital. All was forgotten.

As the night wound down Clyde said, "Let's get out of here."

"Where to?" asked Earl.

"Ma Smith's still operating?"

"Of course. Seven years and going strong."

"I haven't been there in a month of scumdays."

"Let's hit it then."

"What's Ma Smith's?" I asked. "I never heard of it."

"It's kind of an after-hours club," Clyde offered. "You'll like it."

"Okay," I said. "Let's go."

THIRTY-THREE

The rain had started again and stopped by the time we left Boardner's, but the streets were still slick with water and oil. We followed Earl's pickup truck through the city and stopped in front of a house in South Central. The place looked unimposing, a cheap post–World War II stucco job, red shingles and iron bars on the windows. A number of black guys were huddled in the shadows on the porch, talking in hushed whispers. The house was lit up inside, but thick curtains kept the party within safe from prying eyes.

We got out of the car and I said, "This is Ma Smith's?" I obviously said it too loudly because Clyde shushed me and one of the men on the porch came down to meet us at the steel-gate entrance to the fenced yard.

"What's your problem, motherfucker?" the guy said to me in a harsh whisper. He was solidly built and wore a red leather jacket that probably cost more than my car.

"Nothing," I said.

"Get the fuck out of here, boy," the black guy said.

Earl stepped forward and whispered, "Hey, man, it's me, Earl."

"Earl! What the fuck you doin' with this disrespectful bitch?"

Earl and the guy clasped hands in a nine-mutation soul shake. "He's new around here, Tony. Doesn't know the rules."

"Teach him up quick or keep him the fuck away from here. This ain't no auditorium."

"Keep it down," Earl scolded me.

"Sorry," I whispered.

"You fuckers gonna be straight?"

The three of us nodded. The man swung open the steel gate and let us through. We went up the walkway and were stopped by the group on the porch.

"Heeey, Earl . . . and Clydey boeeey," a squat guy wearing a ski cap on his head said in a voice just above a whisper. "How's it going, my man?"

Clyde shook hands with the guy and they gave each other a big hug. "Ain't seen you around here in a loooong time."

"Been working on a new book."

"Finish it?"

"I'm here, aren't I?"

"Fuck, yeah. Go on in and say hello to everybody. First drink's on the house."

"Thanks, man."

"Just for you. Not this shif'less motherfucker and his boyfrien'." Meaning Earl and me, respectively.

Earl laughed and punched the guy on the shoulder. The guy feigned pain and smiled. "Hey, mofo, don't make me bust a cap in your ass." He flashed a revolver stuck in his belt dead center above his crotch.

Earl put his hands in the air and whispered, "I give up. I give up. Don't fucking kill me."

"You niggahs packin'?" Tony, the guy in the red jacket, asked.

"Nothin' but my iron," Earl offered. He turned his back to them, lifted his coat, and showed them a sheathed hunting knife clipped to his belt.

"Don't go flashing that shit in there, Earl. That'd be like lightin' a match in a fireworks factory."

"Don't I know it?" Earl said with a grin.

One of the other men opened the front door and music spilled out of the house: James Brown doing it up big with his hit "Popcorn." We entered the house and I immediately smelled pot and something sharper in the air, probably crack.

The place was hopping with hot chicks and horny guys. It was a mostly black crowd, but it seemed every other race, creed, and color was represented also; there were even a few Samoans present. Everyone was drinking beer, smoking cigarettes, reefer, whatever. People were playing chess in two corners of the room and the kitchen was cordoned off like it was a crime scene. A wooden barrier usually used to keep children from crossing thresholds blocked the bottom of the doorway and yellow crime scene tape was strung in an X above it to keep customers from entering the kitchen.

Two big black women were working the kitchen, serving up beers at seven bucks a pop and bottled water for five. A straight shot of booze would run you ten bucks. Highway robbery, except for the fact that it was three in the morning and this was one of the few places in the city that was serving *anything* at this hour. No one was allowed past the police tape into the kitchen except Ma Smith and her two hefty girls.

Ma Smith herself was three hundred pounds of pure business. No fooling around with her. She had a party house to run and she took no shit from anyone. She made sure that her guests managed to enjoy themselves without infringing on anyone else's rights. No fighting was allowed in the house and guns were frowned upon. She had a couple of guys working for her as bouncers, but it was hard to distinguish them from the customers. They were very relaxed. Everyone was just hanging loose, getting high, making out, cruising the night away.

Clyde covered our first round, then he and Earl split off and drifted into the crowd, reacquainting themselves with old friends and making new ones. Considering Clyde's reputation as a recluse, this form of social intercourse seemed remarkably easy for him.

I was a little tense at first, but I toked up a joint with a couple of hot black chicks and started to melt into the scenery. There was something riding with the pot. It felt like it was laced with some kind of paralyzing agent. Could have been rat poison for all I knew. Whatever it was, it felt gooooood.

I walked over to watch one of the chess matches and felt a tug at my sleeve. I looked down and saw my roommate, Jeff, at the chessboard, locked in a fierce intellectual battle with a tattooed black dude sporting a cornrowed Mohawk.

"Hey, man," Jeff said with a laugh, "what the fuck are you doing here?"

"Me? What about you?" I was completely startled to see him there. What were the chances of that happening? I thought for a moment the dope might be making me hallucinate.

"I've been coming here for years," Jeff said. "It's a good place to blow off steam after the bars close."

"I can't believe I come to a crack house and find my roommate playing chess."

"It's a small town."

"How come you never told me about this place?"

"I figured you were too straight for this scene. You're a boozer, not a druggie. Besides, you usually crash by midnight."

"I can see why you didn't bring Charity down here."

"Yeah. She's crowding me. I wanted to unwind. This is the place to do it. Why bring sand to the beach?"

His inconvenience wasn't what I was talking about. I was thinking more about Charity's predilection for drugs and bad men. I had been friends with Jeff for ten years—we had met while working as temps for the same outfit—but I was beginning to realize that we really didn't know each other very well. We had only become roommates last year out of financial necessity during mutual bouts of unemployment. Even as roommates our conversations rarely went deeper than discussions about which women we had been seeing and that was only to prevent us from embarrassing overlaps. I didn't know him at all, and I was beginning to think I didn't like him very much.

Jeff had been making chess moves as he spoke and the conversation may have thrown his concentration off because the guy with the Mohawk suddenly called out, "Checkmate!" and Jeff began cursing under his breath. Jeff checked the board, then picked up a small mirror lined with rows of coke and presented it to Mohawk as payment for the victory. Mohawk leaned forward and vacuumed it all up his nose, first with the left nostril, then with the right. He played with his nose to rub off any excess, licked his fingers, and said, "Good game." Jeff nodded and got up, allowing the next player to take on the reigning champ.

Jeff and I walked through the room. "So how'd you find out about this place?" he asked.

"I came down with Clyde and his friend Earl."

"Shit. Earl the Carney? What's he doing with you guys?"

"He's a friend of Clyde's."

"Christ, this *is* a small town. Earl's bogus. He can't hook you up. Let me introduce you to Jamaal."

"Hook me up? With what?"

"Whatever you want."

I wasn't sure what he meant but my curiosity was working overtime, so I went along for the ride. He introduced me to Jamaal, a yuppie-looking light-skinned black man. He was a major connection at Ma Smith's. He knew who to go to for whatever your entertainment needs might be: drugs, women, contraband. He was very nonchalant about his job. People had needs and he was there to fill those needs. He was doing the community a service. He certainly didn't look like a drug dealer, but then again who does? Maybe one out of every five.

I assured Jamaal I didn't need any drugs or women or anything else for that matter. The fish paralyzer or whatever that joint was laced with was really wearing me down. I just wanted a place to crash. I found a couch in an isolated corner of the living room and sat there nursing a seven-dollar Heineken, watching the tableau swirl around me. Sometime around five they poured me into the car and Clyde drove us back to the Valley.

THIRTY-FOUR

I slept late the next day, waking only to drain the lizard and down some aspirin. It was Friday, so I used one of my remaining sick days at the studio, saying I had a cold. No one in the office bought that for a second, but I sure as hell didn't care.

Miles Gallo called a half hour after I reported in sick.

"Are you ill, Mr. Hayes?"

"Yes. I told Tom I was ill when I called a little while ago."

"What is the nature of your illness?"

"Well, if you really must know, I'm I.F.D."

"I.F.D.?"

"Ill from drink."

"I see. You told Mr. Feldman you had a cold."

"I do. It's a side effect of the drinking. I *do* have sick days coming, don't I?"

"Yes. You're entitled to sick leave. But I thought you understood how important it is that we finish wrapping things up in Mr. Morton's office."

"I know it's important—*to you.* But when the job is done and my three weeks are up, where will I be, Mr. Gallo? Will you hire me at your law firm if I show unbridled passion for completing your tasks?"

"I don't think you would mesh well with the firm."

"I thought not. Well, then, I don't see why I should kill myself running errands for you. I'm sick. I want to get well. I'll be in on Monday, and you'll get a solid week of ball-busting work out of me. You'll get your money's worth, I promise you. Or is it Dexter's money? Or the studio's? I'm not sure who's paying me anymore."

"It's this attitude that keeps you from achieving."

"True, but I'm a lot nicer when I'm not hungover."

"You should not have been drinking to excess during a workweek."

"You're right. It's very irresponsible of me. By the way, did you find the tape?"

"I believe we did. Mr. Morton had a wall safe behind one of his framed movie posters. Among many other items of a personal nature, we found a tape containing a very hostile conversation between you and another man. I assume it is the tape you were speaking of."

"Sounds like it. What are you going to do?"

"I'm turning it over to the police this afternoon. They are very interested in talking with Mr. Becker."

"Was the money in the safe?"

"The money?"

"The fifty thousand dollars you are looking for."

"No. We will continue trying to trace that money. There seems to be no record of his spending that amount—in cash—at any time."

"Was there any record of Dexter alerting your office about Jim Becker's blackmail scheme?"

"No."

"Maybe that's where the money went then."

"Perhaps." He sounded far from convinced.

"Well, good luck. I'm going back to sleep."

"Rest well, Mr. Hayes. I hope to see you bright and early Monday morning."

"I can't wait." I hung up before Gallo could reply to the sarcasm. The money had become an albatross. I had to get rid of it fast, before it brought me down.

And I had a plan.

I showered, dressed, dug the money out of my bookshelf, put it in my jacket pocket, went out on my balcony, and surveyed the neighborhood. I had a great view from up there, the high ground. I know it was a little paranoid, but I wanted to see if I was under any kind of surveillance. There appeared to be no one watching my building; at least no one in sight. I left the apartment and drove to a pay phone a few miles away. Again, I watched for anyone who might be following me and saw nothing. I realized I was feeling the effects of working so close to the movies. If this were a film, the cops would already be on to me. Luckily they work a little slower in real life. Usually the criminal in question has to make stupid mistakes to get caught. I'd made my share lately and I might be making another one now, but I was going to do my best to set things right, not only for legal reasons, but for ethical ones as well.

Did I say that?

Skip it. Right now I was just trying to save my ass.

I used the pay phone to call Wilkie. Marge picked up after many rings.

"Hello?"

"Marge? It's Mark Hayes."

"Yes, Mark. What can I do for you?"

The frost was back on the bloom. "Is Wilkie there?"

"He's working."

"Well, I hate to disturb him, but it's kind of important."

"Just a minute."

She put the phone down. Wilkie soon picked up.

"Mark?"

"Hey, Wilkie."

"How are you? Any word on Dexter?"

"He's still dead."

"You know what I mean."

"Yeah, I'm sorry. I think I'm punch-drunk today. I was out carousing with your buddy Clyde last night."

"He's really catching up on lost time, isn't he?"

"You can tell too, huh?"

"He drank to excess when we were with him. And you may have some idea what excess is if the word is coming from me."

I shuddered at the thought.

"Wilkie, I need to see you. I've got something for you and I think you're going to be pretty pleased."

"What is it?"

"I'd rather tell you in person. When can I come by?"

"Right now, before I die of suspense."

"Be there in fifteen."

I hung up and went to my car. I took another long look around before I got in and drove away. I cruised down Ventura Boulevard and turned south on Coldwater Canyon. Wilkie had a nice house just off Coldwater up near Mulholland Drive. The door was open when I got there so I walked in and called his name.

"Back here," he replied.

I made my way through the house to the spare bedroom he had converted into an office. The place was crammed with papers, scripts, newspaper clippings, research books, and movie memorabilia. The walls were covered with framed posters of movies he had worked on. A typical screenwriter's work space. Wilkie was sitting behind his desk, staring through the bottom of his reading glasses at a computer screen.

"Just a minute," he said. Then he typed a few words and hit the *save* buttons.

"What are you working on?"

"My spec. The black hole of Calcutta."

"You'll need a new title before we shoot."

"I'll leave that up to you producer types. So what's this big surprise you have for me?"

I pulled the envelope out from under my jacket and laid it on the desk in front of him.

"What's that?"

"Ten thousand dollars."

"For what?"

"It's a bonus you were supposed to receive after the script got the green light from the studio. Dexter died before that could happen, but I figured you should have it anyway."

Wilkie opened the envelope and peered in skeptically at the cash.

"I don't know what to say."

"You don't need to say anything. You earned it."

"I haven't been paid an unexpected bonus in years. I think this calls for a drink, if you'll join me."

"Don't mind if I do."

We went to his kitchen and he showed me a well-stocked liquor cabinet. He said, "Pick your poison."

"A shot of Jack will do."

He got out two thin water glasses and poured them half full of Jack Daniel's.

"That's your idea of a shot?"

He smiled and clinked his glass against mine.

"To Dexter Morton's last act of generosity," he said. "For all I know, it was his first."

We sipped the whiskey and he led me outside to the backyard. He had a small garden and nicely appointed grounds with a wide variety of seating arrangements scattered about, from benches to lawn chairs to a sleepy hammock hung between two elms. It was quiet back there, as if the bustle of the city were a hundred miles away, not just a hundred yards.

"Nice. You do the gardening yourself?"

He raised his glass in front of his face. "Do I look like a gardener?"

"My grandmother was a big drinker, but she had a great garden."

"It's not for me. Marge supervises the grounds here at Tara."

We sat at a patio table under a big green umbrella.

"Where *is* Marge?"

"Oh, out and about. Running errands."

"Because I was coming over?"

"To be honest—yes."

"She doesn't like me much, does she?"

"It's not you, Mark. It's what you represent to her. Maybe her opinion will change when she sees that money."

"My upcoming unemployment should make her happy as well."

"Now, it's not like that. She doesn't wish you ill. She just doesn't want to be around producer-types."

"I thought she was getting over that. She seemed okay at Dexter's party."

"Things had changed for us recently and we were both a bit giddy. We could have been happy in a slaughterhouse that weekend."

"Interesting choice of words."

Wilkie shrugged and laughed. We sat and drank quietly, enjoying the cool air and the solitude of his little oasis. As Wilkie drank I could see the wheels turning in his head.

"Tell me, Mark, why didn't you let me know about this bonus while Dexter was still alive, for instance, when we were talking about the project at the party?"

I had to think a moment to come up with an answer. "Well, the jury was still out about whether the film would actually get the green light or not."

"But Dexter gave you ten thousand dollars to hold while they were deciding?"

"Yeah. Like I said before, he didn't want any connection to the deal. He was using me as a buffer so he wouldn't get into hot water with the Guild."

"I've been a bit worried about that myself. What are the chances of this deal coming to light in the wake of Dexter's demise?"

"The three of us are the only ones who knew about your deal. The three of us and Marge. Dexter is dead. I'm not talking, and I assume you won't."

"And I told you before, Marge will never betray me."

"Then we have nothing to worry about."

"We? Why would *you* be worried at all? You've got no standing with the Writers Guild."

"I was the bagman on this deal. I don't need to get embroiled in any scandals."

"You mean like when you worked for Pete Turner?"

I felt my face redden. "You know about that, huh?"

"Everybody does."

I finished my drink and got to my feet. "Well, I've had enough fun. I guess I should be going."

"I'm sorry. I shouldn't have said that."

"It's okay. I just have to go."

"Stay and have another drink."

"Thanks, but no thanks. I'll let myself out."

"Don't be silly."

He got up and followed me through the house. I stopped at the front door and turned to face him.

"Wilkie, I was wondering something . . ."

"Yes?"

"The night of Dexter's party, what did you and Marge and Clyde get up to?"

"What do you mean?"

"Where did you go?"

"The Formosa, for last call, like we said we were going to do."

"Then what?"

"We came back here and had a nightcap or two."

"What time did Clyde leave that night?"

"He didn't. He slept on the couch. We all slept late the next day and Marge made us a wonderful brunch. Why do you ask?"

"I've just been thinking a lot about that night."

"Doing some amateur sleuthing? Think you're going to catch your boss's killer?"

"I wish someone would. I think I'm looking like a solid suspect to the police."

"Well, if you're guilty, I'm sure you have nothing to worry about. Their track record for nabbing the guilty is nowhere as impressive as the one they have for nailing the innocent."

"I guess I lose either way, then, don't I?"

"Well, you can certainly scratch the three of us off your list of suspects. We were here all night and half of the following day."

"That's very convenient. All three of you hated Dexter."

"Not enough to kill him."

"How much does it take?"

"I don't know. I never killed anyone."

"Me neither, believe it or not."

"I believe you. I don't think you have the stomach for it. Now let me ask you something."

"Okay."

"Were you thinking of keeping my bonus until people started asking questions about the money around the office?"

I felt myself redden again. The crafty old bastard had put it together—after a fashion. Although it appeared he thought it was more a crime of opportunity than premeditation.

"What the hell makes you say a thing like that?"

"It's just curious timing, that's all. You've kept the money under wraps for quite a while."

"Well, since I was the only one left alive who knew about that ten grand, I guess I could have held on to it with no one being the wiser, couldn't I?"

"Not with the police snooping into everyone's business. And I assume Dexter's heirs are wondering where he spent fifty thousand in cash recently. Unless, of course, it was actually more."

"No, Wilkie. It was fifty. You got it all."

"Don't worry, Mark. Your secret is safe with me."

"I'm all out of secrets. I guess you're the one who should worry. You've got fifty thousand of them."

"That sounds like a threat."

"No. Just a reality check."

I turned and walked to my car.

THIRTY-FIVE

I went home, disgusted with both Wilkie and myself. But I was glad to be free of the ten grand. If anyone was going to get into trouble over that money, it would be Wilkie. And it would be union trouble, not prison trouble. He could handle that. Frankly, after the things he said to me, I didn't much care what happened to him. I bring him a gift of ten thousand tax-free dollars, and he practically calls me a thief. I was done with him.

I was lounging in the hammock later that afternoon when I heard the doorbell ring. I went down the stairwell and found Clyde standing at the door. At first I thought Wilkie had called him and told him that I had been snooping into his affairs, but then I saw he was holding a box heavy with manuscript pages.

"What's this?" I asked.

"It's my book. I haven't been able to sleep, so I've been tweaking it in my spare time. I finished the revision this morning. I thought you might want to look at it, tell me what you think."

I felt my neck tighten, like I was back in Dexter's office being asked to read some bomb of a manuscript booby-trapped with secret motives. Did Clyde really want my honest opinion or did he just want me to tell him how great his writing was? I reluctantly took the box and said, "I'll read it tonight."

"Good man," Clyde said, and then he disappeared into his apartment.

I went back upstairs and started reading Clyde's book, knowing that if I put it down, it would be very hard to pick up again. It started with a bang. The dedication read:

For my ex-wife, who stole my son, my livelihood, and my reputation.
You might as well have this dedication too, you sick bitch!

Whew. I guess Clyde had problems with his ex that were similar to what Wilkie was going through. If the rest of the book was that lively, at least it would be entertaining. No such luck. Not only was it not entertaining, it was a real mess. He called it *Chandler's Town.* I don't know if he was trying to make a play of words off *Chinatown,* or if he was being sarcastic. The book was basically just a long rant about how disingenuous a writer Raymond Chandler was, how he was a coward and a mama's boy, possibly even a latent homosexual. And somehow he had managed to lace the text with rants about the studio bosses of the forties and tie it all in with completely libelous anecdotes about the executives he had worked for during his own sordid career. I had a feeling Dexter was chief among them, but Clyde didn't use their actual names. He gave them all pseudonyms. It was his one act of restraint, I suppose in an effort to avoid litigation. Those he attacked would certainly see through his ruse.

The book was scandalous; but worse than that, it was bad. It read more like an angry stream-of-consciousness exercise than a serious work of criticism. I began to doubt Clyde's sanity. If this was what he had been toiling away at so desperately over the last few years, it really was over for him.

The next morning he caught me coming out of my apartment to go get a newspaper. I think he had been waiting to hear me leave. He stuck his head out of his front door and asked me what I thought of the book. I had to reply honestly. "I think it's a little crazy."

Clyde just smiled and said, "Yep."

"Do you think anyone will publish it?"

"I don't know. What's the difference? I didn't write it to be published. I wrote it because I *had* to write it. Now it's done. I feel much better."

"Why do you have such a chip on your shoulder about Raymond Chandler?"

"It's not Chandler who bothers me. It's all the little cocksuckers who have worshiped him to the point of idolatry. They've elevated what were perfectly good pulp novels into high art and thus dumbed down three generations of writers. You know why writers love Chandler so much? Self-pity. He was a master of it. And it feeds into his fans' own deep need to feel sorry for themselves and their lot in life. This entire culture is built on a bedrock of self-pity. Chandler was actually ahead of his time, but not for the reasons he may have thought. The guy took himself way too seriously, but it's not Chandler's fault that the public bought his bullshit lock, stock, and barrel."

"I think you vastly underestimate him."

Clyde looked at me like I was part of the conspiracy. "Not you *too*?"

"And what about all the executive bashing? Was that really necessary? They're going to hate you for this book, if it gets published. You'll never work in this town again."

"I'm not exactly high on everyone's A-list right now."

"It's one-sided. Who says you should be judging these people? It just reads like sour grapes on your part. You don't let the execs have their say."

"Fuck them. They get their say all week long. They strut their stuff and act like little gods, passing judgment on people every day, but they don't have any ideas of their own. They just find out what the party line is and repeat it like mynah birds so they can keep their jobs. The moment they're fired they're faced with the horrifying fact that they have *no skills.* No abilities. See, fixers can't work until someone creative brings them something. Then they whip out their little red pens and start carving and 'creating.' They have been put on earth to judge others, and if that power is taken from them they are hopelessly lost. Without this system they've set up for themselves they're doomed. And *under* this system the rest of us are doomed. But the funniest thing you can ever see is an out-of-work movie executive. I love when a new studio chief comes into power and cleans house, fires all the execs so he can bring his own people in. It's great to see so many fixers suddenly scrambling for work. One minute they're little deities, the next they're bums. It's hilarious."

I thought about how hilarious I must have looked to him. I said, "Well, good luck with it."

Clyde smirked and said, "Spoken like a true D-boy."

THIRTY-SIX

I showed up bright and early Monday morning just as I promised Miles Gallo. Only Miles wasn't there to appreciate it. He and his staff had finished their work Friday night and would not be returning until the following week to gather whatever was left in the office when we were finished with our petty administrative duties. Without Gallo hovering around, the staff got even more lax about their final tasks. No one was taking the job even remotely seriously anymore. It was going to be a slow, lazy week, and then it would be over and unemployment would begin.

I asked Alex what happened Friday, and he said the two cops that had been here before had returned and talked with Gallo for more than an hour in Dexter's office. No one had heard anything new about the Jim Becker situation, Gallo not being one to share gossip for any reason other than probing into someone else's business.

On Tuesday I received a visit from Detective Lyndon, marginally the more pleasant of the two homicide detectives who had grilled me at Dexter's house and followed me home to talk to Charity James. Detective Lyndon caught me hard at work trying to beat the Chessmaster 2000 on my computer. He knocked on my door and walked right in without waiting for a response.

"Mr. Hayes, got a minute?"

I hit my screen saver and looked up, trying not to let my eyes go wide or let out a shout of panic.

"For you? Anytime."

Lyndon came in and stood in front of my desk. "I was in the area on other business and thought I should check in on you."

"How considerate."

"We spoke with Jim Becker over the weekend. He has a rock-solid alibi during the time of Mr. Morton's murder. He was in Telluride with a large group of friends for the entire weekend. The tape was good. It showed a distinct attempt at extortion, but he's not the guy for the murder."

"That's interesting. But why are you telling me?"

"Because Becker was furious that we were talking to him about the tape and it didn't take much for him to figure out who gave it to us."

I leaned forward, a jolt of fear coursing through my body.

"So you told him it was me?"

"Don't be ridiculous. That's not how we operate. But he knew it couldn't be anyone else. You're the only person in this office who knew about the tape—the only person alive, that is."

"Couldn't you have said the executors found it?"

"We did, but he didn't buy it. I just thought you could use a heads up. He's a wrong guy, whether he killed Morton or not. I think he might be looking for you."

"That's terrific. I'm so glad I brought the tape to your attention. Now I've got a maniac on my ass."

Lyndon produced a business card and handed it to me. "If he bothers you, just give me a call."

"From the hospital?"

"I doubt he'll do anything. I just thought you should be aware that it was a possibility."

"Thanks, I guess."

"Oh, and just for kicks, we checked out Jason Ward. He was safely behind the security gates of his Holmby Hills home by 1 A.M. The security guard there saw his car go in and no one left the entire compound until after eight in the morning."

"He lives in a gated compound?"

"Yeah. Looks like the place probably set him back about three mil."

"I'll be damned." I was astounded. I knew Jason had done well in Hollywood, but I had no idea how fat his deals had been. I guess he could afford to go out into the mountains and write the great American novel after all.

"The Ward kid doesn't seem to like you much either," Lyndon added.

"He somehow figured out I mentioned him to you, too, huh?"

"It doesn't take a rocket scientist."

"You guys are going to get me killed."

"On the contrary, we're here to protect you. That's why I came by to give you the heads up."

"You're all heart."

He checked his watch. "I've got to get going. Have a good day."

Lyndon turned and walked out the door.

"You, too," I said, staring at his card.

When I got home that night I saw Jeff going through boxes in the garage. He waved me over as I drove by in the alley. I stopped my car and rolled my passenger window down.

"What's up?"

"A guy came by the place looking for you about an hour ago. He looked pissed."

"Big guy, tight clothes?"

"That's him. What's the deal?"

"He was shaking Dexter down for money and I let the cops know about it last week."

"I'd watch out. He looked crazy."

"Thanks. What are you doing in the garage?"

"Just trying to find some things. I'm half moved already, but I can't find a lot of stuff that I thought I had in storage."

"You don't think your new girlfriend might be hocking it for drugs, do you?"

"I doubt it. She seems to be able to cop at will. She's got a lot more friends than she let on."

"I gathered that. Is she up there?"

"Yeah. She's crashed out in my room."

"I wish you'd take her with you."

"Listen, I've given a lot of thought to what you said that first day she was here and I think you were right. She's trouble."

"This is an interesting time for an epiphany on your part."

"When you move, a lot of things occur to you that don't when you're sitting still."

"So now *I'm* stuck with her?"

"She's *your* friend."

"I barely know her. You've been sleeping with her."

"Tell you the truth, that's another problem. She doesn't let a person get a lot of sleep."

"I feel like moving to Mexico."

"Why don't you for a while? Give you a chance to clear your head. It would also get you out of town until all this weirdness blows over."

"Maybe. Well, good luck with the new place."

"Thanks."

I rolled the window up, drove farther down the alley, and pulled into the parking lot. I gave a good look around before I got out of my car to make sure Jim Becker was nowhere to be seen. The coast appeared to be clear, so I gathered my belongings and walked around the wall to my apartment. Before I could reach my door, Clyde's door opened and he stuck his head out.

"Hey, Hayes? I got a call from Wilkie this morning. In the future, if you want to know my business, just ask me to my face, okay?"

The sudden action had startled me due to my concern over Jim Becker's presence in the area and Clyde's accusation caught me completely off guard. All I could offer in response was a weak, "Okay."

Clyde looked disgusted as he closed the door.

My head was throbbing. I went upstairs to take some aspirin and lay down for a rest. As I came through the door I saw Charity standing naked in front of the refrigerator in the kitchen. She turned and looked at me and did nothing to cover herself.

"Oh, hi," she said. "I thought it was Jeff coming up the stairs."

"No. Just me for a little visit."

"I was thinking about cooking dinner. Can I make anything for you?"

"No, thanks. I'm just going to lie down for a few minutes. I've got a headache."

"Come here. I can fix it."

I put my briefcase and satchel down and approached her beautiful naked body. I had sworn to myself I wouldn't get into a situation like this and her pairing with Jeff had made it easy to avoid, but now I was moving into complicated territory.

She took my left hand in both of her hands and pinched the meaty area between my thumb and forefinger. I grimaced in pain.

"Don't be a baby. This won't take long."

She caught me looking at her vagina, which was shaved perfectly smooth except for a small heart-shaped tuft of hair two inches above the great divide. It was, as they say downtown, a cunning stunt.

"This would probably be more effective if you closed your eyes."

I did as she asked. She pressed hard on the nerve in my hand and after a minute or so I felt my headache starting to lift, but I also felt stirrings elsewhere. I wanted to get out of there before she noticed the angry bulge in my pants. I opened my eyes and said, "That's better, thanks."

"You sure? It usually takes longer than that."

"No. It's better. Really."

She smiled knowingly and looked down at my crotch.

"It's tension. You need to relax."

"Yeah. I'm going to do that right now."

I could hear her giggle as I walked down the hallway to my bedroom.

The rest of the week went by quicker than I expected. Without Miles Gallo and his team hovering around the office, a giddy mood seized the staff. We were wrapping things up fast and we would all soon be off to new adventures: some of us gainfully employed, others kicking back and enjoying the solitude of unemployment until we were evicted from our homes. My cavalier attitude toward Jeff's departure as a roommate was looking foolish now. I had to consider moving to a smaller place or finding someone else to share the rent. I didn't think Charity James was going to make a very profitable roommate. She was used to someone else paying the bills, and that someone else sure as hell wasn't going to be me.

By Thursday we were a lawless bunch, not giving a damn about what

Gallo or even Neil Silverman might think about our comings and goings. We were just going through the motions so we could collect our last check with a minimum of resistance.

The threat of Jim Becker was soon forgotten. I assumed he had come to his senses enough to realize I wasn't worth the trouble of tracking down. I didn't hear anything more about the mysterious fifty thousand dollars, and I didn't speak to either Wilkie or Clyde. I had a feeling I wouldn't get a Christmas card from either of them this year.

I left work early Thursday afternoon, and I was almost the last to go. Only Natalie was still in the office as I departed. She was being professional to the very end.

It wasn't even five by the time I pulled into the Viande parking lot. I got out of the car and looked around. It was remarkably quiet for a Sherman Oaks afternoon. The air was eerily still and the temperature unseasonably high for so late in the day. Classic earthquake weather. It made me uneasy. After months of routine aftershocks, the ground had seemed to settle over the last few days. Was there another big one due to arrive soon?

I walked down the sidewalk and, as I was about to round the corner of the building to my front door, I was suddenly struck in the face by something heavy. I crashed into the bushes against the wall and tried to look up through the pain. My brain felt fuzzy, and I thought for a moment I might black out. As my vision cleared I saw Jim Becker standing over me. He had nothing in his hands, so I had to assume that the heavy object he had struck me with was one of his fists. He leaned into me and grabbed me by my jacket collar.

"Hey, assface, I've been looking all over town for you. You fucked me over!"

I started to speak and he punched me in the mouth. The iron, salty taste of my own blood washed over my tongue.

"Don't talk. You fucking talk, and I'll kill you. I didn't come here to listen to your bullshit. I came here to tell you something. You open your fucking mouth about me again and I'll make goddamn sure the next time you open it you won't have teeth. Got that?"

He shook me for emphasis. I nodded, trying not to challenge his no-talk rule.

The door to Clyde McCoy's apartment suddenly opened and Clyde stepped out and looked at Jim Becker hovering over his bleeding neighbor in the bushes. "What the fuck is going on out here? I'm trying to sleep."

"Then go back in and mind your own fucking business," Jim Becker snarled.

Clyde took another step toward us. "Say what?"

"You heard me. Go back inside and mind your business."

"Who is this asshole, Hayes?"

I wanted to speak, but my jaw wouldn't respond. Becker let go of my collar and stood up, showing Clyde his six-foot two-inch frame and weight lifter physique.

"I'm the asshole that's going to break your fucking neck if you don't get out of here."

Jim Becker approached Clyde. I tried to sit up and warn Clyde to run, but before I could Clyde moved his hand up to Becker's face with surprising quickness. At first I thought he had missed Becker completely because I didn't hear a punch land. I didn't hear a punch because he hadn't punched him. He had done something else, and whatever it was must have been some kind of magic because Becker suddenly grabbed his face and went down on one knee. Clyde reached out and tapped him on the side of the neck, and Becker rolled over onto his side and started weeping with pain.

Clyde leaned forward and looked into Becker's tear-filled eyes. "Break my fucking neck? You and what army, crybaby?"

Clyde looked over at me as I got to my feet and brushed dirt from my clothes. "So who is he, Hayes?"

I moved my jaw with my hand to see if it was broken. It clicked but I found I could use it. "His name's Becker. He's a producer . . ."

"A producer, eh?"

He looked down at Becker again. "I hate producers."

Clyde tapped Becker on the other side of his neck and Becker's hands immediately went there and he started spasming. Becker's eyes were squirting tears now and it looked like he was having trouble breathing.

Clyde leaned down and whispered into Becker's ear, but it was loud enough that I could hear it. "I can make it stop, but you ever come around here and insult me again, I'll kill you? Got it?"

Somewhere through the agony Becker understood that he had been offered a deal he could not refuse and he started nodding his head in affirmation. Tear juice shot off his face like his tear ducts were fire hoses.

Clyde tapped him again on the face and the neck. I think he did it in slightly different spots than he had before, although he did it so fast that it was hard to tell.

Becker stopped thrashing, but it looked like he was still in considerable pain.

Clyde patted Becker down, looking for weapons. He found one, a small pistol in an ankle holster. Clyde stripped the gun from Becker's leg.

"Asshole, I'm sure you've got bigger and better guns in your car or at your house. Let me tell you something. I do, too. You want retribution? I'll clue you to something grim. I shoot even better than I fight. Don't fucking come back here!"

Clyde looked at me and shook his head, then he went back into his apartment and closed the door, taking Becker's gun with him.

I went into my apartment and locked the bottom door. I went upstairs and watched Becker from my living room window. He stayed on the sidewalk crying for a few minutes, finally moving into a sitting position. He stared at Clyde's door for a while, like he was thinking of going another round, and then he seemed to think better of it. Finally he got to his feet and looked around to see if anyone had witnessed his humiliation. He looked up and saw me in the window. I smiled and waved. He shot me the bird. Clyde's door must have opened because Becker suddenly looked at it with shock and ran down the sidewalk in terror.

I waited to see if Clyde would step out and look up at my apartment, but he didn't. I went into the bathroom and looked at my face. My lip was swollen and cracked and my cheek was red where the first blow had landed, but there was no permanent damage. Nothing broken. I licked my lip and went into the kitchen to get a dish towel and some ice for a cold compress.

Charity James came out of Jeff's room and entered the kitchen. She jumped when she saw me pressing the ice to my cheek.

"What happened?"

"Nothing. Don't worry about it."

"Let me see." She approached me and took the dish towel from my hand and looked at my face. "My God, it looks like you got punched."

"Twice."

"Who hit you?" She pressed the dishrag gently against my cheek.

"A guy who knew Dexter. Jim Becker."

Charity's eyes flashed with recognition. She knew him too. But she wasn't about to tell me about it. "Why did he hit you?" she asked timidly.

"He's mad because I told the police he was blackmailing Dexter."

"Really? With what?"

"I'm not sure. I think it was something about you."

"Me? I barely know the guy."

"He seemed to know you. Or at least know *about* you."

"What did he say?"

"He claimed Dexter was pimping you out to executives in exchange for favors."

She pulled the rag away from my face and looked me in the eyes. "And you believed him?"

"I don't know what to believe anymore."

She put the dishrag in my hand and walked back down the hall to Jeff's room. "Believe whatever you want," she said before she slammed the door.

I considered calling the police and filing an assault report on Jim Becker, but then the thought occurred to me that it might serve to enrage him even more. If he did have more guns like Clyde suggested, then he could be truly dangerous.

But Jim Becker seemed less of a threat now in light of the way Clyde had manhandled him. As a youth I had been in and seen my fair share of street fights, but I had never seen an apparent mismatch like that end so tragically and so quickly for the larger party. I'd seen small men dismantle larger men a number of times, but it usually required quite a bit more effort.

I decided to go downstairs and make a peace offering to Clyde. I found a bottle of Bacardi dark that was collecting dust in the back of my liquor shelf, wiped it off with the damp rag that had contained my ice, and went downstairs.

I knocked on Clyde's door. It took him a while to open it and when he did he was rubbing sleep from his eyes. He had gone back to bed even though he had been in combat but an hour before.

"What is it?" he asked with irritation.

"Sorry. I didn't think you'd be asleep after what happened."

"It takes more than that to rob me of sleep. Obviously it takes you."

He was still mad at me. I offered him the bottle. "I wanted to thank you for helping me out like that."

He blinked at the bottle, then looked at me. "Don't take it wrong. I wasn't helping *you.* That guy insulted me."

"Whatever the reason, you still saved my ass. Can we be friends again?" I moved the bottle closer to him. Finally he took it.

"Sure, Hayes. Whatever you want. Who said we weren't friends, anyway?"

"You've been giving me the brush ever since that call from Wilkie."

"That was a troubling call."

"I know. I'm sorry."

"I guess you've been under the gun around the office, huh? Cops still think you did it?"

"I don't know. They don't confide in me."

"They'll let you know when they're ready."

"I'm sure. Hey, that was pretty amazing, how you handled Becker."

"That was nothing. I just messed with his pressure points. That'll teach him to fuck with a guy who dates a third-degree black belt."

"No kidding."

"Thanks for the bottle. Now can I go back to sleep?"

"Sure. Sorry I woke you up."

He closed the door and I went back upstairs to pop some ibuprofen.

THIRTY-SEVEN

I went into work late the next day, but there was practically no one there to notice. Only Alex and Natalie showed up. Everyone else took the last official day of work at Prescient Pictures off as a personal day. No going-away party for this bunch. They were just glad to be out of there.

My face was more swollen than I had expected it to be and I had to tell the story twice, once to Natalie when I first came in and again to Alex, who arrived twenty minutes later. They both suggested I go to the police, but the more I thought about that, the less I wanted to give the cops another excuse to snoop around in my business. When I told Alex about how Clyde McCoy had roughed up Jim Becker, he was astonished. I think it gave him new respect for Clyde. He wasn't just a washed-up screenwriter anymore. He was a washed-up screenwriter who could kick some ass.

This got me thinking about Clyde. And about his relationship with Dexter. I decided to do a little snooping of my own. When Natalie and Alex went to lunch, I found the key to Dexter's private office in Tom's desk, then did an idiot check to make sure I was completely alone.

I entered Dexter's inner sanctum. Boxes of files were lined up against one wall. The studio's legal department, Dexter's executors, and the police had been through everything during the last three weeks. Anything vital to any of their interests had been removed. The files that remained were to be archived at the American Film Institute. I found a stack of alphabetized boxes with PERSONAL stenciled on the sides and pulled out the one marked L-M-N. I nervously sorted through the file tabs and came upon one marked MCCOY, CLYDE. Jesus Christ! I felt like some kind of spy who had hit the jackpot behind enemy lines. The file was thick. I leafed through it briefly but realized I would never be able to read it all before Natalie or Alex returned to the office. I lifted the file, closed the box, and put everything else back where it belonged. I locked the door to Dexter's office, then stored the file in my briefcase, hoping I would not be searched on my way out of the studio on my last day. I wanted to see what was in that file and I didn't care whether some snot-nosed film student of the future would be deprived of the privilege in return. Natalie came through the front door just as I was closing my briefcase. I tried not to look guilty, but I got a strange look from her anyway.

Toward the end of the day I helped Natalie to her car with a bunch of boxes. She had grown on me. I liked her. I didn't want our newfound friendship to end the way most office relationships do when the staff goes their separate ways. I decided to ask her out for coffee the following week, just so we could stay in touch. She took it the wrong way.

"That's very nice of you, Mark, but I'm dating someone."

I was taken aback, not just by the fact that she thought I was asking her out on a date, but by the news that she had a boyfriend. Or girlfriend. Or whatever.

"Really?" I said, not wanting to tell her I didn't mean the invitation the way she took it. I was far more interested in her social life than preserving the integrity of my own meager reputation. I couldn't hold back. "Who?"

"Michael David Blake."

"You're kidding? The underwear model?"

"He does more than model underwear."

"Uh, yeah, I'm sorry. Of course he does."

I couldn't believe it. Our little office mouse was dating a Calvin Klein hunk who had done a season on *Melrose Place*. There was more lurking under those Foster Grants than I would have imagined.

Natalie started her car. "Thanks for the offer though. Give me a call over at Universal when you get situated."

"Sure."

As she drove off the lot I realized I probably would never see her again. Unless I was watching *Entertainment Tonight* and the cameras caught her on the arm of some stud at a movie premiere. No one is ever exactly what they seem in this town.

I went back into the office to gather my things and lock up for the last time. Prescient Pictures had boiled down to a staff of two. Everyone else was gone except for Alex and me. We were the only ones who had not found work yet. We had nowhere else to go and we were in no hurry to get there.

We bullshitted a while, then went out on the terrace for one last smoke.

"What are you going to do?" I asked.

"I don't know. Maybe try to write something. I've got some ideas."

"Really?"

"Why are you so surprised?"

"I thought you had given that up."

"Well, I don't want to just sit around on my ass."

"That's a productive attitude."

"Something will turn up at the studios. I'll keep sending out résumés and work on a new script. Who knows? Maybe I'll put someone else's name on it and try to buy it when I find a development gig."

"That would never fly."

"Worth a try, isn't it? That's how most of these things get bought anyway. Some asshole buddy of some asshole in charge. Right?"

"Right."

"I sure don't want to spend the rest of my life kowtowing to jerks like Dexter."

"They're not *all* like Dexter. I've worked for some good people over the years."

"Executives are like cops. They may not all be bad, but you've got to wonder what was wrong with them in the first place that made them choose the job."

"Hey, *we* want those jobs, too."

"My point exactly. What's wrong with us?"

"How else are we going to get movies made?"

"Crazy, huh?" Alex flicked his cigarette butt off the balcony. "So, what are *you* going to do?"

"Keep looking for a job."

"Good luck, man. But you've got it even tougher than I do."

"How's that?"

"A lot of them think you killed your boss."

My face fell a little. It had occurred to me that the reason I was getting nowhere in my job search was simple fear on the part of potential employers, but to have someone else articulate it flat out like that gave it more weight. Could I blame the executives of Hollywood for not thinking me a good candidate for employee of the year? Who wants to hire a guy who drowns you if you piss him off?

"Don't worry," Alex added with a pat on my back. "I know you didn't kill him. You needed him too much. But you've got to understand the state of things. Until they figure out who knocked off Dexter, you're just as dead as he is in this town."

"Thanks a lot."

"Hey, it's the business. I didn't invent it; I just work here."

We went back inside, gathered the last of our belongings, and locked the office. After dropping off our keys at Human Resources, we went to the parking lot and said our good-byes, each of us promising to keep in touch despite the fact that I was the business equivalent of bubonic plague. I wanted to invite Alex over so he could visit with Charity James—and maybe take her with him when he left—but she was a subject we never discussed, per his request.

The security guard at the gate, a new guy whom I had never met, stripped me of my parking pass before I drove off the lot for the last time. There would be no more free parking for me. Not on *that* lot, anyway.

At least he didn't go through my briefcase looking for stolen files.

When I got home I put on a pot of coffee and watched the sun set from my balcony. There was a preternatural stillness in the air, almost like a battlefield before a decisive conflagration. It gave me the creeps.

I poured a cup of coffee, went into my bedroom, sat down at my desk, opened my briefcase, and pulled out the thick file marked MCCOY, CLYDE.

I sipped the coffee and perused the file. It appeared to consist primarily of letters Clyde had written to Dexter during the years they were in business together. There were a lot of them. The first one was dated July 4, 1983, and it was a simple one-page acknowledgment of Clyde's acceptance of Dexter's terms for a contract binding Clyde to write a movie entitled *The Crypt* for Dexter's new company, Cinetown. I had heard of the film but never seen it. Something about mummies and vampires and things that go bump in the night. The letter was cordial, if not downright optimistic. Their relationship seemed to have started off on the right foot. There were no actual contracts in the file. Those would have been kept with the paperwork of the specific productions they covered.

The next letter was dated two months after the first. It was a short memo criticizing changes Dexter and his staff had suggested for the screenplay Clyde had delivered for *The Crypt.* Again the tone was cordial, but between the lines I could sense Clyde's blood pressure starting to rise.

The next letter was dated December 23, 1983. It was a short rant about changes made to the rough cut of *The Crypt.* It seems Dexter and his foreign buyers hadn't understood that the movie was intended to be a comedy and had asked for reshoots of some of the more humorous scenes. Clyde felt they were sticking their "businessmen's noses where they don't belong, specifically, up the filmmakers' asses."

After a letter like that I would think the working relationship would have come to an end, but sorting through the stack and checking the dates against Clyde's résumé, I discovered that they worked together a lot over the next five years. The pattern seemed to repeat itself often. There would be a letter acknowledging terms, always mutating from the last contract in Clyde's fervent hope of gaining more control over the work as he went along, followed by letters discussing possible changes to either screenplays or finished films. Often there would be a letter toward the end of the series that would lambaste Dexter for his lack of artistic ambition. Poor Clyde. It took him way too long to realize Dexter wasn't in it for the art.

I flipped to the end of the file. The last letter was dated November 12, 1988. It was long. Four pages in total. It read:

Dexter,

Here's one you can stick up on your bulletin board—or anyplace else you feel it will fit. After five years and far too many projects together I have to tell you that I'm calling it quits. If working in the film industry means being shoulder to shoulder with scumfucks like you, I want no part of it. And, frankly, it appears that things are going that way in this town. If I thought you were an anomaly, just a diseased beast who hadn't been weeded out from the herd yet, I would continue on, but I have met far too many evil pricks in the last few years who seem to have been stamped out of the same mold from which you were ejected. Life is too short to be spent lining the pockets of assholes like you.

Your recent comments about the screenplay of *Final Command* were the last straw. This is a project that I created, from scratch. You know that. I then developed it with Kent Buckler as a project for him to direct, and we turned out a pretty good screenplay, or, to put it in your own words, "The best damn action script I've ever read." Remember? Tom Stone at RCA/Columbia even sent you a letter commending the script, saying, "If *Final Command* is not a huge hit at the box office, it will not be Clyde McCoy's fault. It is a finely crafted, suspense-filled tour de force."

Now I also happen to know that you signed a ten-picture deal with Tom a few days after he read the script. This deal was born in no small part from the efforts that Kent and I have devoted to your company over the last five years. Our hands have touched every single film you have ever made. This is something you seem to have completely forgotten as your ego has overridden your memory. For some reason you have decided to fuck over the very people who put you where you are today.

It was bad enough that you paid Kent to leave the picture as director, but when you brought in John Kanowski to replace him, you started a chain reaction that has undone us all.

You said to me on the phone, "The script is too good for Kent. I'm going to get a better director. That way we can get bigger actors. This could be our breakout picture." I argued vehemently for Kent. Each film he had done for you was bigger and better than the last. Why couldn't he handle this one? Because some fucking *casting director* put the bug in your ear that he wasn't up to it? Don't you realize that bitch was just trying to justify her 25K payday by getting Kent fired? Do you think Kanowski actually *did* a better job than Kent would have? *Shiiiiiit.* And did Kanowski manage to draw this A-list cast Barbara said he could? No. Most of the "name" actors Barbara and Kanowski hired had already worked for Kent on other pictures, so the entire reason for his replacement became a joke.

In Kanowski's hands the script that was "too good for Kent Buckler" was suddenly *not good enough* for John Kanowski. He brought his asshole buddy in to help him rewrite it, and the next thing you know we had a straight-to-video-quality piece of shit on our hands that cost you five million bucks to shoot. Do you really still believe you did the right thing this time around?

To make matters worse, the guy is going around town saying he wrote the entire movie and I only have a credit on it due to my "hard-ass contract." This has put me in the unenviable position of having to argue that I contributed to a movie I don't even like. While Kanowski did manage to fuck up most of the scenes I wrote with his clumsy direction, and he *did* add a number of his own scenes, which are completely asinine, by the way, and completely unoriginal, as they are lifted from other, better movies, clearly 70 percent of the film as shot was written by me. This fucking climber ruins my work, then has the balls to claim that it wasn't even mine to begin with! Your assessment last week that I would be receiving solo credit despite the fact that "it isn't your script" stunned me so severely that I could not respond to you properly at the time. I wanted to see the film before I blew my stack. For all I knew Kanowski *was* the genius you had made him out to be and maybe he *had* changed everything, improving it immensely. After the screening last night I realized that it was all just a pack of lies. He's running around taking credit for work he didn't do, trying to get another job before *Final Command* is released and he has his ass handed to him by the critics. I don't know if you are in on this conspiracy of lies with him, but if not, he has completely hypnotized you. For you to say what you said to me, you are either a liar or a fool. Now that I think of it, I realize you are both.

Let me lay it out simple for you. I think you are a backstabbing, two-faced son of a bitch. Not only will I never work for you again, but if I see you crossing the street in front of my car, I will not apply my brakes. If I see you at any of my usual watering holes, you had better be packing heat, because I am going to kick your lying, fucking ass. And that goes double for John Kanowski.

Hope you and the staff enjoy reading this tirade as much as I enjoyed writing it. See you on the playground.

Fuck you very much,

Clyde McCoy

The last paragraph clearly referred to Dexter's habit of sharing his hate mail with the staff—a trait he had brought with him to his studio days. Dexter loved it when he pushed someone so far that they actually took pen to paper to write him a fuck-you letter. He had a bulletin board in the supply room at our offices at Warner's where he would tack these letters up for the staff to enjoy. I think he felt it was similar to posting his enemy's head on a stake out in front of his castle. *Dexter the Impaler.*

I'm not sure what the "see you on the playground" line meant, but I assumed it was a reference to the age-old adage that Hollywood was just "high school with money."

So Clyde had snapped and revealed his homicidal side to Dexter as far back as 1988. This certainly didn't prove he had made good on his threat six years later, but it made him look like a pretty good suspect.

I pulled out my creative directory and looked up Kent Buckler's credits. He had indeed directed most of Dexter's releases for the first five years of Cinetown's existence. And Clyde had either written or rewritten each of those films—as well as two others that Buckler received co-story credit for but that were not directed by him. Dexter had played down

Clyde's contribution to his company when he caught me looking at Clyde's credits in the database, but Cinetown was beginning to look more and more like *The House that Kent and Clyde Built.* Dexter just seemed to be the suit in charge of the business end of the operation. But that's where the real power resides, so Dexter ended up the millionaire. Kent Buckler's career seemed to peter out by 1990. I knew what had happened to Clyde, but I wondered what had become of Buckler.

I decided to check John Kanowski's credits. Clyde had been correct when he wrote that Kanowski was a "climber." He did one more mid-range-budget picture after *Final Command,* then somehow managed to helm a Bruce Willis picture and then a Stallone flick, both of which tanked. He had no credits after '91. I suppose he was in development hell. That pays well enough if you've got the right deals.

I looked up *Final Command* in Maltin:

One star. Jingoistic exercise in mayhem and brutality. A little style goes a short way. Cast of B-movie veterans is hampered by strange dialogue and schizophrenic storyline. Only fans of pyrotechnics will approve.

Sounds like Clyde called it long before Leonard Maltin ever made the screening. And Dexter must have finally come to the same conclusion, because I could find no evidence that he and Kanowski ever worked together again after that picture.

By the time I had sorted through the file it was ten o'clock. I wondered what my neighbor Clyde was up to now. Was he out in front of his apartment, smoking hand-rolled cigarettes and thinking about the producer he had murdered? Or was he down at Boardner's or Ma Smith's getting the night's celebration started? If I ran into him at Viande, could I keep my suspicions about him a secret? It was unlike me to stay in on a Friday night, but I decided to sit this one out for a change.

PART III

Behind every beautiful thing, there's been some kind of pain.

—Bob Dylan

THIRTY-EIGHT

I spent my first official day of unemployment like a bum, watching TV and hanging out in the hammock on the balcony, drinking wine coolers so I wouldn't get too smashed too early in the day. I didn't even bother to shower or get dressed. I was still in my boxers and a T-shirt late into the afternoon.

Charity James was loose in the apartment. Jeff had moved out earlier in the week and I had hoped Charity would go with him. Or that she would find her own place once he was gone. But that hadn't happened. She asked if she could stay on for a while, until she could find a girlfriend who would be willing to split the rent somewhere near Westwood. She was afraid of living alone in the big bad city. Jeff had abandoned his futon and bought a fresh new bed with no miles on it for his new place. Charity promised to keep the apartment clean and run errands for me in exchange for rent if she could stay in his room. I had given her a limited amount of time to find a new situation, but I got the feeling she wasn't trying very hard.

Charity rummaged through the kitchen for about ten minutes before she came out onto the balcony and stood in front of me. She was wearing cutoff shorts and a tube top that accentuated both her curvaceousness and her availability.

"Another lazy Saturday, huh?" she said, taking my wine cooler and drinking most of it down.

"It's the carefree life of the unemployed."

She handed the bottle back and climbed into the hammock with me. It was nice having her warm body next to mine. Too nice.

"I know all about that," she said.

"Can I ask you a personal question?"

"Sure. I have no secrets from you."

"Is your real name Charity?"

"Of course."

"I mean, did your folks actually name you that?"

"Yeah. Why? What's wrong with it?"

"Nothing. It's nice. I just never knew anyone named Charity before."

"My parents were hippies."

"Don't tell me you've got sisters named Faith and Hope."

"No. Nothing like that. They just thought it was a pretty name. 'A pretty name for my pretty girl.' That's what my dad always used to say."

She looked forlorn as she spoke of her father.

"Is he still around?" I asked.

"He died when I was thirteen. Prostate cancer."

"You miss him, huh?"

"Oh yeah. Every day. My mom's still alive, I think, but we don't talk anymore. We never really did. I was a daddy's girl. My dad was everything to me. I think she was jealous. When he died it just drove a bigger wedge between us."

I put my arm around her shoulders and hugged her, trying to comfort her. She took it as a come-on and squeezed the inside of my thigh. I ignored the move, thinking that if I didn't make any further advances she would let the moment pass, but her fingers started making their way higher up my leg. I finally had to push her hand away.

"What's wrong?" she asked.

"I don't think you know what you're doing."

"C'mon, Mark. I know you want me. You've been looking at me like a hungry dog since the day I met you."

"What about Jeff?"

"That's history. He had his fun and he's moved on."

I got up and went to the kitchen for another wine cooler, but there were no more. I had gone through a six-pack in the last few hours. I didn't even like the damn things and now my head was starting to ache. Charity came into the kitchen and grabbed my crotch. Checking. *Testing.* I passed her test and failed mine. Erections don't lie, only their owners do.

"See. I knew it," she said.

I pulled away from her.

"Hey, just because I have a hard-on doesn't mean I want to have sex with you."

"What *does* it mean? You just want to be friends?"

"Don't you get it? You can't just fuck every guy who comes along. It's no good."

I could see a dark cloud come over Charity's expression. "Why are you doing this?" she asked sadly.

"Because I like you. But damn, Charity, you don't care who's fucking you and I can't just jump in the sack with every hot piece that comes along anymore. It's bullshit."

"You're the one who's bullshit. This is ridiculous. You don't want to fuck, don't go putting your arms around someone. You're sending mixed messages."

"A friend can't give you a hug without it meaning sex?"

"Not usually. Not in my experience. No."

"That's sad."

"Don't be so sanctimonious. You have any idea what it's like to be me? I can't go anywhere without some asshole trying to fuck me. Doesn't matter whether I'm trying to get a job or get on a bus, every jerk I meet tries to find a way in on me. Once in a while I let them. I liked you. You took me in and let me live here for free, but I know nothing is really free in this world. At least not for me."

"You think I want you to fuck for the rent? Get real."

"I'm no whore. Don't talk to me like I'm a whore. I thought we had a moment back there and I wanted you because you're a nice guy and it's a hot, lazy Saturday. What's the big crime?"

"I just think you trivialize yourself. You deserve better than what you've settled for."

"You're bumming me out. Tell you what. I'm going to show you something. If you like it, you can play with it. If you don't, you can go back out and swing on your little hammock."

She slid her shorts off, revealing a pink G-string that was no wider than a shoestring. She turned and put her hands on the sink, spread wide like she was ready for a full body search by the authorities. She arched her back and presented me with one of the firmest, roundest asses I had ever had the privilege to see in person.

"Well," she said, "that answer any of your questions?"

"A few."

She reached behind herself and pulled the G-string to the side. "Wanna find out about the rest?"

I dropped any pretense of respectability on the kitchen floor, right next to my boxers. I came up behind her and pressed against her. I reached around in front and rubbed her where she was smooth and wet. I kissed her neck and slid her tube top down around her waist, freeing her beautiful breasts. I rubbed and pinched her nipples with one hand and fingered her with the other, then I slid into her from behind. She pressed against me even harder. I leaned back and we got into a rhythm. I probed her until I found her sweet spot, the area she responded to most favorably, and I focused on bringing her to climax. I didn't know how long I could hold out. It had been a while since I had been in a hot blonde. I pinched and probed and played, my mind becoming completely empty of any thought other than satisfying her. She began to lift herself on her toes and press down harder on me. She was getting close. I was afraid I might be closer. I pressed her sweet spot and held my finger there, holding her against my stroking flesh. She gasped and started to come. If ever there was a cue, that was it. I let go and shot into her like a cannon firing at the moon.

I collapsed on her back and continued rubbing her as I drained the last of my built-up tension into her body. She turned her head and kissed me savagely. I thought she might bite my head off like a giant female praying mantis out of a B movie. For a moment I imagined how silly I might feel if my head suddenly rolled across the floor and my last vision was a low-angle shot of my decapitated body pumping away mindlessly against the ass of this sexy predator.

As our blood pressure began to return to normal, she ground against me a few more times to make sure she got all there was to get, then she moved forward and let me slide out of her. She turned and smiled at me.

"That was nice," she said. "Maybe next time we can do it face-to-face."

She kissed me again, adjusted her G-string back into place, picked up her shorts, and went into the bathroom. I heard the shower come on a few seconds later. I just stood there in the kitchen, half naked, all stupid and totally limp.

THIRTY-NINE

I was eating a TV dinner in the kitchen later that night when the doorbell rang. I went into the living room, opened the window, and looked down at the entrance to the stairwell. Clyde was at the door. It looked like my peace offering a few days ago had worked. He was willing to talk to me again. But now I wasn't so sure that was a good idea.

"C'mon up," I said. "That door's open."

Charity was watching a movie on TV in the living room and it was up loud, so I asked her to turn it down. She stuck her tongue out at me and complied. I went back into the kitchen and opened the door for Clyde, then sat back down to finish dinner.

"Hey, man," Clyde said as he came through the door, "I'm bored. I was thinking of hitting Ma Smith's. Want to join me?"

"I don't think so. I'm kind of tired." I was, but that wasn't why I wanted to turn him down.

Charity bounded into the kitchen happily. "I want to go! Jeff told me about Ma Smith's. It sounds like fun!"

"That's no place for the likes of you," I said.

"Oh, like you have to be a big man or something to go to Ma Smith's," Charity said. "You're just like all the rest. You just want to shuck me. Why have me around if you've already *had* me, right? Fuck me, then shuck me. That's all you guys ever do."

Clyde gave me a knowing look, as in "Banging the hot roommate, eh?"

"It's not like that. I don't think *any of us* should go to Ma Smith's. It's a bad place."

"When did you turn into the voice of reason?" Clyde asked.

"I got a bad vibe down there. That place can't last, and I don't want to be there when it comes apart."

"They've been going strong for seven years," Clyde said. "What do you think's going to happen?"

"About a million different things could go wrong down there. I don't mind a good after-hours club, but that place has some serious fuckups walking about."

"I'm going," Clyde said.

"And I'm going with you," Charity said, pulling on a sweater.

"No, you're not," I said.

Clyde stared at me. "Get off your high horse. You're either coming with us or staying here, but we don't have to hear the rest of your noise."

"So I can go?" Charity asked.

"Sure," Clyde said. "But once we get down there, you're on your own. Don't be bugging me."

"No problem."

That was a recipe for disaster. I decided to accompany them, to keep an eye on Charity. Or at least that's what I told myself. But I knew deep down it was more than that. There is a dark allure to places like Ma Smith's. For people who don't like to see the night end, hangs like that are Shangri-las. Once you get a taste, it's hard to stay away. I didn't feel like going to bed. I knew I wouldn't get any sleep. And if I was going to toss and turn all night, I didn't want to be alone while I was doing it.

FORTY

We took two cars down to Ma Smith's so I could go home whenever I was ready to leave. There was no resistance at the door. Clyde was considered a revered customer and I was now a known entity. And a girl who looked like Charity James would never be turned away from a joint like Ma Smith's.

The place was hopping with the usual mixture of players and pretenders. Perhaps a few more suits than usual. In one corner there was a contingent of entertainment attorneys who had jetted down from Culver City after a hard day of wheeling and dealing so they could get their noses full of inspiration. They were letting anyone into this place! In honor of the attorneys' presence in the house, some smart-ass was playing Warren Zevon's "Lawyers, Guns and Money" on the boom box. Shit, this was a hip room.

Clyde disappeared the moment we went through the doorway. I went to the kitchen and ordered a seven-dollar Heineken for myself and a five-dollar bottle of water for Charity. By the time I turned around Charity was already talking to Jamaal and one of his pals, a big fat guy named Wideboy. They were lounging on the couches in the corner, having a good laugh about something. Wideboy was laying coke on a mirror and dividing it into uniform lines until there was enough for each of them to take two hits apiece. Charity got very serious as the mirror was passed to her. She liked to have a good time, but when it came to coke, she wasn't messing around.

After Charity had snorted her two lines and passed the mirror to Jamaal, I handed her the bottled water.

"Thanks, Mark," she said. Her eyes were shimmering glass.

Jamaal did his ration of coke, then looked at me curiously. "Want to do it up?"

Wideboy looked at me nervously, hoping I wasn't going to snort his blow. I had no interest whatsoever in cocaine. It had never done anything for me other than make me feel like I had inhaled a pot of coffee through my nose. I lifted my beer and said, "No thanks," as if a Heineken would be delivering the same quality high they were experiencing.

Jamaal smiled and handed the mirror to Wideboy.

"You are one beer-drinking motherfucker," Jamaal said. "You don't like blow?"

"Not my thing."

"You ain't a narc or anything?"

"No, man. I just don't do coke. I've got an addictive personality and no job. I get hooked up on that shit and I'd be in trouble."

"You say so."

The explanation seemed to suffice. Barely. I moved over to one of the chessboards and watched two homeboys battle it out. They were playing aggressive street chess. Not very strategic. It was all about how many pieces each of them could capture. They got down to four pieces each. One of them had a bishop, his queen, a pawn and his king. The other had a rook, two pawns and his king, but one of the pawns was just a move away from being promoted. He made the move, turned the pawn into a queen and said, "Checkmate."

"Bullshit on that," his opponent said.

"The fuck!"

The loser moved his king up and to the right, but the rook had him. He moved the king back, then tried for the square above him, but then he was in danger from his opponent's pawn. He tried the next square over and he was on target from the queen in a diagonal move. Finally he knocked his king on its side in disgust.

"Motherfucker, you cheated! Who said you could turn that bitch into a queen? This ain't checkers!"

"Niggah, learn the game if you gonna play this shit."

"Fuck this!" the loser said. He sprang up from the table and threw some money down. He was pissed.

The winner looked up at me and said, "They hate it when they think they're about to win and then they lose." He laughed, then added, "You playin'? It's ten a game, unless you're confident and wanna go for more."

"Ten's fine."

I sat down and we quickly put our pieces in place and prepared for the game. I hadn't played chess in years but I figured a little strategy would go a long way in this house.

Boy, was I wrong. The guy, a friendly fellow named Killer B, was some sort of chess savant. He was a chameleon who adapted his style of play to mimic his opponent's abilities. Only he was much better at playing *my* game than I was. He enjoyed beating me slowly the first time so he could figure out my skill level. On our next go-round he had me beat in nine moves.

"You're good," I said.

"Thanks." He said it like he was only being polite. My compliment meant nothing to him. He was clearly above amateur chess scum like me. A compliment from me was akin to some junkie telling Mike Tyson that he was impressed with the way Tyson kicked his ass.

I got up from the table, handed him a twenty, and let another player sit down.

"Good game," Killer B said to me as I walked away.

"Thanks," I said, but I didn't look back. I didn't want to see him snickering.

I looked around for a familiar face but I saw none. I thought Jeff might be somewhere in the house, but he wasn't. I hadn't heard from him since his move over the hill. I guess he was enjoying his new status as a resident of West L.A.

I went through the house looking for Charity. She was in one of the back bedrooms with Jamaal and three of his friends. They were smoking crack and listening to Rick James on a boom box. I couldn't believe it. Charity was on the pipe. A new low. I approached her gingerly and said, "We better be getting back."

"Go on without me," she said. "I'm going to hang here."

"I don't think that's such a good idea."

Jamaal looked up from the crack pipe and arched his brow. "Why not?"

"She won't be able to get home. She rode with me."

"I'll give her a ride."

"Yeah. Jamaal can give me a ride."

"All the way to the Valley?"

"Ain't a thing," Jamaal said. "Hey, meet my homeboys, Kendall, Poochie, and that there's Crazy Martin. This here's Mark."

Kendall and Poochie got up and hit me with soul shakes. Crazy Martin just nodded at me as he took the pipe from Jamaal. The thing stank. The whole room stank. The three dudes were gangbangers, probably Bloods. They were heavily tattooed and wore the colors. They were obvious where Jamaal was not. I could see the distinct impression of a .38 in Crazy Martin's baggy pants. This was a bad scene and as cowardly as it may have seemed for me to split, I wanted to get out of there.

"Okay, then," I said, trying not to underline my gutlessness, "I'm gonna be heading back."

"Drive safely," Jamaal said.

The other three laughed. Charity didn't even notice I was leaving. She was busy fiddling with the pipe.

I didn't feel good about leaving Charity there, but it didn't seem like I had much choice in the matter. I couldn't force her to go, and her new friends had no interest in helping her make healthy decisions. I looked around for Clyde, but I couldn't find him. The smell of crack wafting through the house was getting to me, giving me a headache. Fuck it, I thought, and got the hell out.

FORTY-ONE

As I drove home I tried to put Charity James out of my mind and my thoughts drifted to Clyde McCoy. Had I inadvertently brought about Dexter's demise by my association with Clyde? Clyde already had a big grudge against Dexter before we went to the party that night, and when Dexter revealed his plans to buy one of Clyde's old scripts that was in turnaround at Tri-Star, Clyde got mad. He dismissed the incident like he didn't care, but I could tell he was fuming underneath. What was it he said to Dexter? *"It's your funeral."* Not good. And on top of it all, Clyde's car hadn't been in the parking lot when I got up the morning after the party. Had he really spent the night at Wilkie's, or were they covering for him? After the way I saw him brutalize Jim Becker, I had no doubt he could have killed Dexter with ease.

Clyde's car was not in the parking lot when I got home. He had left the party house, but hadn't come straight back. Where else was there to go at three in the morning?

I went upstairs and tried to sleep, but I couldn't get the suspicious thoughts out of my mind. Finally I went out on the balcony to see if Clyde had returned yet. His car was in its spot, so I walked downstairs and knocked on his door. To my surprise he was bleary eyed when he opened the door, as if he had been asleep, resting comfortably. He couldn't have been home long and it was unlike him to be asleep at this hour, but I had woken him up. Again.

"What's up, man?" he asked, sounding annoyed.

"Did I wake you?"

"Yeah. I'm beat."

"I'm sorry, but some things are bugging me. Can I come in?"

He opened the door wide and ushered me inside. He stretched out on his couch and closed his eyes as if he were going to go back to sleep while I spoke. I sat in a chair and leaned forward nervously.

"I have to ask you a direct question. Don't get mad. I just have to. It's driving me crazy."

"Go on," he said without opening his eyes.

"Did you . . . er . . . kill Dexter?"

He gave me the horse eye without moving his head. "Are you still high?"

"It's not that ridiculous a question."

Clyde sat up quickly and rubbed his face. "Okay, let's get this out of the way. What's the problem?"

"It's just that . . . you know . . . you hated Dexter so much. And I remember you saying you'd like to see him floating in the pool . . . to see if his toupee would come off, which did happen, by the way, and you told him it was going to be his funeral if he bought your script from Tri-Star . . . and . . ."

"You *are* a little Sherlock aren't you? You think I'd kill a guy to *stop* him from buying one of my scripts?"

"With you, Clyde, I think anything is possible."

"I'll take that as a compliment."

"Where were you that morning, the morning it happened? Your car wasn't in the parking lot."

"I crashed at Wilkie's place that night to keep from driving home drunk. You know that."

"I know that's what you guys say."

"So we're all liars?"

"What about all that crazy stuff you wrote about in your book? You were letting a lot of rage out, and I think most of it was aimed at Dexter."

"It's foolish to make literary assumptions like that. It *is* just a book, you know. I vented my spleen on the page. That's enough for me."

"Okay, then, what about what you said? About the pool and the toupee?"

Clyde stood up and led me toward the door. "Okay, Hayes, you got me. I crowned Dexter and drowned the guy just so I could see him without his hairpiece. Now can I get some sleep?"

He opened the door and I stumbled out into the cold, befuddled and bewildered. It wasn't really a confession, but it wasn't exactly a denial either. I went back up to my apartment but I didn't get any rest.

FORTY-TWO

Charity James didn't come home the next day. She didn't even have the courtesy to call and let me know she was okay. I have to confess I was worried about her. I wondered if my feelings were just friendly concern or outright jealousy. Even though our sexual encounter was less than intimate, I felt connected to her in a way I had never wished. She had gotten her hooks into me like she had so many other men, and I had started falling for her, despite the obvious drawbacks of being involved with a coke whore.

I spent the day like I had spent too many days recently—recovering. I slept, then watched TV until I was sick to death of it. I showered around 8 P.M., got dressed, and decided to go out to get something to eat. I didn't want to sit around wondering where Charity was anymore.

I put on my jacket and went out to my balcony. As I started down my stairs, I heard a thump behind me. I turned to see what it was. Something was on the floor of the balcony, trying madly to untangle itself. I heard footsteps running away in the alley, then the thing in the corner began to rattle loudly. It came out of its tangle, and I saw that it was a large snake. It recognized me at the same time: a startled human standing in a darkened stairwell that probably looked like a nice cave to hide in if it could get past the idiot blocking its path. The snake was angry and frightened and it moved across the floor with great speed. I ran backwards down the stairs as fast as I could. It was not my habit to turn on the light in the stairwell, so it got darker and darker as I descended. I stumbled and fell the last few feet to the bottom of the stairs. As I hit the ground I saw the snake crest the top of the stairs and pour down toward me. It was coming down fast and was soon lost in the darkness. I grabbed the doorknob and pulled myself to my feet. Then I tried to open the door, but it wouldn't budge. I didn't know if the apartment house had settled on itself again or what, but I had no time to think about it. The snake would soon be at my feet, if it wasn't there already. I couldn't tell because the bottom of the stairwell was almost pitch-dark. Panicking, I yelled for help, then grabbed the doorknob to the large storage closet opposite the front door. I pulled on the door and to my relief it opened. I heard the snake rattling just a few feet away. It was on the ground level now. I hid behind the door and pulled it close to me, pinning my back against the wall. I had nothing to defend myself with, but just inside the closet there was a wide variety of things I could use as weapons, from tennis rackets to baseball bats. Unfortunately I had trapped myself on the wrong side of the door.

The snake's thrashing and rattling grew fiercer as it tried to find and attack the imminent threat to its well-being—namely me. I felt something thump on the other side of the door and I realized it was actually striking at me. I wanted to slam the door on its damn head, but if I missed I would leave myself open to attack, so I held the door closer to myself and put the tips of my shoes against the bottom of the door so the rattler couldn't strike my toes under the edge of the door. I was wearing tennis shoes and hoped the snake couldn't bite through the rubber soles. I also hoped it wouldn't be smart enough to come around the front edge of the door and get me through the wedge.

The snake thumped again against the door, but this time closer to the hinges, and I realized that there was a slit of space vulnerable to attack between the door and the door frame. If the rattler got lucky, it could strike me between that gap. The snake struck the door again, even closer to the hinges, and I suddenly realized that it could see in this gloom or at least it could sense what it was doing far better than I could. I grabbed the top of the door and pulled myself up and over until I was riding the door, squeezed between it and the ceiling of the stairwell. At least I was out of striking range of the rattler, or so I hoped.

I heard it slithering about in the darkness below me, trying to find out where the source of its annoyance had gone. I'm sure it would have preferred to just find someplace to hide, but I think it was so damned angry at having been thrown into this strange environment that it wanted to bite something or someone before it settled down for the night.

I felt the door creak on its hinges and start to give way. I moved, trying to balance myself enough to keep from tearing the door off its mooring, but I only made the situation worse. The top hinge snapped and the corner of the door smashed into the wall next to the front door. The bottom hinge had partially held because the door had nowhere else to go. I almost lost my grip and fell to the ground, but I pulled myself back up and held on to the top of the door.

I was momentarily pleased with myself, although I have no idea why. This certainly had to be the low point of the day.

The door creaked again and started tilting backward on its axis. I was going to fall. The snake was reaching new levels of anger with all the movement in the dark. His rattle was so frantic that I wondered for a moment if there might not be more than one of them. I tried to brace my feet on the back wall to hold the door in place but it was useless. The bottom hinge broke and the bottom corner of the door flew up as the top of the door spun toward the floor smashing me against the wall in the process. I hit the ground and groped in the darkness, trying to get to my feet before the snake could attack again.

I grabbed the edge of the loose door and quickly tried to straighten it up in the narrow area. Once clear of obstacles I threw it down on the floor in front of me. It covered most of the space on the floor of the stairwell and I prayed that it had covered the snake as well. I jumped onto the door and bounced onto the stairs, taking them three at a time to the top of the stairwell. I didn't stop or look back until I was at the rail on the far side of the balcony. In my terror I expected to see the snake come slithering over the edge of the stairs hungry for my blood, even though I knew most snakes would not attack unless cornered or provoked. I was prepared to vault the wall and fall the twenty-plus feet to the alley if the snake proved supernaturally pissed off enough to continue its assault. But it didn't.

I got my keys out and opened the door to the apartment. I turned on the light in the stairwell and went back out and looked down to see if I could find the snake. The bulb was very dim and did nothing more than turn darkness into gloom. I could see no details at the bottom of the stairs.

I went to my bedroom and got the flashlight that had sat on my night stand since the week of the big quake, then I returned to the stairwell, the flashlight illuminating the area brightly. There was no sign of the snake. Even the angry rattling had ceased. I wondered for a moment if my paranoid imagination had conjured the beast. I went back into the apartment for a weapon just the same. I got the push broom from beside the refrigerator and returned to the stairwell again. I slowly walked down the stairs, shining the light in front of me, my legs quivering with exertion and fear, the broom held out before me like a lance.

I had to assume the snake was either hiding in the closet around the corner or it was still under the door, hopefully crushed to death. I looked closely at the door. The doorknob was keeping one side of the door elevated off the floor at a slant, so it would have had to have been very good luck to have crushed the snake with the relatively small part of the door that was flush with the floor. My guess was that the rattler was in the closet. If that was the case I could forget about getting out of the jammed front door. I was just going to have to go back upstairs and scale the wall to the ground, or call the fire department to extricate me from my apartment and animal control to capture the snake.

I wedged the broom under the front edge of the door near the doorknob and tried to lift it up, constantly glancing at the corner, fearing that the snake would suddenly shoot out of the closet and attack me again. As the door rose I saw why the snake wasn't rattling anymore. The edge of the door had slammed down on its tail and completely severed it somewhere above the rattle. The snake itself had coiled its bloody body under the door for protection from the evil man who had attacked it, and if it had been mad before it was absolutely livid now. It silently struck out at the blinding light in its eyes, a vicious hiss the only sound it could make as a warning. I pulled the broom back and the door started to drop but it had shifted and it caught on the corner of the closet doorway. I backed up the stairs and considered fleeing, but then I decided to end this now, not just for my sake, but for the snake's as well. It was obviously in a lot of pain and would probably die soon. I turned the push broom over so the wooden top would be facing downward, went back down two stairs, and smashed the snake repeatedly in the head until it was dead. It continued to spin and curl long after its head came off its body. Finally it stopped moving altogether. I had killed it, but I didn't feel good about it. Even though the thing had tried to bite me, I knew it wasn't its fault. Someone had thrown it over my railing deliberately, trying to either hurt or terrify me. It had worked.

I went back upstairs and got a grocery bag. I didn't know what I was going to do with the snake but I sure wasn't going to just throw it in the trash, out of professional courtesy if nothing else. After gathering its various parts in the bag, I picked up the door and leaned it against the open closet. Then I tried the front door again. It still wouldn't budge. I smashed against the door repeatedly until my shoulder was sore. I called out for help, hoping someone, Clyde or a passerby, might pull on the outside of the door. No one came to my aid, so I took the bagful of snake and went upstairs again. I entered the living room and opened the window that looked down on my front door. I saw then why I couldn't get out. A rake was wedged under the doorknob, the handle buried deeply into the ground in front of the door.

I went to the phone and called Clyde McCoy. He picked up on the fourth ring.

"Hello?"

He sounded out of breath. I said, "What are you doing?"

"I just got out of the shower to get this call."

"Didn't you hear me yelling?"

"What are you talking about?"

"I just got attacked by a rattlesnake in my stairwell. I was yelling at the top of my lungs for help."

"What the fuck? Are you kidding? A rattlesnake?"

"Yeah. A rattlesnake. Didn't you hear me?"

"No. I told you I was in the shower."

"Someone wedged a rake against my front door. Can you come out and pull it loose?"

"Huh? Yeah, sure. Give me a second."

I hung up and went to the window again. I wanted to see if he had really been in the shower. If he had, it was remarkable timing. He didn't come out right away, but when he did he had a towel around his waist and his hair was dripping wet. He might have been telling the truth or he might have just quickly jumped into the shower to match his cover story. He looked up at me in the window and looked down at the rake, like he was trying to figure out what had happened. He pulled the rake away from the front door and opened it. I could hear him coming up the stairs and I met him in the kitchen.

"What the hell have you gotten yourself into now, Hayes?"

"Someone threw this onto my balcony."

I opened the bag so Clyde could see the rattler.

"Christ, that's a big one! You sure someone threw that thing over the rail?"

"Unless it's raining snakes they did."

"It's that asshole again. The one who punched your clock."

It was embarrassing to hear him put it that way, but it was hard to contradict him.

"You think so?"

"Who else could it be?"

"Whoever killed Dexter might be trying to shut me up." From saying what, I didn't know.

"And who do you think that might be? Am I still your prime suspect? If so, this should let me off the hook. I'm like Indiana Jones. I hate snakes."

I put the bag on the kitchen table. "I'm going to take this to the cops. I should have told them about Becker when he attacked me. If it's him, he's got to be stopped before he kills me. I just don't know if they'll believe me."

"I'll go with you if you want. I can back up your assault story."

"That might help."

"I'll go get dressed."

He went downstairs, leaving a puddle of water on my kitchen floor. I still didn't trust him.

FORTY-THREE

Unsure of how to proceed, I got Detective Lyndon's card out of my wallet and called him. As I suspected, he wasn't in his office in the Hollywood division at this hour. I paged him and he called me back almost immediately. I tried to explain the situation to him but I'm sure I sounded crazy. After a few minutes of listening to my jumbled rambling, he said, "Can you come down to Hollywood?"

"Yes."

"Meet me at the address on the card. I'll be there in half an hour. I'll see if I can find Campbell, too."

I said okay, but I wouldn't have minded if Detective Campbell stayed home. He made me nervous.

I sat down and tried to steady myself. I thought about having a drink, but realized it wouldn't be a good idea to see the cops with liquor on my breath. After a few minutes Clyde came back up the stairs looking clean and orderly.

I told him about Detective Lyndon, and Clyde said he'd drive us down to the police station since I was so frazzled. We put the bagful of rattlesnake in the trunk of his beat-up old Maserati and we shot down to Hollywood at nearly the speed of light.

Clyde took the Hollywood Freeway to the Cahuenga exit, went

south on Cahuenga, and turned left on Sunset Boulevard. He took a right on Wilcox, and we soon passed the Hollywood police station. He found an empty parking spot two more blocks away, and we had to put money in the meter even at this late hour. We got the snake out of the trunk and walked back to the station.

I was surprised to see stars embedded in the sidewalk in front of the Hollywood police station. I didn't think the Walk of Fame reached this far south. I checked out the names, wondering who had been relegated to spots so far off the beaten path, and realized this was a different kind of walk of fame. The names here were those of Hollywood division cops who had been killed in the line of duty.

We entered the station and the first thing I noticed were the movie posters adorning the walls, one-sheets from the various movies that had used the station as a locale or had hired members of the force as technical consultants. Most of the flicks weren't very good, but that was one thing you couldn't blame on the L.A.P.D.

I asked the uniformed officer at the desk if Detective Lyndon had arrived and she said no, but that he had called in and was on his way. She asked to see what was in the paper bag and I complied. She didn't flinch when she saw the dead snake. I'm sure she had seen worse things in paper bags during her time on the force.

Clyde and I sat and waited for Lyndon to show. About ten minutes later, he and Campbell came through the front door together. Campbell looked ruffled again, like he had been disturbed from another nice sleep. He was cranky enough when well rested. I was beginning to fear the call to Lyndon had been a mistake.

The detectives approached us and I introduced them to Clyde McCoy. Campbell asked why Clyde had come along and I told them he had witnessed Jim Becker's previous attack on me. Campbell looked skeptical, and took the paper bag from me and looked inside. He handed the bag back and said, "You really needed to bring that thing in here?"

"I didn't know if you'd believe me or not."

"And you think that would convince us of something?"

Lyndon raised his hand to interrupt. "Harv, let's let Mr. Hayes have a chance to explain himself. Let's go into a room. You can wait out here, Mr. McCoy. We'll call you if we need you."

Suddenly I felt like a suspect again. Somehow this had gone from my trying to get some help from the police to my being interrogated once again. I thought about what Wilkie had said about your relative chances with these guys depending on whether you were guilty or innocent, and I was beginning to wish I *had* killed Dexter after all.

Campbell and Lyndon led me down a hallway lined with more movie posters. They stopped in front of a door with a small observation window cut into it at eye level. Campbell opened the door and motioned me inside. He said, "Wait here. We'll be with you in a moment."

"Want a cup of coffee or a soda?" Lyndon added.

"No, thanks," I said as I entered the room. Campbell closed the door behind me a little harder than was needed. There was a long table in the middle of the room with four chairs around it. A large mirror on one wall was obviously two-way glass. I assumed a group convened around a video camera on the other side of the wall when a really juicy suspect started to squirm. I was hoping that suspect was not going to be me.

I put the bag of snake on the table, sat down, and drummed my fingers next to it nervously. I knew enough from years of reading screenplays that the cops watched to see if you went to sleep when you were in an interrogation room alone. It was a sure sign that you were guilty of something. You were caught and now you could finally rest. I stayed wide-awake and nervous as a live rabbit at a dog track.

After a few minutes, Detective Lyndon entered the room carrying a steaming cup of coffee. Detective Campbell was not with him, so I assumed he was on the other side of the glass, possibly operating a video camera. What they were hoping to catch on tape was beyond me, but it further led me to believe that I was a suspect in their investigation of Dexter Morton's murder. Maybe their prime suspect.

Lyndon sat across from me at the table. "Sure you don't want something to drink?"

"I'm fine," I said, unsure what lack of thirst meant in the cop code of guilt and innocence.

Lyndon pulled out a small spiral-bound notebook and prepared to take notes. "So, why don't you tell me all about it? Start at the beginning and talk slow, so you don't get tangled up like you did on the phone. It sounds like a lot has happened since I last saw you."

I tried to organize my thoughts so I didn't sound like a gibbering fool again.

"Last Thursday Jim Becker jumped me in front of my apartment. He attacked me. Punched me twice. My neighbor, Clyde McCoy, interceded and scared him off. Tonight, as I was leaving my apartment, someone threw that rattlesnake over the railing of my balcony and I had to kill it to keep it from biting me."

"And you think Jim Becker did this?"

"I don't know who did it, but I wish you would find out. I think someone wants to kill me."

Detective Lyndon scribbled in his notebook. Then he looked at me with a piercing stare and got to his feet.

"Wait here. I'll be right back."

Lyndon picked up the bag of rattlesnake and walked out of the room, leaving his coffee steaming on the table in front of me. I tried not to look at the mirrored glass as I waited for him, but my lack of anything to do was making me nervous. If I ever had anything meaty to confess, I'm sure a night full of this could make me do it.

After about ten minutes Lyndon returned to the room and sat back down in front of me.

"We're checking on Becker's whereabouts. I've got just a few more questions for you and then you can go."

"I didn't know I was being detained."

Lyndon looked at me sharply. "I didn't say you were."

I looked away, but my gaze ended up on the mirrored wall. It was probably my imagination, but I thought I could hear chuckling coming from the other side of that glass.

Lyndon flipped through his notebook until he found the page he wanted.

"On the night or early morning of Dexter Morton's death, what time did you say you left his house?"

I stared at him, finding it hard to believe that we were back on this again. Something must have progressed in their investigation, or perhaps they were going to try to catch me in a lie.

Finally I said, "Around two A.M."

"And the girl, Charity James, she was with you?"

"Yes. Dexter asked me to take her off the premises. It was not my idea."

"But she is currently living with you?"

"She's staying at my apartment, but I wouldn't say she's living with me. She kind of took up with my roommate."

"Roommate? I don't think we've met him. What's his name?"

"Jeff Lasarow."

Lyndon scribbled Jeff's name in his notebook. "Does he have his own phone number?"

"Uh, yes, but I don't have it memorized. He moved out last week and has a new number."

"So the girl went with him?"

"No. She's . . . I'm not sure what she's doing."

Lyndon looked at me sternly again, like I was not helping matters much with my tangled tale.

"So does she live with you or not?"

"I guess so. But I don't see her much."

Lyndon flipped his notebook over and tossed it onto the table in front of him. He stared at the book for a moment, then looked at the mirrored glass and shook his head. I had no idea what was going on, but I had the feeling it wasn't going well for me.

Lyndon stood up and grunted. "We're going to need to talk to you in the next few days. And we may want to talk to Charity James as well. Have you found a new job yet?"

"No." I stood up too, but my legs felt wobbly, like those of a newborn calf.

"So you can be reached at your apartment?"

"Most of the time."

"You're not going on vacation or anything like that?"

"I hope not. But the way you guys are acting, I'm beginning to wonder."

Lyndon smiled and said, "What makes you say that?"

"I feel like you suspect me of something."

Lyndon clasped me on the shoulder. "We're cops. We suspect everyone of something. And you know what?"

"What?"

"We're always right."

He turned and led me out of the room. I was beginning to think that

Campbell might actually be the nicer of these two guys after all and Lyndon just had the better disguise going.

As we walked down the hall I said, "Do you want to talk to my neighbor now?"

"For what?"

"I just thought you might want to verify my story."

"We have all we need for now."

"What about the rattlesnake?"

"What about it?"

"Are you going to give it back to me?"

"Maybe after we have it analyzed."

"Analyzed? For what?"

"Exactly."

He stopped at the doorway to the lobby and offered his hand. I shook it but my grasp was not very firm.

He said, "We'll be in touch," then he turned and walked back down the hall.

As I entered the lobby I saw that Clyde McCoy had stretched his legs out over a couple of chairs and fallen asleep like some guilty criminal who had finally been apprehended after many months on the lam. I nudged him and he woke with a start.

"They ready for me?" he asked drowsily.

"They said they don't need to talk to you."

He got up and cracked his back and wiped sleep from his eyes. "Then this was a merry waste of my time."

"Sorry."

We went outside and walked down the sidewalk toward the car.

"Want to drop by Boardner's since we're in the neighborhood?" he asked as he unlocked his car door.

Remembering our last visit there I shook my head negatively. "I think I've had enough excitement for one night."

He coughed and shook his head with an "it figures" expression. I was really ruining his night.

Clyde and I didn't speak on the ride home. He seemed to be brooding about something. I watched as he darted in and out of lanes on the freeway and my mind drifted back to the night of the party. Something was gnawing at me. Something he or maybe someone else had said that night. But what was it? I felt like I had the answer at my fingertips, but it was just out of reach.

When we got out of the car in the Viande parking lot Clyde stood in the alley and stared at the neon glowing on the La Reina marquee across the street. I started for my apartment, but he stopped me dead in my tracks with one simple sentence.

"Remember when you asked me if I had anything to do with Dexter's death?"

I approached him so that he could speak in a quieter voice.

"Yeah?"

"I gave you a smart-ass answer, acted like I was glad he was dead, but that was just an act. Truth is, I kind of liked Dexter. Sure, he was a scumbag and all, but the guy gave me my first break. I know he took total advantage of me, like he did everyone, but you still have to have a bit of a soft spot for those that brung ya to the dance, even if they go home with someone else. I made a bunch of movies with Dexter, each one better than the last, and then, when he was ready to make the step up to bigger pictures, he cut all ties to the people who taught him the business. It was a smart move on his part. We were his power, but no one else knew that. No one *cared.* He had learned enough that he didn't need us around anymore. See, we were *witnesses* to his original ineptitude. He didn't want us around sharing the wealth or muddying his waters. It was business and he was smart to do it, but it hurt those of us he cut loose. We thought we were all going to ride the wave to the top, but out of the five of us who started Cinetown, Dexter was the only one who made the leap to the big time, to the studios."

I wanted to ask about Kent Buckler, but I was afraid Clyde would realize I had been digging into his past. I settled for, "Five of you?"

"Yes. In the beginning there was Dexter; Kent Buckler, the director; Jeff Weber, the attorney; Maria, Dexter's partner; and myself. Dexter bought Maria out in '87 and Jeff Weber left in a huff later that same year. Dexter fucked him over on some deal. I was never clear on the details. I think Weber ended up in the music business. Kent and I got bumped off in '88."

"What do you mean, 'bumped off'?"

"We had a string of successes that attracted multipicture deals from the top TV and video companies in town. Cinetown suddenly had contracts in place that would keep the doors open for at least another five years, no matter what happened. Dexter decided he didn't need us anymore and shoved us out those open doors."

"Didn't you feel betrayed?"

"Of course, but I didn't want to *kill* the guy. I didn't exactly want to go drinking with him anymore either. The less I thought about him the better. But to tell you the truth, I never blamed Dexter for my failure after it all collapsed. I could have gone on and made the same moves he did, but I didn't. That's not Dexter's fault. I'm not political, and I couldn't treat movies as if they were rungs to be climbed on a ladder. That's not Dexter's fault either. None of it was. The opportunity was there. The video boom of the eighties made it easy. The thing was laid before us; money, fame, the opportunity to do something different, and we blew it. *I* blew it. But most of the rest of them blew it, too. We were like a bunch of spoiled kids who had been handed the world and thought it would be ours forever, but there was no way that kind of fortune was going to last. A few people made the gold rush work for them in a permanent way. Most of us just pissed into the river until it turned toxic."

"What went wrong?"

He thought about it for a few moments, trying to understand it himself and put it into words. Finally he said, "You ever see a flick called *Strangers Kiss*?"

"Yeah. Saw it on tape."

"It was a great little movie. Made by a bunch of young guys back in '83. Independent money. A nice script. Good actors. The crew pitching in for next to nothing, just for the art of it. It's a thinly veiled story about Kubrick when he first started, you know?"

"Uh-huh."

"That movie is what I'm talking about. It was about the *spirit* of filmmaking. Not just in content, but in *deed.* The movie ended up being a perfect example of what the actual subject matter was. And you know what happened to all those guys who made that flick?"

"No. What?"

"Most of them were never heard from again. Except for Peter Coyote. He works a lot. The rest of them never really made the step up, good as that flick was. And you know why?"

"Tell me."

"Because success in this business isn't about making good movies. It's about having cronies in the right places. Those guys weren't hooked up properly. Didn't matter how good the flick was. I'm sure they all got a little work from it, but you can't build a career on good, solid work alone. You gotta have the juice. You gotta know what asses to kiss. I see that flick sometimes on late-night cable and it just depresses the hell out of me."

"Why?"

"It reminds me of the chances we all had back then, how many chances we had to make a difference. But we just didn't have anything worthwhile to say. Oliver Stone was one of the few cats to step up and use the boom years to make a stand. And he's kind of crazy, you know. But at least he used the economics of the times to make a statement or two. The rest of us just made expensive drive-in movies, and there ain't no more drive-ins."

He lit a cigarette, took a deep drag, and let the memories come rushing forth.

"See, I thought we were eventually going to make movies like the great pictures of the sixties and seventies that I grew up on. I thought we were going to be the new Bergmans and Fellinis and Kurosawas and Truffauts, or at least Altmans, Ashbys, and Peckinpahs. But the fact is this town didn't want to replace those guys. Things had changed. Spielberg and Lucas had turned the business blockbuster crazy. Everyone was going for the two-hundred-million-dollar hit. And if your budget wouldn't accommodate that kind of spectacle, they just wanted you to do a cheap version of that *kind* of movie. Forget originality. Forget ambiguity. Forget subtlety. If you weren't pandering to the audience, hitting them over the head with a sledgehammer, the suits weren't happy. I could only do that crap for so long before burning out."

He took another merciless drag off the cigarette.

"I remember a night, not really a night, but a moment when day was turning into night, back in, I don't know, probably '86; we were having a party at Dexter's house. Not the house where he died, but a smaller one off Mulholland Drive. It was a wrap party for *Whirlwind,* this junky little motorcycle flick we made trying to raise coin for a bigger picture we wanted to make, *Final Command,* which was going to cost about four times more than we'd ever spent and it even had a little political content to it. It wasn't just going to be fluff. We'd made *Whirlwind,* and it had been kind of fun and we were looking forward to the next picture. One that might mean something. We were so filled with enthusiasm and hope and things seemed to be going our way. We didn't think we could be stopped. It was an afternoon party and it started to break up around dusk, magic hour. It was one of those great L.A. summer days that just got better when it turned into night. We were going to move the party down to Trancas bar. A bunch of us were walking up the hill to our cars and Kent, he directed *Whirlwind,* he said, 'Look at that sunset,' and we all stopped and looked. It was fucking beautiful. A gorgeous orange sunset right out of a postcard. The sky was on fire with reds and silvers and golds. But as the sun dropped behind the mountains, a cold wind whipped up and blew through us, and I realized right then and there that we had peaked. I don't know how I knew, but I did. I knew things weren't going to work out as we hoped. I had a heavy, sickening sense of doom, and realized we had seen our best days. I knew we weren't going to make the step up. It wasn't going to happen. We had taken our shot and we had blown it. The dream was over. I've blocked out or forgotten almost everything else that happened in the eighties, but I remember that moment up on Mulholland Drive like it was yesterday. In a lot of ways, it was."

He turned and went into his apartment. I stared at the neon sign across the street for a few minutes, ruminating over what Clyde had said, and about how far down his sense of failure had plunged his blackened soul. He had invoked the name of Kent Buckler, but not gone anywhere with it. I knew there was more to the story, but I feared digging any deeper. I had a feeling I wouldn't like what I found.

The air grew colder, a sequel to the chilly wind that had predicted Clyde McCoy's fall from grace back in '86. I wondered where the other people who had started Cinetown over a decade ago were right now.

A homeless guy rolled a shopping cart full of Dumpster treasure down the alley, a loose wheel on the front rattling a horrible tune. I stepped back to give him a clean runway. The bum didn't even give me the courtesy of a little eye contact.

FORTY-FOUR

I goofed off for a few days, not wanting to look for work, not wanting to think about Charity James. I read for pleasure and watched videos and even went to the movies a few times. I drank too much and ate too little and was growing as horny as a rosebush waiting for my sexy roommate to come home. But it seemed she didn't need me anymore. She had found a new home with Jamaal and his banger buddies.

After a quick review of my finances, I decided it was time to return to the workforce. I hit my Rolodex and started looking for gainful employment. I talked to Jim Cameron, whom I had known when he was a production designer for Roger Corman a decade or so earlier. His fortunes had shot through the roof over the last few years with *Aliens* and the two Terminator films. The buzz on his upcoming Schwarzenegger flick, *True Lies,* was that it was going to be the smash of the summer. Cameron had only misstepped once since breaking through with *The Teminator,* when he made the ill-conceived deep-sea flick, *The Abyss.* And rumor had it that *The Abyss* was much better before the studio pressured him to cut it down to a shorter running time.

Cameron told me he was thinking of doing another big movie on the ocean using the Titanic as a backdrop for a disaster-laden romance. He thought he could put me to work in the technical research department when he got closer to preproduction. It sounded screwy to me, but I said I'd check with him again in a few weeks. This project smelled like another big mistake. I had a feeling it would sink faster than the original ship. Hadn't he learned his lesson with *The Abyss*? Maybe it would work—if he could get Arnold to play the iceberg.

I contacted a buddy of mine over at New Line. He said there were no permanent jobs to be had there, but he could give me piecework, reading scripts at twenty-five bucks a pop. For novels they'd throw in an extra ten. I told him I would come over before the end of the day and pick up as much work as he wanted to give me.

I had a late lunch at Viande and then drove over to New Line. Four screenplays and a novel in galley form were waiting for me at the reception desk. My old buddy didn't need to see me in person. I guess he was worried that failure might be contagious.

I stopped at the grocery store on the way home. I had a hundred thirty-five dollars worth of work in the car, and it would take me two days to read the material and write the reports. If that was going to be my new wage for a while, I was going to have to start cooking at home. I was also going to have to file for unemployment. What next? Food stamps? I wondered if they accepted them at Le Dôme?

As I drove down Ventura Boulevard I thought about what Detective Lyndon had said the night before about taking a vacation. It was his way of giving me the "don't leave town" speech, but it had put a bug in my ear. Taking a break from L.A. wouldn't be such a bad idea. I hadn't had a real vacation in years. The cops wouldn't like it much, which made it appeal to me even more. But then I caught myself. What was I thinking? I had already thrown away ten thousand dollars of hard embezzled money. Was I now going to squander what was left of my Development Fund on a frivolous trip to some tropical paradise? And then I realized it wasn't my need to relax that was driving my thoughts; it was the creeping sensation that I had better get out of town before something else bad happened. Either another attack from Jim Becker—or whoever tossed that rattlesnake over my railing—or an arrest by the cops for a murder I did not commit. The snake made me think about Clyde McCoy again. Could he have been the one who threw it? It was very convenient that he was in the shower at the precise moment that I was being attacked and he could not hear my screams. Had he hurled the snake onto my balcony and then run around the building and entered his apartment through the back door? Were my inquiries about Dexter making him so nervous that he wanted me out of the way?

When I got home I made a pot of coffee and started reading the first screenplay. It was crap, as usual. I read the first fifteen pages carefully, then sped through the rest of it, making notes on a legal pad as I went.

The next one was slightly better: a sensitive drama involving incest and rape. It was well written, but far too harsh for anything other than an HBO telemovie. New Line wouldn't go for something like that unless Meryl Streep and Jack Nicholson were ready to party down as brother and sister.

I started reading the novel, hoping for something interesting on more than a cinematic level, but I soon found the book was just an inflated screenplay that some hack had turned into prose with the hopes of coming in the back door with it to get a movie deal. I slogged through it, but, despite the coffee in my system, the exercise made me sleepy. It was only twilight, but I decided to take a nap. I stretched out on the couch and was soon fast asleep.

I was awakened a few hours later by Charity James. She was shaking my shoulder gently and whispering my name repeatedly. I blinked in the gloom of the living room, wondering if I was dreaming.

"Mark, wake up. I need your help, Mark."

"Wha . . . ?"

"Do you have some money you can loan me?"

I knew then that I wasn't dreaming. I sat up and turned on a lamp. We both squinted at each other in the harsh light.

"Where have you been?"

"I've been hanging out with Jamaal."

"Jamaal? Really?"

"He's nice."

Her eyes were shining like polished assholes.

"You look like you've been working the pipe pretty hard."

"I'm not doing that anymore. I'm getting clean. That's what I need the money for. I'm going to get in a program."

"Yeah? I think you're just going to get into some *grams.* I'm not giving you any money."

She squeezed my arm. "Pleeease. I really need your help."

"You disappeared without a trace. Never called. Never came home."

"Home? You said you didn't want me living here."

"That was before."

I immediately regretted saying it.

"Before we had sex?"

"I didn't mean it like that."

"I know. We could do it again though."

She squeezed my cock through my pants with one hand and wrapped her other hand around the back of my neck and leaned in to kiss me. Her breath smelled as if she hadn't brushed her teeth in a week. I pulled away from her and said, "If you want to get into a twelve-step program, I'll take you right now and I'll pay for it."

"I can't do that. Jamaal's waiting for me down in the parking lot. He's going to give me a ride. Over to rehab."

I stood up and looked down at her.

"Who the fuck do you think you're fooling? You just need money to cop and I'm not giving you any. Speaking of cops, they're looking for you. They want to talk to you about Dexter."

"Fuck that. I've said all I've got to say about Dexter."

"That's not up to you. They have more questions for you."

"Let them find me."

She got up and went down the hall to the room she used to share with Jeff. After a few minutes she came out carrying a plastic trash bag full of clothes.

"Are you moving out?"

"If you're not going to help me, I guess so. I'll come back for the rest of my things tomorrow."

"I thought you were going to rehab?"

She stopped and stared at me. She looked like she was going to cry. "Fuck you." The tears came now and she stood there sobbing and heaving. I went over to her and held her in my arms.

"You don't have to do this. I can get you help."

"I just need some money. Is that too much to ask from a friend?"

"If our friendship means so much to you, why don't you stay with me? Maybe we could work things out and be together for a while?"

She pulled away from me and sneered. "You just want to fuck me again. Sooner or later you'd dump me like your buddy Jeff did. Like all you motherfuckers do!"

"That's not true."

"Bullshit. You're no different from Jeff or your old pal Alex. You just want to use me. You all act like you're nice guys, but you're no better than Dexter was. And at least Dexter was straight up about being an asshole, and he gave me a nice place to live. Not a dump like this."

"Sorry it's not up to your high standards. Why don't you give Alex a call? He's got a nice condo on the West side. Maybe you can go live with him. You just have to convince him to forgive you for breaking his heart."

Charity snorted a laugh. "That's funny. Like he has a heart to break. I've already been to see Alex. He fucked me, called me a junkie, and told me to get out."

"I'm beginning to think that's the best way to handle you."

"Are you going to help me or not?"

"If you mean am I going to give you money, no."

"I'm going then."

She went through the kitchen, out the door, and down the darkened stairwell. She slammed the door at the bottom of the stairs as she exited. I walked out onto the balcony and looked down into the parking lot. Charity approached a silver Nissan with custom rims and a purple light glowing on the undercarriage. I couldn't see the driver; he was just a dark shape behind the wheel. As Charity opened the door the light illuminated the face of a man I had never seen before. He wasn't Jamaal. He wasn't even black. He looked Hispanic. Charity closed the door and the car didn't move. I supposed they were discussing her failure to procure cash from her sucker friend.

I turned the overhead light on so the guy could see me standing on the balcony. I stood at the railing, practically daring him to get out of the car.

After a few minutes the Nissan pulled out of the parking lot and cruised slowly down the alley, out of sight.

I went back into the apartment and dumped what was left of the pot of coffee into the sink. I opened a beer, picked up the book galley, and went into my bedroom to finish reading it.

The thing went on and on. My reading was slowed by thoughts about Charity. She had gotten to me, despite my better judgment. I could see how Alex and Dexter and so many others had fallen under her spell. I could also see why they had all gotten rid of her as well. I considered going down to Viande for some serious drinking, but decided to save money and open a fresh bottle out of my liquor cabinet. I had a small bottle of Jack Daniel's that had been given to me for Christmas. It went well with the beer, and I killed a six-pack and half the bottle before I crashed. I still hadn't finished reading the book.

When I awoke the next morning I was somewhat shocked to find my TV, VCR, answering machine, and coffee pot gone from the living room and kitchen. Coffee pot? They even took the coffee pot!

FORTY-FIVE

I checked the garage. Charity and her accomplice—or accomplices—had cleaned out anything worth pawning from there as well. My place had been thoroughly ransacked while I slept. I guess I should have been happy they didn't break my door down and bash me in the head for my wallet, stereo, and computer, which were in the bedroom with me. At least they left the telephone and my movie posters.

I went downstairs and told Clyde that I had been robbed, most likely by my faux roommate and her drug buddies. He suggested I call the police again, but I had seen enough of the police to last a lifetime. By the time they were done with the crime scene, they would probably accuse me of ripping myself off for the apartment insurance. The fact that I had none would be of no interest to them. I also didn't want to get Charity James in any more trouble than she was already in. I wanted to find her, get back whatever they may not have sold yet, and get her some help if possible. Then maybe I'd break her legs myself.

Afraid that Charity and her crew might return to finish the job, I asked Clyde to watch the place while I went to get new locks at the hardware store. He frowned, but grabbed a book, took a chair outside, and sat in front of his door to read.

While at the hardware store I bought three new locking doorknobs and a new padlock for the garage. There was nothing in the garage of any value now, but I was thinking I might eventually be able to rent it out as storage space. Some of the other tenants were getting a hundred dollars a month for their garages.

Lord, is that where I was? Ready to rent out my garage for pocket change? I needed a job. Any job. I did not want the Development Fund to shrink any more than it already had.

I went back to the apartment and Clyde put the new doorknob on the bottom door while I put the other two on the side-by-side doors to the kitchen and the living room. Even if predators scaled the wall, they would have to break a window to get in now.

I told Clyde I was going to go to Ma Smith's later to look for Charity James. He said he didn't think that was a good idea. When I reminded him that she wouldn't have gone down there in the first place if not for him, he frowned and said he would accompany me to watch my back.

I went upstairs, speed-read the remaining scripts—which were as lousy as I expected them to be—and wrote up the reports. It was far from my finest work, but I didn't care much anymore. It was a jerk off job and I knew it and so did everyone else. Why sweat it?

I called New Line and told my contact I was dropping off the work. He said my check would be ready after the following pay period, which was in two weeks. Christ, the hoops you have to jump through for one hundred thirty-five dollars.

I delivered the material and notes to New Line, and asked if they had anything else they wanted covered. I was told they would be in touch.

I went to The Mysterious Bookshop near the Beverly Center to see what was new in the world of crime fiction. A gleeful little man sold me forty dollars' worth of paperbacks and then recommended a new writer on my way out, hitting me up for another $5.99. I practically had to run out the door. I had the feeling I would spend my life savings in there if that guy had his way.

I went home and tried to figure out how to kill the time before we would go down to Ma Smith's. I suddenly missed my television in a big way. It was a twenty-seven-inch Zenith, and even though I didn't like much of the content it played, it was a comforting way to melt the hours. I now found myself with nothing to do but read, and the ordeal of reading all that garbage for New Line had temporarily soured the experience for me. I considered going for a drink, but thought I should remain sharp in case things got rough at Ma Smith's.

It was still daylight. I was hours away from potential trouble, so I figured a beer or two would not dull my senses for any length of time. Luckily I had a few Heinekens left in the refrigerator. I popped one and started looking through my purchases from The Mysterious Bookshop. I settled on the one that the guy had pushed on me as I was trying to leave. It was a first novel, something called *The Black Echo.* The writer already had a second book out, *The Black Ice*—I guess he was going to be the *Black* guy—but it was only in hardcover, and despite the salesman's heavy lobbying, I was restricting my purchases to the more affordable paperbacks.

I went out and sat in the hammock to sip and read. There was a construction crew at the far corner of the Viande parking lot. They appeared to be building a palm tree. I watched with fascination until I realized that they were actually constructing a metal tower to carry cell phone transmissions and it had been cleverly disguised as a palm tree. An ugly palm tree at that. So now those beams were going to be shooting through me. I was going to be microwaved in my own home.

I began reading *The Black Echo* and my exhaustion with the written word soon faded away. This guy was good. He was a crime reporter by day, and you could tell. He had the shit down. I wondered if the suits had discovered him yet. If I was lucky, maybe I could throw some of the Development Fund his way and option the book cheap.

The construction crew finished building their palm tree at about the same time I finished my second beer. The light was fading fast now and the air was growing cold. I went into the apartment, made myself a sandwich, and continued reading. I finished *The Black Echo* a little after ten and made a mental note to check on its availability in the morning.

I washed my face and brushed my teeth and prepared to go hunting for my stolen goods. When I knocked on Clyde's door, Emily answered. I was startled to see her and immediately felt guilty about why I had come to fetch Clyde.

"Emily, hey, when did you get back?"

"This afternoon. I got an early flight and surprised Clyde."

"How was your trip?"

"Exhausting. I've just about had it with out-of-country films."

I hugged her, but she didn't hug me back.

"I hear you guys are going to Ma Smith's."

"You know why, don't you? We're not going there to party."

"The reasons why don't matter. That place is dangerous. Especially for Clyde. He likes it too much."

"We won't be down there long. As soon as we find Charity James, we'll get right out."

"I want to go with you, but Clyde won't let me."

I held back from remarking how ironic it was that Clyde thought *we* would be okay but it was too dangerous for a third-degree black belt martial arts movie star.

Clyde came out of the bedroom. His hair was slicked back and his face was moist, as if he had just gotten out of the shower.

"Ready?" he asked.

I nodded. He kissed Emily good-bye. She didn't look happy about it.

"Be careful, asshole," she said as she closed the door.

Clyde just grinned and we went to the parking lot and got in my car. We headed south on the 405. He was being his usual taciturn self, so I decided to try to break the ice a bit.

"Thanks for coming down here with me," I said.

"After the guilt trip you laid on me, I didn't have much choice."

"Sorry about that. If it's any consolation, I feel guilty too."

"Guilt's for losers. Didn't Dexter ever teach you that?"

"I'm sure he said it more than once."

He had brought up Dexter's name again, but I didn't want to push it. I changed the subject.

"I was wondering, do you have any scripts lying around that you want to sell?"

"You must really be desperate."

"I've been thinking about what you said at Boardner's that night. About going independent. I'm thinking it might be a good idea."

"Especially since the studios won't hire you, right?"

"That's one factor."

"You got any money?"

"Some. And I could raise more."

"I'll think about it."

I headed east on the 10 as Clyde mulled over my implied offer. I could see him taking the bait. He was still a film junkie no matter what he said. I could tell the thought of making another movie was beginning to excite him.

"I've got a few things you could read," he finally said. "Maybe you can find something worthy."

"Great."

I pulled off the freeway and Clyde had to give me directions once we were close to Ma Smith's. Even though I had been there twice already, I had been distracted on both visits and did not know my way around South Central. And in that neighborhood, a wrong turn can get you killed.

Security was at a minimum in front of Ma Smith's. The place didn't really get hopping until after midnight. Inside, the crowd was thin. We found Jamaal in the living room, talking to a very beautiful Asian girl. As we approached him he smiled and said, "Kind of early, ain't it, Clyde?"

"We're here on business, not pleasure," Clyde said. "We're looking for Charity James."

Jamaal's expression darkened. He squeezed the Asian girl's hand and said, "Wait here for me, baby."

He led us into one of the back bedrooms so we could talk in private. "You know better'n that, Clyde, puttin' my business on the street."

I leaned forward and said, "Your *business*?"

Jamaal looked at me. His eyes widened like he might strike me. Clyde put his hand in front of me as if to say, "Stay out of it."

"We just want to know where the girl is," Clyde said calmly.

"Why?"

"She took some things from Mark's apartment."

"No shit? And the bitch didn't bring me anything. She owes me a shit load of money, you know?"

"For what?" I said, ignoring Clyde's warning. I knew the answer, but I wanted to hear him say it. This time both of them looked at me like I was crazy. Then they resumed talking to each other like I wasn't even in the room.

"When was the last time you saw her?" Clyde asked.

"Couple nights ago. We were partying at The Retreat and I got busy with another lady. Charity fell in with Kendall and a buddy of his that did time with him in the Cork. Hostile spick name of Angel."

I said, "She was with an Hispanic guy last night. Drives a silver Nissan."

"That's him," Jamaal said.

"Where's this guy live?" Clyde asked Jamaal.

"You crazy? How the fuck would I know? And if I did, then what? You going to go over there for a shoot-out or somethin'?"

"We're not carrying."

"Well, Angel and his boys sure the fuck are."

"Is Kendall around?"

"No. And good riddance. Him and his homeys are out of control lately. I mean, I'm all for having a good time, but fuuuck, they're stinking up the place. Ma Smith don't want 'em around no more."

"Can you get him on the phone?"

Jamaal's face squinched up and he shook his head. "Damn, Clyde, you are one pushy motherfucker."

Jamaal pulled a cell phone the size of Magic Johnson's tennis shoe out from under his jacket and dialed a number. I was surprised he could fit the phone in his jacket. It was one of the largest I had seen, almost twice as big as Dexter's had been, and even that thing was cumbersome. I wondered if they would ever get them down to the size of a phaser like the techie freaks kept predicting.

"Kendall, Jamaal," he said when the phone was answered. "You got an address on your boy Angel? Clyde wants to hook up with him."

I could hear the tinny voice on the other end of the phone say, "What the fuck for?"

"That girl, the one you call 'Creamy,' she ripped off her roommate and he wants to find her."

The tinny voice now grew louder and was hurling epithets. Jamaal waited for the barrage to end, then said, "I told them all that, but they want to go there anyway. What you care? It's their funeral."

There was more cursing and yelling and Jamaal replied, "The fuck, my boy Clyde ain't no narc, are you, Clyde?"

"Don't be fucking ridiculous. Let me have that phone."

Jamaal handed over the phone, glad to be out of it.

"How long you know me, Kendall?" Clyde said into the phone. "Then don't be such an asshole about this. I just want to find the girl. I know better than to make trouble. Just give me the address."

Kendall got loud again and Clyde waited. Then he pulled a pen out from his inside jacket pocket and wrote something on his palm.

"Thanks, Kendall. I owe you one."

Kendall responded to that with more profanity. Clyde clicked off the cell phone and handed it to Jamaal.

"Kendall said Charity owes him money, too."

"She owes everyone," Jamaal said.

I wanted to ask Jamaal what the current sex-for-drugs exchange rate was because I had a feeling Charity was being shortchanged. Instead I just said to Clyde, "You got the address?"

"Yeah. East L.A. It's in the heart of the barrio."

"I hope to fuck you know what you're doing," Jamaal said.

"Me, too," Clyde replied.

I borrowed Clyde's pen and wrote down my phone number on the cover of a *Penthouse* magazine I found sitting on a nightstand. I handed Jamaal the magazine and said, "Please call me if she shows up here."

He took the magazine from me and was checking out the centerfold as we left the room.

FORTY-SIX

We drove through a neighborhood that made South Central look like Sunnybrook Farm. Clyde gave me directions like he was visiting his old neighborhood. When we finally arrived at the address that had been written on his hand, I began to lose my resolve to get my belongings back. The area was all pit bulls and barred windows. Clusters of shadowy figures gathered in darkened doorways and unlit front porches talking business. It was a tough 'hood, and I wondered if my car or my life might be the next thing I lost.

Sensing my nervousness, Clyde said, "You show fear down here and they'll pick your bones clean."

"You really know how to calm someone down."

"There's a spot."

He pointed at a parking space more appropriate for a VW or a motorcycle than a Camaro. I squeezed in, but pulling out quickly would be impossible if we had to scramble.

We got out of the car and walked two doors down to the house in question. The silver Nissan I had seen Charity get into in the Viande parking lot was parked under a sloping carport next to the house.

We walked up the stairs onto the covered porch and Clyde rapped on the steel mesh outer door bolted over the front door. It took a while but the inner door finally opened. A fat old Mexican man wearing a bloodstained apron stood in the doorway holding a butcher knife. Through the steel mesh I could see my television sitting on a stand in the living room behind him. It was playing, but I couldn't see who was watching it.

"Qué?" the old man said.

"We need to see Angel," Clyde said.

The old man stared at Clyde for a moment then turned to the living room and yelled, "Angel!"

As he turned I could see three other men in the living room, two of them sitting on a couch, the other sitting on the floor at the foot of a recliner. They were watching boxing on ESPN on my twenty-seven-inch Zenith. These men were not fat and old; they were young and lean and mean. One of them got up off the couch and approached the door, spitting curses in Spanish.

Angel was tall and stringy. He wore an unbuttoned blue short-sleeved shirt over a T-shirt and baggy pants. His arms were stringy prison muscles covered with jailhouse tats, and he had a faint blue teardrop tattooed under one eye, indicating he had at least one kill on his résumé. When he saw the two of us on the other side of the door he stopped, probably assuming we were some form of law. The old man stood to the side, smiling at Angel contemptuously, thinking he was about to get into trouble.

"What is it?" Angel said to us with almost no accent whatsoever.

"We're looking for Charity James," Clyde said.

"She's not here."

"Do you know where she is?"

"Who the fuck are you?"

"My name's Clyde McCoy. And this is Mark Hayes, Charity's roommate. She ripped off his apartment last night."

Angel laughed. "Fuck. Kendall said you might drop by. I didn't think you'd have the *cojones.*"

The old man suddenly looked disappointed. He shook his head and walked away, presumably toward the kitchen to continue cutting whatever he had been cutting.

"That's my TV you're watching in there," I said.

"The fuck it is."

"I saw your car in my parking lot last night. You were with her."

"She traded that shit for what she owed me. Said it was hers to trade."

"Then why'd you have to sneak around in my apartment in the dead of night to get it?"

"Nobody snuck nothing. She had a key. We went in and got her shit. We might have been a little quiet because she said you were sleeping."

"I want my things back. All my things."

"Couldn't give that other shit to you if I wanted to. I traded it all to a guy I owed. See how it works? It's a fucking daisy chain."

"How about that TV? That's my TV."

"No. That's *my* TV. I needed a new box so I'm keeping it. The color on my Sony got fucked up in the quake. Won't play nothin' but black and white anymore. I hate black and white."

"I can prove that's my TV. I've got all the receipts."

Angel laughed at the thought that that meant anything down here. "I don't care what you got. It's not yours anymore. Your bitch traded it so she could live another day. Tell you what, homey. You need a TV? Take that fucking Sony out of here. We were just going to throw it away anyway. Chuy, bring over that box on the floor."

Angel clicked the lock on the metal door and opened it wide, but did not move to allow us inside.

Chuy grumbled but got up off the couch, picked up a nineteen-inch Sony that was sitting on the floor beside the TV stand, carried it over, and put it in my arms. Then he returned to his seat and resumed watching ESPN.

"There," Angel said. "Now everybody's got a box."

"I want my TV."

Angel pulled his shirt to the side and showed us a .45 Colt stuck in his waistband over his T-shirt.

"You better get out of here, you Sting-sounding motherfucker. And don't come back."

Clyde looked at the Colt, then looked at me, and nodded toward the street.

"Thanks for your time," he said to Angel.

I couldn't believe it. Clyde just wanted us to walk away, me taking out this drug-dealing asshole's garbage.

"Wait a minute," I said. "I don't want this TV. I want my own. It's mine and I want it back."

Angel adjusted himself like he was going to pull out the gun. I knew if he pulled it, he would fire. Drawing a gun was not an empty gesture down here. If you drew it, you better use it.

"You're holding *your* box. That's final."

"What about Charity James? Where is she?"

"The fuck I know." Angel closed the metal door in our faces. "But if you see her, remind her she still owes me money." He closed the inside door and went back to watching ESPN on my TV.

Clyde turned and walked away, leaving me standing there holding Angel's old television set. I followed him to the car.

"Wait up, Clyde."

He stopped and waited for me to catch up.

"How come you didn't do something when that guy showed us his gun?"

"Like what?"

"Take it away from him or something."

"Are you crazy? You ever try to take a gun away from someone?"

"After I saw how you handled Jim Becker, I thought you could do just about anything."

"You've been watching too many movies. Becker was a pussy. These guys are serious. I'm not getting killed over a Zenith."

FORTY-SEVEN

Instead of taking the freeways back, I drove straight up through the city to get home, Angel's busted Sony in my trunk. Clyde was leaning back in his seat with his eyes closed as we cruised along the winding curves of Laurel Canyon, heading for the top of the mountains dividing the city from the Valley. Some thought of his must have struck him funny, because he suddenly laughed for no apparent reason.

"What is it?"

"I was just thinking about Dexter and all those news stories I keep reading. The execs are really nervous around town, wondering who did it and if they might do it again. Wouldn't it be nice if one of those wizards was knocked off every month until they all agreed to behave? Wouldn't this be a better place to work?"

"Jesus, Clyde. Just because you've been screwed over, it doesn't give you the right to wish people dead."

He opened his eyes and looked at me. "And what gives them the right to carry on the way they do? All those wizards, all those Dexters, fucking us over every day. Killing creativity for a paycheck. How many souls have they crushed with their daily deeds? No one does anything about it. No one makes a move on them because this whole town is chickenshit. They'd rather kiss these scumbags' asses and hope they get a job out of it than actually get proactive about the problem. But ask most writers if they have an executive in their lives who they would like to blow away if they could pull it off cleanly. The list would be long. But we're all gutless. That's what the guys in power are counting on. That's why they know they can get away with what they do. And try suing them. Even if you win, they will tangle you up in so much legal red tape that it will cost you three times your judgment to collect what is rightfully yours. This town is rigged in their favor. But by God if one of these fuckers was killed every month for a year straight, the rest of them sure as hell would grow some common courtesy."

I reached the crest of the hill and turned left on Mulholland Drive. A low fog hugged the ground, and I had to slow down to make sure I wasn't leaving the road.

"So what are you going to do? Go on a murder spree?"

"Hayes, you disappoint me. But I keep forgetting, you're one of them. Or at least you *aspire* to be one of them."

"I just want to make movies."

Clyde snorted. "So you partnered up with the suits? Shit, those guys wouldn't even know which end of the camera to look through. You sided with the wrong bunch."

"I've been wondering about that. If I'm one of the bad guys, why'd you befriend me? Did you just want to keep an eye on me to find out if I thought you killed Dexter?"

"Christ, Hayes, you *are* paranoid. I befriended you because you're my neighbor and because I thought you wanted to be something better than a D-boy. I thought I sensed a *filmmaker* behind your Brooks Brothers suits. I was trying to *save* you from them."

"Thanks, Clyde."

I couldn't focus on the winding road so I pulled the car over at a turnout point on Mulholland. I got out and walked to the top of a mound of dirt piled high and packed down hard so runaway vehicles would be stopped before plunging off the mountainside into the homes below. Through the thin fog I could see a billion lights twinkling down in the Valley like angry fireflies at a picnic that had gone on too long. Clyde joined me at the top of the mound and fired up a cigarette. Did this fucker kill Dexter after all? Was he going to confess to me and then shove me off the mountain? He took a long drag on the hand-rolled cigarette and stared at the shadowy mountain range far in the distance on the other side of the Valley.

"I ever tell you about my friend, Kent Buckler?"

Here it comes.

"The director?"

"Yeah. We started out together. I met him back in my NYU days. We liked the same kind of movies, and when he came out here we collaborated on some things and made a cheap little flick together to get our feet wet. We wrote it together, I produced it, and he directed it. It was crap but it got us some attention. We fell under Dexter's spell not long afterward, and that really was the beginning of the end for Kent."

I had the horrible urge to confess that I had read his letters to Dexter and knew more than I was admitting. I suppressed the urge with all my might. Instead, I simply said, "What happened?"

"We made a bunch of flicks for Dexter, really built up his reputation and his company, and then he stabbed us in the back big time. Not just the little shit he did with every picture—we were used to that—but a major cluster fuck at a critical juncture in our careers. See, I had written this picture called *Final Command.* Ever see it?"

"No, but I've heard of it." An understatement to say the least.

"Don't waste your time. It's a fucked-up mess. But it started out like a dream project. I thought it was going to be our stepping-stone to the bigs, it was so good. I write this thing and everybody loves the script, but Dexter hires this casting agent, a real cunt named Barbara Cleghorn, and she puts the bug in Dex's ear that Kent can't direct a big picture like this and he should be replaced. Dexter offers Kent a payoff and an associate producer credit to leave the flick, and Kent was so insulted he just took the money and walked away. After all he had done for Dexter and the amount of shit he had to walk through to do it, this was the final straw. On top of it all, the new director really screwed the pooch. He fucked *everything* up, and we all ended up looking like talentless assholes. Our shot at the big time turned out to be just another big-time turkey. The whole experience at Cinetown was just too much for Kent. The betrayal weighed heavy on his heart. He burned out, got so despondent about the business that he just fucking killed himself."

Was that it? Had Clyde revealed the true motive for Dexter's murder? Revenge for the death of some long-lost buddy?

"I know what you're thinking," Clyde said. "But, no, I did not kill Dexter, or even have him killed because of what happened to Kent. But it did add to my enjoyment of the fact that *someone* knocked off the rotten son of a bitch. As Dexter would have put it, 'At the end of the day, all that matters is that the job got done.' "

I didn't want to argue the point with Clyde. I was more interested in the back story than his perverse glee over Dexter's murder. "How did your friend—"

"Kill himself? Kent drank himself to death. He was already a drinker—working for Dexter would drive anyone to the bottle—but he got worse and worse after the *Final Command* debacle and finally he just drank so much one night that he didn't wake up. His heart gave out. All the shitty little political moves of the last five years just ate away at him so relentlessly that he was rendered useless. He was damaged goods. He had D.G.S. so bad he was unemployable. He had to *go.* So, yeah, Dexter killed people in his day. He may not have shot or stabbed anyone, but more damage has been done with the flash of a pen than all the guns and knives in history."

Clyde flicked his cigarette into the air. It arched high and dropped into the valley below. He seemed completely unconcerned by the possibility of the dry brush on the side of the mountain catching on fire. I had a feeling he wouldn't have minded watching all of Los Angeles burn to the ground. He'd probably fiddle while it went up in smoke.

We went back to the car and rode home in silence. What more was there to say? When we got back to the Viande parking lot, Clyde invited me in for a cup of coffee, but I no longer felt like sitting around bullshitting with him. The anecdotes and Hollywood war stories would taste very sour from this point on no matter how good the coffee was that washed them down.

I carried the nineteen-inch Sony upstairs and plugged it in. Angel was right. The color was fried. All I could get was a black-and-white picture. I consoled myself with the thought that most of the best movies were in black and white anyway. I could live with it for a while.

FORTY-EIGHT

First thing in the morning I made some calls and checked on the availability of *The Black Echo.* As luck would have it, Mace Neufeld had snapped up the rights to that one as well as the author's next two books at rates that made my Development Fund look like the chump change it was. I had found something of value but I was way behind the curve. That's why people like Mace live in Malibu or Beverly Hills, and I was still operating out of an apartment in the Valley.

I decided to get out of town for a few days to clear my head, cops or no cops. I packed a bag and prepared for a short hop to Santa Barbara.

When I opened my front door to leave I found a paper bag full of screenplays on my doorstep. Clyde had gone through his closet and dusted off the old specs. He didn't realize that I had no intention of going into business with a murderer. What a team we'd make. The guy the whole town thinks killed Dexter Morton partnered up with the guy who probably did. We'd do a lot of business with those credentials. We could call the company Murder, Inc.

Not wanting to go back inside or confront Clyde, I grabbed the bag and threw it into the car.

I jumped on the 101 freeway and sped north, suddenly craving an escape from the insanity that had become my life. The traffic was light and I was lucky that I wasn't stopped and given a speeding ticket because I didn't let the needle drop below eighty until I saw the ocean coming up alongside the freeway in Ventura, sixty miles north of Sherman Oaks.

I rolled the window down and breathed the ocean air, and I could feel myself begin to decompress. I turned the radio up and put on KTYD, Santa Barbara's local rock station. They were playing "Freebird," and by God I couldn't stop from singing along like a madman.

Twenty-five miles farther north I entered the Santa Barbara city limits. Sanctuary.

I headed straight for the El Encanto hotel up in the mountains on the strip they called the Riviera, which overlooks the city. The El Encanto had old-world charm, seclusion, and a killer view. Anytime I had conferences or other overnight business in Santa Barbara, I tried to get my employers to put me up at the El Encanto. I checked for room availability. There were several vacancies. I settled for a bungalow overlooking the plush garden courtyard. It was rumored that over two million dollars' worth of tropical plants had been shipped in and planted in the garden, which also featured a number of waterfalls. It was a very tranquil spot.

I only booked for a night, but let the clerk know I might stay for a second night if the mood hit me. He said he could place the bungalow on hold for no extra charge as long as I let him know my plans by ten the next morning.

I went up to my bungalow and opened all the windows and doors. I sat at a patio table positioned just outside my door. I didn't drink or smoke; I just sat there and breathed. The sun was shining and there was a cool breeze blowing in off the ocean two miles away as the crow flies. The air was crisp and clean. But the air up here is always crisp and clean. Clean air was only worth noting in Los Angeles. Up here they were spoiled. Spoiled rotten.

After listening to the birds chirp for half an hour I drove down to the city and cruised State Street looking for something to do. I considered taking in a movie, but there was nothing good playing that I hadn't already seen. I took note of a huge construction project on lower State. They were building a big, fancy mall where a bunch of mom-and-pop stores and cool restaurants and bars used to be. Christ, the developers were even trying to ruin this place. At least the city's strict building codes were forcing the mall scum to conform to the Spanish design of the rest of the town. It would be a commercial horror, but it wouldn't be an eyesore.

I ate dinner at my favorite restaurant, E. J.'s Café. They boasted of having the oldest bar in Santa Barbara—not the business itself, but the actual bar that you sat at to drink. They had purchased it from Joe's Café a few doors down the street when Joe's had decided to redecorate. The owners of E. J.'s had a sense of history, and it showed, not just in the purchase of the bar, but in the oversize photos that adorned the walls, images that stretched back to the very beginnings of Santa Barbara, at least as far back as could be recorded by photographic equipment. The place had style.

I decided to skip the bar and sit in one of the many booths that lined the south wall. I probably had one drink too many at dinner anyway and I made a mental note to quit drinking as soon as I could afford a healthier hobby. I overtipped the waitress, but she rejected my suggestion to join me for a nightcap at the El Encanto anyway. She said her boyfriend, the same bruiser whom I had watched cook my ribeye in the exposed kitchen near the entrance to E. J.'s, didn't allow her to date other men. He curled his lip at me and made fire shoot up out of a frying pan as I walked past the kitchen on my way out the door.

I drove back up State Street and the town looked sleepy. It reminded me of the first time I stumbled on to this place back in the early eighties while driving up the coast with a girlfriend. It had been a quaint little stop on the map back then, until the news dogs down in L.A. started touting it as the great weekend getaway paradise. Once you clue the world in to a paradise, that paradise will surely be lost. On the weekends it happened here in a big way. But for now it was quiet, almost a ghost town. I cruised the streets and remembered good times had at various bars, restaurants, and movie theaters around town. A kaleidoscope of women were attached to those memories, most of them good women, and I wondered for a moment why I hadn't tried to make it last longer with any of them. That moment passed quickly. Ah, the dangers of vacation time.

As I got out of my car in the El Encanto parking lot, I noticed Clyde's bagful of scripts in the back seat. It reminded me of the bagful of rattlesnake that I had taken down to the police department. I wondered if the material in both bags had been produced by the same man.

I grabbed the bag of screenplays and took them up to my room. What could it hurt to have a look?

I emptied the bag onto my bed. There were four screenplays with Post-it notes stuck to the covers describing the genre and estimated budget of each project. The first script was a big-budget science fiction spectacle. I tossed it onto the floor. The next was a television-worthy rant about the riots of '92. I read ten pages and tossed it on top of the space opera. The next two were crime pieces, Clyde's specialty. One of them had far too much action for the kind of budget I was envisioning being able to raise, but the other one fit the bill nicely. It was called *Blonde Lightning* and it read like a fairly standard detective thriller, but it contained all the required scenes demanded by the shrinking videocassette and foreign sales market: sex, drugs, rock 'n' roll, carnage, and betrayal. Something the whole family could enjoy. The Post-it note on the cover said it was an homage to Dashiell Hammett, but it read more like a low-rent Raymond Chandler rip-off, despite the disparaging words Clyde had for Chandler's work. Still, it was engrossing. It moved right along, had action, but no expensive stunts. Best of all it had a sense of humor about itself. I actually read it all the way to the end and was never bored. For a brief moment I fantasized about raising the budget from private investors—dentists, doctors, accountants—anyone with ten grand to spare, and producing Clyde's screenplay on the cheap.

Then I pictured myself floating face down in my new swimming pool with a big hole in my head. I tossed *Blonde Lightning* onto the pile of scripts on the floor and went to sleep.

I had a nice breakfast in El Encanto's dining room the next morning, but decided I had had enough of the good life. I couldn't stay here indefinitely while the Development Fund melted away to nothing. I had to return to L.A. Besides, I felt the junkie's pull. I had to get back to my source.

I packed my bag, gathered Clyde's scripts, and loaded up the car. I handed the key in at precisely check out time, milking my stay for all it was worth. I took one last stroll around El Encanto's beautiful grounds, then prepared for my descent into hell.

I drove much more slowly on the way home. As I approached Los

Angeles, I could see a very distinct yellow-gray cloud of pollution hovering over the Valley. I was driving into *that*? It wasn't that noticeable when you were under the canopy itself, but I found it odd that I was volunteering to breathe that poisonous air again and I vowed not to return to Santa Barbara until I could manage to live there permanently. I could not afford the depressing perspective it provided.

There were no messages on my answering machine when I got home because Angel's pals were using my answering machine somewhere in East L.A. and I had not replaced it yet. It didn't seem to matter much. I wasn't getting many calls lately. Even the reporters had stopped bugging me. When you're cold in this town, you might as well be dead.

That night I ate at Viande, continuing my spending spree but hoping I'd meet a young lady or at least strike up a conversation with some of the regulars. I struck out on all counts. There were no single women in the place, I didn't run into my usual group of cronies, and even the bartender was new and unfriendly. But the steak was good, and the beer was cold, and I felt like I was home again, whatever that was worth.

It was still fairly early when I went up to my apartment. I thought about what Clyde had said about unemployed movie executives and had to admit he was right: I just didn't know what to do with myself. I was at a loss about what my next move would be. And I had burned a lot of bridges as of late. Maybe it was time to reconsider my father's offer of a career in real estate back East.

I pulled a beer out of the refrigerator and went into my bedroom. I leaned against the headboard, drank the beer, and stared out the window at the big neon marquee across the way currently advertising THE GAP on the electronic display board in the center of the sign. I fell asleep with the beer in my hand.

The phone rang at a little after three in the morning and scared the hell out of me. I sloshed beer everywhere and rushed to pick it up. At that hour, it could not be good news. Jamaal was on the other end of the line. I could hear some fucked-up rap song blaring in the background and Jamaal had to shout to be heard over the noise.

"Hey, man, you told me to give you a call if your girl showed up. Well, she's here and you better come down and get her. She's into some bad shit."

"You at Ma Smith's?" I asked.

"Yeah. You better get over here quick."

That was rich. This guy took what he wanted from Charity, then he dealt her to his friends, and now he wanted me to baby-sit her. It was Dexter all over again. Have fun with the hot blonde, then send her packing when she misbehaves. I wasn't her father or her brother. I wasn't even her "roommate" anymore. Why did this have to be my problem? And, besides, Charity had already ripped me off once. What would she do for an encore? Steal my shitty little black-and-white Sony?

"There's nothing I can do for her," I said. "She told me to stay out of her business, then she robbed me. I'm washing my hands of her."

"You gonna be that way?"

"Yeah."

"That's cold, bitch."

"Hey, you and your pals have been taking advantage of her. You can take care of the problem. Whatever the fuck it is."

"Listen, sucker, I'll fuck you up you talk shit like that to me. I was with her, yeah, but I didn't want her to go the way she's been going. And I didn't take advantage of no fuckin' body. You want me to come up there and straighten you out?"

I guess I should have been frightened, but considering what I had been through recently, Jamaal did not seem like that much of a threat. Matter of fact, he was pissing me off.

"Fuck you, crackhead. You come by my place and I'll have the cops on your ass."

"Little brother, I call you up to do you and the lady a service and now you're threatening me with the *po*-lice. Now what the fuck is that all about?"

"Jamaal, I thought you were an okay guy, but frankly this whole thing has gotten out of control. You made your play for her, now why don't you take care of her?"

"She's in with some bad niggahs. And I mean *bad.* They doing shit with her that I just can't abide. But I got no leverage with them and I got no leverage with her. I thought if you came down here we could get together and work it out. Maybe she'd listen to you. Me and my homeys will back you if you can get her to go, but I don't want to get capped for stickin' my nose where it ain't wanted."

"Hey, man, the last time I tried to get her to leave that place, you told me to hit the road and you'd take care of her. What happened?"

"This is different. I want her out of here. But I want it to go down peaceable. I don't want a lot of heat drawn to the house, and I don't want these nasty motherfuckers hatin' my ass either. You get her out of here and don't let her come back. Get her into a program or something. That bitch needs help."

"I can't do anything about it."

"So that's it, huh?"

"'Fraid so."

"You're one chickenshit motherfucker, you can't help a friend."

I thought about what he was saying. He was right. If not for me, Charity would not have been in that place. She probably would have been just as fucked up somewhere else, but her being at that house, in that specific situation, was my fault. Clyde and I introduced her to Ma Smith's. I should have never let her go down there. If I turned my back on her now, what the hell was I?

"What do you want me to do?" I asked.

"Just come down here. Talk to her. If she says she wants to go home with you, they'll let her go. But it's got to be her idea."

"I'll try. But I don't think I'll have any luck."

"Just get down here quick."

He hung up on me. I got my jacket and my keys and went downstairs. I considered asking Clyde for help, but that might have just made the situation worse. Besides, my previous amazement at his prowess had been tempered with the realization that if things got really dangerous, he was more likely to abandon me than help me. And if Emily was around, it was unlikely that she would allow a second outing to Ma Smith's. The police were another consideration. But if the police raided Ma Smith's house, people might get killed. There were a lot of guns in that place and a lot of messed up heads. The cops come through the wall with the battering ram and all hell would break loose. That's if the cops would have cared enough to bust the joint. It had been operating quietly for seven years now. Surely the police knew all about it and were turning a blind eye. I was on my own on this one. But I'm no Travis Bickle. I couldn't crash that house with guns blazing to save my whore. I had no gun, and she wasn't even *my* whore. No. I'm more the Henry Kissinger type. I'd just go in there and politely ask them to hand over their little blonde plaything and pray I didn't get shot.

FORTY-NINE

I drove down to Ma Smith's house and was met out front by Jamaal. Two serious badasses, Petey Gunn and Big Ted, were standing watch by the front door.

"She's in the back, man," Jamaal said, looking nervous. "There's some bad shit going down and Ma Smith ain't diggin' it. I'm afraid something's gonna come loose around here."

"Well, let's go in."

My legs were weak and my guts felt loose. This was crazy, me going into a place like this, trying to work something out with a bunch of crackheads.

We went into the living room and everything seemed normal. The place was crowded, but not packed. The Reverend Al Green was putting love in the air with his music. Everyone seemed happy, chess was being played, booze guzzled, and lines snorted. A good time was being had by all. There seemed to be no tension in the room. A whiff of crack, yes, but tension, no.

We went to the kitchen and stepped over the wooden divider and under the crime scene tape. Ma Smith and her hefty girls approached me. Ma was about to blow a gasket.

"I want you to get that girl out my bedroom, right now," Ma said. She looked angry, but a bit frightened as well.

I said, "I'll try."

"Don't try. Do it!"

Jamaal and I went to the back bedroom. The door was shut, but not locked. Jamaal eased it open. The room was lit only with candles. Despite the strawberry scent from the candles, the air was stale and acrid.

Charity was on a queen-size bed, naked. Kendall and Poochie, also naked, were using her as a human snort board, dusting various parts of her body with cocaine, then snorting and licking it off. She looked asleep, but I could hear her moaning softly, signaling at least semiconsciousness.

Crazy Martin and some dude I'd never seen before were sitting in rocking chairs in one corner of the room, working crack pipes and ignoring the action on the bed. Crazy's pal was a huge, solid-looking fucker. He looked more like a football player than a drug addict, but I guess he could have easily been both. There was a fifth guy in the room, a skinny white dude sitting on the floor next to the door, shooting something into his veins. He was moving sloooow.

Jamaal and I stood in the doorway, not sure what to do next. Jamaal finally spoke. "Uh . . . Kendall . . . don't mean to bug you, but Charity's cousin's here. He wants to take her home." I was surprised to hear Jamaal's voice crack.

Kendall had his head down between Charity's legs. He felt no inclination to stop what he was doing. Poochie was at her breasts, licking and nibbling. He sat up angrily and yelled, "Can't you fucking see she's busy?!"

Being yelled at seemed to give Jamaal strength. His voice didn't crack when he spoke this time. "Yeah, but now she got to go. Ma Smith wants to close early tonight."

"Fuck dat shit," Poochie said. Then he went back to licking coke off Charity's nipples.

I felt sick again. My legs were turning to Jell-O, but I went over to a pile of clothes wadded up on the floor next to the bed and sorted through it to find Charity's outfit. I felt a pistol stuck in the pocket of someone's pants. I tied the pants in a knot, trapping the pistol so there would be no easy access to the weapon. I found Charity's dress, a slinky little red thing, tossed it down on her body and said, "Get dressed, Charity. We're leaving."

She didn't open her eyes. She just moaned a bit more, as if she thought the dress was another item to be devoured off her body.

Kendall shot up off the bed, grabbed me by the throat, slammed my head against the wall, and said, "What the fuck you doin', niggah?"

I looked over at the door for Jamaal, but he wasn't there. He'd split, leaving me to get my ass kicked, or worse.

"Ma Smith wants us all to leave," I said, trying not to piss my pants.

"We'll leave when we're goddamn ready. Now get the fuck out of here."

He threw me across the room and I slammed into Crazy Martin, causing him to drop his crack pipe. It broke on the hardwood floor, spilling the precious hot rock in the process.

"The fuck?" Crazy Martin yelled, shoving me onto the floor. He looked at his works and saw how I'd wrecked it all, then he sprang to his feet and started kicking me. I tried to get up and the big guy in the other rocking chair put a boot in my face, knocking me flat.

The overhead lights suddenly came on in the room, temporarily blinding us all. Crazy Martin was pulled into the air and shoved against the wall. Jamaal had come back, this time with Big Ted and Petey Gunn. Petey Gunn had Crazy Martin up against the wall, holding him tight and trying to talk sense into him.

"You know we don't do that shit in Ma Smith's house. Chill out, motherfucker, chill the fuck out!"

Crazy Martin was trying to pull away from Petey, but Petey was too strong and had all the leverage going his way.

Poochie and Kendall, still naked as jaybirds, were digging through the pile of clothes, looking for the pistol, but it was all tied up. Jamaal and Big Ted shoved them off their feet. And then I saw the guns. Jamaal and Big Ted both had revolvers in their hands. They shoved the guns into the faces of the two naked men.

"Don't force it, bro," Big Ted said to Kendall. "It's time to go home."

I looked over at the big guy in the rocking chair. He hadn't moved other than when he kicked my face. He was still working his crack pipe like nothing was wrong with the world. It didn't look like he was going to be a factor. The white guy on the floor was staring up at all the action with wide eyes. Wherever he was in his head, the show must have been amazing.

Ma Smith came through the door with a sawed-off shotgun and gave the room the once-over. Her two hefty friends were behind her holding pistols.

"This is some terrible shit in my house," Ma said. "This is supposed to be a nice place, a place folks can come to and have fun. You boys are spoiling my house. Now I want you and that girl out of here. Right now!"

Kendall looked up at Jamaal with hatred. "You done fucked up now, Jamaal. This is bad. You should know better'n ta dis *me.*"

Jamaal leaned forward, inching the pistol closer to Kendall's face. "I ain't showing you no disrespect, Kendall. We're just trying to close the shop. We can't be havin' no white motherfuckers getting killed down here. You gonna get the whole place shut down."

Ma Smith's two lady friends went through the pile of clothes and took any weapons they could find, then handed the clothes to the two naked men.

Petey Gunn pulled a 9 mm from Crazy Martin's jacket pocket and said, "You guys can have this shit back tomorrow when you've calmed the fuck down."

"Bullshit, man," Crazy Martin said. "You ain't keeping my piece."

"Hey, man, we just want to keep the *peace,* and to do that we got to keep your *pieces.* That's the way it is. We're closing up. You done ruined it for everyone. But we don't want you crazy niggers shooting at us for just trying to run a wholesome establishment."

"Dat's fucked up, Petey."

"No, it's not. You're my pal, Crazy. Let's not get federal over this shit. That bitch ain't worth it."

Poochie and Kendall got their clothes on. Ma Smith's two ladies helped Charity get dressed. She was dazed and confused. She blinked her eyes repeatedly when she saw me, unsure whether I was real or a hallucination.

"What's going on?" Charity asked the room in general.

"I came to take you home," I said.

"I'm tired. I don't want to go anywhere."

"You got to go, sweetheart," Ma Smith said. "Everybody's leaving. We're closing early tonight."

Kendall took Charity by the arm and led her toward the door. "Let's get the fuck out of here, baby."

I grabbed Charity by the other arm and pulled her away from Kendall.

"She's not going with you."

Kendall shoved me hard. "Don't play badass now that you got some guns behind you, motherfucker! I'll still tear your fucking heart out!"

Jamaal stepped between us. "Damn, Kendall, can't we just stop this shit? The girl is going home with her cousin and that's it. Start up fresh tomorrow."

"But don't bring it back here," Ma Smith said.

"Why don't we let Creamy decide where she wants to go?" Kendall said, suddenly calm.

We all looked at Charity for her answer. She leaned into Kendall. "I'm really tired, Kenny. Just take me home and fix me up."

"See that?" Kendall said. "We ain't kidnappers. My baby wants to go to *my* crib. Right, baby?"

"Sure."

I pulled Charity around to face me. "Charity, I came all the way down here to pick you up. Please come home with me. You can rest there."

She spoke slowly, but coherently. "That's so nice of you, Mark. But you shouldn't have come. I'm fine. I'm just going to hang for a while. 'Kay?"

"C'mon, baby," Kendall said, leading Charity out the door. He almost had to carry her because she could barely walk. Poochie and Crazy Martin followed them out. Ted and Petey escorted them to make sure they didn't pull anything treacherous. The big guy in the rocker never moved and no one forced the issue with him.

I looked at Jamaal and said, "You can't let them take her out of here."

"Hey, man, it's her decision."

"She doesn't know what she's doing."

"You sure about that?"

I wasn't, but that didn't matter. I said, "Why'd you drag me down here then? Just to get my ass kicked?"

"I thought you could talk some sense into her. Make this go down peaceable. I didn't think you'd go attacking them."

"I didn't attack anyone."

"Man, you don't know how to conduct yourself. A brother's eatin' pussy and you go throwin' dresses over his head and shit. You're lucky they didn't cap your ass."

I shook my head and went through the doorway, trying to catch Charity before she left with Kendall. The house was nearly empty. Ma Smith had been telling the truth. She had pulled the plug early, and everyone who had any sense had scattered fast.

By the time I got out to the porch, Kendall's black BMW was pulling away from the curb. Charity was passed out in the backseat, leaning against Poochie's shoulder. Crazy Martin was riding shotgun. I started down the stairs after them, yelling, "Wait!"

Petey Gunn and Big Ted were standing on the porch, watching the car go. Big Ted hissed, "Shut the fuck up."

"Haven't you caused enough trouble?" Petey Gunn whispered loudly at me.

The car disappeared around the corner and was gone, leaving nothing but a rumble in the distance.

I exhaled painfully, defeated and sore. I turned and looked up at the two men standing on the porch of Ma Smith's party house.

"You could have stopped them. You could have helped me."

"Boy," Big Ted said. "We *did* help you."

Ma Smith stepped out onto the porch and said to me, "This was a nice place until you folks started coming here."

FIFTY

I bought a bottle of Jack Daniel's from Jamaal and headed for the beach, cruising like some lost sea turtle trying to find home. I wanted to be outside under the night sky, not breathing exhaust from crack pipes or listening to P-Funk at four in the morning. I had had it with the party house. If that's how Charity wanted to live, so be it, but I wanted to get my sanity back. What the fuck was I doing going to crack houses anyway? I wasn't a Blood or some work-addicted attorney from Century City. I was just a white boy from the Valley, approaching middle age faster than I wanted to admit, with no clear prospects ahead in either the career or romance departments. It was a fairly desperate situation, but inhaling secondhand crack smoke was not going to make it any better. And now I had received a good old-fashioned ass kicking, like something out of one of those Raymond Chandler novels Clyde liked to mock. Except the guys kicking my ass weren't two-bit thugs or cops on the take. They were just a couple of horny black guys who didn't have much of a sense of humor.

I drove into Santa Monica and parked in one of the sand pits that local entrepreneurs turn into five-dollar-a-spot parking lots in the daytime and I walked through the sand toward the Santa Monica pier. There's a full amusement park on the pier, and the Ferris wheel lights were still illuminated, but most of the other buildings were conserving energy and had shut the power off for the night. A string of white lights trimmed the railing of the pier so the handful of late-night fishermen perched there could see what they were doing. A marine layer was floating in to shore and enveloping the pier. It looked like it might have looked fifty years ago, in its heyday.

I walked down to the edge of the surf and sat in the shadow of the pier, watching the foam roll and curl on the beach, drinking straight from the bottle of JD and thinking about all the weirdness I had witnessed over the last few months. It was time to put my life together again. I needed a new job to revitalize the Development Fund, and a new girl to clear my head of Charity James.

I sat there sipping Jack Daniel's and making plans. My sacking and plundering of Los Angeles would begin anew in the morning. First I would conquer Hollywood, then it would be off to the Playboy Mansion to find a fair damsel!

As if conjured by my sordid imagination, a fat girl and a skinny dude appeared out of the mist walking on the beach just within the light of the pier. They were talking and playing with the idea of getting it on. I could tell they were drunk and new to the idea of screwing each other. He tugged and pulled at her and she would resist, then he'd back off and she'd go after him. She was wearing a blue jean skirt and a halter top and he was wearing a tank top and shorts. He pulled on her halter top and her mammoth breasts flopped free. She punched him in the chest playfully, but it almost knocked him to the ground. He grabbed her and they tumbled to the sand.

Their movements became subdued for a few moments as they negotiated the terms of the deal and restructured the clothing arrangement. Then they were off to the races. They must not have seen me sitting in the shadows because once they got started, it was no holds barred. And it was quick. Real quick. When it was over the guy stood up and acted like it never happened. He adjusted his shorts and suggested a swim.

"No way! I'm not going in that cold water!" the fat girl bellowed.

The guy must have felt the need for a bath because he suddenly half-staggered, half-ran into the ocean and took a dip. I guess anything was preferable to trying to finish what he had started.

The girl got up, pulled up her halter top and tugged her panties over her big legs. I couldn't see her in great detail from where I was sitting, but, as they say around the water cooler, it looked like she had a pretty face.

The skinny guy came running out of the ocean, shivering, his teeth chattering like those of a disturbed monkey. This boy just couldn't do anything all the way. He took his wet shirt off and tied it around his waist.

They began to walk my way, resuming their childish play, shoving at each other as if nothing intimate had just transpired between them. And I suppose nothing *had.* They were like fifth graders who couldn't admit that they liked each other, although in the case of the guy I got the impression he was just using the girl because it was four in the morning and he was drunk and there was nothing else available to fuck. I had a feeling she wasn't going to be getting a lot of calls from him in the future.

As they drew nearer I could make out details of their features. They looked like they had stepped out of *The Hills Have Eyes.* He was pure stupid hillbilly, Confederate flag tattoo and all. She *would* have had a pretty face, if so many cousins hadn't swung from the same branch in her ancestral tree. Her eyes were too wide apart and they didn't exactly point in the same direction at all times. But, hell, they were having a good ole time on the beach.

As they entered the shadow of the pier they noticed me sitting there. They immediately realized that I had witnessed their unspeakable act.

"What the fuck you lookin' at, asshole?" the hillbilly boy snarled.

"You got me, Jethro," I said, not about to take any shit from this redneck peckerwood. "But that was the shortest rodeo I ever saw." The Jack Daniel's was making me brave. At last.

The hillbilly stopped and stared at me defiantly. The girl pulled on his arm and tried to get him to keep walking.

"Come on, Charley," she said. "Don't mess with him. He's one of those L.A. crazies."

Tourists!

The hillbilly spat on the ground near my feet. He didn't hit me with any of it, so I remained seated. I was too tired and sore to tangle with the skinny fuck. Besides, I was afraid his girlfriend might sit on me while I was whomping on him.

They continued under the pier and out the other side. I watched them move down the beach. Every now and then he would pull away from her and act like he was going to come back to kick my smart ass. He had backed down from an insult. Not what a man of his stature would do, 'cept'n, of course, when they's a lady present. I had a feeling this night would be haunting him for some time to come, for many, many reasons. Not all of them having to do with me.

FIFTY-ONE

I fell asleep under the pier, the sound of the surf lulling me to never-never land. I had a nice roaring hangover when I woke up. Despite the fact that the sun was beating down on my face, I was bathed in a cold sweat. The bottle of Jack was empty in the sand next to me. Either I had finished it in the night, poured it out defiantly in a drunken rage, or spilled it while I slept. I couldn't remember, which led me to believe I had managed to consume a good portion of it before passing out.

As I got to my feet I realized that I had bruised a couple of ribs in the skirmish the night before, maybe even cracked them. When I moved my pain moved with me. I threw up under the pier and found I could breathe easier without the additional water weight.

I went to the Denny's on Lincoln, washed my face and slicked back my hair in the bathroom, then ordered the Grand Slam and had myself a meal. The waitress was kind enough to lay a couple of Tylenol on me, even though it was strictly against company policy to distribute drugs to the customers.

By the time I had finished my Slam I was feeling pretty good. I went down to the Third Street Promenade and hung out for a while.

The girls were out in force on the Promenade, looking tanned and sexy. Summer was upon them and they had shed their winter plumage.

Now they were strutting their stuff, and it was a wonderful parade. I knew I should go home, but something kept me from making the drive. I just didn't want to return to the Valley yet.

I drove down to Venice and walked along the boardwalk. It was a hot summer day, and the skaters, bicyclists, and joggers were out en masse. Feeling grimy I bought a pair of shorts, a T-shirt, and a straw hat from one of the venders on the boardwalk, then changed clothes in one of the public bathrooms. It felt good to be out of the dirty street clothes.

I went into the Sidewalk Café and had a little hair of the dog that bit me—a shot of Jack and a draft beer to ease it along. I tossed down some of their free popcorn for roughage.

I dropped into the Mystery Annex at Small World Books next door to the Café, and perused the titles. I was drawn like a magnet to the Chandler section. I felt the spines of his books and memories of the great reads they had been in my youth came flooding back to me. Fuck Clyde and his lame assessment of Big Ray. Chandler may not have had real-life experience in the detective game like Dashiell Hammett had, but the man knew how to write. Clyde was correct about one thing, though. The kind of stuff that Chandler wrote about back then was tame by today's standards. The eleven o'clock news has more murder and mayhem packed into its half hour than all of Chandler's books rolled together.

I bought a copy of Chandler's *The High Window* and read it in the shade of a palm tree near the sand. I had pizza and beer for lunch, then resumed my reading. I finished the book in the amber light of the setting sun. *The High Window* is not one of Chandler's most popular novels. It's not as well known as *The Big Sleep* or *The Lady in the Lake* or even *The Little Sister.* And it's not as highly regarded as *The Long Goodbye.* I liked *The High Window* because it seemed a step up from his pulp writing but less pretentious than some of his later work. It was a quick, easy read, and it reminded me how few quick, easy reads I had encountered during my time covering material for the studios. I made a silent promise to myself to never go back to that life. I didn't know what I was going to do in the future, but I couldn't continue as a creative executive. It was a slow death.

I closed the book and watched the last flaming tip of the sun drop below the horizon. A gust of cold wind put an exclamation point on the event and I thought of the story Clyde had told me about the moment he realized the dream was over for him, almost a decade ago. I shivered and headed for the boardwalk, leaving *The High Window* on a bench for the street folks to enjoy.

I stopped in for one last beer at the Sidewalk Café and watched the light fade from Venice beach. A few skaters and bicyclists whizzed by, but the day was done. The homeless were taking back their turf. I hoped someone would dig the Chandler.

It was the proverbial "end of the day" that Dexter Morton and his brethren metaphorically abused whenever they couldn't find some other way to write off their foul deeds. It was almost nine by the time I finally got to my car and headed home. I had burned the whole day at the beach. I stopped at a liquor store on the way to the freeway and picked up a bottle of Cuervo Gold. I felt like tequila tonight.

Traffic was thick on the 405, but I was home by nine-thirty. I got out of my car, put on my straw hat, and got the bottle of Cuervo out of the backseat. I was halfway to my apartment before I realized there were two men standing in front of Clyde McCoy's door, talking to him. They turned and saw me. They were tall and official-looking. Cops, for sure. But cops I didn't recognize. I froze and for a brief moment considered bolting. I wasn't even sure why. I'm sure I made a pretty sight in my straw hat, shorts, and I ❤ L.A. T-shirt. The bottle of tequila dangling from my hand must have made the picture complete.

One of the men said to Clyde, "Is that him?"

"Yep. That's the guy," Clyde replied. The *fucker*! He had sold me out!

The two men walked toward me and produced badges from under their jackets.

"Mark Hayes?" the first man asked.

"Yes?"

"I'm Detective Ryan, Van Nuys Homicide."

The second man said, "Detective Lutz, Van Nuys Vice."

"Would you mind having a word with us?" Detective Ryan asked.

"What's the problem, officers?" I asked. My heart was jackhammering. Had they finally put it all together and determined, wrongly, that I was Dexter's killer? I wouldn't be the first semi-innocent man to hit death row.

"Do you know a woman named Charity James?" Detective Lutz asked.

"Yes sir."

"She's dead."

Of all the things they may have said, this was something for which I was completely unprepared. I stood there staring at them, totally dumbfounded.

Clyde came up behind them and said, "I think he may need to sit down."

"Do you need to sit down, sir?" Detective Ryan asked.

I tried to get my brain to work. "Yeah," I finally said. "I think so."

"You can come into my place," Clyde said, "But you have to be quiet. Emily is sleeping in the bedroom."

Clyde opened the door to his apartment and led us into the living room. We sat on the couches and he got me a glass of ice water as I prepared for another question-and-answer session, but this time *I* wanted to ask the questions. My first one was, "What happened?"

"That's what we are trying to put together," Detective Ryan said. "She was found on a bus bench at the corner of Sepulveda and Ventura around 8 A.M. this morning. The coroner put her time of death at approximately 6:30."

"Was it drugs?"

Detective Ryan raised his eyebrow at me, as in, "Why, what makes you say that? We never mentioned any drugs. What do you know about the drugs?" I decided to ask fewer questions.

"There was cocaine in her system," Ryan said. "But the preliminary M.E. report suggests she died of toxic shock syndrome."

"Toxic shock?"

Both the detectives reddened as they explained the grim facts to me. It was unnerving to witness hardened types actually embarrassed by the details of someone's death. Charity had fallen victim to a combination of bad hygienics and the side effects of allowing her vagina to be used as a coke snorting board. Her membranes had dried out and she had left something, perhaps a tampon or a contraceptive sponge, inside herself long enough to breed the bacteria and toxins necessary to start the chain reaction that led to a toxic shock fatality.

They asked me where I had been, and I told them of my adventures on the beach. I even showed them the receipts in my wallet from Denny's and the bookstore in Venice. I think I appeared so surprised and confused by the news of Charity's death that they believed my story, which had the added advantage of being the truth. Of course I left out the part about my aborted rescue attempt of the victim at the crack house the night before.

Clyde watched with what appeared to be neighborly concern, but I could tell that he was suspicious of me. When he thought I had the situation under control, he excused himself to go into the bedroom and check on Emily to make sure we weren't disturbing her.

It had taken some canny detective work for the cops to even find me. Charity had no driver's license because of her DUIs. Her California I.D. had an address on it from three years ago, and no one in that apartment complex even remembered her living there. The small phone book they found in her purse yielded a lot of numbers but not a lot of answers. Most of her acquaintances hadn't seen her in months or years, and none of them knew her family. They finally found the key to my apartment in a compartment in her purse and that led them to me. She had taped a tag with my street address on it to the key just in case she got lost or was too messed up to tell whoever she was with where she was going. The intersection where she was found was less than a mile from my address. Thinking they might have found her home, they contacted my landlady and she furnished them with the name of the actual tenant in apartment Four. It was not Charity James but a guy named Mark Hayes, and they wanted to know what he knew about the dead girl who had a key to his apartment.

The detectives didn't know if Charity had died at the bus stop or if perhaps someone had been trying to take her to my place and dumped her when they realized she was dead. I think they also thought she might have died in my apartment and I took her to the bus stop, but they stopped short of saying it. No foul play was suspected in Charity's death. Or so they said. I guess the definition of "foul" has changed over the years. The cops asked me a ton of questions about her habits and associates. I explained what I could to them, but I didn't mention that she used to live with the late Dexter Morton. I didn't want them to start with the conspiracy theories. One thing would lead to another, and somehow it would all come back around to me. And then things might get complicated. I wasn't about to do their work for them. They seemed to buy most of the story and didn't treat me as if they were holding me in any way responsible for Charity's death. They didn't even ask to go up to my apartment to look around. Currently they were looking at this as a death by misadventure, but they wanted to reconstruct her final days to see if an actual crime may have been committed. They also wanted someone to sign for the body. They hadn't been able to track down her next of kin using her fingerprints, and they didn't want the city stuck with her burial expenses. I explained to them that she had no relatives in L.A. that I knew of and that I wasn't sure where her mother resided. They said I would do just fine if no one else could be located. It would put a serious dent in the Development Fund, but who was I to argue?

I felt like ratting out Kendall and his bunch, but I figured I should get more information about what happened before I started implicating people, especially people who could implicate me right back.

My pulse slowed to normal and I felt my panic melt into grief. I always thought it would end badly for Charity. I just didn't think it would be so soon. I wondered if Kendall had tried to get her to my place or to a hospital or if he had just shoved her out of the car when he didn't like the way she was smelling. Or maybe she was with someone else by the time she started to flatline. She may have even been trying to hitchhike. She was a long way from South Central when they found her. I felt a severe pang of guilt for letting her get away last night, but I had tried to make her come with me, hadn't I? Hadn't I done all a person could do in a situation like that? Probably not.

Clyde returned from the bedroom. He said Emily was sleeping peacefully.

The detectives asked if I wanted to come down to the morgue in the morning to sign for Charity's body after they were finished processing her. The thought made me queasy, but I felt that if I rejected them, I would be making a big mistake. They both gave me their cards and their condolences and then they left.

Clyde asked me if I wanted a drink. I said no and bid him good night. As I was leaving he said, "Hey, did you get a chance to look at those scripts?"

I closed the door in his face.

FIFTY-TWO

I got very little sleep. I couldn't stop thinking about Charity James and thoughts of Charity inevitably led to thoughts of Dexter Morton and the strange situation I seemed to be in. Was I a suspect in his murder or not? The Hollywood cops acted like I was, yet I was still free. If they had me, why had I not been arrested? And more importantly, who *did* kill Dexter? Was I living next door to the murderer? Was Clyde so dead inside that he could do such a thing and just move on like nothing had happened? Or did Charity kill Dexter and had the guilt weighed so heavily on her conscience that it hastened her downward spiral?

I dreamed fitfully, as if in some sort of hypnotic trance. Recent events tumbled and jumbled through my mind and I kept thinking the answer was there, buried in my subconscious. I awoke with a start at 5:37 in the morning as something clicked and it all suddenly fell into place.

I got up and showered and prepared for the day. I made coffee and got the newspaper, but didn't open it. At 7:20 I called Alex Richards at his condo. I didn't know if he was employed yet, but I wanted to catch him before he left for the day if he was. He didn't sound like he was asleep when he picked up the phone.

"Hello?"

"Alex, it's Mark Hayes."

"Hey, man, how's it going? Find a gig yet?"

"No. How about you?"

"I started at MGM a few days ago. V.P. of development."

"Nice. How'd you land that one?"

"They had a reshuffle and one of my pals ended up running the department. Max Hertzberg, remember him?"

"Sure." Max Hertzberg was a complete weasel. A brownnoser supreme. I was surprised he wasn't running a whole studio yet instead of just the story department.

"So what's up? Why the early call?"

"I have some bad news."

"Yeah?"

"It's about Charity James."

"What happened now?"

"She had an accident. Uh . . . actually it's worse than that . . ."

"What are you saying?"

"She's dead."

There was silence on the other end of the phone.

"Alex?"

More silence.

"Alex? You there?"

His voice was a whisper when he finally spoke. "What happened?"

"She overdosed." It was close enough to the truth for now. I didn't want to get into the grimier details of her death.

"Oh, God . . . I can't believe it." I thought he might be crying but I couldn't tell for sure.

"I'm sorry, Alex."

"Where is she?"

"They've got her down at the morgue. I'm going down there around ten o'clock. Do you want to go with me?"

"Ye . . . yes."

"I'll pick you up. You don't sound like you should be driving. What's your address again?" I had been to his condo only once, during his housewarming party. He gave me the address and I told him I'd pick him up around 9:30.

I called Detective Lutz and told him I'd be bringing Charity's ex-boyfriend with me. He said he had business at the morgue and he'd meet us down there at 10 A.M. He gave me the address and directions to the morgue before he hung up.

I drank coffee and opened the newspaper. I was stunned to discover someone had killed O. J. Simpson's wife, Nicole, last night. She and a man named Ronald Goldman were brutally stabbed to death in the courtyard of her Brentwood residence. O. J. had caught a flight out of LAX about an hour after the estimated time of the murders. I had a feeling those Hertz commercials had been good training for him.

A little before nine, I got my work jacket out of the closet and headed over the hill. Alex lived in a ritzy West L.A. neighborhood where the cheapest digs ran you at least 300 Gs. No wonder he had been so worried about making those condo payments.

Alex came out of his front door the moment I pulled up in front his place. He had been waiting anxiously.

"Are you okay, Alex?" I asked as he slid into the passenger seat.

"What do you think?" he asked coldly. Those were the last words he spoke until we reached the morgue. We didn't even talk about O. J.

FIFTY-THREE

The morgue is a gigantic mausoleum of a building attached to the Los Angeles County-USC medical center in East L.A. If you die violently or mysteriously in the county of Los Angeles and require an autopsy to determine the cause of your death, you will visit this place. There were news vans parked all around the building. I assumed they were there trying to dig up dirt on the Simpson-Goldman murders.

Detectives Lutz and Ryan were both waiting for us when we got there and they reminded me of the two Hollywood homicide cops who kept haunting my life, oh so subtly. I wondered if I was also now a suspect in the death of Charity James. I introduced the detectives to Alex and he shook their hands weakly. He seemed to be far away.

All the evidence had been collected from Charity's body and the medical examiner was done with her, so they offered us a choice of viewing her in person or from behind a plate glass window or on a videotape shot earlier in the day. At first I thought the videotape would be the best idea, but then the irony of it struck home. If not for the slick lure of the video image, maybe Charity would have never come to this city in the first place and she would still be alive. It didn't matter what I wanted anyway. Alex insisted on viewing her in person, not through glass or electronics. He wanted to be close to her one last time.

We went into the morgue and a friendly man in a white jumpsuit opened a freezer drawer and slid Charity's body out for our perusal. It was definitely Charity James. She was beautiful, even in death. Her eyes were open a quarter of an inch. It looked like she was in a daze, half asleep, or maybe a little high—not gone forever. There was a cut at the top of her chest and Alex pulled the sheet back to reveal some more. There was a stitched-up Y cut right down the middle of her body.

"What happened there?" Alex asked.

"We always do an autopsy if there is an unexpected death," the man in the white jumpsuit said. There was no emotion whatsoever in his voice.

They had opened her up like a suitcase and poked around inside. One last violation before the grave. I looked at the guy in the jumpsuit and noticed that he was staring at Charity's breasts. I wanted to punch his fucking lights out. These ghouls loved it when a beautiful young creature fell into their hands. In L.A. it happened often.

Alex must have noticed also. He covered Charity's body with the sheet, looked at the guy in white, and said, "Touch her again and I'll sue the hell out of you."

"W-what?" he stammered. He probably hadn't had too many people call him on his hobby.

"You know what I'm talking about, necrophiliac. I mean it. Keep your grubby paws off her."

"There's no need for that kind of talk," Detective Ryan said.

"I'm going to call Forest Lawn this afternoon and they'll come get her," Alex said. "I don't want her disturbed again. I'm serious. I'm going to have her checked out, and if cadaver dick here messed with her, I'm going to be pressing charges."

"I don't need to stand here and take insults like this," the man in the jumpsuit said as he stormed off to a far corner of the room.

"I know this is a shock for you," Detective Ryan said. "But those are serious accusations. You should think before you say something like that."

Detective Lutz just smirked, like he harbored the same suspicions that we did.

"Fuck it," Alex said. "This poor girl never had a chance in this town. Creeps like that are everywhere."

FIFTY-FOUR

After viewing Charity's body I had to sit in the lobby to get my bearings again. I was feeling ill. Alex looked worse. He was as white as the necrophiliac's jumpsuit and I thought he might throw up. The detectives had other business in the building, so they said good-bye to us and offered final condolences. They were off to the next corpse.

Alex excused himself to go to the bathroom. As he walked away I saw his chest heave. He was starting to lose it.

I waited for him to return, and as I waited, the last pieces began to fall into place. It was suddenly all so clear, so obvious, that I felt like a fool for not having grasped the truth on the day it all went down.

I walked down the hall. Reporters and camera technicians were milling about everywhere, waiting for news to pop about the most recent celebrity murder. I had a feeling this Simpson thing was going to make Dexter Morton's death old news quick. I wandered into the gift shop. Yeah, even the morgue has a gift shop in L.A. You can buy coffee cups, beach towels, toe tags, posters, baseball caps: all with the coroner's logo and a witty line or two, like, "Just lie down and leave the cutting to us" plastered on the item for fun. I looked over the goods but didn't see anything I wanted, so I returned to the lobby.

Fifteen minutes later, Alex came out of the bathroom. His face was ashen, his gait that of a dying man. Tears had left streaks on his face, but he was not crying. He was moving like one of those brain-eating zombies out of a George Romero film. But he had already claimed his ration of brains back in March, next to Dexter's pool. I had a feeling he might want to talk about it. I reached into my jacket pocket and clicked the button.

Alex leaned against the wall and stared straight at me, but he didn't seem to see me. I got up and crossed over to him and put my hand on his shoulder.

"Are you all right, Alex?"

He blinked a few times and focused his eyes, finally noticing me.

"All right? No. I'm not all right. Can you believe it? Did you see her? Did you see what they did to her?"

"Yeah, man. It's a fucking shame. I'm sorry."

"Who did it?"

"It was basically an OD. But she was hanging with a pretty rough crowd."

"I thought she was staying at your place?"

"She had some things there for a while, but I almost never saw her."

"I wish you'd taken better care of her."

"Me, too."

Alex tried to shake it off. "Forget it. It's not your fault. She was self-destructive. If she'd screw Dexter, she'd screw anything."

Our eyes locked for a moment and then I was sure. He immediately realized that I knew.

"You killed him, didn't you, Alex?"

Alex looked around to see if anyone was within hearing distance. There was no one in the vicinity and there weren't any surveillance cameras in this part of the building.

"How long have you known?"

"Not until now." I thought about it for a second and added, "But I guess I've known subconsciously from the beginning. I don't know why, but it was always there and I just didn't want to accept it. I probably knew the moment I saw Dexter floating in the pool. But I threw out my first impressions and tried to think more logically. I thought too hard about it and came up with all the solutions but the most obvious one, the one staring me in the face during lunch every day. I overrationalized the thing. You even told me what you were going to do at the party."

"How's that?"

"When I asked you to take Charity home, you told me you had 'better things to do.' You had already decided to kill him by then, hadn't you?"

"I guess so."

"That wasn't too smart, Alex. You left a lot of clues for them."

"They haven't come after me yet."

"They will. Eventually."

"Are you going to turn me in?"

"I don't know. I don't know what to do. Why don't you turn *yourself* in? It would save me from the moral conflict."

"Fuck that. I'm glad I killed that bastard. He was a user. He took Charity away from me and he destroyed her. You saw it. Do you think she'd be lying in there all cut up like that if not for Dexter?"

"I don't know, Alex. She was a pretty messed up lady."

"Not when I first met her. She was perfect. She wasn't into any of that shit. Dexter got her hooked up on the coke and that led to everything else. All she ever wanted to do was be an actress. The dope came later. Dexter used it to control her and then she went *out* of control. And when he was done with her, he just tossed her aside and ignored her. What was she supposed to do?"

"I tried to get her help," I said. "Tried to get her to go the twelve-step route. She wouldn't have it."

"She was lost long before Dexter threw her out. Did you know he was pimping her out? He was making her fuck his cronies to get favorable play for his projects. Did you know about it?"

"I had heard things. It's what Jim Becker was trying to use to blackmail Dexter."

"I know. That's when I first found out about it. Becker's got a big mouth. I hoped, when I killed Dexter, that maybe she would come back to me. But she was too far gone. I saw her once after . . . but it didn't work anymore. She wasn't the same girl I had known. I thought, maybe, with time . . . you know . . . Now it's too late. She's gone forever."

The tears came again and they filled the same streaky grooves that had been left by his first crying jag. I took him by the shoulders and tried to make him stand up straight.

"You've got to get your shit together, Alex. You killed a man. He may have been an asshole, a cocksucker extraordinaire, but you had no right to kill him. You want to stand here feeling sorry for yourself, that's fine. But somewhere along the line you're going to have to own up to your actions. It's not my place to turn you in, but you better do something about this. Because what you did was bullshit, and if the cops don't find Dexter's murderer soon, they're going to make my life a living hell."

Alex wiped tears from his eyes and said, "I'll deal with it." Then he turned and walked through the automatic doorway, out into the parking lot.

I went to the water fountain and got a drink. I didn't know what Alex would do. He didn't seem like the type to offer up a confession to the police. He wasn't a fan of anal rape, and he'd be getting quite a bit of it if they sent him to the county lockup to await trial. Then he'd have to turn pro in whatever hard core joint he landed in, for surely he would go to prison for a very long time.

No, I figured Alex would pack his things and split for Costa Rica or France, or he would kill himself. He seemed truly distraught—not about having murdered Dexter, but because he'd seen his lovely Charity James laid out like the catch-of-the-day.

By the time I got out to the parking lot, Alex had regained his composure. He was standing by my car, staring at the morgue, and calmly waiting for me. He was no longer crying.

As I drove him back to his condo he talked about Charity and the good times they had had before it all fell apart. The woman he described to me bore little resemblance to the crack whore she eventually became. Somehow he had blamed her transformation almost completely on Dexter's influence, but I knew it could not have been Dexter alone. It was a cumulative process, and one that probably started years ago, back in her home where she was "the pretty one," the one everyone thought would make it because of her beauty. I'd seen it a million times since I hit L.A.

When I pulled up to the condo Alex asked me in for a drink. I didn't want a drink, but I said okay just to see if he was going to be all right. As we entered the condo, he asked me a question that I was surprised he hadn't asked before.

"Did you sleep with her?"

The abruptness of the question took me off guard. I knew it would be useless to lie, so I said, "Yes. But just once."

His face wrinkled with menace. "What was wrong? She wasn't good enough for you?"

"No. She wasn't interested in me."

"She was interested enough to fuck you at least once."

"It just happened."

"Yeah. It always 'just happened.' You didn't love her. You were just another user."

There was suddenly a very audible click from under my jacket and Alex's eyes went wide as he recognized the sound as that of my minirecorder coming to the end of one side of a sixty-minute tape. I had recorded it on slow speed so I had actually gotten ninety minutes out of the thirty-minute side.

Alex tried to pull my jacket open and I stepped away from him.

"You fucker! You've been recording me! Since when?"

"I started taping right after you came out of the bathroom at the morgue. I had a feeling you had something to say."

"You piece of shit. I told you everything. I told you my innermost thoughts."

"You also told me you killed Dexter."

"So, you're working for the cops, trying to clear your name?"

"I'm not working for anyone. But I have no intention of going to jail."

"Now you're going to turn me in?"

"Only if I have to. It would be better if you turned yourself in, but if you don't and they come after me with any heavy conclusions, I'll have no choice but to play them the tape."

"And in the meantime I'm sitting on pins and needles wondering when you'll ratfuck me. I guess you'll be expecting good coverage on anything you bring to MGM now as well?"

"I hadn't thought of it, but that wouldn't hurt."

"You are a cold motherfucker. Dexter really taught you well."

"This town taught me well. I thought it had taught you, too. It's stupid to go blood simple over a piece of ass. You told me that yourself."

"Can't you spot *spin* when you hear it?"

He was easing his way back toward his fireplace. I had a feeling he was going to grab one of the pokers on the hearth and try to attack me.

"Don't think you can kill me and get away with it too, Alex. Too many people saw us together today."

He stopped moving. "Who says I need to get away with it? I'd do the same time for two murders as one. They can only kill me once."

"You could always try throwing another rattler my way."

I wanted to know if he had been behind the rattlesnake incident or if there was someone else out there who wanted to kill me as well.

"What the hell are you talking about?" He looked genuinely confused by the remark.

"The rattlesnake you threw over my balcony. Come on, you can confess to murder but you can't confess to that?"

"I didn't throw any snake over your balcony. Shit, if I was going to kill you, I'd do you the same way I did Dexter." He took the final two steps to the fireplace and pulled a heavy iron poker from the stand on the hearth. "I'd bash your brains in!"

I moved quickly for the front door and he did not give chase. I opened the door and looked at him.

Alex said, "How's it feel to be scared?"

"It's not the first time. How's it feel to be doomed?"

"We're all fucking doomed." He threw the poker at me and I closed the door just before it crashed on the other side. He had pretty good aim. I moved quickly to my car and I could hear him yelling like a madman inside the condo.

"Run, motherfucker! Run! You can't run from yourself, you chickenshit cocksucker! I'll do you one day just like I did our boss! I'll cave your fucking skull in!"

I believed him.

I got in my car and drove away. I went straight down to the Hollywood Police Department and requested that Detectives Lyndon and Campbell be called in to speak to me. Campbell got me on the line and told me he was busy and if it wasn't damn important, that I should take my ass home. I told him that I had a tape recording of Dexter Morton's killer confessing to the crime. He said he would see me in twenty minutes.

FIFTY-FIVE

I didn't really want to rat Alex out, but he had left me no choice. I didn't want to be looking over my shoulder waiting for him to make good on his threats.

It took the detectives more like an hour to get to the station and they arrived together again. It made me wonder if they were more than just partners on the force. We went to the little interrogation room and I told them the story and played them the tape.

They listened quietly and Lyndon made notes in his spiral-bound notebook. When the tape cut Alex off in midsentence and clicked off, signaling the end, Campbell looked at me and said, "That's it?"

"That's not enough?"

"How do we know who that voice is? And you could have doctored the tape. You *are* in the movie business, aren't you?"

"You've got to be kidding. That's Alex Richards on that tape. I worked with the guy. I'll testify against him if I have to. You've got to get him off the street. He wants to kill me."

"I can see why, you making it with his girl and all."

"She was hardly 'his girl.' "

Lyndon flipped the cover of his notebook over and looked at Campbell. "Quit jerking the guy's chain, Harv."

"Lyndon, you're a spoilsport." Campbell laughed heartily.

I was confused. Something was going on that I did not understand.

"Want to let me in on the joke?"

"I was just playing around for the guys on afternoon shift." He pointed at the mirrored wall. I imagined a few of the fellows were in there having a good laugh at my expense.

"Tell you the truth, we already have enough on your buddy, Alex. We're just waiting for the paperwork before we make a search of his house and arrest him."

"You've known it was him all along?"

"For a while."

"And you've just been toying with me?"

"Just today. All the other times we were just dealing with a pain in the ass. Let me give you a clue. Next time you're up for suspicion of murder, stay out of it! You're no Charlie Chan! You've just been getting in the way."

I got up and picked up my tape recorder. "I figured this one out, didn't I?"

"Big deal. A kindergartner could figure this one out."

"What do you have on him?"

"That's none of your business. It will all be in the papers—when he goes to trial."

"Why haven't you arrested him yet?"

"We like to make sure we've got all our ducks in a row before we pull the trigger."

As I headed for the door, Lyndon spoke up. "Where you going with that tape?"

"You don't need it, so I'll keep it."

"And go to the press and compromise our investigation. Uh-uh. That's evidence now. Leave it on the table."

I didn't know if they could legally force me to do that or not, but I didn't want to argue with them. I popped the tape out of the recorder and started to place it on the table. At the last moment I changed my mind and pulled the tape out of the cassette in long strands, wrapping it around my hand as I did so. They both moved forward out of reflex.

I said, "If you don't need it, what do you care?"

The detectives did nothing to stop me, they relaxed and just sat there looking amused. When the tape was all out of the cassette I broke it free and tossed it onto the table in front of them.

"Feel better?" Campbell asked.

"A little."

"You know, we could arrest you for destroying evidence."

I suddenly realized why they wouldn't and how futile my gesture had been.

"You've got copies. I'm sure you've been running audio and video of this entire meeting."

"Always."

"It's been fun."

I turned and headed for the door again.

Campbell called out to me one last time as I opened the door.

"Mr. Hayes?"

"Yes?"

"About the rattlesnake? Judging by that tape of yours, I don't think Alex Richards was the guy. Might have been Becker or that Ward kid, but I would venture to guess it could be any one of your acquaintances. By the sound of things, you make a hell of a friend."

I stared at him, trying to think of a rebuke. I had nothing.

FIFTY-SIX

I drove down Hollywood Boulevard looking for something to do until the crowd would be gathering at Ma Smith's. I found one of the second-run theaters playing a triple feature that I could not resist: *Platoon, Full Metal Jacket,* and *Hair.* It was 'Nam night in Hollywood. *Platoon* was half over by the time I got my popcorn and Coke and took my seat. Oliver Stone used a sledgehammer to direct that movie, but it worked. I actually heard fully grown men sobbing as the end credits rolled. There was a ten-minute break, then *Full Metal Jacket* began. Damn, it was a good flick. Only Kubrick could have gotten away with that one. *Hair* was up next. I was asleep before anyone got naked. I slept through the rest of the movie and was awakened by an usher after the lights came on and everyone else had left the theater.

I walked out into the night, got into my car, and headed for South Central. I parked near Ma Smith's and looked at the house. They were back in business and nothing appeared different at all. Lights were burning, music playing, and a cluster of men stood on the front porch keeping watch on the neighborhood. Petey Gunn met me at the gate.

"You're not welcome here anymore."

"I've got to see Jamaal."

"He don't want to see you."

"Does he know about Charity James?"

"Who?"

"Creamy."

"She ain't here. Hasn't been since that night."

"No shit. She's dead."

"Say what?"

"She died that morning, right after she left here."

"The fuck you say?"

He opened the gate and let me step inside. He frisked me good, maybe thinking I had come to the house to exact some form of revenge. We went into Ma Smith's. The place was jamming. The early evacuation a few nights earlier had left no scars. We found Jamaal in the kitchen, talking to Ma Smith. Neither one of them was happy to see me.

Ma Smith said, "Petey, I told you no trouble tonight. Don't you listen?"

"You'll want to hear this," Petey said.

I told them what had happened to Charity James, a.k.a. Creamy.

Ma Smith just shook her head sadly and said, "I knew that poor thing wouldn't make it."

Jamaal took it all in stoically, but I could tell a rage was building within him. I asked him if he had seen Kendall and his crew since the incident.

"No. Those motherfuckers have been laying low. Now I know why. I'll fix their asses."

"You ain't gonna do no such thing, Jamaal," Ma Smith said. "What's done is done."

"That's some evil shit," Jamaal said. He went into one of the back rooms where the smell of burning rock was thick in the air.

FIFTY-SEVEN

When I arrived in the Viande parking lot I noticed that the Maserati was parked in Clyde's spot, uncovered, washed, waxed, and looking almost like new. Now that Emily was back I guess his late-night carousing would taper off a bit and he'd have to get respectable. I felt bad having suspected Clyde of Dexter's murder, but he seemed so right for it. Like Campbell said, I'm no Charlie Chan.

But what about the rattlesnake? If Alex didn't toss it onto my balcony, who did? Jim Becker? Wilkie? Or maybe it was Clyde after all? Both Wilkie and Clyde were certainly mad enough at me to throw a little scare my way.

There I go again, accusing the neighbors.

I heard a buzzing sound and realized it was coming from the artificial palm tree with the cell-phone-transmitter coconuts. I'd have to finally break down and get one of those cell phones once I was gainfully employed again. The purchase prices and monthly service charges were dropping. If they could only get them smaller than a field walkie-talkie I'd join the "in" crowd. My reception certainly would be good. At least from my balcony.

A small temblor rolled under my feet, the first one I had felt in quite a while, and I was taken back to that night in January when this all seemed to begin. Nothing had been right since the quake. It was as if the Earth itself had tossed these troubles our way. Perhaps the entire city was suffering from some sort of mass post-traumatic stress. (It looked like even the Juice had flipped his lid.) Or maybe we all just had Damaged Goods Syndrome like Clyde was always saying.

As I went by Clyde's apartment I noticed the blue glow from his TV illuminating his bedroom. The venetian blinds were slightly open so I peeked through the window. He and Emily were lying in bed, watching a late-night movie. At least Clyde was watching. Emily was cradled under his left arm, her head resting on his chest. He was slowly stroking her blonde hair, but he was concentrating on the tube and it appeared that she was asleep. I couldn't get a clear view of what was on the TV screen, but it looked like an old Alan Ladd movie.

It finally occurred to me that I was turning a casual, concerned look into an extended act of voyeurism. I felt a bit dirty, but I watched them a little longer before I headed up the stairs. Clyde was just as washed up as I was, but he was washed up on his own terms. And he seemed happy. Or at least as happy as he could be under the circumstances. Maybe I'd take a portion of the Development Fund and option *Blonde Lightning* from him so we could make a low-budget film. Perhaps I'd call Miles Gallo's bluff and sell my take on the Dexter Morton story to the tabloids to raise the rest of the production coin.

It was after 3 A.M. by the time I got upstairs to my apartment. The sight of Charity's lifeless body wouldn't leave my mind. I turned on my new Sony black-and-white TV (courtesy of my friend in the barrio) looking for replacement images. Ironically enough, *The Blue Dahlia* was playing. *The Blue Dahlia* was the only original screenplay written by Raymond Chandler that made it to the silver screen. It always seemed to play on TV at three in the morning. It was the Alan Ladd movie that Clyde was watching downstairs. I just hadn't had a clear enough angle to identify it. I wondered what Clyde was thinking down there. Was he enjoying the movie, or was he so filled with bitterness and bile that watching a Chandler flick was some form of masochism? And what about his useless book of criticism on the subject? Was this experience proving or disproving his vile theories?

I had a theory of my own. I think Clyde had only written that book to have an excuse to hide himself away from the public and the industry for a length of time. I think it was a psychological defense mechanism. He had been trying to protect himself from himself. And once the thing was completed and he had no more excuses for living like a hermit, he came out of the gate hard and crazy. I had confused Hollywood angst for murderous intentions.

The Blue Dahlia is not a very good movie by most standards, but it is still head and shoulders above most of the films Clyde had been involved with during his career. Was he torturing himself with the knowledge that the whole of his life's work probably wouldn't even amount to a few hours on *The Late Late Show* in the distant future? Was he so jealous of Raymond Chandler that he would make himself watch movies based on his work and then perform ritual self-mutilation afterwards? Doubtful. I had a feeling Clyde had more affection for old Ray than he would ever let on.

I watched *The Blue Dahlia* and felt a strong yearning for Raymond Chandler. I suddenly missed him like I would miss a beloved relative. He had been dead for thirty-five years, two weeks longer than I had been alive, but after rereading *The High Window* and then watching *The Blue Dahlia* so soon afterwards, I felt like I had lost a good friend with his passing. The fact that I couldn't pick up the phone and call him and tell him about all that had happened brought a great emptiness to my heart.

I paced the floor and watched the movie until the final fade out. Damn, it all seemed so simple back then. There were bad guys and good guys. The bad guys got shot and the good guys either got drinks or the girl, depending on their billing. The good old days. This was the kind of movie, hell, the kind of *attitude,* which had drawn me to this town and this business in the first place. But like they say, they don't make 'em like that anymore.

It was a little before five and the sun still hadn't decided to rise. A Randolph Scott Western was up next and I just couldn't get with it, so I killed the TV and walked into Charity's bedroom. I stood in the doorway, staring at the futon. I could still see the imprint of Charity's body in the sheets, left there an actual lifetime ago. It would be the last I'd see of her, so I decided not to disturb the silk sculpture.

I picked up a half-empty pack of cigarettes Charity had left on the nightstand and went into the kitchen. I turned the lights out and opened the venetian blinds. The orange neon trim of the La Reina shopping complex was still blazing, but the rest of the elaborate marquee was turned off. It was just as well. I hated those commercials. The trim accented the building, making it seem dark and lonely in spite of the bright orange light surrounding it. One of the neon strips was flickering, suffering from overuse or wiring problems. Beautiful things need to be maintained.

A light drizzle was falling, the polluted skies draining into the Valley. I don't know if it was the barometric pressure or just the way I was sitting, but my ribs began to ache where I had been kicked.

I stared at the phone on the kitchen table, wishing Charity would call, *could* call. Wishing things could be different and that somehow this whole affair would have a happy ending. A studio ending. But I wasn't sitting on some soundstage at some movie studio, and studio endings just weren't meant to be for the real people of L.A. That was the stuff of fairy tales. "*The stuff dreams are made of . . .*"

The apartment was so goddamned quiet. I was finally enjoying the peace I had craved during the turmoil of the last few months and the silence was deafening.

I thought about what Clyde had said about society when we were discussing his book, that Chandler's fiction appealed to a culture built on a bedrock of self-pity. I decided to get with the program and go digging.

I went into my bedroom and put an old jazz album on the stereo, John Coltrane's *Blue Train,* the only album he ever recorded for the great Blue Note label. Another dead guy reaching out from the past to lend a little comfort to the lonely at heart.

The music was *good.* It drifted through the empty apartment like a winter breeze.

I returned to the kitchen, reached into the liquor cabinet, pulled out a bottle of Jim Beam, and poured myself a shot. Then I sat at the kitchen table and fired up one of Charity's cigarettes. I smoked and drank while watching the orange neon reflect off the wet blacktop of the alley. I didn't do it because I wanted a smoke or a drink, but out of nostalgia for a time and place that no longer existed, and maybe never did. A place I had come looking for fifteen years ago out of youthful exuberance and bald-faced ignorance.

Christ, the things we think when we are young . . .

I moved the phone onto my lap and then I sat there, staring out at the rain-soaked alley, waiting.

Waiting for a call that would never come.

It was *perfect.*

Acknowledgments

Many people gave this book—and its various incarnations—a look over the last six years and contributed positively to its contents. Some of them even provided generous grants that would put the NEA to shame.

I would like to thank, in particular, my sons, Sterling and Brandon, The Pro, Sandra Petersen, Joe Blades, David Pecchia, Scott Phillips, Audrey Moore, Steve Breimer, Marc Glick, Matthew Guma, Richard Pine, Gregg Andrew Hurwitz, John "the Devil" Vogel, Shelly McArthur, Jeff Parker, Jan Alonzo, Joan Kern, Alan Ormsby, Dale Jaffe, Joe R. Lansdale—hisownself, Dr. Rick Lasarow, Diana, Lucy, and Bill Shaffer, and Joey Ito Farina for their words of wisdom and support along the way. Bob Dylan, Tom Petty, John Coltrane, and Warren Zevon also provided much musical inspiration during this long journey. However, the former Heidi Schultz must be credited with the actual completion of the book. If not for her persistence and guidance, I would still be tinkering with this thing to this day.

My gratitude and love goes out to all of them.